THE SOUL CONDUCTOR

C. S. Evans

Copyright © 2021 C. S. Evans

© 2014 C. S. Evans. All Rights Reserved.
No part of this book may be used, reproduced or transmitted in any form or by any means, graphic, electronic or mechanical, including photocopying and recording, or by any information storage systems, without the written permission of the author.
All enquiries:
graveyardmuse@gmail.com
Please visit my blog:
http://graveyardmuse.wordpress.com/
I'm also on Facebook:
https://www.facebook.com/graveyardmuse
and Twitter:
https://twitter.com/graveyardmuse
This is a work of fiction. Names, characters, places, faiths and events are all products of the author's imagination and should not be construed as real, in whole or in part. Any resemblance to actual events, places or persons, living or dead, is purely coincidental.
Cover Art: © 2014 Shannon Milsom. All Rights Reserved.

2nd Edition © 2021. All Rights Reserved.

This book is dedicated to Annie, with eternal gratitude.
Because she believed.
X

I would like to take this opportunity to express my heartfelt thanks (in no particular order) to a few people for making this book possible and for helping me to ensure it is the best it can be. Dr. Mike Johnson, for being a fabulous CW tutor; Craig Russell, for making the time and effort to answer my (many) questions and offer the wisdom of his experience; Warwick Warriors at Warwick Castle, for generously helping me with my research in between their fantastic displays; my editor Michelle Dunbar, for having the patience of a saint; Shannon Milsom, for her excellent cover art and her enthusiasm for the project; Kev Milsom for his assistance with the cover and listening to my wibbles; and all those who have encouraged, congratulated, nagged, cajoled and threatened me along the way – there are far too many of you to mention individually, but you know who you are, and my love goes with you all.

Craig Russell: http://www.craigrussell.com/
Michelle Dunbar: http://michelledunbar.co.uk/
Warwick Warriors: https://www.facebook.com/pages/WarwickWarriors/246401448734101?sk=timeline

2021 Edition
Love and thanks to my wonderful sister, for putting up with my ravings against technology, and the use of office space in her living room! You're amazing, sis xxx

CONTENTS

Title Page

Copyright

Dedication

Chapter 1. Rook.   1

Chapter 2. The Ritual   12

Chapter 3. Awakening.   25

Chapter 4. Accusation.   33

Chapter 5. The Tavern.   38

Chapter 6. A Reluctant Parting.   46

Chapter 7. Fear.   50

Chapter 8. Judgement.   57

Chapter 9. The Keeper.   61

Chapter 10. Renn.   68

Chapter 11. Defence.   76

Chapter 12. Erelas.   81

Chapter 13. Sentence.   85

Chapter 14. Shelter.   93

Chapter 15. Arrow.	98
Chapter 16. Aliena.	104
Chapter 17. Recovery	109
Chapter 18. Revelations.	115
Chapter 19. Walking Away.	122
Chapter 20. Confession.	128
Chapter 21. Galen.	138
Chapter 22. The Sheriff.	148
Chapter 23. In Chains.	154
Chapter 24. A Light in the Darkness.	161
Chapter 25. A Positive Approach.	169
Chapter 26. Threats.	174
Chapter 27. A Desperate Plan.	178
Chapter 28. An Act of Persuasion	186
Chapter 29. Merging.	195
Chapter 30. The Seed of an Idea	202
Chapter 31. Theories.	206
Chapter 32. Weapons and More	211
Chapter 33. Finding Renn	219
Chapter 34. Elyan's Bravery	225
Chapter 35. Sharing the Burden	232
Chapter 36. Journey	237
Chapter 37. Breaking Back In	243
Chapter 38. A Severe Test	249

Chapter 39. Quinn's True Target.	257
Chapter 40. A Crisis of Faith	263
Chapter 41. Toren	268
Chapter 42. A Plea to the King	273
Chapter 43. Duty Done	284
Chapter 44. The Wrath of Aliena	287
Chapter 45. Elyan	293
Chapter 46. Innocence	301
Chapter 47. Comfort	305
Chapter 48. Garin's Gamble	311
Chapter 49. Non-discussion	316
Chapter 50. Good News	322
Chapter 51. Brotherhood	327
Chapter 52. Taking the Bait	331
Chapter 53. Assassin	341
Chapter 54. Torture	347
Chapter 55. Sacrifice	353
Chapter 56. A Precious Soul	362
Chapter 57. A New Quest	367
Chapter 58. Tears of Regret	372
Chapter 59. Adjustment	378
Chapter 60. The Solitude of Self-Reproach	385
Chapter 61. A Promise Made	389
Chapter 62. Einna	393

Chapter 63. A Pact with the Pack	398
Chapter 64. Dawn Attack	404
Chapter 65. Cara Takes Over	408
Chapter 66. Immersion	415
Chapter 67. Alara	418
Chapter 68. Doomed Passion	425
Chapter 69. Maynard	429
Chapter 70. Samien's Tale	437
Chapter 71. Corvus	441
Chapter 72. The Wolves Give Hope	445
Chapter 73. The Archer	450
Chapter 74. A Storm of Thoughts	454
Chapter 75. Morbus	459
Chapter 76. An Unorthodox Introduction	464
Chapter 77. Hostilities	469
Chapter 78. A Companion Returns	472
Chapter 79. The Memory Made Whole	479
Chapter 80. Clash of the Brotherhood	488
Chapter 81. Solace for Erelas	497
Chapter 82. Samien Brings Trouble	500
Chapter 83. Maynard's Motive	503
Chapter 84. Reassurance for Quinn	512
Chapter 85. Anwenn	517
Chapter 86. Marking the Prey	526

Chapter 87. The Perils of Wine	532
Chapter 88. Making an Impression	536
Chapter 89. The Pawn	540
Chapter 90. A Catastrophic Error	543
Chapter 91. The Final Struggle	547
Chapter 92. Fury in Grief	552
Chapter 93. A Promise Kept	558
Chapter 94. Safe	563
Chapter 95. Home	566
About The Author	569

CHAPTER 1. ROOK.

There was blood everywhere; the black pools made the narrow, cobbled alley slick beneath the soles of Quinn's boots, but he ignored it. He was used to that – and worse.

From the look of the man lying motionless on the ground, he had been stabbed through his stomach with a sword, the blade emerging through his back. He had been left - seemingly for hours, judging by the drying blood on his clothes - in the street to die, conscious, gasping, dribbling blood. His dirty, torn clothes, skinny frame and rotten teeth were clues to his low status within the community. For someone such as him, the residents of this poor, frightened town would do nothing. Fear of getting involved in something which might end with them lying right beside him in the filth, breathing their last in the fetid air, kept them at bay. The guards would order the removal of the body in the morning. Perhaps his pauper's grave would be prayed over, perhaps not. Quinn was certain that nothing would be done to bring his killer to justice.

Glancing around to make sure he was alone, his pale face calm in the muted light, he tucked his indigo amulet under his clothes and knelt at the man's side, careful to flick his dark robes clear of the spreading mess beneath him. His silver eyes took on a bright turquoise glow, and he took a deep breath, readying himself for the task in hand.

This was always the most challenging part for any Soul Conductor and Quinn took his time to ensure it was done carefully. It was a risky undertaking – connecting to an often traumatised and pained soul, one who knew it was the end, but did not want to let go of this mortal existence, having no idea what awaited it when Quinn's duty was done.

From his perspective, it felt as if his consciousness, even his very soul, was being ripped from his body, as the dying person tried to hold on with whatever strength they had left. Sometimes pain would course through his body, as his energy was steadily drained. He would shiver with a sudden chill and very often the person's fear would be transmitted into his own thoughts, hampering his work further. Conducting was a dangerous craft.

He clenched his fists, spread his fingers wide and then placed his palms against the sides of the man's head with care. As his slender fingers touched the man's skull, he looked into his eyes, which were still open but losing their light. Deep brown, almost black, they lacked any warmth, a visual sign of what Quinn was already starting to feel from this man's soul. From that moment, he knew this was going to be difficult and unpleasant.

As he fostered the man's energies and merged them with his own, Quinn learned that his name was Rook. He felt no love in Rook's soul – only anger, hatred, joy in the suffering of others, and a belief in his own power to bend people to his will. Evil had become tangible, but in this land, under its current ruler, this was nothing unusual.

Quinn's eyes brightened further, the silver irises now completely obscured by the turquoise light emanating from his pupils. He concentrated hard, his gaze never wavering from Rook's, whose expression registered confusion as he became aware of the stranger kneeling beside him. If anyone had been passing at this late hour, they would have seen just the almost lifeless body of the man lying in its viscous bath of blood – maybe a hint of a dark form beside him, usually dismissed as shadow or their fertile imagination's response to the tableau of death. Realising time was critical, Quinn recited in his deep, calm voice, the words he always used as he locked energies with the dying: 'God, link me with this mortal soul, that I may do my duty with Your Holy Gift.'

There was an instant and violent effect on Rook. He knew now that he was heading for judgement and eternal punishment for his wickedness. It was something he had never attempted to hide in life and could not hope to conceal upon his death. His soul began to fight the only way it could now that his body was useless – by grabbing on to Quinn's energies and holding fast. He did not know *how* he was able to do it; just that he *was* doing it and that he must not give up...

This was what Quinn had been waiting for. As their energies locked together, he recited the phrase he had learned at the age of eleven, right at the start of his training; one which had flowed from him without thought several times a day since his official initiation into the Order of Conductors two years before: 'God, accept my faithful service as I bring to you the soul of this man, for your Holy Judgement.'

Quinn's power resonated in his veins as he quickly severed the soul from the body and took it to a place from which it could never return.

Quinn and Rook were now in what the Conductors had dubbed the Plane of Shadows, but which had no real name at all. Unlike man's idea of Purgatory, a soul did not remain here until it had paid for its sins. Its stay here was brief and, for some, brutal. The Conductors took the name from the fact that once a wicked soul witnessed a shadow passing over them, the huge, black-winged creatures known as Guardians had arrived; then there would be no escape from the hell they had chosen for themselves through sin.

Rook stood before Quinn, his human appearance having followed him to this stage of the 'afterlife'. Quinn's hands no longer held him, and he looked down at the image of himself which had travelled with him, the torn, blood-stained clothes leaving him in no doubt that he had perished in that alleyway. This was somewhere beyond his imagining, but no less real for that. Looking around, clearly alarmed by his new surroundings – a barren, dusty, freezing landscape of reddish-brown sand and a magenta sky – he began to feel fear, a sensation he was unused to and not prepared to accept. He tried to force the feeling back with his anger, glaring at the stranger with glowing eyes. 'What have you *done* to me?' he demanded.

Quinn stood motionless as the sterile sand flew about them, stinging his skin and forcing him to blink. The turquoise glow faded and his eyes reverted to their icy silver colour.

'Answer me!' Rook's face contorted as he drew ever closer to Quinn, the first twitches of his rage serving as a warning.

Rook's face suddenly froze, decayed teeth bared, but his eyes betrayed his terror as a piercing shriek from the skies removed any doubts he may have had about his fate.

Quinn glanced up, searching for the source of the noise. He was familiar with Guardians, having seen them countless times before, but the sight of their enormous black-scaled bodies, lizard-like heads and leathery, dark green wings still filled him with dread.

These were the protectors of this realm, guarding the Keepers with lethal force. The Keepers sent the souls on to their fate but they did not judge. God had already done that. No, the Keepers would receive their instructions and carry them out, but all too often the souls of the wicked assumed they could wield their earthly power here and escape their eternal sentence. Conductors could escape back to the realm of the living with ease, but the Keepers were always here, open to attack. So, whenever evil arrived in this realm, the Guardians would swoop in, their long necks outstretched, foot-long teeth ready to seize the essence of the rebellious soul and drag it to its final destination.

Unfortunately for the Conductors, the Guardians were so zealous in their protection of their masters that any Conductor who did not get out of the way fast enough would also perish in their fury. Quinn feared very little, believing the emotion served no purpose, but the Guardians were not something to be brushed off so easily. The legends were too frequently told – and horrifying.

Rook grabbed Quinn's hands as he saw what he believed were three dragons sent by Lucifer himself. 'Take me back! Right *now*, damn you! I don't belong here!'

He did his best to show in his expression that he believed that, but Quinn knew from the feel of Rook's soul that it was not true. Besides, Quinn was not the one who had judged him. He said nothing. Conversing with the newly-deceased was not part of his duty. All that was left was for him to return to his own world and leave the man to his inescapable fate.

Rook continued to scream at him, adding abuse to his pleas. Quinn merely stared at him steadily as he worked on disconnecting himself, separating their energies. But Rook held on tight. Quinn's body began to pulse with intense pain, causing him to gasp and then hold his breath. He was in for a fight to free himself, and given the number of souls he had transported recently, he was afraid he would not have the strength to fight back for long.

The full force of Rook's rage rushed forth as he realised Quinn was not going to help him. Before Quinn could react, Rook's soul pushed violently towards Quinn's energies and somehow managed to fuse them together, something Quinn had never experienced or even heard of before. It caused him severe pain all over his body and he was suddenly, agonisingly blinded. His head felt as if it would be crushed under the intense pressure and he could not breathe. Despite Quinn's natural strength and refined skills as a Conductor, he had no idea how to get out of it. It was as if the man was planning to take over his body and escape his fate through Quinn.

But that was not how things worked. All he would succeed in doing was destroying them both...

Quinn began to see into Rook's memories, which he hadn't known was even possible. They flashed into his mind with horrifying clarity, each one worse than the one before. He felt sick as the extent of Rook's evil was revealed to him through the images invading his own mind. The killings, the rapes, the sheer terror he had caused others to feel, the brutality inflicted upon innocent people. He tasted bile in his throat as this man's life journey played out in vivid flashes. Rook wasn't going to go quietly...

He steeled his nerves and began a casting out loud as best he could, his violent shivering causing the words to fail several times. His vision began to clear in his left eye, but he could see nothing with his right. He turned around, confused. The form of the man had vanished.

Quinn panicked. If he was carrying this soul of evil within him, he had no idea how to expel it and save himself. The Guardians circled ever closer, as his legs gave way. He slumped to the dry earth, falling onto his back. It felt as if his limbs were made of granite and he gasped for air, crying out as his agony intensified. He needed to fight, not really knowing how to, but as sure as night followed day that if he did not eject Rook's soul he would perish, his own soul would be lost forever.

Rage swelled inside of him. He was not going to be destroyed by this vile human being, this man who had no respect for life and no concept of love or compassion. His eyes emitted sparks of turquoise light and glowed with an intensity he had never experienced before, obscuring his already limited vision. He summoned all of his remaining power to save his own life. He attempted to shout out the castings he thought might help, but his voice shook, the words interspersed with cries of agony, his focus interrupted by the proximity of the three creatures overhead. Their shrieks deafened him, almost drowning out his voice. His breathing became laboured, and he soon lost the ability to speak at all. He had to plead with God silently as visions of the man's depraved acts fought their way in once more. Almost inevitably, his body quickly lost the last of its reserves of energy.

He knew then that he was defeated. He had nothing left to defend himself with. As his body convulsed with of pain from the incredible force of Rook's will to live, he gathered up one last breath. *'God, save me!'* The words barely escaped his lips as more than a whisper. His chest seized up and every fibre of his being felt like it was being burned in a flash of white hot energy. He clutched desperately at the raven-black, sweat-soaked hair at the sides of his head, squeezing his eyes shut, wanting to tear the pain away. In that moment, convinced it was all over, he felt his heart break, crushed by the injustice of it. He had only ever wanted to help the dying, good or bad. This was his reward.

But then, to his confused relief, the pain began to fade. The storm in his mind seemed to be blowing itself out. He found he could breathe again and gasped the hot, dry air. A spark of hope fluttered in his chest. Could he prevail after all?

When he opened his eyes, that spark died as quickly as it had been born. One of the Guardians had landed, mere feet away from him, while the others continued to circle above, screeching with fury. Quinn gave a weak, derisive laugh as the Guardian showed its teeth. 'Get it over with,' he breathed.

But the Guardian did not move. Quinn had been warned by scholars many times over the years that these creatures would destroy without mercy – and three times since his initiation they had received word from a Keeper that one of their missing Conductors had been a victim of the Guardians. There was never anything left to be sent back, buried or mourned over.

Quinn could not understand why this one didn't move to strike him, but lingered, staring at him, increasing his unease with every second that went by. He looked into its huge, golden eyes, trying to read its intention, but seeing nothing. Then, though he could scarcely dare to believe it, the creature started to back slowly away. He could do nothing but watch, too afraid to risk even the slightest of movements.

It stopped moving after only a couple of steps. Quinn prepared for the end, whispering a few last words to God – no longer asking for salvation, but seeking forgiveness for his failure. The Guardian stretched out its long neck, its head coming within inches of his face. He could feel and smell its hot, sour breath on his cold, clammy skin and he fought the urge to turn away, still not wishing to provoke it by moving a single inch.

The creature screamed at him, a mournful

noise that thickened the atmosphere, causing a painful vibration in his head. His own cry, at the renewed agony, was lost in the power of the Guardian's voice.

Then the scream of the Guardian in turn was drowned out. A noise resembling thunder came from somewhere behind Quinn as a wave of energy slammed into him, rolling him over several times in the dust. He came to rest on his front, shrouded by the frenzy of sand that had stirred by the blast. The air seemed to have been sucked from his lungs and at that moment he decided it was pointless to fight any longer.

He closed his eyes and accepted that this would be the end of his life. He was too young, it was too soon, and he had been beaten by pure evil. He silently asked God to bring peace to his parents, to his friend, Erelas, and to his fellow Conductors, before giving in to the deep, cold darkness.

CHAPTER 2. THE RITUAL

'This is *most* unorthodox, Erelas,' the Archdeacon said, continuing to change his robes as he spoke to the young Conductor before him.

'I know, Archdeacon, but that's how she wants it.' Erelas shuffled, nervous of the senior Conductor. 'She is uncomfortable with the idea of the whole of Delmoril watching her take her vows. She wants our wedding to be as private as the other aspects of our lives.'

'Well, Anwenn has always been reserved, I understand that. And with that *friend* of yours involved in the ceremony, who knows what might happen. Maybe it's better that as few people as possible get to see it.'

'Quinn would *never* do anything to undermine the sacred nature of our marriage.'

The Archdeacon raised an eyebrow. 'I wish I shared your certainty—'

A young scholar burst through the wooden door so fast it almost rebounded into his face, which was a picture of alarm. 'Archdeacon, you must come quickly,' he gasped. He glanced at Erelas. 'It's Quinn!'

The Archdeacon frowned at Erelas. 'What the blazes has he done this time?'

'Nothing, Sir – I...I mean...' stammered the scholar.

'Spit it out, for heaven's sake!' the Archdeacon snapped.

'He's hurt!'

Erelas started for the door. 'Where is he?' he said, panic clear in his voice.

'Outside the chapel, by the fountain.'

Erelas sprinted away. The Archdeacon pressed his lips into a barely visible line, wrapped his cloak around his shoulders and followed.

***

Several scholars and Conductors had gathered around Quinn by the time Erelas reached him. He uncharacteristically shoved them roughly out of the way and knelt on the grass, which was still damp from an autumn shower, his face a mask of concern.

'God...' he breathed, as he took in the situation. Quinn was lying on his side; his arms were clutched to his chest, one hand gripping his amulet so tight his knuckles were white. His legs were stretched out, and his feet kicked as spasms coursed through his body. His eyes were closed, his breaths short and wheezy and blood trickled from his nose. He was covered in red dust and as the Archdeacon arrived, Erelas looked up at him. 'He's come from the Plane of Shadows...'

The Archdeacon bent over Quinn and took

in his appearance, his frown so deep his white, overgrown eyebrows seemed to merge. He opened his mouth as if to reply, but seemed as confused as Erelas.

Erelas leaned over Quinn and turned his face towards him. 'Quinn...can you hear me?'

There was no response from his friend, but as the blood trickled to the back of his throat his breathing worsened, so Erelas slowly let his face rest against the grass. 'Archdeacon—' he said, without looking round. 'Can you help him?'

The Archdeacon didn't answer directly, instead summoning two Conductors. 'Take him to my quarters. Lay him on my pallet. Erelas,' he added. 'I'll need your help.' Turning to the small crowd that was still growing, he shouted: 'The rest of you, back to your duties!'

The spectators shuffled away, avoiding the Archdeacon's stern glare, but they stole a surreptitious glance over their shoulders before moving away. The chosen ones gently lifted Quinn between them. Erelas followed; relieved the Archdeacon wanted him present, although he would have insisted on staying with Quinn, even if he was no good at confrontations with the ruler of Delmoril...

As they reached the quarters, Erelas felt a hand on his shoulder.

'What's happened to Quinn?' Anwenn asked. Wide-eyed, she wrapped her pale blue cloak around her against the sudden chill in the air.

Erelas took her hands. 'I don't know. He—' Erelas broke off, realising he never thought to ask the scholar who had found Quinn how his friend had actually got there. 'I don't know. But he's in bad shape. The Archdeacon is going to help him – I think.'

'I pray he is alright. I'll find his parents for you.'

Erelas kissed Anwenn's cheek. 'Thank you.'

She hurried away and Erelas entered the quarters he had left only minutes before. The Conductors had laid Quinn on the Archdeacon's pallet and stood back, awaiting further instructions.

'Leave us!' barked the Archdeacon, surprising them all with his tone. He seemed angry, but with whom?

Erelas sat next to Quinn, who was motionless now. The spasms had subsided and his arms lay limp at his sides. Erelas lifted an eyelid, shocked to discover his iris still held a turquoise glow, but with sparks of red dancing within the light. He opened Quinn's right eye and gasped. 'Archdeacon...' The pupil was so widely dilated it was difficult to tell where it ended and the iris began...the iris was such a deep purple colour that it, too, was almost black.

The Archdeacon arrived at the bedside, handing Erelas some clean cloths as he took in what the young Conductor was showing him.

'What is that?' Erelas asked.

The Archdeacon's lips tightened and he

drew a deep breath through his flared nostrils. Erelas looked up at the sound and frowned at his superior's obvious displeasure.

'I do not know, Erelas,' the Archdeacon said in a flat tone. He prised the amulet from Quinn's hand. 'But I have a suspicion, and if I am right, you should not get your hopes up for a recovery.'

Erelas felt sick. He could not bear the thought of anything happening to Quinn. He was his brother in all but blood.

They had known each other for almost their entire lives, since before their training had begun at the age of ten. They had been virtually inseparable once they began to learn the ways of the Conductors together. They even looked alike – beyond the silvery-grey eyes of all the Conductors – with their sometimes unruly black hair, wiry strength and mischievous smiles.

Quinn helped him get through that training. Although Erelas was strong, enthusiastic, and possessed all the compassion and sense needed to fulfil their duties, he often struggled with the physical training. He lacked Quinn's natural ability with the sword and dagger. In turn, Erelas would aid Quinn in the academic subjects, ensuring he passed the tests on things he often lacked the patience to grasp.

However, in addition to this, Quinn had been the rebellious one. He disliked the Archdeacon's use of authority, often challenging decisions based on his unshakeable desire for justice and fairness. Erelas would always defend his friend – albeit in a subtle way – and often wound up in the same amount of trouble. Then there were the practical jokes; Quinn ensured that Erelas – who would never have thought up such things on his own – got his fair share of fun when he devised pranks against the scholars and, on occasion, the Archdeacon himself. Their parents had given up trying to keep them apart early on in their friendship. Instead, they had grown accustomed to being called to the Archdeacon's quarters when their sons had been disciplined yet again. When Erelas' parents died in separate accidents a couple of years before, they had grown even closer as Quinn helped him in his sorrow. Even the maturing relationship between Erelas and Anwenn, due to be sealed in their marriage very soon, had not affected their brotherhood.

Erelas could not imagine life without Quinn and the very thought of it turned his insides upside down.

'*Erelas!*' The Archdeacon was glaring at him, holding out an old, leather-bound herbal. 'If you want him to have any chance of surviving this, I suggest you pay attention!'

Erelas glared back, hurt by the words. He snatched the book from him, but the Archdeacon took no notice of his anger. He returned to the numerous shelves lining the walls of his cramped quarters, examining cloths, bottles and both dried and living plants. Selecting what he wanted – a white cloth, a candle, a silver leaf, a bottle of sanctified water and a dove's feather – he set the items down on the tiny table next to the pallet.

Erelas stared. 'You're going to give him the Rite of the *Dying*?'

The Archdeacon didn't answer. Instead, he went back to his desk and fetched an ornate-looking dagger. The blade glinted in the orange light from the fire, which burned in the small hearth between the desk and the pallet. The smell of wood smoke mingled with the pungent aromas of the herbs and potions cluttering the shelves and the room seemed shrouded in a thin fog, which did nothing to lift the gloom.

He placed the dagger on the table and grabbed the herbal from Erelas. He strode to the desk again and returned with a black, leather-bound book – which looked even older than he did – and thrust it into Erelas' still-open palm. Erelas glared at him, wondering which of them was really lacking in attention, but again was ignored. The Archdeacon flicked through the herbal and once he found what he was searching for, made for one of the uppermost shelves in the room. He took down a small jar of oil and a bottle of thick, black liquid, returned to the table and set them down by the dagger. He threw the herbal back onto the desk.

'Why are you giving him this Rite?' demanded Erelas, fear paradoxically lending him courage. 'You haven't even *tried* to help him!'

'Hold your tongue!' snapped the Archdeacon. '*If* what I am going to attempt fails, there may not be time to gather these items ready for the Rite. I *told* you not to raise your hopes; I am merely preparing for the possibility that he may not survive!'

Erelas dropped his gaze. He bit hard on his lip as the Archdeacon readied himself. He tried to swallow his fear and concentrate, knowing that if the Archdeacon could not save Quinn, nobody could, and he, Erelas must not do anything to increase the risk of failure. He squeezed his eyes shut and prayed silently: *Please, God, let him live!*

'Do nothing until I tell you, and then do *exactly* as I say.' The Archdeacon sat opposite Erelas on the pallet and reached across for the oil. He removed the lid, and muttered in such a low voice Erelas could not make out the individual words. He wanted to hear; if he could hear the words he might recognise the rite and be reassured that Quinn's case was not a hopeless one. But all he heard was the soft buzz of the man's deep voice, as he dipped his fingers in the oil and anointed Quinn's pale forehead with it.

The Archdeacon took the black book from Erelas and placed it on Quinn's chest. He laid the dagger on top of the book and then leaned right over Quinn. He placed his palms against Quinn's temples, his long, wrinkled fingers curled into his sweat-soaked hair. He continued to speak in not much more than a whisper, but Erelas could at least see that he was doing something: something that required a great deal of effort, as if he were channelling energy into Quinn. Erelas could see the effect on Quinn, too – he was barely breathing, his fists clenched slowly and his back went rigid.

Quinn's eyes snapped open and he stared at the Archdeacon. The darkness of his right eye was unchanged, and seemed to Erelas to be even deeper, like an abyss that shouldn't be looked into, for fear of never escaping. But in his left eye, the turquoise light intensified, along with the red sparks. Then the Archdeacon's eyes changed, too. A deep indigo glow appeared and bright blue sparks danced outwards from them, flitting around the space between the two men, mingling with – no, *devouring* the red sparks emanating from Quinn's. His body stiffened further and the Archdeacon fought to hold on. Tears streamed down both their faces as the opposing forces between them battled it out.

A strange voice began shouting in an unrecognisable language. It took Erelas a second to realise it was coming from Quinn. The Archdeacon tightened his grip as Quinn's hands shot up and grasped his wrists, trying to force him to let go. Erelas made to assist the Archdeacon, but the Archdeacon bellowed '*No!*' at him and he flinched back. The Archdeacon resumed his recitation and eventually Quinn – or whatever it was that controlled him – began to lose the battle. Little by little, his hands lost their strength and then dropped to his sides, dislodging the dagger and the book.

Erelas made no move to catch them as they clattered to the floor.

Quinn took in a great gasp of air and cried out, '*God save me!*' He writhed as if in pain, and more tears emerged from his closed eyelids. Blood poured from his nose again and he coughed, spraying the Archdeacon's face.

'The cloth, Erelas,' the Archdeacon said, in a much gentler tone than he had spoken thus far.

Erelas wiped the Archdeacon's face clear of blood and retrieved the book and dagger from the floor.

'The book – put it back on his chest,' instructed the Archdeacon. Erelas did as he was told. 'Now, take the dagger. When I take my left hand from his head I need you to make a cut, small, but deep, on his left palm. Then, make a cut on his right hand, when I take *my* right hand away from his head – at those *precise* moments. Do you understand?'

Erelas was incredulous but nodded his assent and readied himself.

The Archdeacon resumed his work. He spoke louder, but Erelas was too focused on waiting for the moment he had to cut his friend's flesh to take heed of the words. He gripped the handle of the dagger tightly and held his breath as he stared, wide-eyed. The moment soon came; Erelas' hands shook as he grasped Quinn's left wrist and sliced into his palm. He pointed the blade at a steep angle to ensure the cut was deep enough. Quinn tried to pull away, but Erelas held on and the deed was done. The Archdeacon continued to speak. Mere seconds later, he removed his right hand from Quinn's temple. Erelas dropped his left wrist and reached for the right, almost flinging himself in the Archdeacon's way in the process, but he managed to make the cut in time and breathed again. The Archdeacon nodded his approval.

'You may let go of him now,' he said, out of breath and sweating. Tears stained his aged face.

As Erelas released him, Quinn clenched his fists and dug his fingertips into the blood on his palms. It dripped on to the rough, grey blanket beneath him. His eyes were still shut and his nose still bled. Erelas found it hard to see any improvement in his friend's condition, but at least he was calmer now.

'Is it over?' he whispered, not sure he wanted to know the answer.

'For us, yes. The rest is up to him.' The Archdeacon sounded exhausted. He stood up and backed away from the pallet. Quinn weakened and relaxed his hands. 'One more thing for us to do, then he will sleep.' He took the bottle of black liquid and pulled out the stopper. 'You will have to hold him, Erelas – he will not like this.'

Erelas sighed. *He won't like* me *at this rate*, he thought, and shifted closer to Quinn's head. He steadied it, one hand across his forehead, the other holding him by the jaw. As the Archdeacon leaned in, Erelas prised Quinn's mouth open. He expected a fight, but Quinn had no energy left. He attempted to turn his head away from the foul-smelling liquid as it was poured quickly into his mouth, but Erelas was able to still him, preventing too much from being spilled. Quinn swallowed, tried to clear his throat of the potion and swallowed again. He sucked in air and coughed one more time before he surrendered to exhaustion. He had not opened his eyes and, as Erelas released him, his head rolled to the side, his breathing becoming slower, steadier.

Erelas did not move from the pallet as the Archdeacon lit the candle on the table and laid the silver leaf on Quinn's pillow.

'He must rest now,' the Archdeacon said. 'There is nothing we can do but wait.'

'I'm not leaving,' Erelas said without looking away from Quinn's face.

The Archdeacon paused. 'As you wish,' he said, almost with empathy. 'I will go and speak to his parents. I am sure they will want to see him and I am sure you will respect their wishes if they ask you to leave.'

'Of course, Archdeacon. Anwenn went to fetch them. They will be here any moment.'

'Very well. I will speak with them outside. Try to clean his face and hands up a little before they see him.'

When the Archdeacon had left the quarters, Erelas gently washed the blood from Quinn. He prayed to God to spare his life as he did so. His thoughts did not stray to the mystery of what had befallen his friend in the Plane of Shadows – all he cared about was Quinn's survival.

The Archdeacon, however, could think of little else as he waited for Anwenn to return with the young Conductor's mother and father. They would need answers and he had none he was willing to give...

CHAPTER 3. AWAKENING.

The sight in his right eye had not returned. Quinn did not linger on this realisation; he had a hundred other questions in his mind to deal with first. Not least of which was how he had even survived his ordeal.

As he looked slowly around, he learned he was on a low bed, but that it was not his own; the light was coming from the wrong direction. He peered towards that light and Erelas came gradually into focus. He was dozing in a hard-backed wooden chair, his chin almost on his chest and his long legs stretched out in front of him.

He blinked hard, his head still pounding, and was surprised to recognise the Archdeacon's quarters.

It was a place which produced mixed feelings in him. He had loved this room since the start of his training, and was frequently found snooping around it when he should have been at study – usually dragging the unfortunate Erelas into trouble alongside him. It had been a treasure-trove to his young mind. The shelves were crammed full of all manner of items – herbs, potions, silver goblets with strange inscriptions on them, dusty old books neither boy could read, maps and feathers of all shapes, colours and sizes. The warmth and the smells were a comfort on cold winter days. The enormous desk with its locked drawers had them guessing what secrets it hid for hours on end. Best of all, the numerous candles, silver ornaments and crystals stilled even Quinn's playful mind and gave him a few moments of peace, which he found nowhere else except in the chapel.

But, being the quarters of the man who seemed to despise him to his very core, this room also brought out feelings of dread, frustration and resentment. Quinn was under no illusions that he wasn't partly to blame for the Archdeacon's attitude towards him, but he was hurt that nothing he did ever seemed to please him – the most he ever got for doing well was a forced grunt of admission.

He wondered where the old man was – and how he had ended up here. The last thing he remembered was being face-to-face with a Guardian and he wondered if he was really here or if this was just some strange, afterlife conjuring of his imagination. But as he moved to raise his head from the pillow, the pain became all too real and he slumped back with a groan. He was alive, by some miracle.

'Quinn?' Erelas sprang from the chair and peered at him. He placed a hand on his forehead.

'Erelas,' Quinn said, his voice little more than a whisper. 'Your snoring woke me up.'

'Liar.' Erelas smiled slightly, concern not allowing him to relax. 'How do you feel?'

'I'm just getting used to being alive, give me

a moment to decide.'

'According to the Archdeacon, you shouldn't be.'

'Is he terribly disappointed?'

For once, Erelas could not tell if Quinn was joking or not. He decided to ignore the question and replied with another of his own. 'Do you remember anything about what happened?'

Quinn went to rub his face with his hands, but flinched as he felt the pain of the cuts on his palms. He looked from the dressings to Erelas. 'Well, I remember most things – I don't remember *these*.'

Erelas looked uncomfortable. 'I'm sorry. That was me. The Archdeacon made me do it as part of the ritual he used on you to…well…to save your life.'

Quinn opened his mouth to reply, but the enormity of what he had experienced hit him like an armoured guard barrelling into his chest. He closed his eyes and took in a deep, shuddering breath instead.

'Are you alright?'

Quinn looked up at Erelas, his frown a feeble attempt to curb his emotions. 'My God, Erelas, I have never been so scared. The Archdeacon is right – I should be dead. The Guardians had me…three of them. I don't know how I…' He swallowed as Erelas put a hand on his arm. 'The soul I was conducting…it did something. It was so strong. I did everything I could to fight it off—'

'Slow down, Quinn. You need to take it easy for a while. There will be plenty of time to talk this over when you have rested and grown stronger. God knows the Archdeacon will make you go over it enough times, not to mention your parents. They've hardly left your side; they're only not here now because they were ordered to rest by Anwenn.'

'But...I don't understand *how* I survived...or how I got *here*. Did I get back to Cara and I just don't remember?'

'No. You just appeared outside the chapel, covered in dust from the Plane of Shadows. The best guess right now is that one of the Keepers sent you back.'

'A Keeper? But why? They never...' Quinn closed his eyes as a wave of nausea engulfed him.

'Quinn, please...not now. It can wait.'

'But Cara...' Quinn pressed his trembling fingers to his temples. He would never forgive himself if something had happened to his beloved horse...

'I went to find her. She's fine.'

'Thank you...' Quinn's hands drifted back to his sides. Gradually he relaxed, his frown faded and he closed his eyes once more. He sensed Erelas' warm palm upon his forehead again, as he felt the world tilt violently beneath him. He trusted Erelas to prevent him from falling and gave himself up to rest.

***

'So...How in the name of all things natural did you end up in such a state that even the Keepers took pity on you?' Erelas asked as he poured fresh water for Quinn.

Quinn had thought about the Keeper's intervention in the short time he had been awake, before Erelas had arrived straight from breaking his fast. The Keepers were powerful beings, but under constant threat from evil, hence their need for the Guardians' protection. They had neither the time, nor the inclination, to watch over Conductors working inside their realm – after all, the Conductors knew better than to delay returning to this world. If they were caught by the Guardians, the Keepers did not intervene. In fact, the Conductors had not even known they were able to until now.

'I don't know why a Keeper saved me, *if* that is what happened...' Quinn took a sip of the water, wincing at his sore throat. 'But if he did, I'm more than grateful. I was faced with three Guardians. One landed right in front of me. I could feel and smell its breath on me. I should not be here.' He shivered violently, almost spilling the water. Erelas took the cup from him and he sank down beneath the blankets, feeling exhausted again.

'Well, we don't have to talk about it now,' Erelas said gently. 'I just thought you might like to go over it with me, before the Archdeacon decides you're ready for interrogation. He's been in an utterly foul mood since it happened. You've been here three days now and it's *really* starting to grate, let me tell you.'

Quinn raised an eyebrow. 'I am, or he is?'

'Oh, it's becoming hard to choose,' Erelas said. He tried to look glum, but failed as the faintest curl of a smirk formed at the corners of his mouth. 'You're the talk of Delmoril. I'm only in here talking *to* you to avoid having to talk *about* you...'

Quinn gave a short laugh. 'Well, I appreciate the company. At least you talk to me.'

'What do you mean?'

'My father...Mother seems her usual self, but he hardly said a word to me the last time he was here. He looked at me strangely, as if I'm no longer me. And I don't mean he's fascinated by my right eye, for all its novelty value. Mother came to see me without him last night. She didn't know what to say when I asked her why he was like that...she wouldn't tell me why he hadn't come either. It's obvious he can't bear being around me. But all she says is that she thinks it's just the shock.' Quinn scoffed, unable to stop himself. 'He thinks *he's* had a shock?'

Erelas put a hand on his friend's arm. He knew how important his relationship with his parents was to him. 'He will be fine, Quinn. Nothing like this has ever happened before – that anyone knows of – and you're his only son. I don't need to tell you we could so easily have been in mourning for you right now. Go easy on him.'

Quinn was quiet for a while and Erelas left him to his thoughts as he busied himself around the room. He folded the extra blanket Quinn had needed during the night, adjusted the width that the single window was open to let in more fresh air, and replaced the candles. He turned back to the bed when Quinn said: 'Has the Archdeacon said anything about why the Keeper sent me back, instead of leaving me to be...to my fate?'

'No. I don't think he knows. But does it matter why, Quinn?'

'Well, yes. I don't know. I just...'

Erelas sat down on the bed, worried by the expression on Quinn's face. 'What? What's bothering you so much about it?'

Quinn looked at Erelas with a steady gaze, but took a deep breath before he replied. 'It's just that the Archdeacon seems *angry* about it. Angry with *me*. He's never liked me and I wouldn't want my near-death to be an excuse for him to suddenly start being nice to me, but...' He rubbed his face with his hands, now free of their dressings. He was exhausted and doubted his thoughts made any sense, let alone his words. 'If anything, he's worse now. If it was just getting into that situation that angered him he'd have let me feel his wrath by now. It's as if he's angry that a Keeper got involved. Or angry that I survived.' As he saw Erelas' cynical look he raised his hands. 'I know – I know...it sounds ridiculous, but I'm so used to his treatment of me over the years, I can feel the difference now. Something feels very wrong in all of this and I wish I could work out what it is...'

Erelas sighed. 'Look, Quinn. Keep this in perspective. As I said, this kind of thing has never happened before and nobody knows how to react. On top of that, the ritual the Archdeacon had to perform took quite a bit out of the old man and he's making sure everyone feels the effect of it, not just you. It's not right he's treating you the way he is, you will get no argument from me there. But your perception could be a little off, you know. You were completely drained, as well as almost being killed. You've not grown much stronger in the three days since and anyone would have been traumatised to the core by what you went through. Give yourself some time. If he's still bothering you when you have recovered more – a lot more – then *ask* him why. You've never been afraid to go up against him before and I hope you won't start to be now.'

'I'm not afraid of him, Erelas. I'm afraid of whatever has *him* so rattled...'

CHAPTER 4. ACCUSATION.

Arion shifted with unease as his son stared at him. 'I'm sorry, Quinn, but that's the only thing we can think of that could have caused such a thing.'

'*We?*' Quinn said with barely concealed anger. 'Meaning the *Archdeacon*.' He tried to sit up, feeling nauseous at the notion his father had just explained to him, but he still lacked the strength to do so by himself, so he gave up trying before he was offered help – help he was too angry to accept.

'Well...yes – we have had several meetings about this. God knows he has more experience and knowledge about conducting than the rest of us do.'

'That is *not* what happened, Father. I can't believe you would even *think* such a thing of me!'

'I think it because there is no other explanation!' Arion's frustration and distress was evident.

'That *you* can see! That doesn't mean there isn't one! I did *not* kill that man!'

'Then how do *you* see it? That this man had a power we're not aware of? That it somehow enabled him to force his consciousness into you, as you put it?'

'*Yes* – why is that less believable than me

being a murderer? The Archdeacon plants an idea in your head and you just accept it, against your own *son*!'

'You have hardly been a model of self-control over the years, Quinn. The Archdeacon knows that better than your mother and I were perhaps willing to admit, because we love you. But now...'

'Now *what*?' Quinn was trembling with anger at the Archdeacon's character assassination of him to his own parents. Although he had rarely been in the Archdeacon's favour, he thought this was far below the level the ruler of the Order of Conductors would ever have stooped to. 'Now you've woken up, or something?'

Arion did not answer, which was all the answer Quinn needed.

'What can I do to convince you? Yes, I *did* feel the evil in Rook, but it didn't make me angry. I was sickened and hurt, not angry. And even if I *had* been, I would not have severed his soul early or tried to destroy him myself. That would make absolutely no sense, since I wouldn't have even *been* there unless he was dying anyway! And what would be the point of trying to destroy his soul when I knew the Keepers would deal with him? Conducting has become second nature to me, Father, you know this! I know what I'm doing. Why would I be so stupid and reckless?'

'Why, indeed?' The Archdeacon appeared in the open doorway and Quinn glared at him.

'What do you want?' he snapped as anger

made him forget any courtesies afforded to the Archdeacon's rank. 'Have you come to make sure the poison you have fed my father is working to your satisfaction?'

'*Quinn!*' Arion's face was a mask of horror at his son's outburst.

'How *dare* you?' shouted the Archdeacon. His eyes widened and his cheeks flushed. 'I had a feeling your faith in your own abilities and the arrogance with which you carry yourself would get you into serious trouble one day. Do not try to shift the blame onto me when *your* actions are all that got you into this mess!'

'I did *not kill* that man!' Quinn cried, choosing to ignore the insults. 'I explained what happened. Your theory is ridiculous!'

'Quinn, that's *enough!*' Arion rose from the chair and glared at Quinn. 'This is not helping matters!'

Quinn covered his face with his hands, unable to grasp what was happening. He felt like screaming, like shaking his father, like slapping some sense into the Archdeacon, feelings which were alien to him and which filled him with as much dread as the Archdeacon's presence. Drawing in air until he could draw in no more, he dragged his fingers over his eyes and cheeks. He looked from one man to the other, hoping his emotions weren't visible. 'What do you intend to do with me, now that you have tried and convicted me in my absence?'

'Don't be so dramatic,' the Archdeacon spat. 'I don't plan on doing anything. The man is dead, and you have received just punishment for your actions. And –' he added quickly, seeing Quinn about to protest once more. 'I'm not interested in going over the matter any further, Quinn. This is the end of it. You will recover and resume your work. I cannot afford to have a Conductor removed from duties. Had the Keepers thought that to be a preferable outcome, you would not have been sent back to us alive. I will not discuss this matter further with you.'

'Then get out.' Quinn's voice had an eerie calm to it. He held his focus on the Archdeacon's cold eyes, despite the dizziness which threatened to overwhelm him.

The Archdeacon's mouth tightened in his familiar expression of intense displeasure, but he said nothing. He turned and walked away, brushing past Erelas, who had just arrived, out of breath, clearly wondering what the shouting was about.

Quinn looked at his friend, his emotions now almost impossible to hold back. He shut his eyes tight. 'Please go, Father,' he said.

Arion looked deflated and older, Erelas thought, as he tried to fathom what on earth had gone on in this room. Arion walked slowly out of the quarters. He did not look up from the floor as he went.

Erelas watched him go and after checking that neither man would change their mind and return, closed the door. The room lost its brightness as the sunlight was shut out, and took on the muted glow of the fire and candles, with little assistance from the small window at the northern end.

He went to the chair, pulled it closer to the bed and sat down. Quinn had not opened his eyes and the hand pressed over his mouth trembled. Sweat ran down his temples and his skin was paler than usual. Erelas was worried – four days after his return, he had made very little progress in his recovery.

'Quinn...what the hell just happened?'

Opening his tear-moistened eyes, Quinn took his hand away and mumbled: 'I think I'm going to be sick...'

CHAPTER 5. THE TAVERN.

Quinn could see the inside a tavern. He could smell the acrid smoke, and a foul stench which stung his nostrils and made his eyes water. His throat was sore and there was an intense, bitter taste in his mouth. He moved slowly forwards, further into the main room. It was dark; dimly lit by poorly maintained, flickering oil lamps and a dying fire in a grate at the far end. It was quiet – too quiet. He knew something was wrong. In the darkness he could make out the vague shapes of people sitting at tables, but his focus struggled with the inconstancy of the available light – and none of the shapes were moving.

He saw himself pick up a lamp from one of the side tables and move towards another, one with a short, rounded shape sitting at it. As the light got closer he saw a plump woman in her late thirties slumped over the table, a tankard upset at the side of her arm. Its contents dripped over the edge of the table and onto the floor. He moved the lamp closer to her face. The eyes were wide, but saw nothing. A splash of red, up her fleshy neck, on to her chin and a flood of darkened blood down towards her large chest showed her throat had been slashed.

Quinn felt his body flinch, but in his mind he heard himself laugh. His consciousness panicked as he tried to fight free of this vision. He seemed to have very limited control over his physical form and he moved forwards again. The lamp provided him with a brief view of the rest of the room and the rest of the mutilated corpses, before lighting the way up a rickety wooden staircase. He saw himself smash a door open with a heavy, dirty boot and walk into a well-lit, but smoky chamber.

In the middle of the room, on the floor, sat a young man. His mouth was gagged, his feet were shackled together and his wrists bound with rope. He looked up in terror and shook his head; muffled protests came through the cloth between his teeth.

Quinn desperately fought to be free before he witnessed any more of this horror, but no matter what he did, he was trapped...

***

For several moments Quinn did not know where he was and panicked, trying to fight against the strong arms pinning him onto his back. He could not see properly in the dimly-lit room, and tears hampered his vision further. It took him a while to realise the arms belonged to Erelas. He froze, still not trusting that he was not in any danger.

'You were dreaming, Quinn. You're alright now.' Erelas' voice was calm and Quinn was able to relax a little and take in the familiar surroundings of his own quarters. Erelas released his hold and reached for a damp cloth. He dabbed Quinn's sweat-soaked forehead. 'What were you dreaming about?'

'That man…Rook. I think I was seeing into his memories again. I don't think it *was* a dream, Erelas.' He felt sick again and closed his eyes, but when that made it worse, he inhaled sharply and tried to sit up.

'Slowly…' said Erelas, assisting him. 'What did you see, exactly?'

'A tavern. Dead people everywhere. And a young man, bound and gagged in an upper room. I was seeing it as if – I don't know…' He shook his head, as he looked up at Erelas. 'I don't know if I'm losing my sanity, Erelas. I was him. I saw it from inside Rook, as if I were the one doing whatever he was doing. I'm glad you woke me when you did.'

'You're not losing anything, Quinn. I'm certain the dreams will stop when you have recovered physically. Your fever is slow to break. Try not to worry about them so much; it will only slow your progress.'

'Erelas, please…I've had enough of people not believing me. It was *real*. I could smell things, taste things. I knew I had killed those people. I knew what I was planning to do to that poor man…I know that's not much in the way of evidence, but please, trust me – I have Rook's memories stuck inside of my head and they are starting to reveal themselves. I don't know what to do…'

Erelas could see he was close to breaking down and placed a hand on his arm. 'Alright, I believe you. I know you wouldn't exaggerate such things. But there is nothing we can do until you're well again and we have a better idea of what we're dealing with. They may go of their own accord when you're fully recovered.'

'I hope you're right. I wish I felt stronger already – it's been five days now and I still feel as weak and sick as I did the first day. And I'm still blind in this eye,' he added miserably, indicating the dark right eye that nobody could seem to avoid staring at.

Erelas opened his mouth to reply but the door opened and the Archdeacon strode in, his face as stern as ever.

'Out,' he snapped at Erelas. 'I want to talk to Quinn alone – for a change.' The contempt in his voice was plain and Erelas frowned. He did not understand why he should be on the receiving end of the Archdeacon's anger.

'I have nothing to say to you.' Quinn's voice was quiet, but held all the determination he needed to get his point across to his master.

'I have plenty to say to *you*, Quinn. And you are not exactly in any state to avoid hearing it.'

'Archdeacon...' began Erelas, shocked by his lack of compassion.

'*Out!*'

Erelas looked to Quinn for guidance. Although he did not wish to be left alone, Quinn did not want to bring more trouble to Erelas and nodded his assurance that it would be alright. Erelas flung the damp cloth onto the table and strode out, daring to give the Archdeacon a withering look as he passed. As usual, however, the Archdeacon took no notice.

The Archdeacon waited for Erelas to close the door behind him, before he stepped forwards and stood at the end of the bed, his hands crossed in front of his formal robes. The deep purple, edged with gold, made the old man's skin seem even more pale and sickly, giving his whole appearance a disturbing aspect when paired with the glare in his eyes.

'I heard your conversation with Erelas,' he announced.

Quinn sighed and looked at the master. 'So now you take away my privacy, as well.'

'As well as what?'

'As well as the love of my father, my reputation among friends, my dignity…I could go on.'

The Archdeacon scoffed. 'You assume you had much of a reputation to begin with, Quinn. You over-estimate yourself.'

'Where does this hatred of me come from, Archdeacon?' Quinn asked, tired of the constant battles. 'I admit that I have always been difficult and contrary, but nothing to warrant such treatment as you have given me for as far back as I can remember!'

'*Hate*? No…that was not hate. You would have really felt my hate. That was merely irritation and constant disappointment. You showed such promise at the beginning of your training. You could have been so much more than you are. You are an excellent Conductor, but you have settled for that and wasted your talents. Proper application of your intelligence would have ensured you a place among the scholars and a chance of advancement. Now look at you...'

'I am *happy* as I am!' Quinn snapped.

'And now that is all you will ever be. I hope your contentment lasts, because there will be nothing else available to you now. Everyone will look at you with contempt and distrust and you will have to live with that. But no matter – I see it as just reward for your behaviour.'

'I don't care how you see it. Tell me what you came here for, or get out.'

The Archdeacon bristled and Quinn saw for just a moment that he was fighting to remain in control of his temper. He was pleased to have rattled the Archdeacon so much – he was tired of the abuse being one-sided.

'As I said, I heard what you said about your dreams. And they *are* dreams. What you were proposing to your friend is ridiculous. Thankfully, I am not as impressionable as he is. You will accept that they are dreams and leave it at that. You have two weeks to recover your strength and then you will resume your duties as a Conductor.' He slammed Quinn's amulet down onto the small table by the bed and stepped back. 'And – if anything like this happens again, rest assured I will leave you to your fate.'

Quinn could not speak. He could not understand what was going on in the Archdeacon's mind. Why would he not believe what was happening when Quinn's testimony should have counted above all else? Why was the old man so incensed by everything he had said about his experience? There was nothing he could have done to alter what occurred in the Plane of Shadows, any more than he could help what was happening to him now.

But, no matter what Quinn felt about the injustice of it all, he knew in that moment that there was nothing he could do about any of it. He would return to his duties with his relationship with his father spoiled, his relationship with the Archdeacon worsened, not to mention what the other Conductors thought of him now that word had spread about the murder he knew he hadn't committed.

Thank God for Erelas, he thought. If anyone could lift him and get him back on his feet and ready to carry on, Erelas could.

'Do you understand?' the Archdeacon demanded.

'Is that all?' muttered Quinn, exhausted once more.

The Archdeacon's jaw clenched. 'For now.'

'Then get out and leave me alone.'

The Archdeacon strode to Quinn's side and leaned in close, his eyes ablaze with fury. Quinn was so surprised he instinctively shrank back against the wall. 'Do not forget that I could still have you executed for murder,' he hissed. 'Your word counts for far less than mine. This attitude of yours had better cease *immediately*, or I will see you publicly tried and convicted! And if you think I would not dare, *try me*!'

Quinn remained silent and his heart hammered in his chest. The Archdeacon had him and they both knew it.

CHAPTER 6. A RELUCTANT PARTING.

'Stop fussing, Erelas. She'll bite you in a minute...' said Quinn, tucking the indigo amulet under his plain linen shirt and wrapping his robe tight around his body.

Cara snorted as if in agreement and Erelas stepped back. He gave the massive, glossy black mare a reproachful glance. 'She wouldn't...would she?'

Quinn smiled and raised an eyebrow. 'I wouldn't put a wager on it. The girth is fine – thank you for your help.' He placed his foot in the stirrup and shifted his seat in the saddle. It felt as if he had not ridden for months rather than just a couple of weeks.

'If you ask me, the fact you needed help with it proves you're not as strong as you ought to be before you go back out there.' Erelas' face resumed the same fretful expression it had worn frequently over the three days since the Archdeacon had ordered Quinn to return to his duties. The allocated time for rest was over and whether anyone else believed it or not, he pronounced Quinn fit and refused to allow any more delays.

'I have to go back. Refusal to do as he says will just result in more threats to have me formally tried. And he holds all the strings of his puppet scholars. I'd be convicted the minute I walked into the Great Hall.'

'He's a bastard.'

Quinn looked shocked. 'Erelas!'

'Well he is,' Erelas snapped. 'I know I've never spoken out against him before – I don't have your courage, but he's gone too far—'

'You're not to get yourself into trouble, Erelas.' He hesitated, concern in his eyes. 'I appreciate your support, you know that. I wouldn't be as ready as I am today without you. But leave it alone now. It's time to move on, however angry we might feel about it. Very few people believe my side of it. Even my own parents side with the Archdeacon. I don't have the energy to go up against them all again, and even less inclination to drag you down with me. There is no sense in getting yourself in bother with the old man with your wedding so close. Focus on that.'

'I can't help but worry, Quinn. I think you should travel with me – just for a while, until we know how well you will hold up when the time comes.'

'The Archdeacon won't *allow* it!' Quinn was frustrated with the constant travelling in circles they had been doing, and the horrible feeling of being trapped on this path caused him to speak more sharply than he intended. He felt guilty when Erelas closed his mouth and looked down. 'I'm sorry,' he said. 'But he insists he needs every

Conductor he has out there, with the guards cracking down on the civilians all over Rivallen, and the civilians killing each other because of poverty and frayed nerves. I hate to admit it, but sitting around here for three days, knowing I have to get back out there has only made the task more daunting. My eye is not going to get better, I've accepted that, but the rest of me will get stronger in time. Maybe getting it over with is the best thing to do – *alone*.'

'But he wouldn't have to know...'

Quinn could sense the desperation in Erelas' voice. He slowly stepped down from the saddle, placed his hands on Erelas' shoulders and looked into his eyes. 'I will be alright, Brother. I'll come back to Delmoril after each journey and rest. The Archdeacon cannot argue with that.'

Erelas considered this for a moment and nodded. 'I'll check on you when I can. If I'm not here, Anwenn will look in on you. Please, make sure you rest – and eat!' he added as he looked Quinn up and down. 'You're a bag of bones; even with the robes on you look thinner than Anwenn!'

'And you're fussing again,' Quinn said with a smile. 'Go and finish those wedding plans, before your betrothed runs off with a scholar...'

Erelas laughed and punched Quinn's arm in mock protest. 'Get going, then. I can't fuss if you're not here.'

Quinn shook his head and grinned, showing a glimpse of the old Quinn. He climbed back into the saddle and wheeled Cara slowly around.

'See you soon,' he called as the big horse broke into a trot. 'And stay out of trouble!'

CHAPTER 7. FEAR.

Quinn managed to travel for several miles before he had to pull Cara up. He leaned forwards in the saddle, rested his head against her hot, damp neck and breathed in her scent, a smell he loved and had missed these past two weeks. He was shocked and frustrated as he could not stop his tears from falling on to her shiny black coat. Why could he not have just confided in Erelas and been honest about how he really felt? It might have relieved a bit of the pressure he felt that was weighing him down, drowning him, not allowing him to hang on to hope.

He was experiencing a sickening mix of emotions. He felt a deep, painful grief at the loss of his close relationship with his parents, the loss of some friendships in Delmoril, and the respect of nearly everyone who knew him and was convinced of his guilt. He felt anger at the injustice. He felt trapped by his position and his inability to fight back with any effect whatsoever. Most of all, he felt absolute terror at the prospect of it happening again.

He knew he had not killed Rook. But the Archdeacon's refusal to look into alternatives meant he had no idea what caused the violation of his consciousness, the brutal assault on his mind and body and his own near-death. He was not sure whether Rook's soul had perished, or was locked within him, whether the memories he experienced were due to the trauma of his ordeal or if the soul was trying to fight Quinn for some continued level of existence. Trying to assemble these thoughts into some kind of coherent order had proved impossible in the weeks since it had happened.

And now, despite feeling mentally exhausted and physically weakened far below his usual level of fitness, he had to face the prospect of conducting another soul.

As Cara waited for Quinn to compose himself, he wondered whether he could go through with it at all. What if he froze at the crucial moment and caused the soul of the dying person to be trapped in this realm for eternity? What if the same thing happened and the Keepers were unable to rescue him a second time? What if he could not begin the ritual at all? He was nothing if he was not a Soul Conductor. It was what he was born to do. It was all he had known, and he had loved it.

He and Erelas were both good Conductors; powerful servants of God, able to use abilities that would turn most liberal-minded believer's hair white. They loved their work, although Erelas lacked the self-assurance that often got Quinn into trouble with the Archdeacon and the scholars. Quinn stood out from the others in terms of strength, stamina and an almost uncontrollable desire for justice. He willingly shouldered the blame when they had been called in for disciplinary measures during their training. His disregard for authority irritated the Archdeacon on a regular basis, but even he could not deny Quinn's natural skill and potential. They had both been eager to finish training, which they did at the age of twenty. On that day, Quinn decided the joking around and pranks would end.

He became one of the best Conductors anyone had seen for many years, capable of conducting souls that would have destroyed a weaker one. Even though Quinn's experience with Rook had never happened before to anyone's knowledge, some of the worst souls could exhaust a Conductor to the point that they never recovered. They lived in a permanent state of catatonia, sometimes for weeks, sometimes for years, before eventually dying. Less traumatic experiences could put even a strong Conductor out of action for days at a time. But that had never happened to Quinn, despite his young age and relative inexperience. Indeed, the Keepers often reported their satisfaction with his skills to the Archdeacon – views the Archdeacon had grudgingly passed along to him. But Quinn had felt he still had a long way to go before he could say he was as good as he would ever be. At twenty-two years of age, he – perhaps arrogantly – believed he had hardly begun.

And now, one man, one single soul, had managed to do something to him that nobody had ever heard of, and almost killed him in the process. He had only survived due to the unprecedented intervention of the Keepers and the skill and hard work of the Archdeacon. If it were all to end now because he could not face his fears, it would all be in vain. There would be nothing left for him to do with his life and he would have broken his own heart.

He knew he had to call on his hitherto strong sense of duty, his reserves of strength and stubbornness and tackle his fear head-on.

But as he breathed in the scent of his beloved horse and felt the comfort of her warmth in the cool autumn breeze, he decided a few more minutes of peace wouldn't hurt. He had been relieved that Erelas had tracked Cara down and taken her home – she would have remained where he had left her for days otherwise, waiting for him to return. She had been his companion since the last day of their training, when *she* had chosen *him*, as was tradition in Delmoril. They had developed a special relationship of mutual trust and respect. If he had had a particularly difficult time conducting a person's soul, with little energy to do anything but slump to the ground upon his return, she would lie down next to him, always careful not to crush him. He would lie against her back and there she would stay, waiting for him to recover his strength. He would talk to her about everything and she would listen, seeming to understand how he was feeling – knowing when to nudge him, to comfort him, or just remain still and let him get things off his mind. He did not know what he would do without her.

He sat up, took a deep breath and patted her neck. 'Where shall we go today, Cara?' he said, looking around at the quiet forest.

Cara tossed her head a couple of times and then turned to the right. Quinn allowed her to lead him; it did not matter where they went.

***

Quinn and Cara travelled overnight, deep into the Kingdom of Rivallen, guided by a brilliant full moon. They met very few people on the forest trails or open tracks. Most people were afraid to go anywhere after dusk, and a curfew was in place after midnight.

People eyed them with suspicion and passed them by as quickly as possible, but Quinn was used to being treated that way. Many people were wary of strangers; the Conductors, especially, looked as if they did not belong there. Their pale skin and silver-grey eyes made them stand out against the brown or blue-eyed, tanned population of Rivallen. Quinn was fully aware his appearance was even more striking now his eyes didn't match in colour.

They were usually taken for travellers and largely ignored or avoided. Even the notoriously brutal sheriff's guards took little notice of them.

They dressed like poor pilgrims in plain robes, which helped to hide their strength and agility. The only things they carried of any value were their weapons – a magnificently crafted sword and a small dagger, which also doubled as a useful tool. They were always kept well-hidden.

Only one man had spoken to them, a dirty, poorly-clothed and poorly-fed old man who rubbed Cara's ears and blessed Quinn, wishing them both a safe journey before he strolled into the shadows. He didn't appear to notice Quinn's odd eye colours. He had perhaps assumed the dark one was normal and he was blind in the grey one – rather than the reverse – which was not uncommon among the poor. They suffered more from disease and misfortune than the rest of the population.

Early the next morning he broke his fast by a stream. The autumn sunshine was bright and promised a little warmth later in the day. It sent blinding flashes of white light into his working eye as it was reflected from the tumbling, clear waters.

He considered catching a fish, but decided he was not hungry enough, so he settled for some bread he had brought with him, and some berries he had found on the edge of the forest. Cara grazed on the unspoiled grass of the riverbank, her saddle and bridle on the ground at the base of a tree. She would not stray from Quinn.

As he refilled his water-skin after eating, the amulet at his throat began to vibrate. He pulled it out from under his shirt and saw the same turquoise glow that would soon shine from his eyes – or one of them, at least. He fought down the sudden lurch of nausea, proof of the nervousness that threatened to rise up and take control of him. *I just have to get through this one*, he told himself. *After this first soul, things will surely be easier...*

'Cara – it's time.'

Cara snorted in reply and carried on grazing.

Quinn raised an eyebrow and shook his head, smiling. 'I'll miss you, too.' He took a short drink from the skin, placed it on the ground next to his pack and stood up. '*Don't* steal the bread from my bag!'

Cara raised her head and nodded at him, lips curled back.

'Bad horse.' But he was grateful she had made him smile.

Quinn closed his hand around the glowing amulet and spoke in a low voice: 'God, deliver your servant to the soul awaiting your judgement.'

Slowly, in a creeping, swirling shroud of white mist, he disappeared from Cara's side.

CHAPTER 8. JUDGEMENT.

He found himself inside a tiny, single-roomed house that stank of stale ale, sweat and urine. He tried to ignore the stench, as he listened to the irate yelling of a man who stood a few feet away from him, beside an upturned table. The man had not seen him yet and Quinn took a moment to allow his sight to adjust to the lack of light – the single, small window provided very little. Broken crockery littered the room, and through the dust and smoke of the fire in the hearth, Quinn noticed a small shape on the dirt floor, beyond the bulk of the man. He moved around the man and inhaled sharply. The figure was a small boy, he guessed around eight or nine years of age, lying motionless and bleeding.

All his fears evaporated. Fury took over.

'Get up, you useless piece of *shit*!' The man was screaming at the boy, slurring slightly. 'You're just like your mother was – good for nothing! Get *up*!' He kicked the boy hard, shifting his whole body several inches across the floor.

Quinn took one long stride towards the man. He grabbed him with both hands, gripped his skull and forced the man to face him. The man went from rage to terror in an instant, as he realised he was not strong enough to fight the power of the stranger who had appeared from nowhere. Quinn's face conveyed his feelings, frightening the man further as he spoke a rapid stream of words he could not follow. His right eye remained dark, but his left began to glow – this time however, red sparks darted from it and shot straight into the widened eyes of the man, who screamed and squeezed them shut. But that could not stop the power from taking its hold on him.

Quinn's body did not suffer the pain he would usually have felt when conducting a violent person's soul. He felt no fear that this man's wickedness would pose a threat to him the way Rook's had. Instead, he felt a rush of energy shoot through him, and a feeling of immense strength. He even felt his mouth break into a smile; he had never felt so alive. It should have alarmed him, but all he felt was the pleasure of it. He did not want it to end...

The man struggled, clawing at Quinn's arms and hands in a futile effort to free himself from his grip. Quinn held on and continued to speak as he glared into the man's eyes – and then everything changed. The screaming ceased abruptly and the hands lost their grip on Quinn's arms. The darkness of the cottage dissipated into hazy, roseate light.

They were in the Plane of Shadows.

The man stood petrified in the silence. 'Who are you?' he asked in a shaky, weak voice.

Quinn did not answer. He looked around

and saw two Guardians circling in the distance. The man followed his gaze and after a few moments of squinting into the murky, dirty red sky, he spotted the massive creatures. A feeble cry escaped his lips. His knees buckled, but Quinn grabbed him by the throat and held him tight.

'Please...' the man croaked.

Quinn waited until the Guardians were close enough to see the two figures standing on the barren sand, then he looked at the man with pure hatred in his glowing eyes. He thrust the man away from him, making him stumble backwards and sit heavily on the ground. The feelings of euphoria disappeared that same instant, replaced by a wave of intense pain and sudden weakness. He fought to stay on his feet as his vision blurred a little. But the anger did not fade.

The Guardians screeched, a terrible noise that made the man freeze. He looked in turn at them and at Quinn, his eyes so wide they looked as if they might break loose from their sockets.

'Please!' he shouted. 'I'm *sorry*!'

Quinn's expression changed to one of disgust and as he took the amulet in his hands, he spoke in a quiet voice. 'You will be.'

Remaining calm, he said the words which would return him to the dying boy. There was a flash of pure white light, a flutter of sparks like turquoise fireflies...and he was gone.

All the man could do was scream, as the Guardians swooped in to control him until a

C. S. EVANS

Keeper arrived.

CHAPTER 9. THE KEEPER.

Quinn stepped over the corpse of the man and bent down beside the child. His body was failing, but there was a hint of life left in his open, unseeing eyes. However, Quinn would not have been called here if the boy had been destined to survive. Without intervention, which was strictly forbidden, it would soon be over.

Quinn wanted to cry for this child, this innocent boy who had done nothing to deserve the beating that had brought a Conductor to his side.

He had conducted the souls of many victims of violence, but never a child. In fact, he had never conducted anyone under the age of nineteen, and realised with a jolt of alarm that he could not do it. He just couldn't. He would have to break a fundamental rule and attempt to revive the boy…

Fear gripped him. It formed like an ice crystal in the pit of his stomach. He did not know if he was capable of saving this child or not, but even trying to save him would break the laws of the Order of Conductors, set down over the centuries by the Keepers. They were not to contest the will of God.

In the killing of the boy's father he had already disgraced himself in the eyes of God, without adding further insult by trying to change the boy's fate. He had broken one of the core tenets of the Order. He had manifested the very crime the Archdeacon had accused him of. Execution seemed inevitable now. Execution and eternal punishment.

But he could not let it be in vain. He had to try. Placing his hands over the sticky mess of hair that partially concealed the injury to the boy's head, he prepared to cast...

'Quinn.'

The deep voice from behind him made him jump so badly he almost lost his balance. Twisting around as far as he could, he inhaled sharply when he realised it was one of the Keepers, bearing a solemn stance beneath his dark, hooded cloak. Quinn let go of the child and stood, bowed in reverence, and then looked up, anxiety clear in his eyes. He knew he was in serious trouble.

'What are you doing, Quinn?' The Keeper's voice was quiet, calm. 'You have taken a life and now you are trying to change the fate of another. You must not do this.'

Quinn swallowed, his mouth dry. When he spoke, his voice seemed hoarse and feeble. 'He's just a child, Keeper. I cannot let this happen to him.' He could not find any words regarding the murder he had committed. He was far too frightened to say anything about that.

'It is not your place to decide who passes over unless you are defending yourself. You have known this since the start of your training.' The

Keeper folded back the hood of his long, black cloak and looked at Quinn steadily, paying particular attention to his right eye. They had the same, piercing silver eyes as the Conductors, the same pale complexion, the same fine, black hair. But there was an air of perfection about these beings that commanded obedience and respect.

'I am sorry, Keeper. I always thought I was strong enough to deal with anything I had to do. I don't know what has happened to me. That man...' Quinn glanced at the body between himself and the Keeper. 'Something took over. I cannot explain it. But I cannot bring myself to do my duty for this boy. His life has barely begun and it's been ended by the one person who was supposed to protect him.' He felt a hot stinging sensation in his eyes, the left of which had now turned back to its normal silver-grey. 'Take my soul, if you have to – I deserve it – but I will not take his.'

The Keeper said nothing. He stood still, just looking at Quinn, and Quinn felt the full weight of his gaze. The moments passed and he became more fearful for the boy's life. Surely soon it would be too late...

'It is not your compassion for this child which is of the most concern to me, Quinn. You went against *God*. You were not forced to protect yourself but still you took a life. And you took that life without hesitation and with violence.'

Quinn looked at the floor; remorse and dread burned inside him like acid.

'What are your intentions?' asked the Keeper.

Quinn looked up again, a look of confusion on his face. 'I have not thought of my intentions, Keeper. I was not aware I had a choice in front of me.'

The Keeper remained silent for a moment and then stepped over the man's corpse to stand directly in front of him. 'You are well known in our realm for your skill, courage and strength as a Conductor. You have commanded respect among the Keepers, although you have not been aware of our observations. Conducting Rook's soul would have killed even some of the strongest of Conductors, and you do not fall far below the ranks of the very best.'

'What *did* happen to me that night, my lord?' Quinn dared to ask, trying desperately not to break down. 'Archdeacon is convinced I killed Rook. I didn't...'

'I know you did not kill him, Quinn. I am afraid we do not know what happened to you, or why it changed you, but I have faith that you can recover.'

'My lord...' Quinn clenched his fists when he realised his hands were shaking. 'Please...I have no wish to be sent to the Guardians, but—'

'Speak plainly, Quinn. I will not object to your honesty.'

'I am broken. This –' he said, a hand gesturing to the sorrowful scene before them. 'This proves I am no longer what I was. I do not know what I am now. Something dark is within me and I cannot get rid of it. I don't see how I will ever be what I was again...or what purpose is left for me in this life...' He could no longer keep his feelings in check and tears sprang from his tired eyes. He looked at the floor, wishing he could feel gratitude instead of shame. '*God forgive me...*' he whispered, almost choking on the words.

The Keeper stretched out a pale, slender hand and lifted Quinn's chin until he had no choice but to look into his eyes. He smiled, and his compassion was plainly visible. 'You are still Quinn. You are not an event, or a circumstance. You are not a triumph, or a tragedy. You are not your crime. I *know* you did not kill Rook. I know why you killed this man and while that does not make your actions right, or allow for them to go unpunished, they *do* demonstrate that you are still the man we have come to know recently. You have not killed for power, money or pleasure. Yes, you were devastated by evil, but you survived. Do not let these things define you, my son. *Fight back.* Bring back the man who was loved and respected. It may take time – maybe years – but that man *is* still within you. Make sure he becomes the victor, not the victim. God *will* forgive you. Have faith in his love, if not in yourself.'

The Keeper let his words sink in, watching Quinn until he slowly nodded. 'You lend me courage, Lord. I am grateful for your leniency and wisdom, more than I feel I can express.'

'You're exhausted, and in shock. It is to be expected. But there is something you need to do for me in return.'

'Name it, my lord.'

'Your healing would not have helped the boy. However, I can restore him, *if* it is God's will. I will do this only to prevent your crime from being committed in vain. But in return, you must go to the Archdeacon and make a full confession. I do not take you for the kind of man who would hide from his responsibilities, but I would like your solemn oath that you will face the consequences, whatever they may be.'

Quinn nodded his assent without hesitation. 'You have my word, Keeper. The boy's life is worth whatever will be done to me as punishment.'

The Keeper's expression softened a little. 'I hope he repays you by living an honourable life. I will send word to the Archdeacon that your life has been spared by me and he is not to pass a sentence of death upon you. Neither is he to imprison you. You are no use to anyone dead or locked inside a cell. Now, let me see to the boy.'

Quinn remained where he was as the Keeper moved past him and bent over the body of the child. With a silent movement of his hand over the boy, the invisible power he asked of God descended onto him. Moments later, the boy gasped and began to cough. As he started to cry, he looked around the room in fear, while the Keeper turned back to Quinn.

He placed his hand on the young Conductor's arm and gave him a sympathetic smile. 'I *do* understand why you did what you did. I wish you well. But I must take my leave of you now. We shall meet again.'

Quinn bowed his head once again, and then looked deep into the Keeper's luminescent eyes. 'Thank you for your mercy, Lord. I fully expected to be sent to the Guardians.'

The Keeper inclined his head, looking serious once more. 'Some souls are too important to be lost.'

CHAPTER 10. RENN.

The boy struggled into a sitting position. Still crying, he looked fearfully at the stranger in his house and the body of his father in rapid turns. Quinn remained where he was, unsure of what to say or do. He would keep his promise to the Keeper, of course, but what was he to do with the boy?

The boy's cries calmed and he pushed himself backwards, further away from both Quinn and the corpse. Quinn held out a hand to reassure him.

'Do not fear me; I did not come here to harm you.'

The boy stopped shuffling and looked up at him with red-rimmed brown eyes.

'What is your name?'

The boy hesitated, blinking hard, then said, 'I – it's – I'm Renn.'

'My name is Quinn.'

'Is he dead?' Renn said, his voice strengthening.

'Yes. I had to stop him from hurting you. You do understand that, don't you?'

Renn nodded slowly.

'How old are you, Renn?'

'Eleven.'

Quinn raised an eyebrow. The poor child had not been looked after for a number of years for him to still be so small at that age.

'Do you work? Are you apprenticed to anyone?'

Renn shook his head, sniffing. 'My father is a cottager. I just work with him. Nobody will take me as an apprentice. They say I'm too weak.'

Quinn frowned. I'm not surprised, he thought. He again felt pity for the boy. He had lived a life of poverty and cruelty and must have had no hope of bettering himself.

'Do you have any other family here in this village, or nearby? Someone you can stay with?'

Renn shook his head as he got to his feet. 'It was just me and...' He glanced at the body on the floor and struggled to keep himself from crying again.

Quinn was stuck. He did not want to leave this boy alone, but he could not possibly take him to Delmoril. He bit his lip as he looked the boy up and down.

The door burst open, making them both jump violently. The boy cried out, ran to the upturned table and crouched behind it. Two members of the kingdom's Royal Guard rushed in, took in the scene and grabbed Quinn by the arms before he had a chance to react. He tried to free himself, but they were heavy, thick-limbed brutes and it was useless – exhaustion washed over him too quickly.

'Hold fast!' growled one of the guards. His weather-worn, chunky face frowned down on

Quinn, a satisfied smirk beginning to form. 'You've got no chance.'

Quinn slumped, giving in to their physical dominance, and looked over at Renn. 'I'm sorry. I would have found you somewhere safe—'

'*Quiet!*' shouted the second guard, causing Renn to sink lower behind the table.

'What will happen to the boy?' Quinn asked, but all he got in reply was a strike to his face with the back of the guard's hand.

'Speak again and I'll cut out your tongue!'

Blood ran from his nose. He squeezed his eyes shut as the guards twisted his arms behind his back and forced his head down. They turned him around and half-dragged him out into the open. Villagers stood around, too frightened to move or speak themselves.

As he was hauled away, he saw a man and a woman enter Renn's house; he prayed they would take care of the boy far better than his father had.

***

He was forced to walk several miles, getting soaked by the sudden downpour that started as soon as they had left the village. The guards pulled him along behind one of armoured horses, with his hands tied in front of him so tightly the rope was chafing the skin on his wrists. He had stumbled many times, his fatigue not helped by the mud – where his boots didn't stick, they slid. If he had to go much further, they would have to drag him along the sodden ground.

The guards said nothing to him on the trek, but he knew enough about the Kingdom of Rivallen to know where he was going. He would be taken to the sheriff, who was notoriously harsh and used fear and cruelty to keep the people in line.

Rivallen's king, Mattias, was a weak man. He had changed from a young, strong, charismatic leader to an ageing recluse after the accidental death of his beloved Queen. Without being conscious of it, he had gradually handed the main responsibilities of ruling the kingdom to Sheriff Garin. The king spent his time brooding in the castle, looking after his only son, shielded from the trials and troubles of life inside and outside his court. He no longer gave banquets, or held tournaments for the knights of the Royal Guard, or took any interest in the lives of his subjects. He cared not what was happening to them under Garin's rule, as long as he and his prince, Toren, were safe in the castle.

Garin took full advantage of his new power. He ruled by intimidation, taxed everyone heavily, imposed trade limitations and curfews and regularly beat people who did not conform. Most of his own guards were afraid of him, but there were some who craved power and were just as cruel as him.

But Quinn remained calm. All he had to do was wait for the physical connection between himself and the horse and guard to be broken and then he could use the amulet to travel back to Cara. He would ride hard for Delmoril and the sheriff and all his guards would not be able to find him. All he needed was a little patience…

**

As Cara galloped smoothly up the grassy slope towards the seemingly impenetrable forest, Quinn reached into his shirt and grabbed the amulet. Saying just one word aloud, he heard the familiar fizz as an opening formed in the screen of thick undergrowth which hid his home from Rivallen's people.

As the gap closed behind them, he felt his heart leap. He was safe from Garin and his guards, but he still had to face the Archdeacon's wrath. He hoped the Archdeacon would understand his reasons for doing what he had done and that he would be shown at least *some* degree of mercy, but for the first time in his twenty-two years, he was afraid of the ruling man's power. Even the knowledge that execution and life-imprisonment were options not available to the Archdeacon gave him little comfort.

Then there was his sheer, personal horror at the crime he had committed. Whatever his methods of getting his viewpoint across to others were, Quinn was essentially a pious man who cherished the gift of life and had always respected the laws of God. Nothing would ever dull the painful disgust and self-loathing that would remain after the Archdeacon's fury had been unleashed upon him, despite knowing the extent of God's mercy and forgiveness that had been passed down to him through the promise of the Keeper.

Cara slowed to a trot, happy to be on home ground, where she was free to amble around on her own until Quinn needed her again. He leaned forwards and patted her warm neck. This could be the last time he saw her, and another pang of sadness struck him in his gut.

He pulled her up and jumped down from the saddle. Taking it and her bridle off, he decided to let her go right there, in the forest. Placing everything on the floor, he murmured to her, not wanting her to canter away with a swish of her tail as she usually would. She looked at him and pushed her nose into his chest, snuffling softly at his shirt. He pulled her muzzle up and rested his forehead against her face, breathing in her scent. She seemed to sense something was wrong, keeping her head still. Man and beast ignored the rain that was still pouring down; both were soaked through anyway.

He wanted to stay with Cara, in this moment of tranquility and safety, away from the evil that seemed to be enveloping him. He forced himself to face his thoughts, to think about why he had snapped the way he had. Of course, it was only natural that he would want to save Renn from more abuse and fear, but Quinn wondered *how* he was suddenly capable of snatching a man's life away like that, without thinking about it. Had the violence in Rook's soul remained with him, even after the Archdeacon's insistence that he was experiencing only dreams? If someone with the Archdeacon's strength had not helped him, then even without whatever punishment he was about to face, he could not continue his life as a Conductor. What would he be, then? What *use* would he be, trapped in his hatred of himself and his actions, trapped in a world where everyone would turn from him, where he could never be trusted again, where it would be made plain to him that he had brought shame to the Order of Conductors?

He tried to trust in what the Keeper had told him, but he could see no way to change his circumstances and *not* become a victim of them. At that moment, he knew what true despair felt like. He turned his face to the sky. The rain washed the tears from his stinging eyes and he silently pleaded with God for forgiveness and mercy – not truly believing he deserved either, despite the Keeper's reassurances. Then he closed them and leaned against Cara, trying to prolong the inevitable for as long as he could. But eventually, he knew he had to keep the pact he had made with the Keeper. He kissed her muzzle and looked up at her with a smile. She nodded her head in reply.

'Be a good horse, Cara,' he said.

She lifted her head, snorted at him and then

whinnied as she caught scent of one of her own kind nearby. He patted her neck again and pushed her away.

'Go on then – enjoy your freedom. Think of me now and again. I won't forget you.'

Cara tossed her head, as if in agreement, and then she was gone, cantering through the trees and flicking her tail. Quinn watched her go and then picked up his equipment. The walk would be a long, lonely one and would tire him further with all that he had to carry, but he had to gather his thoughts before he presented himself to the Archdeacon and faced his fate.

CHAPTER 11. DEFENCE.

The Archdeacon sat expressionless in his fireside chair as a sodden and exhausted Quinn relayed the events of that morning. As time passed, he felt more and more uncomfortable, until, at last, every fibre in him strained to keep from running out of the door and into the forest again. He wished the Archdeacon would say something, anything. Even if he stood up and bellowed in Quinn's face, it would be better than this silent stare. He did not know how much longer he could remain standing there, as he started to feel dizzy with fatigue. He could do nothing but stare back at the Archdeacon, desperate for his master to release him from his torment.

At last, the Archdeacon stood up. 'You seem afraid of me for the first time.' His voice was flat, but his eyes seemed triumphant.

Quinn blinked hard, trying to focus and find the right words. 'I fear God. I fear not receiving His forgiveness, His mercy. I'm afraid of your power to make my life even more miserable than it already is. I'm not afraid of *you*.'

'I *am* my power. We are one and the same. Perhaps you should consider that and put aside your stubborn insolence for once in your life!'

Quinn did not reply as nausea rose in him.

He clenched his jaw and fought to keep himself steady as he continued to meet the Archdeacon's icy glare.

'Soul Conductors are not allowed to pass judgement on men. You have always known this! This man was not attacking *you*, so you had no right to attack him. How do you explain your sudden arrogance, your violent disregard of this fundamental law? Of *God's* law?'

Quinn's indignation lent him courage. 'It was not *arrogance*! I had to do something–'

'It was not your place to do *anything* other than the task you were born to do!'

'I couldn't! I have no excuse, other than the fact I could not bring myself to erase the last spark of hope for that poor child, while that brutal, vile man, who was supposed to love and protect him, escaped any kind of punishment!' Quinn could feel the anger swell inside him, despite the fatigue. 'You *know* what the men of Rivallen are like. There would have been no justice for the boy!'

'How do you know that? You said yourself the guards came to take you to the sheriff. How do you know they would not have done the same to the father, had you not interfered?' The Archdeacon's tone was one of barely-disguised contempt and mockery of Quinn's good intentions. Quinn felt increasingly sick to his stomach as the attack continued. 'What makes you think he is any better off now? How do you know what kind of people are now taking care of him? He's alone in a society that you claim is indifferent to the suffering of its people, especially the poor – so how much better will his life be now that he has to live with someone else? You sent his father to the Plane of Shadows and he will suffer for his wickedness, but you have done *nothing* for that child!'

Quinn looked at the Archdeacon with defiance. 'You're wrong.' His voice was low, almost calm.

'Am I?'

They stared at one another. Quinn struggled to find an answer in the fog of his mind. His logic had been undone and he knew the Archdeacon was right about the boy's future, but he could not bring himself around to such a negative way of thinking. He still believed deep inside his heart that he had done the right thing by the boy, if not the father.

The Archdeacon sighed. 'I will need to discuss this matter with the scholars. This is unprecedented. No Conductor has *ever* broken our laws in this way. You must prepare yourself for the worst; you will be punished in a way that reflects the seriousness of your actions. I will not disguise my displeasure at the Keeper's instructions against death or imprisonment – for execution is exactly what you deserve and imprisonment would have been my next choice.'

'You should have just let me die when...' The sentence went unfinished, as Quinn struggled to draw in a breath through his grief.

'The thought crossed my mind,' the Archdeacon said coldly.

Quinn closed his eyes, hurt, but not surprised.

'You're not to leave Delmoril.'

'I don't intend to,' Quinn snapped, looking his master right in the eye once more. 'I gave the Keeper my word.'

'Your *word* does not mean very much to me right now. Go to your quarters, or the chapel. You're not to go anywhere else without my permission. I will summon you in due course.'

***

The chapel was empty. Quinn was not surprised, given the hour and the number of Conductors being called to duty of late, but he was relieved. It was dark and cold inside – just a few candles lit the small, sacred space. The light of the autumn sunshine could not penetrate the tiny, high windows to any effect, neither could its warmth – the ancient stone walls were too thick.

As he half-staggered down the central aisle, he looked at the paintings on its walls: a prophet teaching the laws of God to a crowd of people; a terrifying depiction of the plane you would find yourself in if you led a life of wickedness; a king committing suicide, with evidence of his sins strewn all around him. These paintings had been here for decades, and Quinn was familiar with them down to the finest details, but suddenly they scared him, as if they were there to judge him. He felt his guilt wash over him again and averted his gaze. He looked at the altar, with its candles and flowers. Even that failed to bring him the comfort it usually offered.

As he reached the steps leading up to the altar, he found he no longer had the strength to hold himself up, physically or emotionally. He collapsed to his knees and pitched forwards, hands thrown out to break his fall. Slumping down on to his chest, he lay with his arms at right angles to his body, ignoring the chill of his wet clothes and the cold stone floor beneath him. With his forehead pressed against the stone, he whispered urgent prayers, placing himself wholly and humbly at God's mercy. The words were broken, and his thin frame shook as he fought to draw air into his lungs through his grief and despair.

CHAPTER 12. ERELAS.

Erelas saw the sleeping figure of his friend on one of the pews as soon as he entered the chapel. He walked down the softly-lit central aisle of the sandy-coloured stone building and scolded himself for not realising this was the first place Quinn would have come to, instead of wasting time waiting for him in his quarters. He should have remembered this was Quinn's favourite place to visit when he needed to meditate on the stress in his life.

Erelas slipped onto the pew behind Quinn, not wanting to wake him just yet. Instead, he passed the time in prayer, knowing he would be doing a lot of it in the coming days.

He knew Quinn would have spent time praying equally hard before tiredness had overtaken him; he would be struggling with the fact he had taken a life, even if on the outside he had been focusing on rescuing the boy. Quinn would be locked in a terrible battle with his conscience. It would not matter what the Archdeacon's decision was in the end – Quinn's self-hate would destroy him from the inside. Erelas felt awful on his behalf, and felt completely powerless to help in any way.

Suddenly he stood up, bumping his heel on

the bottom of the long pew. He glanced at Quinn, relieved to see he had not woken him. He made his way back to the aisle and crept out of the chapel as fast as he could.

***

'Archdeacon!' Erelas called as he jogged across the grassy area in the centre of the settlement towards the old man. 'May I speak with you?'

The Archdeacon tightened his robes against the chill of the evening breeze as Erelas reached him. 'I am about to have another meeting with the scholars, Erelas. It will have to wait,' the Archdeacon said, continuing to walk towards the Great Hall next to the chapel.

'It *cannot* wait!'

The Archdeacon stopped and scowled at him. 'If this is about Quinn, I would advise you to stay out of it.'

Erelas opened his mouth to speak, but faltered as the Archdeacon moved off. He had taken a couple of steps before Erelas clenched his jaw and followed him. Cutting across the Archdeacon's path, he stood tall and looked his master in the eye. 'I'm sorry, Archdeacon. I can't do that. I don't think you realise what this is doing to him. I'm asking you to show mercy. I know his actions would ordinarily warrant the strongest of responses, but –'

'There are no *excuses*, Erelas!' The Archdeacon stepped closer to Erelas and looked down on him with fury in his eyes. 'And you cannot convince me that his crime is something that can be dealt with *gently*!'

Other Conductors paused on their journeys around the centre of Delmoril, to watch the usually mild-mannered Erelas challenging their leader.

'Quinn is the *best* Conductor of all of us and you *know* that to be true! What happened to him in the Plane of Shadows *has* to be the cause of his actions in Rivallen this morning. What if the rituals you performed didn't remove all of the evil inside him?' Erelas ignored the stiffening of the Archdeacon at the suggestion his powerful abilities were not good enough. 'You *cannot* punish him for something that was and *is* totally beyond his control!'

'Do not *dare* to tell me what I cannot do, Erelas! You are putting yourself in danger of reprimand if you do not control your tongue and leave this matter to myself and the scholars!'

Erelas frowned and straightened up a little more. He could not match the Archdeacon's height or build, but he was not going to be made to shrink away as he usually did. 'Punish me if you must. It will not change my opinion. Quinn is a victim as much as that poor, defenceless boy. Whether you like his methods or not, Quinn has removed an evil man from this world and even *God* would not treat him as if he were not better than –'

'*Silence*!' The Archdeacon glared at Erelas,

and Erelas glared back. 'Before I decide to put *you* on trial for harbouring such abominable opinions about murder! Go back to your quarters – *immediately* – and remain there until you are released by me. Think about your own future, Erelas. Too often you have put it at risk to follow your friend and his reckless ideas and actions. This time you have gone too far!'

He strode off, the breeze forgotten, his robes flapping freely. Erelas stared after him, while his heart hammered in his chest.

CHAPTER 13. SENTENCE.

The sound of rustling cloth woke Quinn from his exhausted slumber inside the chapel. For a moment he could not fathom where he was, and when he remembered, the memory of everything that had happened came slamming back into his thoughts. He eased himself up slowly, stiff from lying on the hard, wooden seat and chilled from not having changed out of his still-damp clothes. He looked around and saw Anwenn, Erelas' betrothed, standing in the aisle. She had a nervous smile on her face.

'Erelas has asked me to come to you,' she said. 'You look terrible, Quinn.'

'Is he alright?' he asked, rubbing the fatigue from his grimy face and reddened eyes.

'Yes. Well, no. He's been confined to quarters.'

Quinn sat up straight and frowned at her. 'What for?'

Anwenn looked down at the floor; her shyness prevented her from meeting such an intense stare. 'Speaking out for you. To the Archdeacon.'

The *Archdeacon*?' Quinn stood up and shivered as the cold air inside the church touched more of his body. 'I hope he's not got himself into trouble…'

'He believes in you. As I do,' said Anwenn, looking back at him. Her eyes were moist and he could see she was struggling to keep her emotions under control. 'This is so *wrong*, Quinn.'

Quinn paused for a few seconds, before replying. 'My father doesn't think it is.'

Anwenn's eyes widened. 'What do you mean?'

Quinn rubbed his face with his hands, then brought them forwards, as if he were about to pray. Swallowing hard, he glanced at the altar before looking back at Anwenn.

'He has disowned me.' He paused, taking a deep breath in to prevent himself from breaking down again. 'He came to see me here. The Archdeacon gave him his version of events. Even though Father saw the state of me after the incident in the Plane of Shadows, he doesn't believe that it has anything to do with what happened in Rivallen. If anything, after the row we had then, this has just confirmed things for him. I have never seen him so *angry*, Anwenn. Plus…he's always been afraid of the Archdeacon. I should have expected a bad reaction, really.'

'But – he *disowned* you?' Anwenn could not stop a tear from escaping a silver eye and it rolled down an unusually flushed cheek.

Quinn nodded. 'He said he had forgiven me for many things, but could never forgive this. I have gone against "the very fabric of existence of Conductors". He said I would never be one again and I could never be his son again. He assured me Mother felt the same way, and then he left.'

Anwenn did not know what to say. They had all known each other for so many years and she would never have expected Arion to turn his back on his only son, no matter what he had done. Certainly, not when it seemed that it had all been beyond Quinn's control…

'Anwenn, do you know what the Archdeacon is going to do to me?' Quinn said, taking her hands in his.

Anwenn nodded as more tears coursed down her cheeks. 'Banishment.'

Quinn's stomach turned over. 'For how long?'

'For good. Forever. You can never come back.' She broke down at last and leaned her forehead against Quinn's chest as she sobbed.

He wrapped his arms around her and attempted to digest the information. He would lose everyone he cared for and be thrust out into a world he did not fully comprehend, never having been a part of it before; the Conductors existed on the fringes of it, but now he would be forced to live among people he did not understand, and who would not understand him. There would be no safe haven to return to, friends to cheer him up, family to comfort him.

If only the Keeper had *permitted execution*, he thought, as a gaping hole seemed to form in his heart.

***

The centre of Delmoril was filled with concerned and confused Conductors. They waited, murmuring to one another in bewilderment. Nothing like this had ever happened in their lifetime and they were all gripped by a morbid sense of curiosity...

Quinn knew some would take the same view as his father. He had always been viewed by some as a reckless trouble-maker with a complete disregard for authority, with a stubborn streak that caused him to do things he should not do – things the others would never do. He had come to accept their opinions over the years and had never let it get to him.

Until now. The Archdeacon's suspicions regarding the incident that almost killed Quinn had spread around Delmoril and more and more people were beginning to share that view. To those Conductors, he would be getting what he deserved; some may not have even been surprised that he had ended up actually murdering someone, even if they did not believe he had killed Rook.

To the rest, however, he was a strong personality, with a driving desire for justice. He was courageous, even to the point of carelessness about his own safety, but he was also kind and gentle. He could make people laugh in spite of any upsets or troubles that might concern them. He would listen to any problems they had, no matter how small, and come up with wise and practical solutions. He believed in the joys of life, which was one of the reasons he was disciplined so often during his training – life was nothing without fun. They would now be wondering what kind of life he would have outside of Delmoril, and also considering how much poorer Delmoril would be without him. To those people, the Archdeacon was being extremely harsh, but there was nothing they could do to change his mind, as Erelas had discovered. The Archdeacon was not the kind of man to tolerate being challenged…

Everyone in Delmoril knew the story about an event many years ago, when the young Archdeacon had come to the rescue of an inexperienced Conductor. Trouble had broken out between some men from Rivallen and intruders from neighbouring Kilora, right on the border between the two lands. Conductors from Kilora – known as Saloreans after the secret place they had lived in until it had been destroyed by a flood decades before – had arrived at the scene of the riot, which had left many dead from both sides, and had attacked the Conductors from Delmoril. One had been in grave danger of being destroyed by a particularly powerful Salorean. The Archdeacon defended him, killing the Salorean and – so the legend went – fifteen of his fellow Conductors. Over the years the number grew – twenty, twenty-five – it didn't matter. The Archdeacon was the strongest Conductor in their history, and not a man to be crossed.

Quinn, however, who was not one for believing the legend, frequently crossed him. But he was powerless now.

He could not bring himself to look at the faces of the other Conductors anymore. The pity and disgust in their eyes shamed him and, fighting to keep himself from searching for the face of his father in the crowd, Quinn looked down at his feet and bit his lip. He felt hollow and nauseated and his limbs felt weak. All was lost to him. He just wanted it over and done with now.

He stood a little way in front of the rest, with Erelas looking grim behind him, Anwenn clutching at his arm, her eyes still red from crying.

Erelas had been released by the Archdeacon so that he could watch the sentence being passed. In the chapel, Quinn had had just enough time to thank him for pleading for mercy on his behalf. Erelas had not been able to speak; anger and sorrow held his tongue prisoner. They had embraced one another instead. Both felt as if they were losing a brother. The fact they would probably still manage to meet up in Rivallen on occasion had offered little comfort to either of them.

Then one of the scholars had entered the chapel and ordered Quinn to present himself to the community. They had trudged out to the appointed area in gloomy silence.

The gathering suddenly fell quiet and

Quinn looked up. The Archdeacon approached from his quarters, his face set in stern determination. Despite already knowing his fate, Quinn felt afraid of their leader's power once again and shivered. He summoned up the remains of his courage as the Archdeacon stopped in front of him. Quinn met his glare, knowing that nothing he did would change his sentence now, so he might as well face it with dignity.

'As all of Delmoril seems to know the punishment I have decided upon,' the Archdeacon said, 'I will not bother repeating it. Neither will I go into my reasons for this decision. Your conscience knows what you have done, and I shall leave that for you to discuss with God in your prayers.'

Quinn said nothing.

'I know you have had support from your friends and I will forgive their transgressions, *this* time.' The Archdeacon's stare shifted to Erelas, who looked back at him, unashamed of his efforts to help his friend. 'They were merely misguided by their attachment to you,' the Archdeacon went on, looking back at Quinn. 'I hope this will provide you with some comfort.'

'I'm touched by your concern for my comfort,' Quinn spat as the anger returned, giving his pale face a little colour. 'However, as you are giving me so much *discomfort* with your sentence, I doubt I will feel anything but *that*.'

The Archdeacon's jaw tensed. 'You will give me your amulet.'

Quinn stared at him a moment longer, desperate to defy the Archdeacon, but he knew it was beyond hope now. He reached into his shirt and with a quick tug, snapped the fine silver chain that held the indigo-coloured stone. Glancing at it one last time, he squeezed it into his palm and then handed it over. With it went his ability to ever enter Delmoril again.

The Archdeacon pocketed the amulet. 'I trust you have said your farewells?'

Quinn felt he had not, but the Archdeacon cruelly did not wait for an answer.

Throwing his palm out towards Quinn, there was an intense burst of blue light, forcing him to squeeze his eyes shut. All view of Delmoril, and all possibility of seeing his friends again inside it, was gone.

He landed painfully, in a crumpled heap, on a sparsely vegetated hillside riddled with rocks and sprinkled with dark, sandy soil. As he coughed and tried to get his breath back, he felt as if part of him had died. He lay back on the wet ground and let out a long, agonised cry of grief and frustration.

Nothing stirred around him. He was alone.

CHAPTER 14. SHELTER.

Quinn felt as if he were about to experience the land of Rivallen for the first time. Although he was familiar with its gently sloping hills and meadows and the dense pockets of woodland which offered him shelter overnight during the summer, he had no experience of actually living here as a *citizen* of the Kingdom of Rivallen. As a Soul Conductor, he would just 'jump in', complete his task for the soul of the deceased and then return to Cara – the time he spent among the people, taking notice of their lives, their world, their habits, passions and troubles was, out of necessity for their own protection, kept to an absolute minimum.

He knew their beliefs better than they did – after all, he knew as truth things that they could only take on faith. He knew their dress, from expensive silks to filthy rags, as he'd learned to blend in with his surroundings. The language was the same. He also knew all too well how they died. But he did not know much about how they lived.

He was soaked through to his skin once again and he stumbled from lack of energy. He had no money for food, or any items he could barter with. All he had been able to find was ice-cold water from a spring on the hillside that he had been dumped upon. Resting there was out of the question as it was growing darker; he needed to find shelter for the night, but had no idea how he was going to find anywhere to stay. He had no time or strength with which to earn a bed for the night through some menial tasks. He knew how to look after horses exceptionally well, but was willing to have a go at anything – if anyone would take on a strange-looking outsider in the first place, which was unlikely. If he could not find regular employment, he might have to stoop as low as scavenging to survive. He would live like society's least-valued members. Like Renn.

As these black thoughts sapped his energy further, he slumped onto the sodden ground, not caring how much filthier he became. It all seemed so hopeless and it had only been a short time since he had been thrown out of Delmoril. He felt bereft already; he could not imagine how he would feel when he had not seen his friends for a month, let alone a year and beyond. He did not even have Cara for company.

Thoughts of Renn came back to him after a while and they made him open his eyes. He blinked away the rain as he turned sideways on the grass. It was for Renn that he was going through this, and the boy was worth every bit of suffering he might endure.

After berating himself for his wallowing, he took a deep breath, coughing at the remnants of rain that had trickled into his mouth, and stood up. He would find some basic shelter in the woods, or on the outskirts of town, and remain there for the night. He would start afresh in the morning, with dry clothes and some sleep behind him. Cold, fatigue and hunger always made things seem much worse than they were. He would at least be warmer and less exhausted. One task at a time…

***

In the end, Quinn decided to take a risk and crept into a barn a mile or so from the nearest town. A tiny stone cottage stood a little way away from the wooden barn but when he stole past it in the near-dark, he could see no candles burning within. He hoped the owners were inside and preparing to sleep. He would be able to rest in the dry barn in relative warmth and be gone before first light – they would never know he had been there.

A dull-brown, horned cow ate hay in the far corner of the barn and made no noise or fuss at the sudden appearance of a stranger. He walked up to her, murmuring gently, and she looked at him with disinterest as he ran his hands along her flank. She did not object when he crouched down and squeezed a teat, squirting a jet of creamy milk into the straw under her. He then caught the milk in the palm of his hand and drank it. It was like ambrosia to him at that moment, and he continued to take it from the cow until she began to fidget. He stood up, patted his thanks on her rump and looked around the barn for a safe and warm hiding place to rest in.

He chose the darkest corner opposite the cow. A small cart obscured any view of him from the door, and there was plenty of clean, dry straw piled up for him to sleep on. He lay down on it, his joints and muscles aching from the accumulative effects of recent events. Feeling a huge sense of relief that he would at least get some of his strength back with a night's rest, he closed his sore eyes.

A faint rustling sound made his eyelids snap open. From the slightly open doorway of the barn a magnificent black wolf stood and watched him. Quinn inhaled sharply and held his breath, not daring to move. But the wolf just eyed him calmly.

Quinn wondered if he was hallucinating from fatigue – wolves were rarely seen in Rivallen. They had been mercilessly driven out by men centuries before. When they did appear, it nearly always ended badly for those unlucky enough to cross their path. Even the power the Conductors commanded was largely useless against them. If this wolf was real, he was likely to be in grave danger.

But still the wolf continued to stand in the doorway, watching. No growling or baring of teeth – just a strange, silent vigil.

Finally Quinn had to breathe and he let the air from his lungs slowly, blinking hard. His eyes began to sting and his eyelids felt heavy. He could feel his strength leaving him and he lay still, watching the wolf until his eyes would stay open no more. He sank into a void of darkness, his last thought being whether the wolf might kill him as he slept.

CHAPTER 15. ARROW.

The sudden light from the opening of the barn door startled Quinn from his sleep. In a moment he realised he had slept much longer than he had planned and he panicked. Whoever had opened the door would find him here and he did not want to guess what their reaction might be.

Trying to shake the fog of sleep from his senses, he scrambled to his feet, lurched sideways, unbalanced, then felt a sudden, sharp and intense pain in the side of his neck. His breath caught in his throat and he slapped a hand to the area, confused by the warm stickiness he found there. Taking his hand away, he saw it was bright with blood. More ran down his neck and seeped into his clothes. He looked around in confusion, trying to fathom out what had happened. A movement caught his eye, in the upper level of the barn. He looked up just in time to see the dark shape of a cloaked man vanish without a sound through the winnowing door. He winced in pain, held his hand to the wound again and looked around him for what had struck him. He soon saw it; sticking up in the straw not two feet from where he wavered on his feet was an arrow. Someone had *shot* him, but his unsteadiness had saved him from a far worse injury...

He stooped to pick up the arrow, but a wave of dizziness and nausea swept over him, clouding his vision. He slumped to his knees, groaning as pain spread around his body. He didn't understand why he was in pain beyond the site of the wound and tried to think of a reason as he reached once more for the arrow.

A moment later he heard a scream and the clatter of a dropped pail. Shaking all over, he forced himself up again and turned around, hand still clamped to his neck. A wide-eyed woman of no more than twenty stood frozen in fear and stared at him in confusion. It had been she who had opened the door and woken him.

So who was..? He tried to think, but his mind would not obey. Desperate to ignore the pain shooting through his body, he took a hesitant step towards her. He held out a trembling hand in front of him as a gesture of reassurance.

'Please,' he said, his voice surprisingly weak. 'Don't be…afraid of me – I mean n-no harm. I just took for –' He gasped again, swallowed and tried to make himself make sense. 'Shelter, here for the night…slept longer than I in-intended to. I'm sorry for fright…*frightening* you.'

Pain gripped his chest and he bent his body over, grunting in his effort to not stumble again. Somehow he maintained eye contact with her, fighting hard to stay focused. He knew something was wrong, beyond a simple arrow wound, but his thoughts were becoming more and more clouded, out of reach, indecipherable…

The woman stood still, looking him up and down, as if equally unsure of the situation. He realised he must have looked disturbing, with blood staining his already scruffy, filthy clothes and his dirty face, unkempt hair and strange-coloured eyes that did not even match. He did his best to keep his posture and expression from looking threatening, but the pain was an increasing distraction.

'Help me…*please*,' Quinn finally gasped. His body turned cold as sweat began to soak into his clothes.

A young man burst through the door, still pulling his shirt on against the chill of the morning. '*Aliena!*' he shouted, but skidded to a halt when he saw the woman staring at the stranger who faced her. Gathering himself a little, he strode towards them both.

Quinn could see he was only around seventeen years of age, but tall and strong-looking. He wanted to step back from the forceful advance, but did not want to unbalance himself. Thankfully the young man stopped just in front of him, scowling. Quinn remained where he was.

'Who are you?' the man demanded, then turned to Aliena without waiting for a reply. 'Are you alright?'

'I am unhurt, Elyan – I was just startled.'

Elyan looked back at Quinn, still frowning. 'What are you doing in here?'

Quinn's vision almost failed as the pain reached every part of his body. He could not help but groan through his gritted teeth. His knees started to buckle but he fought to hold himself up. 'I...am sorry...trespassed,' he said, starting to sway alarmingly. 'But, I...a man...shot me...arrow...'

Aliena touched Elyan's arm to stay him and stepped towards Quinn. 'Someone *shot* you with an arrow? In *here*? Just now?'

Quinn nodded, instantly wishing he had not, as his dizziness increased. 'Something –' He gasped for air as the barn seemed to darken. 'Poisoned...'

Aliena's expression changed as the realisation of his plight hit her and she rushed to him and grabbed his arm just as he began to slump to the floor. 'Elyan! *Help* me!' She managed to hold him up just long enough for Elyan to reach them. They lowered him to the ground between them with care.

His eyes glazed over and his breathing grew rapid, but shallow. Pain made it impossible to focus on anything and his mind started to wander. Flashes of his life in Delmoril, along with glimpses of his nightmares came to him. He blinked furiously and struggled to get back up.

Aliena pressed her hand to his chest to keep him still, and brushed the dampened hair from his eyes, trying to give him a reassuring look. 'Do not worry – I can help you.' Then, to the young man, she said: 'Elyan, fetch the arrow, quickly – I need to know what kind of poison is on it. But be careful!'

Quinn shook his head and fought against Aliena's gentle restraint. '*No!* Don't *touch* it!'

'It is alright...Elyan will take care not to touch the arrowhead. I need to know what poison it is so I can help you – but you *must* keep still!' Her tone became more desperate as he struggled against her grip. '*I must stop the bleeding*!'

He stopped fighting and looked back at her. He blinked hard as he struggled to stay conscious. She let go of his wrists and tore a strip of cloth from her apron, folding it several times. Looking apologetically at Quinn, she pressed it down on the wound on his neck, quenching the flow of blood. His body tensed up and she placed a cool palm on his burning forehead. As she leaned closer to him, her long, dark hair fell around her neck and brushed against his shoulder. 'Do not worry,' she said again, her voice gentler now. 'I will take care of you. What is your name?'

'Quinn...' His voice was barely more than a whisper. The effort it took to speak was tremendous.

'I am Aliena. Elyan is my brother.' She smiled and then looked up. 'Elyan?'

Elyan crouched beside them, holding the arrow by the shaft. 'I can't see anything on it...' he said.

'I will find out what it was, don't worry,' Aliena said. She turned back to Quinn. 'Who shot you?'

Quinn shook his head, his eyes slowly closing as the last of his strength waned. 'I didn't see… where is…the wolf?'

'What wolf? Aliena raised an eyebrow. 'There are no wolves in Rivallen. You must have been dreaming…' She touched Quinn on the shoulder and he opened his eyes again, fighting to focus on her. 'I can help you,' she said. 'But you *must not* give up – do you hear me? You *fight*, and you don't stop fighting!'

Quinn nodded, unable to speak.

'Do you swear it?'

He held her gaze for a moment and nodded again, with more conviction. Then the pain took over and he gasped. His fingers clutched at the cloth of his shirt, searching for the amulet that was no longer there. He could hear a wolf's mournful howl from somewhere in the distance and desperately tried to hold on, afraid he was losing his mind. Its heart-wrenching song continued and he cried out, almost as if in reply. Aliena grabbed his hand and squeezed it tight, encouraging him to stay with her, but he could not. A few moments later, his senses left him and he lay still.

'Elyan – help me get him into the house. We don't have much time!'

CHAPTER 16. ALIENA.

The room Quinn found himself in was quite dark, and it took him a long time to make out anything about his surroundings. The fire in the hearth not far from where he lay – on a low bed of sorts – had died down, and gave off no more than a weak orange glow. He could see sombre grey stone walls with wicker baskets hanging from nails, along with a few simple tools. There was a large, odd-looking table, with some wooden bowls, some vegetables and two cups on it. Two low stools were pushed underneath. He could not see beyond the end of the table and could not tell how large the room was.

The light increased at the far end of the room and he watched through his blurred, watery vision as it seemed to approach his bed. He closed his eyes again; the movement of the light made him feel nauseated, so he lay still and pieced his memories together. He tried to think past the thumping in his head, the pressure in his chest and the searing pain in his neck. He recalled Aliena and the way she had ignored his invasion of her property, in order to tend to his wound and his sudden sickness.

He opened his eyes and saw her there before him. She looked even more beautiful than he had remembered. He thought for a moment that she might be a vision, an angel. His heart thumped alarmingly as he realised the possibility that she could even be a *Conductor*, and that he was about to die. He blinked hard and looked at her again. Her soft eyes looked down at him with compassion and her hair flowed like a warm, chestnut-coloured river over her shoulders. She smiled at him, but it was not until she felt his cheek with the back of her hand that he realised she was really there with him, sitting on the bed. He jumped a little, as if waking up again.

'Lost in your thoughts?' She reached to a low stool and wrung out a cloth over a wooden bowl.

Seeing the cloth, he knew then she was no Conductor, and felt relief that he wasn't about to lose his life. Yet. 'Remembering,' he said feebly. 'Trying to –' He coughed and Aliena put the cloth back into the bowl. She reached for a small cup of water and helped him to lift his head, holding the cup to his lips as he drank. He winced at the pain the movement caused his neck, but he had not realised how thirsty he was and the cool, sweet water was welcome.

'Not too much.'

He stopped and she let his head down gently on the folded blanket under it.

'Thank you,' he said, his voice clearer.

She smiled and swapped the cup for the cloth. As she pressed it to his forehead, he closed his eyes, appreciating its coolness. But he felt nauseated again, so he looked back at her to give his eyes something to focus on.

'I'm sorry,' he said. 'I should not have been in your barn. This wouldn't have happened...'

'Shush...I'm sure it's not the first time a weary traveller has taken refuge in there. Although...' She paused, and looked anxiously into his eyes. 'We still do not know who shot you. Elyan found no trace of anyone having been in there except you. Do you have any idea of who it might have been? Or why they did it?'

Quinn noticed how the question came with a tone of concern, not suspicion, and he was grateful for that. 'I have no idea,' he answered. 'I have only just arrived in Rivallen. I had not spoken to anyone – let alone made any enemies.'

'Well...a lot of the guards around here are archers, and nasty with it. Or, maybe it was a robber, who hadn't seen me coming. I must be scary.' She gave him a thin smile that was not reflected in her eyes. 'You were lucky the arrow did not penetrate deeper.'

'Do people use poisoned arrows around here?' Quinn asked, although he already knew the answer. He'd never conducted anyone who had been killed in that way.

'Not that I've ever heard about. Who knows, maybe they are changing tactics.' Aliena placed a hand on his arm as she spoke. 'You will come to find, very quickly, that Rivallen is not a nice place, but there *are* good people here, too.'

Quinn smiled as well as he could, but he did not make it convincing enough. Aliena's own smile faded and she frowned as she took the damp cloth from his feverish skin. 'What is it, Quinn?'

'I feel very…oh, God…' With that, he lurched sideways. Aliena held another bowl for him, but despite the painful retching that gripped him for several minutes, there was nothing but the water for him to bring up. He lay back, exhausted, while Aliena wet the cloth again and dabbed the sweat from his face.

'I'm afraid this will go on for some time,' she said. 'The wound itself will heal in time, but the poison was venom from a Forest Asp. I could tell just from the smell. The herbs are keeping you alive, and you are young and strong, but you have yet to face the worst of it. I am sorry.'

'I have never been ill. It's come as a shock.'

Aliena raised her eyebrows. 'Never?'

'Fell off a horse once. Knocked myself out and broke my arm.'

Aliena smiled. 'Not sure that counts. Just don't give up. No matter how bad you feel. You swore, remember?'

He was prevented from replying by the sound of the door opening and footsteps coming into the small dwelling. Aliena gave Quinn a quick smile and stood up. She took the cloth and bowls with her as she walked away. She had not gone far before the gloom enveloped her. He gave up trying to see her and closed his eyes.

'Elyan, he is awake,' he heard her say.

'Has he said anything? About where he is from? What was he doing in our barn?' Elyan made no effort to keep his voice down or hide the anger in his tone. Quinn felt embarrassed and knew that must have been Elyan's intention.

'*Elyan*!' Aliena hissed. 'Do not be so uncharitable! He already told me what he was doing in the barn. He also said he was sorry – several times. Leave him alone, do you hear me?'

Elyan said nothing for a moment, and then quietly muttered: 'Alright.'

'Do not forget how fortunate we are in these times of trouble,' she said, her voice softer now.

'Forgive me. I just don't like strangers being here. He could be outlawed. He could be one of the sheriff's spies. He could be *anything*. I worry about you.'

'I am the one who does the worrying for both of us, remember? Now – what news from town tonight?'

Quinn did not hear what the news from town was as exhaustion overtook him. He sank back into oblivion once again.

CHAPTER 17. RECOVERY

The next two days were mostly a fog of sleep, sickness and nightmares for Quinn. He kept dreaming he was back in Delmoril, facing the Archdeacon, then being banished all over again. Except that, in his dream, each time he was banished, he returned to Renn's cottage and murdered the boy's father again – and taking *pleasure* from it. Then the man would turn into his own father and he would be filled with unbearable pain and terror. He tried to fight and let go before his father died, but would end up waking in a sweat, yelling, and would then try to vomit yet again. With nothing left to come up, he would merely exhaust himself, pass out, and return to the horrors in his subconscious mind. The nightmares he experienced in Delmoril, however, did not reappear and he was grateful for that.

Most of the time it would be Aliena who was there to help him when he awoke from the dream. Sometimes – when he was raving so badly he had to be held down – Elyan would be there, too.

On one occasion, he awoke to the sound of them both shouting frantically at him, Elyan nervously shaking him by the shoulders. He'd apparently been so desperately ill that he had experienced some kind of seizure and had stopped breathing for a few seconds. Aliena had shed tears of relief as he came back to her, and she repeatedly begged him to fight for his life, as she cradled his head and stroked his hair. He could do nothing but lie there, staring into the candlelight, his breathing ragged and his pulse hammering in his head. It had frightened him so badly that he fought against sleep for as long as he could before he simply could not keep his eyes open any longer.

At other times it was just Elyan watching over him, who would stand and watch Quinn suffer for a while, an unnerving expression on his face. He seemed to grow ever angrier with Quinn, and Quinn could not work out why. After a couple of days it was as much as Elyan could do to hold the bowl for Quinn to be sick into. There was certainly nothing comforting in his tone when he spoke, which he rarely did. Quinn was relieved whenever he woke up to find Aliena trying to soothe and calm him. She would rub his back as he tried to be sick, wipe his face with a cool, damp cloth and give him water to sip. Once he woke up sobbing, and she put her arm around his shoulders and squeezed onto the bed with him, staying with him until he fell asleep again. Sometimes she would give him something that tasted foul and his sleep would be a little more restful.

'It's Lenara root,' she told him on the evening of the second day. 'It eases the pain a little. I wish there was more I could do for you, Quinn, but other than this and trying to keep your fever down, it's up to you. You *must* keep fighting.'

He willed his heavy eyelids to stay open as she supported his head and helped him to drink from the small cup. He had to force himself to swallow the dark, bitter liquid, but he trusted her completely.

She lowered his head back and he coughed feebly. The wound in his neck was starting to hurt less with movement. He just wished the rest of him felt better, too. Looking up at her leaning over him, her gentle face awash with concern, he knew he had to fight, for her if not for himself. She was giving of herself freely and he'd made a promise to her. Whatever horrors this land might hold in store for him, he did not want her kindness and generosity to go unrewarded.

But he had another favour to ask of her.

'Please…will you pray for me?' he asked. 'I… the words will not come to me.'

'I have been praying for you, Quinn. Morning, night and every time you are gripped by these dreams and the fever takes hold again. God is with us. Have faith.'

Quinn longed to share with her all he knew of God, and his own role in the lives and deaths of men and women, but he remembered his exclusion from that life and lost all sense of who he was and what he could show her. All he had left was *his* faith, *his* truth. So, instead, he squeezed Aliena's hand in thanks and allowed the dizziness to spiral him back into darkness.

On the third day, he awoke in the morning feeling as if he might finally be over the worst of the poisoning. He no longer felt as sick as before, his head no longer ached as much and he thought he might actually manage to stay awake for more than just a few minutes.

He lay still for a while, looking around the room. Even the daylight did not make it very bright in Aliena and Elyan's little home, but he could at least now see everything in it.

Boots – clean but not polished – stood just inside the doorway. A lady's grey cloak hung on the back of the closed door. Pots and cooking utensils hung on the side of the hearth, where a low fire glowed once more. He could see a ladder reaching up to the small roof space, which he guessed was where his hosts slept.

Everything was tidy, but sparsely furnished, with very little in the way of personal or sentimental items. Quinn liked it, although it was very different to the dwellings in Delmoril, which held an abundance of things for every conceivable purpose crammed into every space available.

But this was not his home. He was an intruder here. He had lost his home and all that was close to his heart. He cursed himself for having thought of Delmoril at all. It was pointless and would only serve to keep the gaping wound in his heart wide open.

He struggled to sit up, propping his back against the cold, hard stone wall behind him. He was dressed only in clean undergarments, and wondered where the rest of his clothes were. He felt no shame at the thought that someone had stripped him, washed him and clothed him in fresh linen – it was too late to worry about dignity after the helplessness he had felt for the past three days.

He pushed back the thick, woollen blanket from over his legs. He had a quick look about the room once more, then swung his legs slowly around the side of the bed and dropped his feet the mere inches to the floor. There was a single animal fur under his feet, the rest of the floor being of compacted dirt that was swept as clean as could be expected. He shivered with the sudden change of temperature and his legs felt as if they would not hold his weight, but he did not retreat back under the blankets. He had to try. The sooner he could get out of this house and let Aliena and Elyan have their lives back, the better it would be for them, especially Elyan. The young man clearly had an issue with Quinn, and he would rather not stay around long enough to be confronted with it.

Looking around again, he spotted his clothes, clean and folded, on the big wooden table in the centre of the living space, which had been cleared of everything else.

Raising himself from the low bed, he felt sick and dizzy again, but he would not give in to it. The table was just a step or two away, and with his clothes on, he would feel less dependent and hopefully a little warmer. He took the first step, but his left knee wobbled alarmingly. In an effort to correct his balance, the other leg lurched forwards and he practically threw himself at the table. Being so large and heavy, it did not tip over, so he was able to lean on it and regain his equilibrium for a while. When he felt safe enough, he straightened up and took his clothes from the table. They were spotless and he was grateful, remembering the state they had been in when he had fallen asleep in the barn.

He slowly returned to the bed and, in time, managed to dress himself; his arms felt heavy and ineffective and pulling his coarse linen shirt over the bandage around his neck was excruciating. His legs refused to go where he wanted them to at first, and at times he thought he might run out of strength or pass out half-dressed. He was relieved – and exhausted – when he finally had everything on except his boots, which he could not see anywhere.

Fighting nausea again, he lay back down under the blanket and curled himself into a foetal position, waiting for the blood to stop thundering in his ears.

For the first time in three days, he slept and did not dream.

CHAPTER 18. REVELATIONS.

'You've been busy…'

Quinn's eyes flickered open. Aliena stood beside the bed, smiling down at him. It was night-time; the fire was ablaze in the hearth and several candles had been lit. The room had a soft, comforting orange glow, and was far warmer than it had been when he had ventured from his bed.

He slowly sat up, feeling as if he had some energy at last.

'You were supposed to await the orders of your physician before getting dressed,' Aliena said, an eyebrow rising as she reached over to feel his forehead.

'My physician, it seems, was elsewhere,' Quinn said, a hint of humour in his eyes.

Aliena held up a small wooden cup. 'Gathering ingredients for your sleeping draught.'

'Have I been having that since I've been here?'

'No. Not a sleeping draught. You have hardly needed one. The herbs I used against the poison I got into you every chance I could – which was no easy task, I can tell you! But the worst seems to be over now. You fought back well.' She smiled as she handed him the cup.

'Literally fighting, I seem to recall. I'm sorry

about that. I've been having dreams...'

'Yes, we were very worried for a while. You were in a state every time you awoke. Elyan said you talked a lot during some of them, but he could not make sense of what you were saying. Do you remember what it was you were dreaming of?'

Quinn hesitated. He wondered if Elyan was telling the truth, or whether he did not want to tell his sister they had a murderer in their home.

'Quinn?'

'I'm sorry. I do remember, but I don't know how to explain it. It was to do with how I came to be here, but it's all a bit of a mess in my head at the moment.'

'Where is it you are from? Is there anyone we can get word to, to tell them you're here? Was anyone expecting you?'

Quinn ignored the first question. 'No, thank you. There is nobody. Nobody is expecting me. I wasn't sure where I was going, to tell the truth.' He looked down. Hoping his overwhelming guilt over his banishment did not show in his expression. 'Which makes someone trying to kill me all the more puzzling. If I've made enemies, I'd like to know how.'

'We'll try to find some answers for you, when you're stronger. I'm only curious, Quinn, not suspicious. You have nothing to fear from me. I can tell you have no desire to harm us, so I'm willing to help, if I can.'

'I promise I will tell you more when I have

made sense of my thoughts,' he said. He had not decided how much he could safely reveal about his previous life to her, or to anyone in Rivallen, but he believed he owed Aliena more than he had given her so far. He would not leave without explaining himself to her, if only in part.

'You still need a *lot* more rest. All of that can wait. Just get yourself better. You have fought well, as I said, but the battle may not be over. I'm sure the dreams were just due to the fever, which was dangerously high at times and hard to keep down for long. The sleeping draught should help you to rest without having any more of them.'

Quinn nodded, but was not convinced, and it showed in his expression.

'Don't worry,' Aliena added. 'If it doesn't help, we can always try something else tomorrow. There's a plant out there for everything.'

He tried to push his fears away. 'I am grateful,' he said, smiling faintly. 'And does my physician recommend I get out of bed now?'

'Tomorrow.' Aliena smiled as she added: 'But only as far as the table.'

***

Quinn sat on the grass between the cottage and the barn. It had been an unseasonably warm morning and the dew had gone from the grass quite early. He had been sitting alone for a while, lost in his thoughts, just gazing ahead, his elbows resting on his knees.

He was avoiding Elyan, whose surly behaviour grated his nerves and tested his patience. He was unable to react to any of the bitter comments out of respect for the fact that Elyan and Aliena had saved his life.

He felt much better now, six days after the attack by the still-unknown assailant. He had more energy and was able to pick at a little food now and then, but he was nowhere near his usual strength. No casting power had as yet returned to him; the familiar hum of the energy of his gift through his veins was still absent. He knew it was because of his weakened state, as the Archdeacon could not have removed it from him. Despite the loss of his amulet, he was born a Soul Conductor, and a soul Conductor he would always be. He did not, however, really know what *kind* of a Soul Conductor he was anymore. There was not just the issue of his banishment and the resulting loss of his ability and right to carry out his duty. The attack on him in the Plane of Shadows seemed like a distant event in his memory now, but in real terms it had taken place less than a month before. Some Conductors had taken longer than that to recover from less traumatic or physically damaging encounters than the one he had experienced. He'd been sent back out into service far too early. To then have to deal with someone like Renn's father, who had been both violent and strong, would not have helped Quinn.

It had been the Archdeacon's decision to send him back into Rivallen to resume his duty. So did the responsibility for what occurred not rest with *him*?

He closed his eyes and shook his head to clear that thought from his mind. It was useless to question the Archdeacon's actions now – that part of his life was over for good. He needed to build a new one for himself and he would not manage it by dwelling on the past.

'Are you alright?' Aliena appeared behind him, jolting him from his reverie. 'Sorry – I didn't mean to creep up on you.'

Quinn smiled. 'No matter. I was miles away.'

Aliena sat on the grass beside him and began to pluck blades of it from the ground. 'So… are you alright?'

Quinn nodded. 'It's good to be outside in the sun again.'

Aliena looked up at the cloudless sky and nodded. 'It's warm today. Warmer than I expected.'

'I thought I would try to enjoy it while it lasts. Last night was cold.'

'You slept well, though. You had no nightmares.'

Quinn looked at her and saw that she was genuinely pleased for him, not merely relieved that he had not woken her and Elyan up with his screaming. 'I am sorry I caused so much of a disturbance on the other nights.'

'It's alright, Quinn. I'm just happy to see you

improving. You'll be back to your full health soon.'

'And then I must think about moving on.'

Aliena's expression changed and she looked concerned again. 'Where will you go?'

'I don't know yet.'

'I don't even know where you're from…'

Quinn looked at her and remembered his promise to explain a few things to her when he had made sense of them himself. He now knew what was real and what had been his fevered imagination, but he still did not want to tell her everything. He did not think she would understand. As for Elyan…

'I am from a place…other than here. I left after getting into some trouble with my friends and family. Or, I should say, it was *decided* that I should go. So here I am – trying to start again and making a terrible job of it so far.'

Aliena looked unsure of what to say for a moment. She threw the blades of grass away and looked at him. 'I will not ask what kind of trouble. As I have said before, that's your business. Judging by the state you were in when we found you, I would think you've suffered enough already.'

Quinn again thought of the attack on him. He still had no idea who might have done such a thing, or why, but he could not shake the feeling that it was more than just a failed attempt at robbing him – after all, he possessed nothing but the clothes he was wearing. The more he thought about it, the angrier it made him – he'd done nothing to provoke an attempt on his life, and, as at so many other times in his life, his overpowering desire for truth and justice increased his frustration at his lack of understanding.

'Quinn?'

He looked up and saw that Aliena was staring at him in alarm. She shuffled away from him and then stood up, not taking her eyes from his. He frowned, not comprehending, then he realised what she must have seen in his silver iris. His ability to use the gifts he had received from God must finally be returning to him…at least in part.

He looked away sharply, as he became aware of the increasing tension throughout his body. He forced himself to calm down and looked back up at Aliena. She looked a little less fearful now, but very confused.

'I have to get back to the house…'

Quinn could think of nothing to say as she walked away from him. Her hurried steps made it clear that whatever she had seen in his eyes frightened her.

It was time for him to leave.

CHAPTER 19. WALKING AWAY.

'I don't think you're well enough, Quinn,' said Aliena. She sat at the table on one of the low stools preparing a handful of vegetables for the main meal of the day. Elyan was out gathering more wood for the fire.

'I have imposed upon you both for long enough. I should not have been here at all and you have been more than generous. I will not forget that you saved my life.' Quinn stood in the doorway, watching the rain pour down. 'I need to find a way to sustain myself, now. I refuse to take advantage of you or your brother now that I am recovering.'

'I know that Elyan had been...difficult. I will have a word with him. You must not let his behaviour influence you. I don't think you are strong enough yet.' She looked at him and stood up. 'Quinn, I saw something in your eyes yesterday. I'm sorry I reacted the way I did. It frightened me. But I've never seen anything like that before. I know of people who practice witchcraft, but I don't think you're the same as them. But I know it could be dangerous for you if the wrong people discovered you here, in Rivallen, with some form of..."magic". Even I have to be careful with my herbs and potions so that I am not accused of being a witch. The penalty is death, and they make it impossible for anyone to prove their innocence. You're…different, and will be even *less* likely to be accepted by the people here.' She sighed. 'I've always tried to teach Elyan to not be afraid of what he does not understand, yet I could not follow that teaching myself. I am ashamed of that.'

Quinn was not sure of what to say, but he did not want to lie to her, or insult her by trying to deny it. 'You need have no fear of me. I do have a kind of "magic", I suppose some might call it. But it comes from *God*. I was born with it. All of my people are. My abilities just…well, they seem to have mostly deserted me right now. Even if they had not, I would never hurt you or Elyan.' *Intentionally*, he thought with an inward shiver. Could he ever guarantee anyone's safety anymore?

'I am not afraid. Not now.' She tried to smile. 'In fact, I would have loved to have learned more about it – and you. If you were willing to share with me…'

'I cannot stay.' He avoided answering her directly. He was the one who was afraid – afraid to trust.

'Is it just because of Elyan? Because if it is, I will talk to him. He has been very unfair to you, for reasons I intend to get to the bottom of –'

'Elyan has been perfectly within his rights to protest about my being here. I did not exactly arrive under honourable circumstances and I don't blame him for wishing I would leave you in peace again.'

Aliena looked stern for a second. Quinn wondered if she was aware he had deliberately shifted the focus of the conversation. 'Go *where*, Quinn? You told me you were made to leave the place you came from and look at the state you ended up in, not to mention the fact that this is a dangerous place for strangers. Do you know anything about Rivallen and the kind of rule we live under?'

Quinn could not help turning a little defensive. 'Yes, I do. Just because I am not *from* here, it does not mean I know nothing about the place. I have spent a lot of time here in the last two years, I just haven't *lived* here. Just because I've been cast out with nothing, that does not mean I am completely incapable of looking after myself. You saw me the day I was made to leave and an awful lot had happened to me before that. I was a mess, I admit, but I'm not a child!'

Aliena bit her lip and turned away, sitting back down on the stool. Quinn realised his words had come out in a much harsher tone than he had intended. He walked over to her and placed a hand on her shoulder.

'I am sorry. It is just very difficult for me to feel comfortable about living off the labours of other people. I have never had to before.'

Aliena looked up at him, frowning. 'Quinn, don't imagine that people always expect something in return for what they give. Not everyone is like that. Certainly not me.'

'That is not what I meant –' he began.

She stood again and walked over to the fire. As she tried to look busy tending to the smouldering wood, Quinn knew he had upset her, but he did not know how to undo it. He could not bring himself to give in to her and stay longer. They had formed a bond in the last couple of days and he was loathe to walk away from that, but he did not want to bring his troubles to her and Elyan, or cause a rift between them when it was clear Elyan had a huge problem with him being there.

'Aliena, I am sorry. You are right. I do not understand this place as well as I need to and I don't know how to fit into it yet. A lot of things are going to be new to me...'

'Quinn, the first thing you do in order to understand a new land is to make a friend in that new land. You've done that. Why walk away from it now?'

A sudden urge to capitulate and stay there gripped Quinn and his heart seemed to contract as he wrestled with the choice in his mind.

'*I* don't want him here.'

They both turned and saw Elyan standing in the doorway, cradling half a dozen logs in his arms.

'*Elyan*!' said Aliena angrily.

'I know you think I'm being rude and unforgiving, but I'm being truthful –'

'Unforgiving?' Aliena was confused.

'I love you, Sister, but I cannot always agree with you. You don't know anything about him, or where he is from, or why he was sent away. How can you ask him to stay when he has not been *honest* with us? Someone wanted him dead – they must have had a reason!'

'What has happened to him is no concern of ours unless he *chooses* to talk about it, Elyan. You should not judge things you know nothing about!'

'I know more than you!'

Quinn felt panic building up inside his mind, but he had to hold himself together. 'Please,' he said, holding up his hands. 'Don't quarrel over me. I am leaving, Elyan. I am sorry you feel you cannot trust me when I have meant no harm, but I do understand.'

Elyan ignored him and looked at Aliena, who stared back, angry, but also torn.

'This is not *right*, Elyan,' she said. 'Imagine if you were in his situation!'

'Aliena…' Quinn said. He went to her and took her hands in his. 'It is alright, please. Don't be cross with Elyan. It was my intention to go before he said anything – and he is just protecting you. I will go, but I hope I leave you with the knowledge that I will never forget what you have both done for me. You have given me hope – I had none when I arrived at your barn. Maybe we will meet again, under better circumstances.' He bent towards her, and kissed her cheek.

Aliena did not move, except to hold his

hands a little tighter for just a moment, before he gently pulled himself free and turned towards the door. Then he looked back at them both, wanting to say more, but unable to find the right words. He turned and left the house, leaving Aliena and Elyan to look at the rain in silence.

CHAPTER 20. CONFESSION.

Quinn wished he had a cloak of some kind as he walked away from the little cottage. The rain was heavy, but he could not have delayed his departure a moment longer. He had never felt as uncomfortable as he had just then – stuck in the middle of a disagreement between siblings who obviously loved each other. It had not been right for him to be there, causing it all, and he was sure Elyan had been about to reveal what he knew. He breathed a sigh of relief as soon as he was a few steps away from the door.

He did not know where he was going, but he knew he had to secure legitimate shelter for the night – he would not risk trespassing again. He would just walk until he came across some work, and a place to stay as payment. He tried not to consider another attempt being made on his life…

'You there!'

Startled, Quinn looked up to see two heavily-armoured but bare-headed guards approach him, swords drawn. Confused, he stopped and stared, dread piercing his stomach.

They wore dark red and black surcoats, decorated with the coat of arms of King Mattias, which consisted of crossed swords over a crown, flanked by two falcons. The guards looked enormous, even though Quinn himself was tall and reasonably muscular, despite his thin frame. He had come across guards before, having conducted several in the last two years, but never in this way. Back then, they had just been souls to deliver to the afterlife – but, like this, they were extremely intimidating and without any way to defend himself, he was afraid.

'Identify yourself!' demanded one of them as they reached him, standing close to discourage any ideas he may have had about escaping. 'Show me your papers!'

'What papers?' Quinn asked, genuinely at a loss. This was one part of life in Rivallen he had no knowledge of.

He staggered sideways as the other guard viciously backhanded him with his gauntlet. 'You are to have identity papers with you at all times!' he shouted, as Quinn steadied himself and gingerly felt his cheek, his eyes watering with the shock.

The first guard spoke again. 'Where are you from? I don't recognise you.' He stared at Quinn with a cold intensity, examining his mismatched eyes with a mixture of curiosity and distaste.

Quinn did not know how to answer; bizarrely, all he could think of was how much this would please the Archdeacon…

The guard who struck him moved past Quinn and walked up to the door of the cottage. 'You in there – come outside! And bring your papers!'

Quinn felt sick. It seemed he was to unintentionally bring more trouble for Aliena and Elyan. He watched as they emerged from the house clutching small pieces of paper. The guard snatched them from their hands and studied them. He nodded at his colleague, who looked at Quinn again.

'Your papers!' he snapped.

'I have none – I do not know how to get papers. I am new here!' Quinn stood fast, ready to be struck again, toying with the idea of fighting back if he was.

The guard looked him up and down, as if he were something gruesome to behold. He peered again at Quinn's distinctive eyes and suddenly looked a little less sure of himself. His voice a little lower, he said: 'So, where have you travelled from? Vagrancy is outlawed in this kingdom.'

Quinn stood silently. These people, these violent, prejudiced children of God, knew nothing of Delmoril, its inhabitants, or their abilities – and it *had* to remain that way, no matter the cost to himself.

The guard grew angry. 'I will have your answer!'

Quinn glanced at Elyan, who looked at him with a mixture of disgust and fear, then at Aliena, who looked terrified. He had to fight for them, and he had to do it with the only way still left open to him.

Before the guard could react, Quinn punched him hard in his unprotected face, aiming upwards. He broke the guard's nose, knocked out some of his rotting teeth and sent blood spattering in all directions. In the same moment, he lunged at the sword with his other hand and grabbed it from the guard, whose grip had been weakened by the power and surprise of Quinn's attack. As the guard fell backwards and landed in the dirt with a splash, yelling in pain, Quinn swung the sword expertly around and with one long leap had the point of it at the other guard's neck.

'Drop it,' he said. The menace in his tone was unmistakable.

The guard dropped his sword and Quinn crouched to pick it up, never taking the blade from his throat. He pointed the second sword towards the guard on the ground, who was now trying to sit up, dazed, his face covered with blood. He glanced from one guard to the other, unfamiliar feelings of rage beginning to course through him like a drug. Although it gave him a level of energy he had not felt for weeks, the feelings were unwelcome – they were not part of the real Quinn. At least, not the *old* Quinn.

'I was trespassing on this land,' he told the guards. 'You have no cause to be intimidating these people. Give them back their papers. *Now!*'

The guard at the door handed the papers back to Elyan, who stared wide-eyed and open-mouthed at Quinn. 'You will not get away with this!' the guard said.

'Really?' said Quinn, moving closer to him. He tickled the guard's retreating chin with the tip of the blade. 'If I kill you, there will be nobody left to recognise me and hand me over to your sheriff, will there?'

The guard fell silent. Quinn looked at his partner, who was coughing and retching, desperately trying to stem the bleeding from his nose and mouth with a dirty rag.

'*Please...*' said Aliena quietly, making Quinn look up in surprise. He stared at her, praying she would not say his name and ruin his plan. But she did not. 'Don't kill them...' She looked as if she were about to weep and Quinn realised she was as scared of him as she was of the guards. That knowledge crushed him, but he knew all of this was necessary to get them out of trouble.

He did not answer her, feeling it was safer to not speak to her directly, thus lessening the risk of the guards punishing her or Elyan later on. He had no intention of killing the men, but they could not know that – not yet.

Instead, he grabbed the guard by his surcoat and thrust him towards his colleague. 'Get him up,' he instructed.

The guard helped his friend to his feet and supported him under the arm. Quinn stayed behind them, swinging both swords around to make his grip safer and more comfortable, with a skill and strength that amazed Elyan and Aliena. Elyan even looked impressed, in spite of himself.

'Start walking,' Quinn ordered.

He did not look back as he marched the guards away from the cottage. If he had, he might have seen a third guard – an archer – taking aim at him.

Everyone heard the whisper of the arrow as it flew to its target, but it did not register with any of them until Quinn was thrown over by the force of its impact into his left shoulder. He landed heavily, the swords clattering to the ground. The sudden, agonising pain of the wound told him what had happened.

Aliena screamed and Elyan shoved her back into the cottage, looking around for the source of the shot as he did so.

Before Quinn could even think of moving to escape further attack, the uninjured guard grabbed him and hauled him to his feet. 'Now we have a different situation,' he leered, as the archer ran up to the group. 'You and your friends are going to pay *very* heavily for this!'

Quinn could not answer, the pain rendering him speechless, along with a sense of relief that the arrow did not seem to be poisoned.

'We're *not* his friends!' Elyan shouted from the doorway. 'He *was* trespassing, looking to steal, until I caught him!'

'Lying will not help you, boy,' said the archer.

Quinn's heart sank as Aliena started to cry.

Nothing any of them said now would make any difference. He feared he had only made things worse for them all.

'He was holding us hostage!' Elyan screeched, desperately trying to wriggle out of trouble.

'More lies, I am sure,' said the guard holding Quinn. 'You are only making it worse for yourselves when you join your friend at the castle.'

Quinn struggled against the grip the guard had on him, wanting to smash his face in just as he had done to his colleague.

'Oh, no you *don't*!' The guard twisted Quinn's body down and grabbed the arrow shaft sticking from the back of his shoulder. He pushed down on it, making Quinn scream in agony, until it finally snapped under the pressure, leaving the arrowhead embedded in his flesh. Quinn fell on to his hands in the mud and stayed there, feeling nauseated and dizzy, gritting his teeth and shaking with rage. After a moment he looked up through the rain at Aliena, who was standing in the doorway beside her brother now. She discreetly shook her head at him, tears still falling from her sad, frightened eyes. He dropped his head down again and closed his eyes, fighting down his fury. Despair spread through him instead, as he realised the situation was hopeless.

Then Elyan spoke again. 'We can make a deal!'

Everyone looked at him – Quinn in shock,

Aliena in horror and the guards with mild interest.

'What could you possibly offer us that would be good enough to stop us from punishing you for harbouring a vagrant?' said the archer.

'He's not just a vagrant. I know what else he has done!' Elyan had now given up hiding his contempt for Quinn and glared at him, daring him to argue.

'Go on...'

'First we want your word that you will let us go.'

'*Elyan*!' Aliena protested.

Elyan ignored her. 'Give us your word!'

The injured guard slowly stepped towards Elyan, snorting like a boar as he tried to clear his nose and throat of blood. 'You have it,' he said, the words rattling their way forth. '*If* the information is worth anything.'

Elyan swallowed, sudden doubt flashing across his face.

'Well?' shouted the guard, sore and out of patience.

'He *killed* a man.'

Quinn felt the blood drain from his face, as Aliena gasped and stepped away from her brother.

'And you know this *how*?'

'He was sick. He talked in his fever. I don't know who the man was, but wherever *he* comes from –' He jabbed a finger at Quinn. '– they banished him for it! He's a murderer! Someone even followed him here and shot him with a poisoned arrow. They didn't want him here and neither did I! Check for yourselves – it's all true!'

Quinn looked at Aliena. She stared back at him, her eyes filling with fresh tears. Her lip trembled, along with the rest of her slight frame. Her gaze held a silent plea for him to tell her it was not true, but he was trapped. He had to protect her and Elyan – even if he had just been horribly betrayed by the young man who now stared at him with something resembling triumph in his dark eyes. If the information was worthless, the guards would not keep their word.

The archer dragged him to his feet, thinking nothing of the extra pain he caused his prisoner. 'Is this true?' he demanded.

Quinn looked up, defeat plain to see in his face. 'It's true.'

Aliena sobbed and he could not bear to look at her again.

'Then I suppose the capture of a murderer may be worth us overlooking the hiding of a vagrant,' said the archer, looking at the guards, who were slow to nod their agreement. The archer turned back to Elyan. 'You have been fortunate today, boy. We could still have you punished at any time. If you so much as look at one of us the wrong way in the future...'

Elyan nodded his understanding, relief paralysing his tongue.

The archer waved him away. 'Be gone into your house. We are finished with you.'

Quinn glanced at Elyan one last time as he ushered Aliena into the cottage. He did not see her face, but he could see her shoulders shaking as she gave way to her sorrow. Looking down at the ground once the door was shut, Quinn wondered if he had ever felt so wretched in his life.

'You're going to see the sheriff,' announced the archer, as the guard who had hold of his shoulder swung him around to face the direction of the nearby town.

Quinn straightened himself up as best he could and began to walk, determined not to be dragged along to Castle Rivallen like a dog.

But inside he felt destroyed.

CHAPTER 21. GALEN.

The cells in the western tower of the castle did not smell as bad as Quinn had anticipated. He was already feeling sick with pain, however, and the musty, dank air made it difficult for him to breathe. His rain-soaked clothes stuck to his skin, and the chill in the air made him shiver violently.

The guards pushed him up the steep, spiral, stone staircase. Soon it was so dark he could barely make out the walls or the steps. He stumbled on several occasions, but was roughly forced onwards by one of the guards, who had no sympathy for the intense pain it caused his wounded shoulder.

Glad to finally reach a break in the climb, he watched as the guard pounded on a solid door he could barely see. He heard bolts being drawn back and the passageway they stood in was flooded with a gentle, orange light. He was shoved through the open door into a narrow tunnel, lit with torches on both sides. The guards left him with this new colleague and stomped back down the staircase.

The new guard did not push him along; grabbing a torch, he merely indicated with his free hand that Quinn should move along and he obeyed, not wanting any more pain inflicted upon his wound. The tunnel soon gave way to another, colder staircase. An icy draught swept through narrow slits at various intervals along the outer wall, and he felt weaker with every step. He just wanted to reach the place he was required to go to and get whatever he was facing over with.

They reached another thick, oak door. The guard took a heavy key from his belt and unlocked it. Quinn knew he must go through it, but he hesitated – suddenly the prospect of only coming back out to face his execution filled him with an almost uncontrollable urge to fight and run. The guard slammed the heel of his hand between Quinn's shoulder blades, knocking him through the door. He stumbled, landing heavily on his front on the dirty floor. He gritted his teeth as pain and fury coursed through him, but before he could recover enough to do anything, the door was slammed shut and the key was turned.

'*Bastard*,' he muttered.

He slowly rolled on to his side and lay still, eyes closed, as he waited for his anger to pass. When he opened them, he looked towards the small arrow loop in the outer wall of the cell, which was letting in the weak light. Rain still poured down and the roaring wind drove it through the loop. It was trickling on to the floor and running between the thick, wooden boards. A large rat sat under the loop, lapping at the water, taking no notice of Quinn.

As he looked around, he saw that part of the large cell was not visible to him from his position

– the light was not strong enough to illuminate the far end of the room and he could not tell how big it was, or what might be hiding there. Sitting up, he saw heavy chains and shackles attached to the outer wall and he pondered for a moment why he had not been put into them. He thought that maybe they considered him too weak to put up much of a fight – and they were probably right.

His shoulder seared with pain again, making him groan. He did not know how he was going to get the arrowhead out, but he knew it was not worth trying to. He would just have to bear it until such a time as the sheriff decided to have him put out of his misery…

He got slowly to his feet and felt the queasiness in him increase. His face seemed to tingle and grow cold. He staggered to the wall and steadied himself with one hand held against it, the other hanging uselessly by his side. He fought to control his shivering, but could not. Without realising it, he was tipping slowly sideways. His senses faded, and as all pain drifted from his body, he did not feel himself crash to the floor once more. The darkness returned, enveloping him with its mercy; he was not aware of the skinny, filthy figure shuffling towards him in the gloom.

***

'You're not from these parts,' said a man's voice as Quinn's eyes flickered open.

Quinn looked at the inquisitive face that was slowly appearing before him as his vision cleared. His head pounded and he was already shivering again. He was very thirsty, but the pain in the wound on his shoulder seemed to have eased and he no longer felt as if he might vomit at any moment. He was lying where he had fallen as far as he could work out, but now he had a threadbare, scratchy blanket draped over him.

'Can you sit up?' asked the man, smiling at him.

'I think so…'

The man helped him to sit, and when he was relatively steady and comfortable, held out his right hand. 'I'm Galen. Resident of this cell for two years.'

'Quinn. Sorry to barge in on you like this…' He shook Galen's hand and managed a faint smile.

'You're *special*. And special people make the best company. Think nothing of it.'

Galen sat down in front of him, cross-legged. Quinn noticed how filthy and sparsely clothed he was, yet he did not seem to feel the cold. He was shirtless and bootless, his only attire a pair of thin, leather trousers that were too big for him, held in place with some dirty string. Quinn guessed they had fitted perfectly two years previously.

He had a rough-looking face, but it had a kindness about it that Quinn had rarely seen among the men of Rivallen. His wrinkled and pock-marked skin was of a deep tan colour, his eyes a piercing blue and what was left of his brown hair had grown to his shoulders. But he had no beard, and Quinn was both surprised and pleased that the poor man was at least allowed the 'luxury' of shaving.

'Why do you think I'm special?' Quinn asked him.

'Because, my son, the sheriff kills everyone but the special ones. He's keeping you alive for a reason.'

'So you're –'

'His uncle.'

'You're his *uncle*?'

Galen laughed, a deep, gentle sound that Quinn could not help warming to. 'You have much to learn, it seems, Quinn. More proof that you are new to Rivallen. My nephew is a hard man, but not without his weaknesses. Let me explain. He is fond of executions – they are a great deterrent and also spare him the bother of needing many guards to watch over the prisoners here. But even he can't bring himself to murder one of his own family. So, here I rot…'

'But *why* are you here?'

'Because I told him he was becoming a tyrant. I threatened to expose some of his actions to the king. He's quite fond of coming up here from time to time to tell me how right I was.'

Quinn was silent for a moment, wondering how Galen stayed in such good spirits and talk about it in such a carefree manner, after being treated in such an appalling way by one of his own family.

'Don't feel bad for me, my son,' Galen said, as if reading his thoughts. 'I learned a long time ago that feeling sorry for myself is a waste of time and energy. And it seems you have your own troubles to occupy you.'

Quinn decided to drop the subject for the old man's sake. He might not be as blasé about his predicament on the inside…

After a short pause, Galen said: 'I was checking you over while you were out of your senses. I've never seen eyes like that in Rivallen. And I've lived over sixty years.'

Quinn looked down at the floor. 'I knew I was bound to stand out. But, as it happens, I had no time to worry about it.'

'Oh, I don't mean the colour of them *now*. I've seen plenty of people with blindness in one or both eyes that turns them milky-white…'

'My right eye is the blind one, not that that's important…what did you mean if not now?'

Galen peered at Quinn's dark eye, frowning. 'That is indeed unusual. But, I mean, they *glowed*. Not for long, mind. But they turned a bright blue colour a couple of times. Never seen that in my life.' Galen smiled, as if he had no fear at all of this strange new being with eyes that changed colour.

Quinn felt a flutter of hope – his powers were still returning, despite the fresh injuries to his body. '*Both* of them?'

The old man nodded. 'You have magic.' His face turned grim. 'And, unfortunately, the sheriff must know about it.'

'I don't understand…'

'As I said – you're special. You would not be alive now if you did not have something about you that the sheriff thought worth *keeping* you alive for. What was your crime?'

Quinn inspected the floor again for a few moments. 'I killed a man,' he said, careful to keep his voice low.

'Something which would normally mean immediate execution in my nephew's eyes. He likes to be the only one with a say in who lives or dies around here.' Galen showed no sign of surprise, reproach or distaste at Quinn's confession. 'He must know you have magic.'

'It's not *magic* - and I've never met him,' Quinn snapped. 'How could he know anything about me?'

'He must have found out from somewhere, whatever you call what you have. Be careful, Quinn. Garin must have plans to use you for his own benefit. And, knowing him, it won't be for anything good.'

Quinn rubbed his temples hard, unable to focus on any theory about the sheriff right then, however much he understood its importance. 'I'm sorry,' he said. 'But is there any water?'

'Of course – forgive me. I should have

offered it straight away.' Galen shuffled to the darkest part of the cell, returning moments later with a dirty pewter tankard.

Quinn took it gratefully and drank as if it was water from the freshest mountain spring. He started to feel better almost at once, which led him to another question. 'Did you take the arrowhead out?'

Galen smiled as he nodded. 'I was a physician in my time. I'm afraid I had no equipment and very little water to clean the wound with, but it should start to heal now. It did bleed a lot, though, as it took me a while. Thankfully, you slept through the whole thing – you've been here a day already.'

Quinn looked up at him, confused. Galen nodded his confirmation.

'Does the sheriff usually have prisoners executed as soon as they arrive?' Quinn asked.

'If he's here, yes. He was not in the castle yesterday when you arrived, but he came back late last night. He had a quick look at you when you were still out of it, but didn't say anything – at least, not in my presence. Normally he'd have dragged you straight off to be hanged. I've seen him do it to two others. He *knows* you have magic – what do you call it? I'm sure of it.'

Quinn ignored the question, not knowing how to begin to explain his abilities. He knew most ordinary folk would call it magic, as Galen had, but he'd never liked the word himself. It was bandied about far too much, with little appreciation for the true skill and complexity of what he could achieve.

'So…with me being here a whole day already, someone has had plenty of time to give him that information,' he told Galen. 'The guards who seized me did not know about it.'

'Do you know who it might have been?'

'I have a couple of ideas.' There was bitterness in Quinn's voice, which did not go unnoticed by Galen. 'It was either the unknown archer with the poisoned arrow tips, who must be someone who knows me, or the person who gave me up to the guards – he must have seen the same thing you saw in my eyes.'

'You were shot with a poisoned arrow?'

Quinn nodded and pointed out the still-vivid wound on his neck.

'I wondered how you had come by that. I've never heard of such a thing being used by the guards here…you have no idea who did it?'

'None. Beyond the possibility that someone from home hated me enough to follow me here. Banishment obviously wasn't enough justice in their eyes.'

'You admit you killed a man, though?'

'I did kill a man. But not without good reason.'

'Is there ever a good reason?'

Quinn looked up at Galen and saw that there was no challenge in his question, only curiosity about Quinn's viewpoint.

'He'd beaten his young son almost to death.' He decided to leave out the fact that the child had actually died and been brought back to life – Galen might be open-minded about 'magic', but was he ready to know the extent of the supernatural in his world?

'Ahh.' Galen sat down again. 'Then you stood up for one who could not stand up for himself. That has honour in it. But taking a life – that does not.'

'I have already been punished by my own people for it. I accepted that. I'm not sure I can accept *this*!' He gestured violently at the cell around him. '*Your* people do not rule me,' he added, feeling his anger rising. He fought to keep it in check and gave Galen an apologetic look.

'My son, it seems that – for now, at least – they do.'

Quinn fell silent, trying to understand the spiralling disaster that was his new life. He was locked up, tired, wounded and grieving. He could see no way out.

Galen patted him on his good shoulder and stood up, leaving him to his thoughts. As he shuffled over to the dark side of the cell, he said: 'There is *always* hope. Right up to the last beat of your heart, Quinn. Don't forget that.'

Quinn thought of Renn's resurrection and knew the old man was right.

CHAPTER 22. THE SHERIFF.

The guard made as much noise as possible turning the key in the lock, then threw the door open with almost theatrical vigour. Galen did not look around from the arrow loop, where he gazed out at the limited view of the murky moat, the grass beyond and the forest in the distance. His body blocked out most of the daylight, but the guard carried a torch. Quinn saw the dark form of the infamous sheriff behind him.

'On your feet, stranger!' demanded the guard.

Quinn stood up slowly, his body still feeling weak and his head spinning. As he straightened up, Sheriff Garin pushed past the guard and stood in the middle of the cell. He looked Quinn up and down with a mixture of interest and distaste.

As he studied Quinn, so Quinn studied him. He was a young man for a sheriff, perhaps thirty-five years old, with a clean, untroubled face that suggested a life of luxury, contentment and perhaps an unshakeable belief that he was right in everything he said and did. His dark hair was neatly cut and his beard expertly trimmed. He stood with a practised air of authority, which he clearly enjoyed. He was dressed in full armour, carrying a beautifully crafted broadsword that even Quinn felt admiration for, despite Delmoril having the finest weaponry anyone could imagine.

His dark eyes sparkled with malice as he glared at Quinn, thoughtfully scratching his chin for effect. 'What are you?' he finally asked.

Quinn raised an eyebrow, but said nothing.

'What are you? Garin asked again. 'Where are you from? Why have I never seen your kind in Rivallen before?'

'*My kind*? I'm no different from anyone else.'

Garin stepped forwards and thumped Quinn hard in the stomach. Quinn doubled over, all his breath gone, then his legs gave way and he sat down heavily with a groan. The guard rushed to him and dragged him to his feet, holding him as upright as he could – Quinn was taller and almost a dead weight in his weakness.

'You will answer properly – and you will address the sheriff as "my lord",' said the guard.

Galen looked around, finally, pursing his lips in disgust.

'Let's try a different question, shall we?' said Garin. 'Why are you in Rivallen? I was told you were banished for murdering an innocent man.'

'Then why are you asking me?' replied Quinn, his voice weakened, but with defiance in his eyes.

The guard shook him by the shoulder, making Quinn wince, but the sheriff held up his hand and stopped him. 'It is alright,' he said. 'He will answer me soon enough.' Stepping closer to Quinn again, he went on: 'You see, Quinn, you and I could be very good for one another. You have something I could use and you would be well-rewarded for it.'

Galen turned and leaned against the wall, listening intently.

'I have nothing,' Quinn argued. 'Why do you think your guards arrested me for vagrancy?'

Anger flashed in Garin's eyes as he glared at Quinn. 'You might want to forget about playing games with me. I know much more than just your name. There is no point in denying that you have magic. It has been witnessed.'

'"Magic"? By a boy who just wanted me out of the way and wanted to save his own skin?' Quinn scoffed. 'Quite gullible, aren't you? *My lord.*'

Garin moved far more quickly than Quinn imagined he could and slammed his forehead into the bridge of Quinn's nose. The guard let go of him and he dropped to the floor in a heap, blood streaming down his face and his eyes watering. The sheriff pushed him on to his back with his boot and pressed his sword to Quinn's throat.

'I *know* you have magic. But, I also imagine that you would have used it to escape from here if you could. So just remember who has all the *relevant* power, right here, right now.'

Quinn coughed as blood trickled back his throat and he spat it at the sheriff, making him leap backwards. Galen stiffened, expecting retaliation from Garin, but the sheriff merely sheathed his sword and laughed.

'You will keep.'

The guard opened the cell door and held it as the sheriff stalked through, then followed, closing the door and turning the key quietly.

Once he was sure they had gone, Galen rushed to Quinn and helped him to sit up. 'Why did you do that?' he asked, trying to hold Quinn's head still while he examined his injured face. 'It makes no sense to antagonise Garin further! He wants your power, we know that now, but his patience is not endless. You may push him into deciding that your power is not worth the irritation you are causing him.'

'I would *never* give him my power, even if I could,' Quinn said, flinching as Galen touched his tender nose. 'I don't understand what he thinks he can do with me. Maybe this way he will put me out of my misery sooner rather than later.'

'Is that what you want?'

'I will not be his puppet.'

'No – indeed, I know you wouldn't agree to that. But you seem to have forgotten what I said to you before. You have already given up hope of your fortunes changing. And hold still – your nose isn't broken but if you keep fidgeting it will continue to bleed.'

Quinn stopped moving and allowed Galen to continue inspecting the injury. The pain was distracting, but at least his head was clearing a little. 'The sheriff is right about me not being able to escape. Even if my power was at full strength,

I could not do it. I would need my amulet, which was taken from me when I was banished. I would need my sword at the very least and I don't have that, either. Everything was taken from me.'

'Stop sulking like a petulant child.'

Quinn frowned at Galen's sharp tone.

'Don't look at me like that. You *are* sulking! So, you were banished. You say you have accepted that, but you haven't. You pine for everything you had. You've had a rough time of it, I don't deny that. And it's got worse. I don't deny *that*, either. But are you really just going to give up and provoke Garin into executing you?' He sighed and softened his tone at Quinn's weary look. 'Just because you cannot see the mountain's peak for the clouds, does not mean the peak is not there. Hmm?'

Quinn looked down, knowing the old man had a point. Galen made him lift his head again, raising a finger. 'Stop weakening yourself by inviting this sort of treatment from Garin. Gather your strength and think about how you can change your situation. God gave you these gifts, my son, along with the gift of life. Don't fight to preserve one while throwing away the other. That's how evil works inside us.'

'Quinn looked confused. 'I thought your priests said that "magic" is evil and that it does not come from God.'

'I don't know what sort of faith you have in your world, Quinn – hopefully a simpler one than ours. You are right; some do see it as evil. But others take a more tolerant view, as long as it is not used for harm. They are, sadly, in the minority. To me, God created everything and that includes whatever power you hold within you. Some do use it for evil, but that does not make the power itself evil. If you beat a man with a stick, is the stick then evil?'

Quinn smiled. 'All I've known about – until now – are the punishments meted out to those suspected of what they call witchcraft. That is why my people hide from men as much as we are able, and try to at least blend in when we are not.'

'The people who accept these things are afraid to say so. They hide themselves, just like you. Or they leave. Kilora seems more tolerant towards healers and suchlike, but you exchange prejudice for even more violence if you go there. It's a lawless country and a sad world we all live in.' Galen changed his troubled look for a gentle smile. 'One day, my nephew will be gone and then perhaps it will change for the better.'

'How do you carry on and keep hope the way that you do?'

'By reminding myself that no man can take certain things from me that I do not *allow* him to take – except my life, and that will be the will of God. Nobody can take my hope, or my dignity. I won't let them.' He patted Quinn on the arm and stood up. 'Pray to God, Quinn. Draw strength from wherever you can. Refuse to accept this, by action, not anger. In time, the answers *will* come to you.'

CHAPTER 23. IN CHAINS.

Quinn was lying on his front on the floor. His head rested on the folded blanket while Galen did his best to clean the arrow wound in his shoulder. It had started to bleed again after the rough handling by the guard and Galen was worried about it becoming infected. Knowing that Quinn was a valued 'prize' for the sheriff, Galen had asked the guard to bring clean water and muslin cloths so the wound could be given the best chance of healing without Quinn suffering a fever. The guard had agreed and had even given them a small amount of wine to pour over the wound.

'An intelligent guard for once,' Galen had muttered after the guard had left and locked the door.

Despite the occasional searing pain, Quinn was beginning to drift off to sleep as Galen finished tending the wound. But then they heard the key rattling in the lock again. Galen stood up quickly, going to his usual spot by the arrow loop, while Quinn struggled to shake the fatigue from his brain and sit up. His expression remained passive as the guard let Garin into the cell – he wanted to at least try to follow Galen's advice and not allow his anger to provoke the sheriff into weakening him further.

'On your feet!' said the guard.

Quinn stood, feeling the cold crawl around his bare skin. His tunic and undershirt lay in a heap on the floor, but he doubted Garin would grant him permission to put them back on, so he made no move to pick them up. Instead, he stood motionless, levelling his gaze upon the armoured sheriff, unable to hide the contempt from his expression. But it was slapped away with his gaoler's next words.

'Chain him.' Garin's voice was chillingly calm.

Quinn's eyes held a silent protest, but he did not resist. The guard pushed him firmly back to the outer wall of the cell and told him to raise his arms above his head. As he did as he was told, he could see Galen's fists clenching, but the sheriff's uncle said nothing.

The rusted irons were clamped to his wrists. Heavy chains were pulled taught and fixed, via a large metal ring on the roof of the cell, to a hook on the wall. Quinn found himself pulled up so far that his toes barely touched the floor and his shoulder protested so strongly he groaned involuntarily. He did not miss Garin's brief smile at his pain.

The guard was not done yet. He removed Quinn's boots and placed even heavier clamps around his ankles, which dug into flesh and bone as they sagged. Quinn could not help but wince as the guard rattled them to check they were secure.

'Now – don't assume I have done this because I am afraid of you,' said Garin, walking over to stand directly in front of Quinn. If you cooperate, you will be let out of the chains again. If you don't, we'll find out how long you manage to last before you pass out.' He took out an ebony-handled whip with around a dozen leather tails on it, each one with a tight knot at the end.

Quinn's whole body stiffened. He glanced at Galen, who had turned at the sheriff's words and had stared, open-mouthed, at the sight of the implement. Quinn's eyes widened, trying to send a message to Galen to stay where he was and not get involved. Galen hesitated, but then seemed to understand, slumping against the outer wall, a look of fear on his gentle face. He knew, as did Quinn, that Quinn would find it almost impossible to curb his anger under this kind of treatment. This would be no sudden, one-off injury. The only hope they had was that his body would give out before his temper did, which they both knew was unlikely.

Quinn looked Garin in the eye as he swung the whip around in his hand, pacing a little just in front of him. He could do nothing but pray silently and wait for the inevitable.

When the first strike on his back came, the pain was so shocking that he could not, at first, draw a breath in. He tensed every muscle from his jaw to his toes, until he was finally able to suck some air in through his teeth. Before he could recover further, the whip sliced into his flesh again and again, until he could not help but cry out in agony.

Garin had been waiting for him to do just that. He lowered his arm and sneered in satisfaction, a look not missed by Galen.

Moments later the assault began again. Now Garin worked his way around Quinn's body, covering his chest and back in red welts, some of which began to bleed. He ignored Quinn's weakening protests and his uncle's pleading eyes.

At last, as Quinn's legs began to buckle, he stopped. Garin rubbed his striking arm as he surveyed his achievement with unconcealed pleasure. 'I have your attention now?'

Breathing hard and fast, Quinn looked down with watering eyes at the bright, angry cuts on his pale skin. As he looked back up at Garin, he tried to stifle the rage that was building up inside of him.

'Good. Now, listen carefully. You have magic. I have a different kind of power. Together we could offer the people of Rivallen a safer, more secure life, don't you think?' He spoke in a smooth tone, as if he were offering Quinn an equal partnership in a new merchant's venture.

Quinn said nothing, unable to do anything but attempt to supress his emotions as his skin burned. His body instinctively wanted to curl up, but the chains stretched him still and it was all he could do to stop himself from unleashing whatever strength he had left on the sheriff. He would not lower himself to that level, risking Galen's safety in the process.

'You see, not *everyone* in my Guard is as loyal as they should be – as loyal as this fellow here,' the sheriff said, indicating the guard standing beside Quinn, who seemed to draw himself up in pride at the sheriff's words of praise. 'With *your* help, I could seek out the traitors to the king and deal with them appropriately.'

'It's not the *king* they want to rebel against,' said Galen.

Quinn watched in alarm as Garin marched over to his uncle and pointed a finger in his face. 'And what could you possibly know about it, old man?'

'I know *you*, nephew. Isn't that why you keep me here? I also know that the people and the guards are basically good underneath the fear and distrust you've instilled in them. I've spoken to enough of them over the last two years. I know they would get rid of you in a heartbeat if they knew how. But you rule by terror, as I've always said. Using whatever you think Quinn possesses would do nothing for these people except make them fear you more.' Galen pointed at Quinn. '*He* does not deserve the same kind of infamy you have.'

'Uncle, do you imagine for a moment that the king could have survived on his throne this long, without *me*? He is a weak and an ineffectual ruler! He thinks of nothing but hiding away in the castle with his boy, pining over his dead wife. He is not a monarch – he is merely a man wearing a crown. This kingdom would be in utter chaos if it were not for me!'

'That is your *ego* talking. Nobody else believes that –'

'It needs a strong ruler, someone to keep the people in line. And a strong ruler needs loyalty. That is where *he* comes in.' The sheriff gestured towards Quinn, who had listened intently to the exchange, keeping his mind from the agony his body was in.

'What do you propose to do with him, exactly?'

'He will root out the traitors among my guards and kill them.'

'I am not a mind-reader, and whatever you believe I can do – I will not kill!' snapped Quinn.

Garin crossed the cell in an instant. He stood so close Quinn could smell the foul, stale wine on his breath. 'That is a *lie*! I know you have already taken a life using your magic. If you can be made to do it once, you can be made to do it again!'

Quinn stayed silent.

'You suspected that boy of passing us the news of your magic, but it was not him. He merely knew of the murder, which we then investigated. You were *seen* that night. We know what you did to the boy's father, and how you did it. You were seen by two others. You have no defence!'

Quinn considered the sheriff's words. His anger, his desire to bring Renn's father to justice had made his presence visible to others – more proof that his ordeal in the Plane of Shadows had affected his ability to conduct. He should not have been visible to anyone but the occupants of that tiny house. But he stayed quiet. The sheriff was right – there was no way he could talk his way out of it now. But there was also no way he would ever agree to help Garin.

'You will bring peace to this land by killing the enemies of the king. And *my* enemies. You could do it without suspicion ever being laid at my door.'

'I will never be your assassin. You're *insane*.'

The sheriff laughed and looked at his uncle. 'So I'm told. But the fact remains,' he added, glaring back at Quinn. 'You will eventually agree to do as I bid. Everyone has a breaking point. It matters not how long it takes – I will find yours. And with more...*efficient* tools than this.' He twitched the whip close to Quinn's face.

Quinn stared defiantly. 'I will never work for you. I'd rather *die*.'

'That would be far too easy for you. Oh, no... we won't be letting you die.' The sheriff smiled and patted Quinn's cheek, making him flinch away. 'We will see how long it takes. How long you last. But you will break. Trust in that.'

CHAPTER 24. A LIGHT IN THE DARKNESS.

'Quinn, you must sit *up*!'

Galen fought to lift the larger, heavier man upright, straining with the effort it took and feeling the protests from his old joints. Quinn tried to help himself, but his limbs felt heavy and he shivered from being in a cold sweat. He was fighting the urge to just lie down and sleep.

'Come on – you can't stay on the floor, you will get all sorts of filth in those wounds.'

'I've got to get out of here, Galen,' Quinn said drowsily. 'But how..?'

'I don't know yet, dear boy, but at least your head is on straighter now. Come on – that's it – up you get.'

Eventually Quinn was sitting up, leaning gingerly against the wall and panting, his arms hanging limply by his sides. His wrists and ankles were red and sore, but that was nothing compared to the injuries to his back and chest. They were mostly small and not too deep, but there were dozens of them, criss-crossed over his skin like the desperate scratchings of a long-dead prisoner on the cell wall behind him. They collectively buzzed with so much pain that, although he was very cold, he knew he could not yet put his clothes on over them.

It was hard for him to see a way out or prevent himself from being overwhelmed by a dark cloud of despair that seemed to lurk in the already-gloomy depths of the cell. But he knew he must act, however small that act may be, for now.

'I need the candle,' he said, resting his head back against the wall and closing his eyes.

'What for?' asked Galen.

'It will help me to focus my power...whatever is left of it. I have to try some healing – this is too much for you.' He opened his eyes and looked at his companion apologetically. 'I don't mean to be disrespectful.'

'It's alright, Quinn. I know what you mean. I cannot be of much use with just a bit of wine and some cloth, even if the guard would agree to bring me more. I am sorry Garin decided to be so brutal. But you kept your temper – he hasn't won.'

'This time,' Quinn said, miserably. 'I don't know how much time I have before he pays me another visit, but I can at least try to get myself stronger. He knows I have some power, I can't deny it now, so I don't care if he knows I'm using it.'

'But what if he decides to increase the punishment because he knows you can heal this kind of injury?' said Galen, indicating Quinn's traumatised skin.

'I will just have to take that chance. Maybe there will be an opportunity to change my circumstances somewhere along this path. I have to at least have the strength to take any chance I can of getting out of here.'

'You have a plan?'

'Short of killing him and the guards? No.'

Galen was thoughtful for a moment. 'I will help you in any way I can, Quinn. I know I said there is no honour in taking a life, but I believe you to be an honourable man. You do not deserve this and the fact that my nephew wants to use you and your power to increase his own hold over this kingdom means I will – indeed *must* - help I whatever way I am able, to prevent such a thing from happening.' He held up his hand as Quinn was about to speak. 'No, no – I know you will not let it happen if you can possibly help it, but your death should not – *cannot* – be the only way to prevent it. I will not sit here and allow your life and your gift to be wasted because of the evil that runs through Garin's veins. You were created by God for *good*. We have to keep you that way.' Galen paused, rubbing his face as frustration seemed to creep into him. 'Whatever it takes, Quinn. For too long I have sat here in my own thoughts, keeping cheerful, accepting things are what they are – trying to ignore the brutality I could predict, but not prevent. It's time I made my nephew regret bringing it to me and reminding me just how wicked he really is.' He managed a conspiratorial smile.

Quinn tried to sit up straighter, wincing. 'Well, let's start by making him regret giving us a candle.'

Galen fetched the candle and made a small indentation in the soft, dry dirt on the floor to set it in. Once it was ready, he stood up. 'Do you need anything else?'

Quinn shook his head. He wondered if he had the strength to do this, but had to try. 'No. Thank you, Galen. Don't worry, this will not harm you. It may look a little alarming, that's all.'

'All the same – I'll take my place by the wall, out of the way.'

Quinn nodded and settled himself, legs crossed, leaning towards the candle, the flame dancing as if in greeting. He held his hands over the flame, spreading his fingers as far as he could and creating a kind of spherical shape with them around it. Moving his hands lower and closer, he looked as if he were about to interlock his fingers, but stopped just short of them touching and held them as still as he could. He waited until his cold hands began to acclimatise to the heat, then spoke in a low, soft voice: 'O God, grant me the blessed gift of healing, that I may continue to serve You as You intended when You created me.'

As he spoke, Galen watched open-mouthed as the flame began to grow. It changed from its normal, cold yellow to a beautiful, deep purple. It began to spread, tickling Quinn's fingers and licking at his wrists. At first, he did not appear to even notice, let alone feel any pain from the flames as they worked their way up his arms and seemed to disappear into his body. But, as he finished speaking, he gasped, as the power of God spread right through him. He started to shake and had to fight to keep his hands over the candle. He cried out in pain and Galen froze, unsure of what to do – if anything at all. He watched in fearful awe as the flames spread all over Quinn's body, rushing around him and showing bright sparks of red in amongst the intensifying purple light. Then there was a blinding flash of blue, and Quinn yelped in pain as myriad sparks fizzed around him for a few seconds. When they had burned themselves out, the candle died and he slumped to the ground, shivering and wide-eyed.

'*Quinn*!' Galen rushed to his side and knelt down, lifting his head gently and resting it on his lap. Moving the sweat-drenched hair from Quinn's eyes, he gasped as he saw that they were glowing – the left one a beautiful turquoise-blue, but the right one a vivid, angry red. 'What's happening? Your eyes…they are different from when I saw them glow before…'

There was no time for Quinn to answer, as the key turned in the door and it was flung open by the guard. He stood there alone, frowning at the two prisoners.

'What's going on in here?' the guard asked.

Galen cradled Quinn's head, ensuring his eyes were hidden from the soldier. 'Nothing is going on, except that the sheriff's prize prisoner is going to *die* if he's not given warm clothes and a blanket or two. Look how he shivers!'

The guard looked, but said nothing.

'Who do you think he will blame if this man dies?' Galen asked.

The guard thought about it for another moment, then said: 'I will have something brought to him.' He closed the door and locked it again.

Galen slumped with relief that he had not been punished for his insolence and then turned back to Quinn, who looked up at him, clearly confused.

'I don't know what happened, Galen. The flame was meant to help me to focus…when it grew, I found I could not move away from it.'

'You are not burned…'

'But it hurt. It was like being stung by a swarm of angry bees. And I feel so cold now.'

'You will be warm soon, Quinn, when the guard returns. I hope.'

'Did you see red sparks?'

Galen nodded.

'They have appeared before,' Quinn said, as Galen helped him to sit up. 'I fear that something that happened to me has not yet been properly undone and now I am stuck with a flawed power that I cannot control.'

'But it has worked – look at your wounds!'

'They both watched as the welts on Quinn's body began to fade. Soon, the evidence of Garin's recent torture was gone except for some drying blood and some long, silvery lines that would serve as a permanent reminder of his trauma. Even the arrow wound was rapidly vanishing. His eyes began to lose their glow and Quinn rubbed them with trembling fingers.

'You're healing up fast.'

'But the red...'

'How do you feel? Do you feel stronger?'

'A little.' Quinn looked at Galen, his eyes now fully back to their previous, mismatched colours. 'It was not supposed to hurt. Something is *very* wrong with me, Galen...'

'Try not to think about that now. Worry about it once you have recovered your strength fully. I think you are still a little giddy from it all.'

They fell silent as they heard the guard unlocking the door again. He opened it and threw a clean linen shirt and an old but thick blanket at Galen, who just managed to catch them before they landed in the dirt. The guard left without a word.

'Put this on and wrap the blanket around you. I will lay the old one on the floor. It's not much, but you will be able to rest without getting damp and covered in dirt all over again. See how you feel after some sleep, then we'll talk. I don't know anything about your gift, but I'd like to help – if you'll tell me about what happened to you before.'

Quinn nodded as he put the shirt over his now completely healed, but scarred skin. He shivered as he wrapped the blanket around his shoulders, but knew it would not take long for his body to warm up. Watching as Galen laid out the other blanket, he felt grateful for the plea the former physician had made to the guard.

He felt grateful for Galen.

CHAPTER 25. A POSITIVE APPROACH.

'So, let me see if I've got this...' Galen said. He paced the cell in the dwindling light as Quinn sat against the wall, shivering again. 'No – sorry. I don't think I have.' He stood still and thought for a moment, scratching his chin.

'I'm sorry. It's a lot to take in. I've never told anyone what I am before. There's never been any need to. I've very rarely interacted with your people and when I have it's only been at a basic level – traders, those I've passed on the road.'

'I thought you were just a man from somewhere outside this kingdom, not from an entirely different *race* from a hidden world *inside* the kingdom. It's fascinating! I would love to hear more about your people, when the time is right. But I want to understand this first, to help you if I can. So, let me try again. You killed this man...'

'I didn't kill the first man. He was dying of wounds someone else had inflicted on him. I was there for his soul.'

'I see.' Galen began to pace again, 'Yes. Forgive me. So, you think that this man, at the very point of death, or thereabouts, managed to do something to you. Or to your ability to do your duty.'

'Yes. He locked his consciousness into mine – at least, that's my theory. It was never really explained to me properly. I don't think anyone really knew what had happened. But then I was trapped in the Plane of Shadows and one of the Keepers rescued me.'

'Keepers. What an idea! Our priests would eat themselves from shock if they could hear this.'

'Galen…'

'Sorry. Go on.'

'I thought you were telling me what *you* think happened?'

'Oh. Yes, I was, wasn't I? Let me sit down – I think my mind is wandering as much as my feet. So many questions…' He sat, cross-legged, beside Quinn, who inwardly winced at the stark ribs and hollow stomach of his poor companion. 'Your Archdeacon was supposed to have removed the effects of that incident.'

'That's right.'

'And you think he failed. You think that's why you killed the boy's father? Because this "remnant" has made you feel rage that you cannot control?'

'There's no other explanation for it. No other Conductor has severed the soul of someone who was nowhere near death. We're not even taught *how* to do it. That's why my father reacted the way he did.' Quinn looked at the floor in shame and sorrow. 'I think he was also scared of me…'

'Why did your Archdeacon – wait…does he

have a name?'

Quinn shook his head. 'Once they take the position they become known simply as "Archdeacon". I was just a baby when this one was elected. I've never known what his was.'

'Why did *he* not think that this might be the reason, when you returned to tell him what had happened?' Galen asked, probably deciding it was better if Quinn did not wallow in his feelings about his father.

'That's another strange thing. The Archdeacon has never liked me, but even so…he just decided he was going to banish me and that was the end of it. Erelas even tried to argue with him over it and Erelas has never spoken out against the Archdeacon in public before. He's a far gentler soul that I am.'

'So Erelas believed it was possible?'

'He thought of it without me suggesting it. The Archdeacon wouldn't entertain the idea at all. He had already decided to just be rid of me for good, the only way he could, since the Keeper had forbidden execution or confinement. Maybe he just didn't like to admit his own failure.'

'No. That's not it, Quinn.'

Quinn looked up at his friend, catching the odd tone in his voice. 'What do you mean?'

'I think the Archdeacon must be hiding some important knowledge about what happened to you. He tried to get rid of it without explaining what it was in the first place. And, when that failed, you were dropped as quickly as possible. I'm sorry to say, he probably hopes you won't survive long out here. He knows *something*. And he's afraid of it.'

'That doesn't make me feel any better.'

'I know, my son, but I don't think this has anything to do with his pride. When you get out of here – and you will – you need to find a way of discovering what really happened to you. Can you contact these Keepers?'

Quinn shook his head. 'I would need to travel to the Plane of Shadows – which I can't do without my amulet.'

'Well, we can worry about that later then. Where were we?'

'Where were you, you mean,' Quinn said, smiling a little.

'I'm getting it, I'm getting it!' Galen protested light-heartedly. 'If the rite the Archdeacon performed failed, then this "evil" – for want of a better word – may be the reason you killed Renn's father, the reason you keep feeling rage that you're not used to – and why that prayer almost blinded the pair of us.'

'Don't…I feel bad enou–'

'Ah-ah! Don't even think of saying it. You're not to give up. Your powers *will* get you out of here. You just need to practice. You need to learn how to use your power again, even with this added problem.'

'It's too dangerous.'

'Look, Quinn. I'm an old man, trapped in here until the end of my days, as God wills it. You're a young man who doesn't deserve to be here. That nephew of mine is an insane man who must be prevented from forcing you to use your skills for his own gains. I know – you wouldn't – willingly. But there it is. We either sit here or we *work* at it. If we blow ourselves up, then at least we die trying. And he doesn't get his way. So we keep going.'

'I still don't see how my power is going to get us out of here.'

'I don't, either. But that's *your* job.' He patted Quinn on the leg and stood up. 'So get thinking!'

Quinn smiled and shook his head as the old man started pacing again.

CHAPTER 26. THREATS.

The key rattled in the lock late that night, clattering away the sleep that both prisoners had struggled to find just an hour before. The guard opened it and stood aside to allow another guard carrying a torch to enter the cell. Galen and Quinn were still trying to get their bearings when Garin strode in, pointed at Quinn and barked: 'Chain him!'

The guard shoved Quinn towards the wall and gestured for him to raise his arms. Quinn was feeling a lot better because of the effects of his healing prayer, but he was still very tired and did not appreciate being woken up and chained with his arms in the air again. He did not disguise his annoyance as he glared at the sheriff, who was now standing in front of him.

Garin lifted up Quinn's shirt. 'Glad to see you have healed so…miraculously. Perhaps I will have to set your magic a bigger challenge.'

'What do you want?' spat Quinn.

'You know what I want.'

'You're not getting it. I don't care what you do to me. If your alternative plan was to kill me, get on with it.'

In the background, Galen shook his head, which Quinn saw, but the sheriff did not. Quinn realised the anger within him was rising again already – in his weary state he had not held it at bay. He sighed. 'Look – what is it you actually plan to do with me? You can keep hurting me. I'll just keep healing myself.'

'I don't just want you to help me and your king with your magic –'

'For the love of God – it's not magic. And he's not my king.'

'He is as long as you're in his kingdom.'

Quinn shook his head and looked away, too tired to argue.

'I want to know where you are from and if there are others like you.'

'So you can enslave them, too?'

'Oh, no,' Garin leered, standing close to Quinn. 'I only need one of you, maybe two. The rest will be put to death. I can't have people with your kind of abilities running unchecked through my kingdom.'

Quinn's blood ran cold, but he tried not to show his horror at the prospect of all his people being slaughtered. '*Your* kingdom?'

'In all but name.'

'You really are insane. But that matters not. I'm not giving you any information, any more than I am giving you my abilities, or any control over what I do with them.'

'Perhaps I will send some guards to pick up that beautiful young lady you were staying with – I'm told she really is a sight to behold. Maybe you told her a few things about yourself and your people…If she's as reluctant to share as you are, well…' The sheriff sneered at Quinn, knowing his rage was building up. 'I have many different ways of persuading lovely young women to talk.'

Quinn thrashed against the chains that held him, making Garin step back. 'You *bastard*!' he shouted. 'I'm going to rip you apart!'

Garin laughed. 'I have allowed the bargain between the boy and my guards to be honoured thus far. But…if you do not cooperate and start to tell me what I want to know, *and* do exactly what I want you to do, then that bargain will be ignored. I will kill the boy and she will join me here. And she will not leave again!' He scoffed at Quinn's fury. 'You are powerless, Quinn. The sooner you accept that, the better it will be, especially for the beautiful Aliena.' He turned around and stalked towards the door, a self-satisfied smirk on his face. 'Leave him there until the morning,' he told the guard.

As the two left the room, Quinn could do nothing but glare as the door was slammed shut and locked. He was still staring with a mixture of hopelessness and disbelief on his face, fire raging through his body, when Galen appeared in front of him.

'I am sorry, Quinn. I did not dare say anything. I'm afraid we have run out of time.'

Quinn tried to stem the flow of rage through his veins. 'I will kill him – and every one of his guards, if that's what it takes!' The position of his body began to make breathing difficult and he pushed himself up onto his toes as far as he could.

'Settle down. Think this through…'

Quinn felt drained. 'I *can't* think, Galen. This anger won't let me.'

'Don't start giving into it, or all will be lost. And don't tell me you cannot control it. I don't believe that and neither do you!'

Quinn stared at Galen. Where would he be without this wise old man? He had just as much reason to hate the sheriff, yet he remained calm and used his brain. He took a breath, fighting the pain, and exhaled slowly.

'That's good. You can do it,' said Galen. 'And I don't want any more sulking, thank you.'

Quinn raised an eyebrow.

'Do you know what you are going to do? Galen asked, ignoring Quinn's expression. 'Think quickly, but with your head, not your heart.'

Quinn nodded. 'I'm getting us out of here, as soon as they have let me out of these chains.'

CHAPTER 27. A DESPERATE PLAN.

'*This* is your idea of thinking with your head?'

'My head knows Aliena doesn't have much time,' Quinn said, trying to look down at the ground outside through the arrow loop in the tower's wall.

'It cannot be done, Quinn.'

'Of course it can. I need the amulet to pass through Delmoril's hidden barriers, not to open a hole in something tangible. I used to do this kind of thing with Erelas when we were children, albeit on a smaller scale – besides many other pranks. It's fairly easy.' *At least, it used to be,* he thought.

Galen paced again. Quinn let him get on with it. He knew he could do it. It would not require him to have physical contact with the walls of the tower, so they could stand out of the way while the hole was made. Then it would simply be a case of reaching the ground.

Galen should have been tired – he had stayed up for the rest of the night talking to Quinn, trying to distract his mind from the discomfort of being forced to stand with his arms chained above his head for all that time, until the guard had released him at dawn. Galen told him stories about his earlier life – before Garin began his rule of tyranny. Quinn's admiration for the old man had grown further when he heard how much he had endured and lost because of his nephew.

Galen had been a respected physician in the king's court. He had lived in relative luxury, had trained three men to follow in his footsteps and had been in a happy marriage for many years. His wife had died four years before his imprisonment. His only 'crime' had been to raise concerns over the sheriff's methods of keeping the people in line; when he'd voiced those concerns more publicly than he'd intended one day, Garin ordered his execution. But, as Galen had told Quinn on that first day, even Garin had his limits and he decided to lock his uncle away instead. However, the whole court and all of Rivallen believed he *had* carried out the execution, which made them even more fearful of the sheriff. There seemed to be no limits to the lengths to which Garin would go to ensure the obedience of the people.

As far as Quinn was concerned, Galen deserved to be free more than he did...

'You are coming with me, aren't you?' he asked. 'I can't just leave you here. Garin will kill you for helping me.'

'Only if I won't slow you down. I'm not a cripple, but I'm not as young as I was.'

'I have no intention of making you live life on the run, Galen. I just want to give you back your freedom. We'll find a safe place for you. You have helped me to get this far; when I do this, when we are free, it will mostly be due to you.'

'Nonsense – '

'Don't argue.'

Galen grinned. 'Alright. I will go. But how far is the drop to the water, and how deep is it? You can't tell from up here.'

'I guess we'll find out when we've got a hole to look through.'

Galen raised his eyebrows in alarm. 'What if it's too high?'

'Galen – sometimes you can think too much, you know.'

Galen sighed, and stood well back against the inner wall of the cell, while Quinn positioned himself in the centre, facing the arrow loop. He held out his right hand, palm pointing towards the outer wall. This time he said nothing out loud, but squeezed his eyes shut as he focused his energy and power on his task.

A sudden purple flash of light and a deafening crash had Galen throwing himself to the ground. Quinn was thrown backwards in the same instant to end up sitting on the floor against the wall, right where Galen had been standing a second before. As the dust slowly settled, they sat and coughed, both looking shocked at the result of Quinn's evidently unstable power. A gaping hole had been blown in the wall, taking a wide circle of stonework from around the arrow loop, far larger than Quinn had intended it to be. Rubble had been blown inwards as well as outwards, and as they stared at it, more chunks of broken stone clattered to the floor, sending up even more dust.

'*By God…*' whispered Quinn, scrambling to his feet. 'Galen! Are you hurt?'

The old man rubbed his eyes, shaking his head. 'No,' he said hoarsely. 'We *must* go, Quinn. Guards will be on us in moments!'

'Come on, then,' Quinn said. He hauled Galen to his feet. 'Let's see how long that drop is!'

They hurried over to the hole in the wall. Quinn stood in the gap and peered over the edge at the murky, still waters of the moat below. 'We can make that, I think. I just hope it's deep enough.'

Galen gasped as he heard the key being rapidly clattered into the lock of the cell door. 'Quinn, they are coming!'

'You first!'

But before Quinn could protest, Galen gave him an almighty shove, unbalancing him. He fell through the gap in the wall, letting out a shout of surprise. It seemed an eternity before he hit the water and when he did, it badly winded him. He sank a considerable way before his momentum ran out, then he kicked furiously for the surface. As he broke through, coughing the water from his throat, he turned himself towards the tower and looked up.

'Galen, jump! It's plenty deep enough!'

Quinn's heart seemed to pound even harder. There was no reply, and no sign of his friend.

'*Galen!*'

Galen appeared at the hole and looked down, ashen-faced. Quinn felt sick when he saw Garin standing behind his uncle, immobilising the old man with a hand across his forehead and holding a short sword to his throat.

'*Go!*' Galen shouted.

Before Quinn could say or do anything, the sheriff drew the blade across Galen's neck. His body twitched as blood sprayed from the deep wound. Then he went limp and Garin gave him a push, disgust in his expression. Galen's lifeless body tumbled over the edge and fell for what seemed like an age, then landed so close to where Quinn was treading the water than he was momentarily blinded by the wave that washed over him.

'*No! Galen!*' Quinn grabbed Galen's arm and dragged his body closer, turning him over. Cradling his head, he let out a sob as the blood of the brave old physician seeped into the water and slopped over Quinn's arm. 'I'm so sorry, Galen…'

Quinn knew it was hopeless, but he did not want to let go and it was not until he heard the hiss of an arrow and the zip as it entered the water mere inches from him that he knew he had no time to mourn, or even give Galen back some dignity by removing him from his watery grave. He looked up at the hole in the tower and saw the sheriff standing to one side as his archer aimed again.

'I'm going to personally escort you to *Hell* one day, Garin!' he yelled, rage competing with his sorrow.

The sheriff merely smiled as the archer released the arrow. Quinn felt sickened as it thumped into Galen's chest. Knowing it was folly to stay and rage over his death, he kissed Galen's head. 'May we meet again, my friend,' he said, and then let him go. Turning, he dove under the water and swam as fast as he could along the moat, desperate to get out of range of the archer. Surfacing only when he was sure he could no longer be seen, he scrambled breathlessly up the muddy bank of the moat and ran shakily away from Castle Rivallen as fast as he could. He could hear the shouts of the guards as they spread word of his escape. They would be on him in no time if he did not find somewhere to hide.

He ran and ran, out into the open countryside, past farmsteads, upsetting sheep and pigs as he flew past. People looked up in alarm, some shouting angrily, as he hurdled their small fences and crashed straight through their meagre crops.

On reaching the sprawling grassland beyond the farms, he started to panic as he heard a horse's hooves thundering behind him, growing louder with every second. He would not be able to outrun a horse and the woods in front of him were still too far off for him to hope to conceal himself in time. Nevertheless, he kept running, refusing to give in, not wanting Galen's death to end up being in vain.

The horse was getting closer and closer, and from the pace he knew it was being ridden hard – the rider was definitely pursuing him. He had mere moments left before it ran him down.

'Quinn! *Wait!*'

Quinn spun around in shock and stumbled, falling heavily and lying on the grass gasping for breath. His mind was racing – he knew that voice, but how could it be..?

The horse skidded to a halt, whinnying. As Quinn pushed himself up onto his elbows, he recognised its gentle, noble midnight-black head and blinked, unable to believe his eyes.

'Cara?'

The horse nodded and pushed her nose into his chest as he lay on the ground. Snorting at his dripping wet clothes, she lifted her head again and he could see Erelas, grinning despite the peril Quinn was clearly in.

'Anyone would think you're more pleased to see her than you are me!'

'Erelas! Thank God!' Quinn said. He took the arm Erelas offered him, but struggled to stand up. His legs shook and his lungs burned. They embraced each other, Erelas ignoring Quinn's soaked clothes dampening his own. Quinn fought back the urge to sob against his shoulder as waves of sorrow and relief washed over him, compounding his exhaustion.

'Come on – we must get out of here,' said

Erelas as he released him. 'The guards won't be far behind us.'

'Did you come for Galen?'

Erelas looked blankly at him.

'My friend,' Quinn said, his legs weakening. 'He's dead...'

Erelas looked down at his amulet. 'I haven't been called. We've been out here looking for you for days...'

'But his soul – he'll be *trapped* here!' Tears began to form in Quinn's eyes.

'Quinn, someone will be with him. There must have been a Conductor closer to him than I was at the moment he...' He put a hand on Quinn's shoulder. 'Come on – he will be taken care of, I'm sure of it.'

Quinn nodded and rubbed his face, trying to focus on the other immediate problem. He needed to get to Aliena and Elyan...

Erelas mounted Cara and helped Quinn to get up behind him. Then they were off, racing towards the woods and away from danger.

CHAPTER 28. AN ACT OF PERSUASION

Erelas pulled Cara up as soon as he felt they were at a safe distance away from pursuit. Jumping down as quietly as he could, he waited, listening intently for any sound that gave away the presence of men or horses. He heard nothing out of the ordinary, so he took Cara's bridle and led her to a fallen tree. The woods were peaceful, if a little damp and chilly, with only the flutter of a startled pigeon and the oblivious song of a blackbird to break the silence. Erelas knew he had to get Quinn to shelter where he could dry off and get warm, before he succumbed to the cold that made him shiver so violently. Erelas could hear his teeth chattering from three paces away. But he needed to know what had happened, in order to decide what they should do next.

'Stand still, Cara,' he said. 'We need to take a breath or two.' He patted her neck and looked up at Quinn. He was staring, unseeing, into the distance, breathing heavily through his nose and looking as if he was trying to control a rage building up inside him.

'Quinn…come on. Get off and sit a while. Tell me – what in God's name was going on back there?'

Quinn didn't move.

Erelas squeezed his ankle. Quinn jolted as if he'd been struck. 'Why have we stopped here?' he asked, looking around, clearly alarmed. 'We have no *time*...'

'No time for what?'

'We need to get to the farm – to Aliena!' The sheriff and his guards will go straight there and take her to the castle...'

'Quinn, I don't know what has been going on. You'll have to explain...'

'Then I'll explain on the way. *Please*, Erelas, she doesn't have long!'

'Alright,' said Erelas. He took Cara's reins and passed them to her master. 'Cara led me to a farm while we were searching for you. Is it the same one?'

'Yes!'

Erelas nodded and jumped up behind Quinn as Quinn patted Cara's neck.

'Clever horse,' Quinn said. 'Find my friends!'

Cara snorted and then she was off, almost unseating Erelas as she burst into a swift canter.

***

Quinn jumped down from Cara's back before she had even stopped at the gate to the small farmhouse. He grabbed Erelas's sword before his friend could react, and sprinted for the door, alarmed to find it flung wide open, despite the chilly wind that had picked up since their flight from the castle.

'Quinn – *wait!*' called Erelas. He dismounted and pulled his dagger from his boot, leaving Cara at the wall as he went after Quinn. The events he had been told about spun in his mind, the uppermost thought being how the Archdeacon could have left Quinn to this kind of fate...

Quinn half-stumbled into the cottage. As his eyes adjusted to the dimly-lit interior, he saw that nothing had been upset there: vegetables from their garden were piled on the table, ready to be sorted for market; the fire glowed gently in the hearth, with a pot of water steaming over it; clothes were hanging between the walls to dry.

He looked up at the roof space. 'Aliena?'

There was no reply. As Erelas skidded in behind him and looked around, Quinn pushed past him and headed back out towards the barn. Erelas followed, hoping they would not find that anything terrible had happened.

'*Aliena!*' Quinn rushed into the barn, startling the cow and sending some pigeons flapping to the rafters.

'Quinn?'

He spun around, his heart pounding. 'Oh, thank God!' He rushed over to Aliena and took her hands in his. 'I was so afraid we were too late when I saw the house was empty!'

'What's going on?' She looked surprised to see him and, Quinn noticed with dismay, a little afraid of him. Her alarm increased as Erelas rushed in.

'There's no time to explain. The sheriff and his men are probably on their way here right now, to take you to the castle.'

'But *why*?' She snatched her hands away from Quinn's. 'I have done nothing!'

'I know…please, you must trust me! I know you must be confused because of what Elyan said about me – '

'Which you admitted – '

'I know – and I promise I will explain everything to you, if you will give me the chance. But right now, you are in danger. The sheriff threatened you to try to make me do things for him against the king. Now I've escaped, he is bound to come straight here for you. We must *go*!'

Aliena looked into his eyes, clearly frightened now.

'Where is Elyan?' asked Quinn, looking around.

'I do not know…'

'How long has he been gone?'

'Not long – is he in danger, too?'

'Possibly. We need to find him, and fast. This is Erelas – ' he added, waving a hand towards his friend. 'Erelas, meet Aliena.'

Erelas gave her a slight bow and she gave him a nervous smile in return.

'Erelas,' Quinn continued. 'Take Aliena on Cara and get her away from here. I will find Elyan and meet you. Go to the river to the west.'

Erelas nodded, but Aliena looked reluctant.

'I will not hurt him, I swear,' Quinn said, holding up Erelas' sword. 'This is just in case the sheriff arrives before I can get Elyan away. Aliena, please…'

Suddenly Cara whickered and all three of them jumped.

'Someone is coming,' Erelas hissed. 'We must go!'

Aliena was frightened into complying with their pleas and she took Erelas' proffered hand. Quinn put a hand on her arm, stopping them both. 'I promise I will explain everything, Aliena – I know you are afraid of me and nothing hurts me more at this moment than that. But I swear on my own life that you can trust us with yours. And Elyan's. I will bring him safely to you. I hold no grudge against him.'

Aliena tried to smile through her fear and nodded. Quinn stood back and watched Erelas lead her out to Cara.

***

Once he heard Cara's hooves thumping away, Quinn raised the sword defensively and looked around the barn for signs of life, but apart from the cow and the birds, there was none. He glanced up at the spot where the unknown archer had taken his shot and shuddered, remembering how close to death he had felt. He tried to clear the thought from his mind; there was no time for such things at that moment.

Elyan was not there, but he could have seen their arrival and hidden himself somewhere, afraid of what Quinn and his friend might do to him. Creeping out of the barn, he stole around the back, where he was hidden from both the cottage and the road. He stood behind a thick, evergreen shrub, straining to hear what it was that had made Cara give them a warning. He could hear nothing above his own shuddering breaths as he fought against the cold that seemed to seep as deep as his bones.

Then he detected movement among the trees, beside the dirt track which swung around Aliena's land and away towards the river, where she had been taken.

Studying the layout, he knew he could get to whoever it was without being seen and take them by surprise. He retraced his steps around the barn and, looking fervently towards the road, darted between objects that would hide his approach: the cart, which had been moved outside of the barn; another large shrub; a piled of logs stacked against the cottage wall. He then crept along the path, out to the road, and jumped to the other side, where he was hidden by a fence marking the boundary of a neighbour's land, which was overgrown with nettles between its posts. He kept his head low and ran along the fence until he guessed he was parallel with the spot where he had detected the movement, and waited.

Soon the movement caught his eye again. It was directly across from him, and he saw Elyan.

Quinn sprang up, vaulted the fence and leapt at Elyan, knocking him forwards onto his knees. Elyan cried out in alarm, but could do nothing, for in a moment Quinn had grabbed him by his hair and had pressed the tip of his sword against his throat. Elyan let out a squeak, and an image of Galen invaded Quinn's mind, the old physician looking terrified and hopeless. He gritted his teeth and dragged the young man to his feet.

'Hold still, Elyan!'

'*You*!' How did you – '

'*Shut up*!' Quinn hissed. 'You are coming with me – quietly. Guards are on their way here and I have Aliena – '

Elyan struggled to get free and Quinn began to feel the rage building inside of him.

'*Hold still*!' he growled. 'Do you think I won't use this on you? After what you did to me?'

Elyan stopped fighting, his eyes wide with a fury of his own. 'You're a *murderer*! What did you expect?'

'Yes, I am. And don't think I won't kill again, because I will if I have to.' Quinn switched his grip to Elyan's shoulder and shoved him forwards. 'Now, *move*! Across the fields to the river. And don't try anything stupid – I have a friend looking after your sister, so if anything happens to me, or you get away, you are putting her in danger. Understand?'

'*Bastard*!'

Quinn threw Elyan onto his back and pressed his arm across his throat. Holding the tip of the sword an inch from Elyan's left eye, he glared at him. His anger was mounting and he knew he could not allow the boy to rile him further. 'Not another word! You have no idea how much trouble you have caused me. *Don't try my patience*!'

Elyan froze. He looked petrified and Quinn guessed he could see red sparks in his eyes.

'Do we have an understanding?'

Elyan nodded, now tongue-tied.

'Good. Now get up and move!' He dragged the boy to his feet and pushed him again, aiming the sword at his lower back and keeping his fingers gripped on his collar. Elyan complied, staying silent.

Quinn fought to control his feelings as they marched away from the farm and away from imminent danger. He had been telling the truth when he had told Aliena that he harboured no bad feelings against the boy for his betrayal to the guards. He understood that Elyan had been trying to protect his sister and himself, and had, in fact, done a better job of it than Quinn. But for some reason, seeing him again had raised feelings of anger, a desire for revenge and even a level of hatred towards him for what he had done – feelings he neither understood nor wanted. What was happening to him? Why did he seem to have two different personalities – was he *still* under the influence of Rook?

As they walked on, keeping low and under the cover of trees and shrubs, Quinn thought back to that terrifying episode. Who had Rook really been and what had made him so powerful? Had Galen been right about the Archdeacon knowing more than had been said?

He did not want to remain this way for the rest of his days. He felt as if he was a slave to the rage that kept flaring up inside him, even when his own mind had worked hard to accept how things were now. He wanted to be himself again – not some kind of rogue Conductor, forever on the run because of things he did not have the strength to control. He was sure this was not what the Keeper had planned for his life to become when he had spared him.

It was the fear he saw in Elyan and Aliena which hurt him the most. He did not want anyone to be afraid of him – not this young man, who was just protecting his only family and fighting to survive in this land of bloodshed and fear. And especially not Aliena, who had given Quinn hope that there were some people the sheriff's tyrannical rule had not poisoned and could not prevent from being compassionate and caring, no matter the cost to themselves.

CHAPTER 29. MERGING.

There was no conversation between Elyan and Quinn as they trudged unhappily towards the river. Quinn was weary, wet and cold and Elyan was frightened and angry. However, Elyan seemed to have curbed his temper enough to do as Quinn had told him, so there was no need for Quinn to keep a hold on him to keep him moving forwards. He stayed just in front of his captor, careful not to stray too far or drift to one side. Quinn was glad, because his own anger was gradually abating and he did not like being mean to the boy. Also, he did not want Elyan to become aware of just how much his hands were shaking…

They heard no sound of any pursuers and Quinn hoped that they had been lucky. When they reached the river, they both looked around anxiously for Aliena and Erelas. Elyan looked worried when there seemed to be no sign of them, but Quinn quickly picked up Cara's trail and followed it along the grassy bank. He found the place where they had crossed the shallow, fast-flowing water and soon they came across a group of caves in a steep, forbidding gorge that scarred the otherwise gentle landscape.

Quinn gave a low whistle and was answered by a gentle whinny from Cara. They were in the largest cave, the entrance to which was well-screened behind wildly growing ivy and thorny shrubs. Skirting around them, Quinn could see Erelas standing at Cara's shoulder, waiting for them. Aliena rushed forwards when she saw her brother and Quinn did not object when Elyan ran to her. He walked to the back of the gloomy cave after giving Cara a quick ear-rub and placing a reassuring hand on Erelas' arm.

He had run out of both physical energy and strength of mind. He just wanted to be left alone with his thoughts for a while. Even so, he would be forever grateful that Erelas had found him, with no fear that the Archdeacon would find out or even care.

As far as the Archdeacon was concerned, Erelas had told him, he was just out performing his duties as a Conductor and leading his usual nomadic life in between. Even the fact that he had taken Cara had raised no eyebrows – she had not wanted to stay and would not allow anyone else to work with her. Quinn was relieved he had both of them here with him now. It felt as if he had part of his family back, even if it was only temporarily. They would also take care of Aliena and Elyan, while he, at the moment, could not. The death of Galen, along with everything else he had been through, had sapped his strength and he was just thankful that they were safe for the time being.

He found a dry, dark corner to sit down in as Erelas worked to improve the natural barrier of branches across the cave entrance. They could not be seen from the narrow deer trail several metres away and, as long as they kept as quiet as possible, Erelas was confident that they were well-hidden.

After a few minutes, Quinn stood up again and approached Elyan, who was in a hushed discussion with his sister. As he reached them, Elyan looked at him accusingly and drew himself more upright, as if in defiance. However, he seemed to think it best to hold his tongue.

'I'm sorry I was so rough on you, Elyan,' Quinn said. 'I didn't mean any of it. I thought it was the only way I could make you come with me, with no time to explain everything. I hope you will forgive me for the way I treated you. I do not have any bad feelings over what happened with the guards – I just needed a reason to pretend to be angry with you. As it happens, I have enough anger over other things to make it a very convincing act. I'm sorry I frightened you.'

Without waiting for a reply, he turned and walked dejectedly back to the corner of the cave, leaving Elyan open-mouthed. Aliena put a comforting arm around her brother.

Erelas sighed as he watched Quinn's retreat. This was not the man he remembered from mere weeks before. He resolved in that moment to do whatever he could to help bring that Quinn back. His own life, even his marriage, could wait.

***

Erelas busied himself tending to Cara's feet and brushing the worst of the mud from her legs. He knew better than to disturb Quinn when he was lost in his thoughts. Aliena and Elyan remained locked in whispered conversation and he did not interrupt them, either.

They all needed Quinn to help piece together the events of recent days, but he would do so when he was ready.

Quinn was not sure if he would be ready any time soon, despite the urgency of their situation. He remained at the back of the cave, wrapped in the thick blanket that had been under Cara's saddle, while his outer clothes were laid out on a rock to dry near a small fire Erelas had built in the centre of the cave. Everything was spinning through his thoughts like a kaleidoscopic storm, but frequently to the fore was Galen. Over and over, he played the scene of the murder in his mind, trying to decide if he could have – or should have – done anything differently.

In such a short time, he had come to value Galen's presence and freely-given friendship and he wondered how he could go back to any sort of life in Rivallen without his guidance. I the seemingly endless hours of his imprisonment, Galen had been there, to keep him sane when he had been left chained up all night, or to talk to him when he had woken from a nightmare and had been unable to get back to sleep. Quinn had talked to him about his parents, and Galen had given him comfort and hope that one day things would be different between them. He had given Quinn strength when he had none, tended his wounds as best he could and given him a stern talking to when he was beginning to lose his way. He felt as if he now had two people to turn his life around for – Renn and Galen.

Thinking logically, as far as he was able, he knew that there was nothing he could have done to save Galen. There had been so little time after the blast that took the wall out that the sheriff had to have already been on his way to the cell when he had spoken the words that caused it. Galen had pushed Quinn through it knowing there was no time for them both to escape. He had chosen Quinn's life over his own and had died heroically. Quinn would miss him terribly and he felt sickened by the fact that Galen would not be given an honourable burial. Worse still, his soul would be stuck in this plane, unless Erelas had been right about another Conductor being summoned to his side. Quinn knew he must hang on to that hope as there was no way to know for certain, and he'd only drive himself to distraction if he brooded on it. He knew Galen would have told him off for dwelling on such things when their situation was still so perilous. The four of them were trapped; even though Erelas was not known to the sheriff or the guards, Quinn knew he would be in it for the duration and would never abandon them.

Eventually, he decided it was time to merge their stories. He stood up, feeling stiff, but dry and a little warmer. He walked over to where his three companions were sitting, close to the fire. Cara was standing beside the wall, sleeping with one hind foot poised on its front edge.

Quinn sat down next to Erelas and looked at them all in turn. 'I think there are a few things I need to explain to you all, about why today went as it did.'

'Hold on, Quinn,' said Erelas, holding up a hand. 'They need to know the whole story of why you were banished, and *I* need to know about the attack on you with the poisoned arrow...'

Quinn looked uncomfortable.

'Don't look like that. You were unfairly judged, and not just by our own people.' Erelas shot a look at Elyan, who quickly looked at the floor.

'It's not Elyan's fault, Erelas. He *could* have asked me to tell him the whole story instead of judging me by what I said during my fever, but I don't blame him for telling the guards about it.' Quinn looked at Elyan, who had looked up again, surprise in his expression. 'He was just trying to protect himself and Aliena when I had failed to keep the guard from threatening them with imprisonment – or worse.' He glanced at Aliena and looked quickly away again, avoiding her puzzled stare. 'If truth be told,' he went on, 'this is entirely my fault for trespassing in their barn in the first place.'

'Please, Quinn. Tell them what happened. It is not right that they do not know the *real* you.'

'You promised you would explain everything to me, Quinn,' said Aliena quietly. Her eyes pleaded with him and he knew he could not refuse her.

For the next hour, Aliena and Elyan were introduced to the enigmatic world of the Soul Conductors and their extraordinary abilities. As Quinn explained everything that had happened to him, he was relieved to see nothing but forgiveness and relief in Aliena's eyes. Erelas was horrified to hear of the poisoning he had barely survived, and he brooded about it long after the conversation drew to a close, which had brought no conclusions as to who might have carried it out. Some things were left unsaid by them both – things neither of them wanted to contemplate.

Quinn no longer felt alone with the two of them to support him in whatever happened next, Aliena having pledged to help in any way she could. About Elyan, however, he was still unsure. If anything, the news that he and Erelas were capable of things ordinary folk could dream of seemed to alarm the young man further still. Quinn knew he would continue to be suspicious and unpredictable – and hard work for them all.

CHAPTER 30. THE SEED OF AN IDEA

'It's an *insane* idea!' said Quinn. He paced back and forth in the dim firelight, glancing at the dancing shadows on the glistening walls of the cave, so the others would not see the hopelessness in his eyes. 'It can't be done!'

'Of course it can,' said Erelas, still sitting by the fire with the others. 'You know the king is easily influenced, although usually by the wrong people. But if we can't persuade him to pardon you on the evidence alone, there must be another way…'

Quinn shook his head. 'We'd never get near Castle Rivallen without being seen by the guards. If we *did* get near, we'd never get inside!'

Erelas sighed and stood up. 'Quinn – you're tired and you've been through more in a month than most of us go through in a lifetime. I can understand why you're scared.'

'I'm *not* scared!' Quinn snapped, stopping his pacing and glaring at his friend. 'I'm just not as reckless as you seem to expect me to be all of the time. Since when did *you* start feeling so brave?'

That remark hurt Erelas and Quinn knew it. However, the anger rising in him stopped him from making amends and instead they both stood in awkward silence.

Aliena stood up and went to Quinn's side. 'Please – don't fight, Quinn. I know it sounds like a totally mad idea – '

'It is,' Quinn replied curtly.

'But, if you stop and think about it, anything is possible if we plan it properly. What about Renn?'

Quinn frowned at her, not comprehending her meaning.

'Renn could help you,' she went on. 'If we could find the boy, he could tell the king what you did for him and what kind of life you saved him from. The king has a young son himself. He would understand, and it would surely help your case.'

'Even if we could find him, we'd still have to get him and us into the castle…'

'You just broke out of the castle, Quinn,' said Erelas warily, unwilling to provoke another backlash from his oldest friend. 'What makes you think you couldn't break back in?'

Quinn thought for a moment and sat down by the fire. He crossed his legs, leaned his forehead on one hand and closed his eyes. All the confidence he had developed in his life seemed to have disappeared in just a few devastating weeks. He could see no way forward – but he had to start trusting the judgement of the others if he could not rely on his own. Their lives could not continue in this way, no matter what became of him.

'I'll help you find the boy, Quinn. I'll go with

you.'

Quinn looked at Elyan in surprise.

'It's the least I can do,' said the young man, looking at his feet.

Quinn sighed, staring into the fire. 'You don't owe me anything, Elyan. I know I was rough on you before, but as I said, I didn't mean it. It's too dangerous.'

'I can use a sword if I have to.' There was pride in Elyan's words that reminded Quinn of his old self.

'He taught himself,' Aliena said. 'Living under the sheriff's rule, it's something almost everyone now owns and knows how to use. It's just a shame not everyone will pick one up and fight back against that snake and his despicable guards...'

'One battle at a time,' mumbled Erelas, making everyone look at him. He looked back at them as he noticed the sudden silence. 'Sorry. Go on.'

Quinn smiled and then thought of what he had said before. Guilt slammed into his heart. 'I'm sorry for what I said to you, Erelas. I should not have implied that you have no courage. You have far more than I do right now – you took on the Archdeacon, after all.'

'For all the good it did.'

'Still, I shouldn't have said it. I don't like what is happening to me. The slightest bit of anger turns me into something I'm not. As much as it convinced Elyan to come with me, I don't *want* to be this way.'

Erelas sat next to Quinn and placed a hand on his shoulder. 'We can work on that later. Right now, as much as you may loathe the idea – '

'I do.'

'It may actually work to our advantage. We will go for Renn in the morning.'

CHAPTER 31. THEORIES.

The rain had started again, adding to Quinn's black mood. He was sick of being soaked through and feeling cold all of the time. As they made their way cautiously along a little-used forest trail, he swore he was going to steal a cloak the first chance he got...

They were silent as they walked, lost in their own thoughts. Yet again, Quinn was thinking about Galen and his horrible death at the hands of his own nephew. He had been unable to sleep much because of the memories, and barely touched the food Erelas produced for them all from Cara's saddle pack. His stomach hurt from a kind of hollowness that was born of more than hunger, as he remembered the old man's kindness and wisdom, freely offered in spite of his own predicament.

'Quinn?'

He looked up at the sound of Aliena's gentle voice, but hadn't managed to hide his sadness quickly enough.

'Are you alright?' She looked down from Cara with concern. Cara stopped without instruction and Quinn stood at her side. He leaned against the beautiful black mare, feeling comforted by her warm presence.

'I keep thinking about Galen.'

Aliena held out her hand to him, and he took it. 'What was he like?' she asked.

'It sounds improbable given the short time I spent with him, but he was a great friend. And wise. He seemed to see so much in the situation that you wouldn't have expected him to because he barely knew me. He never met the Archdeacon, or anyone else who was involved in it all, yet his theories…'

Erelas stopped and turned around. Striding back to where they stood, he said, 'What do you mean? What did he say about the Archdeacon?' The seriousness of his expression troubled Aliena.

'When I told him that you and I had both come to the same conclusion that something had affected me in the Plane of Shadows, he said he thought the Archdeacon knew more about it than he was letting on. I've not really had a chance to think about it since he said it, but I suppose it's possible.'

Erelas clenched his stubbled jaw before replying. 'It is possible. The Archdeacon has refused to discuss it since you were sent away. He won't even tolerate your name being mentioned. Which – I'm sorry to say – is something your parents are happy to accept.' Erelas watched Quinn's reaction, knowing the words had hurt him, but knowing he could not give him false hope. Quinn kept his feelings under control, but his face betrayed his pain.

'This is so unfair,' said Aliena. 'I don't know

anything about you or your people, Quinn, but it seems to me that this Archdeacon is not a nice person. He should have been more understanding. And less arrogant.'

'Arrogant?' said Quinn.

'Yes. He sent you back out to do your work without really knowing if you were completely recovered from the ordeal. He merely *assumed* that his ritual had been a success. He should have devised a way to – I don't know – *test* you?'

'But I didn't make much of a case against his deadline. I knew I needed to get back to my duties…even felt desperate to, in a way.'

'If I was being treated the way he was treating you, I'd have been desperate, too,' said Erelas. 'That doesn't mean you should have gone out when you did.'

'There you go,' said Aliena. 'That was reckless of him. He placed you on a path that was always going to land you in some sort of trouble. So, to me, the responsibility for everything that has happened lies with *him*, not you.'

'I agree,' said Erelas. 'And Galen has raised a question I had not thought of. Why did I accept his authority, almost blindly, instead of considering other possibilities? We will talk about this when we have more time,' he added quickly, noticing Quinn about to argue with his self-criticism. 'Right now, we need to keep moving. We're getting nearer to the village now and the guards could be close by.'

***

They trudged on through the rain, keeping sharp eyes on their surroundings for any signs of trouble. Quinn, in particular, was worried about archers and was glad that the woods offered at least some protection against one being able to get a clear shot at any of them. But autumn was well under way now, and the leaves were falling around them with the persistent drizzle. The cover was not as good as he would have liked.

Cara kept close, matching her pace to his. She nudged him for attention from time to time. He patted her neck and scratched her ears, glad to have her back at his side. He tried to relax a little, knowing she would warn him if anyone approached, but he could not.

Eventually the trees began to thin out as the land sloped downwards and the village came into view. All of them stopped and surveyed the small group of houses and plots of land in front of them. One or two people could be seen out among their crops or tending to their animals, but they could see no guards.

'Where do we start, Quinn' asked Elyan.

'We need weapons before we can do anything.'

Erelas drew his sword. 'I've got mine, but I will search the village for more. Aliena said most people have one.'

'Not alone,' Quinn said.

'It will be safer. I will get them as quietly as possible, with a few "tricks" to help me. Nobody will recognise me, even if I am seen. The guards will not know you are here. If you were to be spotted, the village would be swarming with them in no time.'

Quinn considered this for a moment. 'Take Cara. At least then you can get away quickly if you need to. We'll move around the edge of the woods and meet you at the bottom of the valley on the north side of the village. It's not so far for you to come back to us.'

Aliena dismounted and Erelas jumped up in her place. Cara stamped a hoof and snorted, clearly not happy at having to leave Quinn again, but took hold of her bridle and pressed his cheek against her muzzle, talking to her in a soft voice. She nodded her head, snickered quietly, and then she and Erelas were away, cantering noiselessly along the muddy, leaf-strewn track.

CHAPTER 32. WEAPONS AND MORE

Erelas guided Cara down the hill and slowed her to a walk, swinging around the outskirts of the poor village of Otterbroc. To the three people who had glanced up from their chores, he just looked like a traveller passing by, who had no plans to stop in such a small and insignificant place. Once out of sight of all those who were out and about at this early hour, he dismounted and searched for a place to hide Cara. Choosing a spot among some apple trees, still heavy with fruit, he looped the reins lightly around a branch, so that she could come to him quickly if he needed her.

'Be good, Cara. I won't be long.'

Cara nuzzled him, over her earlier disapproval about leaving Quinn. She trusted Erelas as much as she trusted him. She stood still but alert, and Erelas patted her sleek shoulder.

He moved off towards the cover of a windowless rear wall of a timber-built thatched cottage. He flattened himself against it, drawing his sword slowly and listening for any sounds of activity within.

All was quiet. Erelas crept around the side of the building, bending low to avoid his head brushing against the low eaves. He moved past rusting tools and dirty buckets stored against the wall, his eyes darting around him all the while. Crouching down as he reached the corner of the cottage, he listened for a moment. He could hear a man cussing at some unseen animal in the distance, but he was safe where he was. Taking a deep breath, he slipped around to the only door of the cottage. The window was on the far side, but he did not want to risk taking a look through it – it would be too dark inside and would take too long for his eyes to adjust.

He slowly raised the latch on the door, trying to be as quiet as possible. Once the door was free, he flung it open and darted inside. Sword raised, he glanced around the room. There were no shouts of surprise, no sudden movements of a startled resident. Nobody was here.

Closing the door, he drew a hand over the latch, whispering; his silver eyes sparkled turquoise for a moment as he caused the latch to seize just enough to give him a warning if someone tried to enter – he could hide himself if necessary. Relaxing slightly, he took a more leisurely look around the tiny cottage.

People lived simply here. There were sparse furnishings and very little in the way of comfort. A fire glowed in the hearth, but no lamps had been lit. Empty food bowls stood on the table, with an empty water jug and smaller drinking bowls. No outdoor garments were hung on the back of the door. It looked to Erelas as if the occupants had eaten their early morning meal and had gone out to do their day's work, taking a meagre lunch with them, and would not return until late afternoon, when it began to grow dark.

He crossed the room to the low bed set against the rear wall. Crouching down, he felt underneath and pulled out a large, old, wooden chest. His eyes glowed again as he unlocked it. Lifting the heavy lid up, he was pleased to find two swords and a dagger. He lifted them out and unsheathed them in turn, nodding with appreciation – they had been crafted with very little decoration, but with great skill. The swords were a good weight and well-balanced, with handles that would pose no problems with grip in the wet weather. They had been maintained well and were both clean and sharp. The knife looked new, its leather-bound handle spotlessly clean.

Concealing the knife in his boot, he returned the chest to its hiding place and hoisted the two swords under his left arm, keeping his own ready for use in his right hand. With just a few words of Latin, he released the door and left the cottage.

He hurried around to the back and gave a low whistle. In moments Cara was with him. He mounted the mare and, holding all three weapons, urged her forwards.

Without warning, Cara reared up. Erelas fell backwards with a shout of alarm. He landed heavily, dropping the swords and narrowly avoided being injured by them. Scrambling to his feet, filthy, winded and dazed, he looked at Cara, who was treading on the spot, snorting and nodding her head furiously.

In front of her, sprawled on his back with a dent in his helm, lay an unconscious guard.

***

As Cara skidded to a halt in front of the waiting companions, Erelas threw the guard's armour to the ground. Jumping from the saddle, he ignored their surprised stares and gave each of them a weapon; Quinn and Elyan got the sword sand Aliena was given the dagger.

'Care to explain that?' Quinn said, pointing at the armour's various components.

'It's for you,' Erelas announced proudly.

'And how did you manage to get it?'

'I didn't – Cara did.'

Cara nodded, snorting.

Quinn smiled, shaking his head. 'What did you do, you clever horse?' he said, taking her reins.

'Well,' said Erelas. 'There's a reason the helm has a dent in it…'

Quinn laughed. 'Cara! Well done, girl.' He scratched her nose, then said to Erelas: 'What did you do with the guard?'

'Hidden in a bush. He won't wake until dark – at the earliest.'

'Good work.' He skilfully swung one of the

swords around. 'These are good swords, too.' He didn't notice Elyan watching him with reluctant admiration, holding his own weapon with a little trepidation.

'There will be other guards, though,' said Erelas. 'Which is why you need the armour. At least there's a chance nobody will recognise you, unless they get too close.'

'If they get close enough to recognise me in that, they won't live to talk about it.' As soon as he had said it, Quinn glanced at Aliena and saw the smile vanish from her lips. He looked away quickly. He did not like the fact she would probably have to watch him kill someone.

'It's alright, Quinn,' she said, walking over to him. 'I know what has to be done if we run into trouble. It doesn't frighten me, nor does it make me think the worst of you. I wish there was no need for killing – but that is not your fault, either.'

Quinn took both of her hands. 'I just keep thinking of your face when I attacked that guard. I don't want you to be frightened of me – I'd never do anything to harm you, or your brother.'

'I know that now, Quinn. I was shocked, that is all. I saw the real you for all that time you were recovering from the poison – this side of you is not who you really are, it's just who you need to be for a while. I understand that.'

He smiled and gave her hands a gentle squeeze before letting her go and turning to Erelas. 'We should hurry—'

'I'll help you with this,' Erelas said, gathering up the armour.

Elyan went up to his sister and took her arm. Turning her away from the two men, he said quietly: 'I don't want you to be close to whatever goes on at the castle, Aliena.'

'Don't worry about me, Elyan. I will stay with Cara – it sounds as if she is more than capable of looking after me.'

'Even so...'

'Do you still have doubts about Quinn? And Erelas?'

Elyan shook his head. 'No. That is, I don't know. Their tale is just so strange. The power they use in the name of God, the guiding of souls – it scares me. And I know they are helping us, but...he scares me. He can say he holds no grudge all he likes, words are easy to use. You didn't see his face when he caught me. He's a killer who wasn't honest with us. Don't ask me to think the way you do, Aliena. I just can't...'

'Elyan, were you not listening to them earlier? They explained all of that. He's not a killer in the same way that the men who get executed by the sheriff are. Or the sheriff himself. You shouldn't be so harsh in your judgement of someone you don't understand. I don't understand it all either and I'm a little scared by their powers too. But we have always believed there to be more to the world than the church teaches us, have we not? Now that we see proof of it, shouldn't we be trying to understand them, not be prejudiced against them? Shouldn't we rejoice in what it means for us?'

'You seem so calm about it all. These are people who take souls from bodies. They can kill with their bare hands!'

Aliena sighed. 'Listen to me,' she said, her tone sharpened to match the look in her eyes. 'Think about the little boy, Renn. You should not need more proof that these people are using their powers for good, not evil. Look at the way Quinn has resisted Garin, and escaped so that the sheriff cannot use his powers for evil. He came straight here to protect us, too, when he could have just forgotten about us and gone into hiding elsewhere!! We have nothing to fear from the Soul Conductors. They are on our side. Don't you see that?'

Elyan looked at her for a moment, then nodded sulkily.

Aliena squeezed his hand. 'Trust me – and them. And do not worry about me. We will find the boy and sort this mess out, for the good of all of us.' She pulled her brother towards her and kissed his cheek. 'Now, go and get a feel for that sword. Quinn is nearly ready.'

They looked around to where the two friends stood. Erelas was trying to get the helm on Quinn's head.

'Give up, Erelas!' Quinn said, unable to resist a smile at his antics. It's not going to go on…Cara dented it too much.'

'No – you just have a big head!'

'Thank you! I think I'll just have to do without it.'

'That makes the disguise rather pitiful...'

'Not really. The coif will help a little. I just hope I don't have to wear it for long. I've never worn anything so uncomfortable.'

'Stop complaining. Cara, look how ungrateful he is!'

Cara snorted and put her head down to pull at some grass.

Quinn rolled his eyes. 'Alright, alright,' he said, throwing his hands up. 'I'm ready – I think. Elyan, let's go and find Renn.'

CHAPTER 33. FINDING RENN

There were no humorous exchanges between Quinn and Elyan as they made their way into the village of Tarley, where Renn had lived. It was only a few miles from Otterbroc and further away from Castle Rivallen, so they did not feel the need to hurry, saving their strength in case of any problems that may arise.

Each was lost in his own thoughts as the rain still fell on them and a cold wind blew down from the north, as if shoving them ever closer to the danger. While Quinn was sure Elyan was gathering his nerves for what would be his first real confrontation with the sheriff's Guardsmen, he himself was wondering what he was going to say to Renn if they found him. The boy had last seen him on that traumatic night, when he had taken another beating from his father – one that had resulted in his death. Did he know that he had died? Did he really understand why Quinn had killed his father, or was he still scared of him? Perhaps worst of all, for their current situation, would he view Quinn as a murderer and someone who should be executed?

Quinn tried to put these thoughts from his mind as they neared the village. It was useless to try to predict what might happen – they just had to find the child and take things from there. He glanced over at a solemn Elyan and was glad that he was with him, despite the obvious awkwardness between them. He would hopefully help the boy to relax – events in the dark cottage aside, Quinn had no doubt that he would look even stranger in daylight, with his odd eyes and part of a guard's armour.

'Which house was it?' asked Elyan as they managed to reach the main track through Tarley without attracting attention.

'I'm not sure. I only saw the inside, and then a view through the doorway out on to this track before I was dragged along it behind a guard's horse.'

Elyan looked along the muddy track at the tiny houses. 'Well, it shouldn't take us long to find it. There aren't very many of them.'

Quinn nodded his agreement. 'Let's work our way down.'

At the first house on the left they saw a faint glow from the window and crept to the side wall. His hand shakily on the hilt of his sword, Elyan crouched low and made his way slowly around the corner. Careful not to block too much light, he peered in through the window and took in the gloomy scene as quickly as he could. An old man sat in a chair by the fire, dozing. There was nobody else in the cottage that he could see, so he reversed back to Quinn and shook his head.

Quinn quickly surveyed their surroundings

and led the way across to the opposite dwelling. Smoke came through the hole in the roof on this one, as with many of the others, but it did not necessarily mean anyone was in there, as Erelas had found. Again, Elyan crept to the single window and glanced inside.

Immediately, he dropped as low as he could, wide-eyed. He turned on his heels, careful not to overbalance himself, and worked his way back to Quinn.

'There's a man in there. He looks about forty years old. Big,' he whispered.

'Anyone else?'

'I didn't see properly. He startled me...' Elyan looked sheepish.

'It's alright – I'll take a look. Wait here.'

Quinn stole around the corner and straightened himself up, flat against the front wall. With a smooth and gradual motion, he turned and looked through the window at the narrowest angle he could manage. It was brighter in this cottage, with a roaring fire and two lamps, and the man was easily visible. Taking in the scene as quickly as he could, he then stepped back into hiding and drew close to Elyan.

'He's alone. And there is only one set of bowls on the table and one bed in the corner. There could be another hidden where I cannot see, but it looks as if he lives on his own. Let's move on – around the back so he doesn't see us.'

Elyan nodded, regaining his composure.

They moved swiftly along the rear wall of the cottage and darted in between it and the next one. This cottage was larger, with a window either side of the door. Elyan looked increasingly nervous, so Quinn signalled for him to stay put while he took a look at the place. Elyan nodded gratefully and flattened himself against the wet wall, careful not to make a sound.

Quinn worked methodically, checking one window, creeping past the closed door and then checking the other – all the while keeping a sharp eye on the rest of the street. He felt very exposed here, but this was the only way other than knocking on doors and asking about the boy – and he was not prepared to draw attention to himself in that way. They needed the boy to be on his own to give them a chance to explain everything before trying to take him with them. Quinn realised there was every possibility they might have to force Renn to go with them, but he would do everything he could to avoid that situation.

The cottage was empty. There were signs of at least three people living in it – more bowls, spoons and jugs on the table, three chairs and two adult-sized cloaks draped over two of the chairs. A large pair of men's boots stood close to the fire. He did not linger. He darted around to the back of the building at its far end, startling Elyan as he appeared, shaking his head. As Quinn looked at him, Elyan suddenly pointed behind him, open-mouthed but not saying anything. Quinn raised his sword and spun around in an instant.

There, at the back of the next cottage along, stood Renn. He looked dirty, hungry and tired and Quinn suspected he was being neglected by whoever had taken him in. His heart ached for the boy – he had hoped Renn would be living a better life after his father had gone.

The three of them stared at each other for many moments, before Quinn snapped himself out of his surprise and smiled. 'Renn,' he whispered. 'You're safe...'

The boy looked suspiciously at the two men, raising his eyebrows when his name was mentioned.

'You may not remember me, Renn. Will you talk to us? We have a great favour to ask of you.'

Renn looked surprised but a little less suspicious – these men did not look threatening, despite the armour one of them was wearing.

'Will you come and talk to us? Where we won't be disturbed?'

'Who are you?' Renn asked, keeping his voice as low as Quinn's.

'I was here the night…the night your father died.' Renn frowned, then looked alarmed. Quinn put his sword back in its sheath and raised his hands. 'It's alright, please. We're not here to harm you. We need your help.'

Renn looked at Elyan, questions in his wide, brown eyes. Elyan smiled, hoping he looked reassuring rather than nervous and nodded, backing up Quinn's words.

Renn did not move. Quinn started to get worried.

'Renn,' said Elyan, moving to Quinn's side. 'I live in Foxvale – do you know where that is?'

The boy nodded as Quinn looked at Elyan, surprised at his sudden interaction.

'Well, I have a little cottage there, with a spit of land. I live there with my sister. You'd like her, she's a very kind lady. This man,' he went on, indicating Quinn, 'helped me and my sister when we had some trouble with the sheriff. He might seem a bit scary, but he's on our side. That armour isn't his, he's not a Guardsman – he just borrowed it for protection. Will you come and talk to us – me, him and my sister and another friend? Please? It is very important. You see, we have a problem that we can only sort out with your help.'

Renn thought about it for a moment longer and then nodded. He walked over to Elyan, giving Quinn a wide berth. 'I don't like the sheriff,' was all he said.

CHAPTER 34. ELYAN'S BRAVERY

As he moved slowly down the length of the tavern's creaking wooden floor, Quinn saw himself picking up one of the dirty, inefficient lamps from a table once more. Crossing diagonally to the second table, he heard the drip-drip this time, before the woman's lifeless form came into view in the dim, flickering light. Her eyes still did not see and her neck was still a shocking contrast of red blood and white skin.

Hearing the laughter that did not belong to him, his view moved on, through the long room, taking in more corpses: an old man, two middle-aged women, an old woman sitting with a younger one and a youth, whose body lay on the floor. It looked as if he had resisted death for mere seconds before it claimed him.

Quinn could feel fear in his mind, but still the laughter continued, as he saw hands that were not his wiping the blade of a knife that was not his, onto the front of a tunic that was not his.

He stopped at the hearth for a few moments and, turning, surveyed the carnage before moving back the way he had come, more quickly this time and with a purpose. The smell of the blood mingled with the stench of the evacuated bowels and emptied bladders of the victims, but strangely this body – Rook's body – did not seem to care.

He mentally struggled to free himself from the image as he was taken by Rook on the same journey, up the ancient, creaking stairway to the bedroom door, where he witnessed the filthy boot smash into it again.

The bound and gagged young man was there, as before, as expected, just as terrified.

This was no dream. This was real.

Quinn heard the voice that was not his, yet seemed to come from him. 'Shh,' it said, at the young man's panicked cries. 'That won't do you any good now, will it?'

Quinn was able to pick out the words 'please,' and 'no,' from the man's muffled response. Then he sobbed and looked at the floor, spent of all hope.

'That's it, lad. Give up. It's easier that way. He likes 'em quiet. Helps him to get ready for his "moment", as he calls it.' Quinn saw himself draw a finger across his own neck and start laughing again, a terrible, evil sound, lacking any humanity or compassion.

Suddenly the young man vomited. It sprayed out of his nose and through gaps between the gag and his lips, dribbling down his chin. He choked, mortal fear in his eyes as his lungs fought against the liquid that he had inhaled into them. His face grew red and his eyes seemed to bulge. To Quinn's horror, he saw himself take one full stride forwards and kick the young man full in the face. The boot made impact with such force that the back of the man's head slammed into the floor and he lay there, no longer choking, but twitching. Soon even that stopped, too, and a dark stain grew at his crotch and spread to the wooden floorboards.

***

Cara whinnied nervously as Quinn slumped sideways to the ground in the midst of his nightmare. Erelas got up and, as he walked around Cara, who was carefully getting to her feet, he saw what was happening and rushed to Quinn's side. Aliena and Elyan also got up, sleepily wondering what was amiss.

'Quinn...' Erelas crouched at his head and shook his shoulder gently.

Quinn did not wake – his breathing was coming in short panicked gasps and he was soaked in sweat. Erelas held his head still and lifted an eyelid. There was a faint turquoise glow, but it was tainted with red sparks.

Cara backed away, snorting. Aliena went to her side and held her muzzle, whispering words of comfort.

'Quinn! Come on, wake up,' Erelas said, more urgently, as Elyan appeared at his side, looking down anxiously. Quinn did not respond and Erelas knew he had to bring him back quickly. Holding his jaw with one hand, he slapped his face sharply with the other. Elyan took a step back as Quinn's whole body jerked at the shock of the strike and his eyes snapped open.

For a moment Quinn did not seem to see

Erelas, but then he looked straight at him, staring into his eyes with a mixture of confusion and anger. 'Are you alright? You were dreaming again, like you did in Del—'

Quinn's hand shot out and grabbed Erelas around the throat. With a roar of rage, Quinn pushed him backwards and down, scrambling to his knees as he did so. He slammed Erelas flat on his back. Cara threw her head up and leaped backwards, away from Aliena, snorting in alarm, eyes showing their whites. Aliena was rooted to the spot in shock, staring in disbelief.

Quinn had Erelas pinned to the floor by his neck and one arm. He tried to prise Quinn's grip from his throat with the other, but could not make any difference to its force. He could not believe what was happening and could only stare at his friend as Quinn looked down on him with absolute fury. His head was starting to spin from the lack of air and his throat was burning with the pain of Quinn's hold on him.

Unseen by anyone but Aliena, who was unable to react in time, Elyan grabbed the gauntlet from the Guardsman's armour Quinn had discarded on the floor. Hauling it on in a panic, he rushed up to Quinn and hit him with the back of his armoured hand as hard as he could manage, impacting Quinn's right cheek and temple. The force of the blow instantly made him lose his grip on Erelas and he landed heavily on the floor of the cave – on his side, motionless and bleeding.

Erelas struggled to get up, choking violently and unable to see properly from the dizziness and the watering of his eyes. Aliena snapped out of her shocked daze and, as Elyan threw the gauntlet down, shaking, she rushed to Quinn's side.

'My God, Elyan,' she said, her voice trembling. '*What have you done?*'

Elyan stared, saying nothing, but backing slowly away as Erelas finally managed to stand, swaying slightly.

Aliena placed a hand softly against Quinn's uninjured cheek and raised his head. There was no flicker of movement behind his eyelids and his breathing was weak and shallow. Elyan's strike had split his right eyebrow, covering his temple with blood, some seeping into his black hair. A second cut on his cheekbone was adding to it and already his pale skin was turning half the colours of the rainbow around the wounds.

'Erelas, you must help him! Healing prayers – he mentioned one before?' Aliena said, turning to look at him. He was standing as still as he could, rubbing his violated throat with a shaking hand and blinking hard. '*Erelas!*'

Erelas looked at her, then Quinn, then Elyan, piecing together what had happened. He staggered forwards and fell to his knees at Quinn's side, trying to focus on the condition of his friend.

Aliena placed a hand on his arm and looked at him, examining his face and neck. 'Are you alright?'

'I will be,' Erelas said, in not much more than a whisper. 'I don't know what all of that was about—'

'We can think about that later,' said Aliena a little sharply, turning her attention back to Quinn. 'Can you *help* him?'

Quinn coughed suddenly and groaned at the pain it sent shooting through his head. Squeezing his eyes even more tightly shut, he took a shuddering breath, his jaw trembling.

'Quinn – just lie still,' said Aliena.

He opened his eyes and looked up at her face and for a moment he could not be sure of where he was. Was he back at the farm, still recovering from the poison? But then he saw Erelas and he recalled what had just occurred. He was horrified.

'Quinn – I don't understand. What is it you think I have done?' Erelas asked, sitting back slightly as he noticed the red sparks still in his friend's eyes.

Quinn could only feebly shake his head. He turned over on to his side again, covering his head with his arm as the pain became unbearable. Aliena put her hand on the back of his head and leaned in close to his face.

'It will be alright, Quinn, don't talk now. Erelas will help you.'

Quinn coughed, the pain exploded in his head and he lost all his senses again. Aliena returned him gently onto his back, and then pulled at Erelas' sleeve.

'Please, Erelas…*quickly*!'

CHAPTER 35. SHARING THE BURDEN

Quinn was awakened by Cara snuffling at his shoulder from behind him. He opened his eyes to find he was lying covered in Cara's blanket, his head on Erelas' folded cloak. He did not know what had happened to his head; he knew he had been hurt somehow, that was all. It no longer screamed with pain, but it hurt enough to keep him from moving just yet. He was warm and comfortable and felt as if he had slept deeply for many hours, although he still felt exhausted.

Cara kept up the nuzzling and Quinn reached around and touched her velvety nose. She moved slightly, breathing on his neck softly. He rolled onto his back to look at his beloved mare and as she looked at him, the full memory of the night before flooded back to him and he closed his eyes again. He felt both sickened by the memory of the young man's horrific death and mortified that he had, beyond reasoning, lashed out at Erelas. He had been out of control again.

Cara lifted her head as Aliena stepped up to Quinn and got down on her knees beside him. She smiled with more than a little uncertainty and Quinn knew he had a lot of explaining to do – to everyone. This thought led him to another and he grabbed Aliena's hand and attempted to push himself up onto his elbows.

'Where is Renn?'

'Lie still, Quinn. Renn is fine. He slept through the entire thing. He's still sleeping now – it's only just dawn. He knows nothing about last night.'

Quinn let go of her hand and slumped back with relief, blood thundering through his temples. 'Erelas?'

'He's gone out with Elyan to gather some more wood.'

Quinn nodded slowly, closing his eyes.

'How do you feel?

'Better than I deserve to feel.'

'What was that about, Quinn? We are all mystified; why would you attack Erelas like that? Who did you think he was?'

'I don't know,' Quinn said. 'I must have thought he was the man in my dream...' Quinn rubbed his eyes with the tips of his fingers and then drew them up around his temples to try to push away the ache. 'Except...they are not dreams, they are the memories I was telling you about, the ones that the Archdeacon was supposed to have taken away with the rituals he performed on me. Last night they came back, worse than before.'

'Why don't you tell me what happens in them?' said Aliena, settling down at his shoulder and taking his hand again.

Quinn looked at her face, searching for

strength in her that he felt was lacking in himself. 'They are frightening...'

'Tell me anyway. I want to help you to understand what is happening to you, if I can.'

Quinn was reminded of the similar statement Galen had made and felt less alone in the darkness.

***

'I'm sorry...I did warn you it wasn't very nice.'

'Aliena smiled, the disgusted look gradually fading from her pale face. 'It's alright.'

'I didn't kill those people.'

'I know, Quinn...I know it wasn't you.' She placed a hand on his. 'I'm just sorry you have to see it and carry that memory around with you.'

'I feel like an idiot.'

'Don't. You have no reason to. You were in shock, and Erelas woke you up quite roughly.'

Quinn knew she was probably right, but kept quiet. He did not feel he deserved such understanding. After all, anything might have happened if—

'What happened to me, anyway – who hit me?'

'Elyan.' Aliena bit her lip.

'Elyan? With what? It felt like Cara had kicked me!'

'The gauntlet. Are you angry with him?'

'Angry? No, not in the slightest! I was out of control...I'm glad he did it. And, actually, impressed.' Quinn smiled as well as he was able.

Aliena relaxed, returning his smile. 'He will be pleased to hear that. I told him, once I'd got over the shock myself, that he'd done a brave thing, but he said he was terrified of what you'd do to him for it. He still is.'

'Bravery isn't about feeling no fear. It's about facing that fear and doing what needs to be done anyway. I'm sorry I put him in that position. All I will do to him is thank him and apologise.'

'He could hardly wait to get out of here this morning, as he was so afraid you would be furious with him.'

'The only person I am furious with is myself.'

'Well, I will let you have until noon and then you are banned from any such feelings. They will get you nowhere and we have other things to think about. We need to make a move on the castle...' Aliena swallowed, hoping she sounded more courageous than she felt in her heart. 'In the meantime, you and Erelas can talk.'

Quinn nodded. 'There's nothing I want more right now.'

'He will understand, Quinn. He knows you were not yourself. We all saw the red sparks in your eyes. He is far more worried about you than about himself.'

'Sounds like Erelas.' He smiled ruefully. 'But

even he must have limited patience. I insulted him yesterday, now this—'

'With all the trouble you've got me in over the years, Quinn, do you really think that what happened last night would make me hate you?'

They turned and saw Erelas standing by the fire. He dropped a great pile of logs on to the floor of the cave. 'Believe me, last night was nothing compared with you getting us trapped at the Falls of Esa that time.' He smiled at Aliena. 'Biggest damned spiders you ever saw...'

CHAPTER 36. JOURNEY

The rain stopped by the time they left the safe, secluded cave and started the risky journey to the castle. The sun was leaking through the milky clouds, filtering down through what leaves were left on the trees. There was little warmth, however, and the only one of them apparently not feeling the chill was Renn, who was sitting proudly upon Cara wearing Erelas' cloak. It swamped him, but he thought it made him look regal, which he considered an absolute necessity when travelling to the king's castle. He asked Aliena if he looked like a prince, as she led the mare along the forest path. She assured him that he looked every bit a son of royalty and he beamed. He was beginning to trust her, but he kept his distance from the men of the group.

Quinn walked at the back of the small convoy, frowning as he watched his steady footfalls on the soft bed of the woodland. He was desperately trying to fashion some kind of plan before they reached the edge of the forest. He knew that once out in the open, they would be a significantly noticeable group and the last thing they needed was attention, even from civilians. He had no wish to split them up, but he realised that dividing them into two – one led by himself and one led by Erelas

– might be the only way they would be able to enter the castle without being seen or heard.

He also had grave concerns over using his warped abilities to gain entry into the castle. His escape from the dungeons had proved that things could, and probably would go wrong and the last thing he wanted to do was blow another hole in the walls, if he expected the king to listen with a sympathetic ear to their tale of injustice.

'Erelas,' he called to his friend, who was walking just in front of Cara. Everyone turned around, and all but Renn noticed the seriousness of Quinn's expression. As Erelas turned and joined him, they all stopped and waited to see what was amiss.

'Did you get any sense of the layout of Castle Rivallen when you were near it?'

'Not really. I was still quite a distance away when I heard the explosion. Once I made my way round to that side of the castle, my focus was on getting to you. I do know where the gate tower is in relation to where you were being held, but that's really all...'

'No matter. I just wondered if you had an idea of the guard presence there. We need to get across that moat somehow, but if we can't, the only option left will be the main gate.'

Erelas nodded. 'There may be a postern gate somewhere – if the moat doesn't reach all the way around.'

'Can't you use that amulet?' asked Elyan,

joining them. Erelas had explained with honesty what the amulet had been for when Elyan had spotted it earlier that day, dangling from a beautiful silver chain around his neck.

'No,' said Erelas. 'It can only transport one person. And that person has to be a Soul Conductor.'

Elyan looked disappointed.

'Don't worry, my young friend,' said Erelas cheerfully. 'We have lots of other ways and means to call upon.'

'Hopefully one that includes getting all of us across that moat,' said Quinn flatly. 'Elyan, I want you to take the armour. Just in case…' Quinn added, noticing Aliena's flash of concern. 'When we get near the castle, you should go with Erelas and Renn. Erelas will be in front should you meet any guards. Renn, will you stay with Elyan, while Aliena comes with me?'

Renn nodded, suddenly not excited about going to the castle any more.

'It will be alright, Renn,' said Elyan, smiling at the boy. We just need to get in. The rest will be easy.'

Aliena doubted that Elyan believed that any more than she did, but she smiled at Renn, too. 'You have two strong warriors escorting you, Renn. You'll be very safe.'

Renn's smile returned.

'Elyan would make a fine guard…under a different sheriff, of course,' Erelas said to the child as they watched Quinn help Elyan with the armour. 'Maybe you will too, someday.'

'I'd much prefer that to what I am right now,' said Elyan.

Erelas and Quinn looked at him in surprise.

'There's nothing wrong with what you are now,' said Erelas.

'Maybe not for my father. But I want more from life than tending a farm. It's *boring*.'

'Maybe you should try looking at it in a different way,' snapped Quinn. 'A life of adventure isn't all it's made out to be. I'd give anything for a peaceful existence. Just remember, Elyan, that when your people are wishing they could rise up against the tyranny of the sheriff and the apathy of the king that allows it to continue, a "boring" life is what they are longing for.'

'I'm sorry,' said Elyan quietly. 'I didn't mean to—'

'Let's move on,' Quinn cut across him. 'It's getting late and although less light will help us, complete darkness will not.'

Elyan glared with hurt pride, as Quinn walked away, leaving Erelas to finish helping him with the armour.

***

They left Cara at the edge of the forest at dusk and continued on foot. Quinn led the way, with Elyan, dressed in the armour, close behind him. Aliena held Renn's hand as they followed. Erelas was bringing up the rear with his sword drawn, but with calm expectation rather than anxiety.

Quinn's eyes strained to see the slightest movement ahead of them, but there seemed to be none – at least from this distance. They had a clear view of one side of the castle wall and two of the wall towers, but not the gate tower. The moat did indeed seem to go all the way around and Quinn was disheartened.

As if he had read his thoughts, Erelas appeared at his shoulder. 'Don't worry, Quinn. We knew we might need to do some casting.'

'It's not the use of castings that bothers me, Erelas. It's the use of *my* castings. I don't trust it.'

'Think of the end result, not the means. We can always put you to work rebuilding the castle when this is all over.' Smirking, Erelas clapped him on the shoulder. 'Come on,' he said, taking the lead and making Quinn smile in spite of himself.

Aliena overtook Quinn, leading Cara. She turned as she passed and gave him an encouraging smile. He bowed his head to her and turned to see where Elyan was.

'This damned armour,' Elyan hissed. 'It hurts.'

'Arrows hurt a lot more.' Quinn's smile had vanished and he gestured impatiently for Elyan to move on. Taking up his new position behind them all, he began to wonder if this was going to be just a journey to their deaths...

CHAPTER 37. BREAKING BACK IN

As the light faded and the castle grew large and intimidating before them, the group split up. They could make out the shapes of Guardsmen patrolling along the ramparts as they passed between the towers. They would need to be quick, quiet and time their moves to perfection and that would be much harder to do in a group of five.

Erelas took Elyan and Renn towards the west tower, while Quinn and Aliena headed for the northern side. Part of Quinn wanted to stay with Erelas, in case his skill was needed to get in to the castle, but he knew they had to take the relatively safer option. If the guards caught them, they would only end up in front of the sheriff, never getting near the king.

He led Aliena to a low, evergreen shrub and they crouched behind it. Watching the others make their way towards the massive wall, he said a silent prayer to God for assistance – after all, this was not just about his life anymore, thanks to the sheriff.

They watched until their companions were just a few dozen metres from the castle wall, and started to make their own way across to the moat along the north side. It was slow going – they adopted the same method as the others, lying flat and crawling along when a guard disappeared behind a parapet. As they got closer, they could just about see in the dim light that the guards were lax in their duty; they stopped and chatted to one another as they went, and didn't seem to be paying much attention to anything outside the walls. The castle gates remained closed during curfew and as it was quite a walk from the nearest village, nobody would risk a pointless journey and punishment to come here at night.

The moat was partially lined on the outside by very tall grasses and reeds, so when they finally reached its banks, they found they had good cover.

Sitting on the damp ground, Quinn spoke to Aliena in a low voice. 'We should keep following this bank until we find some way to cross over. There may still be a postern gate somewhere, as Erelas was hoping.'

Aliena nodded. 'Don't look so worried, Quinn. If we have to swim across, we'll get in.'

Quinn raised an eyebrow and looked at her long layers of clothing made from heavy materials. 'I don't think that's going to happen,' he said. 'Trust me – that water is freezing and you're hardly dressed for a swim.'

She smiled. 'We'll think of something. I have faith in you.'

Quinn tried to smile back but it was not very convincing and reflected the doubts flashing through his thoughts. 'Let's go,' he said, then moved off before she could say anything else.

They crept along the bank, periodically checking the position of the guards by peering through the reeds. It was difficult to see them from that angle, but they could hear the clank of their armour and the thud of their boots on the stone walkways.

There were two Guardsmen on this section, moving in opposite directions to each other and meeting in the middle. Quinn decided the best place for them to find a way to cross would be at a section where a guard walked alone, and a little distance from the tower to their right. He stopped at a place he thought suitable, looked across the still, dark waters at the foot of the curtain wall and sighed. There was no entrance here. The solid stone wall was built on a rock bed, which jutted out several feet before sloping steeply into the moat four feet below. Quinn remembered how different it had looked where he had made his escape. There was no way he could have missed those rocks if he had fallen at this point in the walls. He stared at the rocks and the water and the smallest seed of an idea began to form in his mind.

'Stay here,' he told Aliena. Before she could protest, he moved on his hands and knees, back the way they had come. As he went, he scanned along the bottom of the wall, taking in the distance the rocks reached out, the drop from the ledge and how wide the ledge looked.

Eventually, when he was almost out of sight

from Aliena, he found what else he was looking for – a small postern gate, as Erelas had predicted, created at a wider part of the ledge. This was where people could escape from the castle if it came under attack. As Quinn looked at it, feeling hopeful again, he considered the possibilities of how it was used; there had to be a way for them to cross the moat once they came out of the gate and followed the ledge around the bottom of the wall – but where was it? Was it further around the moat than he and Aliena had travelled?

He crept back along the bank to where he had left Aliena, a look of excitement on his face that made her raise her eyebrows questioningly at him.

'Have you found something?'

'Yes. There is a gate. The ledge on this rock bed must be wide enough all the way around to wherever it is they cross the moat – it's an escape route. All we need to do is find the crossing and we can follow the ledge around to that gate. I should be able to unlock the gate. I just hope I can do it without blowing it up.'

They crossed the moat over a narrow stone walkway, which was just wide enough for them to traverse in single file. Aware of how exposed they were, they scuttled across it as fast as they could, crouched as low as possible. The relief Quinn felt when they reached the ledge brought a smile of triumph to his tired face and Aliena was pleased to see his hope returning.

The ledge itself was damp, slippery and dangerous and they had to go slowly, making as little noise as possible. Quinn held on to his sword to prevent it scraping the stones. Aliena held up her skirts a little, fearful of tripping over them on the uneven surface. When they reached the gate several long minutes later, it was almost too dark to see where they were going. Quinn hoped Erelas had found similar success…

They stopped by the iron gate and peered through, their eyes and ears alert to the slightest sign of life within. Satisfied there was nobody nearby, Quinn examined the lock and took a deep breath.

'You can do this,' Aliena whispered, placing a hand on his arm.

Quinn smiled nervously. He turned his attention back to the lock, raised his right hand and pointed his palm towards it. Closing his eyes, he spoke in a low voice. His eyes opened and his focus on the lock became determined. They flashed their brilliant turquoise colour and a fizzing sound was heard. Quinn stepped back instinctively. Then came the almost imperceptible click of the lock turning, freeing the gate. There was no explosion, no destruction, no pain.

Aliena smiled broadly, squeezing Quinn's arm as he stared, almost not believing he had managed it.

After a brief pause to listen for anyone approaching, Quinn slowly pushed the gate open and

they stepped through.
> They had done it – they were in.

CHAPTER 38. A SEVERE TEST

The darkened passage beyond the gate led sharply upwards by way of stone steps that were almost as treacherous as the ledge outside. The air smelled stale and damp and Aliena could have sworn she heard the high-pitched chatter of rats.

Quinn held his cupped hands in front of his mouth and whispered: 'Find Erelas.'

Blowing gently into his palms, as if he were blowing out a tiny candle, a turquoise wisp of light curled from his lips and formed a tiny sphere over them. It hovered for a moment, its light pulsing, before it began to float slowly away from him, up the dim passage. Ignoring her look of delighted amazement, Quinn took Aliena's hand and pulled her close. Carefully, they began to follow the light up the steps.

It was not long before the narrow staircase joined a wider passage that was lit periodically by small torches. Apart from these, the walls were bare and there was no sound from either direction. Although it was too soon to assume that the passage was little-used and relatively safe, Quinn hoped the guards would be concentrating on the outside of the castle rather than its interior, and that the only place that would be heavily guarded would be the area around the king's and the prince's chambers. By the time they reached them, with God's grace, they would have met the others and be better prepared to take the guards on if they had to.

As they followed the little glowing orb, Quinn suddenly wondered how they were going to approach the king with their pleas for help; aside from the difficulty getting past the guards, the fact that they had invaded the castle at night to gain a pardon for himself, Aliena and Elyan was not going to be accepted graciously.

'Are you alright?' Aliena whispered.

Quinn realised he had been frowning. He nodded. 'Just not enjoying making this up as we go along. We need a plan to get to the king and at least some idea of what we are going to say to him when we do...'

'One thing at a time, Quinn,' she said. 'Let's just find the others.'

He nodded in assent and they moved on. But almost immediately, he stopped dead, frowning again. Aliena met his eyes, questioning him. He looked at her with what seemed to be a sense of growing panic and she glanced around the passage, trying to see what it was that had startled him so much. The orb paused, as if it somehow 'knew' it had to wait for Quinn.

'We can't kill any guards,' he said.

'What?'

'If we come across any guards, we can't *kill* them. It would summon another Soul Conductor.'

'Wouldn't they be on your side?'

Quinn shook his head. 'I cannot trust to that. And besides, if Erelas is seen to be killing guards, even in our defence, he will be tried and executed. He shouldn't even be here...'

'So what do we do?'

'We will have to rely on castings. Which in my case, could be a disaster.'

'You have managed perfectly well so far, Quinn.'

'But those are simple ones I've been doing since I was five. Immobilising a guard – or several – is going to be much harder.'

'I still have faith in you. You need a little more in yourself. Don't forget that when we find Erelas, you will not have to do them alone.'

Quinn bit his lip, unnerved by his own realisation. 'We had better hurry up and find him, then.'

The bright turquoise sphere of light led them along the passage contained within the curtain wall. Eventually, without having met any guards, they turned and climbed a short flight of stone steps into the main body of the castle. This passage was more brightly lit by torches placed at shorter intervals along the walls.

Quinn signalled to Aliena to stop. Both listened, hardly daring to breathe. They could hear the rattle of armour and the heavy footfalls of a guard. Their luck had run out.

He ushered Aliena against the wall in between two of the torches, where it was a little darker and sheathed his sword as silently as he could, knowing it would be disastrous if he were to use it here.

Standing in front of her, and pressing his back against her body, he stretched his arms out and back slightly, forming a shield around them, the backs of his fingertips just touching the wall. Closing his eyes, he took a deep breath and whispered something Aliena did not understand.

An almost imperceptible haze spread from his outspread palms and met in the middle with a flurry of silver sparks. His eyes glowed turquoise, but then he flinched as a sudden and unexpected pain shot through his body. Aliena placed her hands on his shoulders as a gesture of support. The shield flashed momentarily, but held and then became transparent. They were enclosed and concealed, along with the orb.

They held their breath as a Guardsman rounded the corner. He strolled along the passageway, paying little attention to his surroundings. Aliena's legs felt like they would give out as the guard drew level with them and paused – even though she trusted Quinn and his power. The seconds stretched out; the guard seemed to be taking an eternity to move on. She could feel Quinn's strength start to sag under her fingers and she squeezed lightly, letting him know he was not alone. Feeling him inhale as far as his lungs would allow, she closed her eyes, pressing them as tightly shut as she could and waited, praying in her mind for their deliverance.

Quinn watched the guard's feet. His eyes were wide and he could feel the hammering of his heart in his chest and the blood thundering in his ears. He felt the pain again and did not know how long he could hold this shield in place. If it failed now, they were lost. He silently mouthed another prayer. It was all he had left...

The guard coughed heavily, making them both flinch – but then he moved further on, his strides lengthening, his movement more purposeful. After the longest moments of Quinn's life, the Guardsman eventually disappeared around the corner and soon they could hear him no more.

Quinn exhaled sharply. The shield failed with a delicate fizz and he fell to his knees on the hard stone floor. Tipping forwards, he stopped his fall with his hands and Aliena bent down at his side, a hand on his shoulder. She lifted his face to hers with a gentle touch and saw the pain in his odd-coloured eyes; both were bloodshot and weary.

'You did it, Quinn, you did it – we're safe!' she whispered, smiling at him, trying to hide her concern for him. He did not look as if he would cope with having to do that again, but she did not want him to know that. 'Can you get up?' she asked. 'We should keep moving.'

But he could do nothing and slumped sideways into a sitting position. Drawing his knees up slowly, he interlocked his fingers behind his head and rested his forehead on his knees. The blood was still racing through his ears and his whole body ached as if he had been running for miles up a hill. He was breathing rapidly, trying to suppress the nausea that was washing over him.

Aliena pulled at his arm. 'Quinn, I'm sorry,' she whispered. 'I know you feel tired, probably worse than tired; I can't begin to understand. But we *must* keep moving. He could come back.'

'It wasn't meant to feel like that,' Quinn said. 'Something is wrong.'

'Let's get to Erelas – he can help you.'

She took his hand and he gripped it tight as she helped him to his feet. He staggered and bumped against the wall, blinking furiously. He gathered his senses for a moment, taking deep breaths and bending forwards, still holding Aliena's hand. Soon he felt able to stand up straight and pushed himself away from the wall. His head cleared and he allowed Aliena to lead him along the corridor. In his mental fog, he relied on her to pick up on any indications of movement up ahead.

They passed a door leading deeper in to the castle and hesitated, listening for signs of life on the other side, but they heard none. The orb led them on and Quinn began to wonder how much further they had to go – or if Erelas and the others had even made it in to the castle yet.

Something scraped lightly against the stone wall up ahead, around another corner and out of sight. Quinn looked at Aliena with dread. He drew his sword as quietly as he could; he knew he could not cast anything again and they would have to fight, after all. Aliena let go of his arm and reached under her dress, drawing out the knife she had concealed by tying the sheath to her girdle.

As they edged towards the source of the noise, Quinn could feel his emotions changing. He was becoming less scared and more angry with every step and he could feel the blood beginning to rush around his body again, fizzing with an unnatural heat. He did not want to be forced into a battle with the Guardsmen, some of whom were forced into the service of Garin. They were only there to protect the king, after all. It was not fair that he would have to attack them. He was the villain now, and that thought infuriated him. He had spent the last two years trying to guide souls to justice. There was satisfaction in delivering the wicked for punishment and a deep joy at delivering the pure of heart to peaceful eternity. This – this life as some kind of outlaw – was the last thing he could ever have envisaged himself doing. He did not want to break in to the king's home and frighten him and his son. This was all the sheriff's doing and he was furious. He would happily run his sword through the man's black, cold heart if he was standing in front of him at that moment—

'Quinn?' Aliena's frightened whisper cut through his thoughts and he looked at her, startled.

'What?' he said impatiently.

'Are you alright? Your eyes...' Aliena seemed afraid to say more and Quinn realised he must have worked himself up so much that his eyes had begun to emit the red sparks again.

Inhaling deeply, he struggled to regain control of his feelings and looked at her, shame in his eyes. 'I'm sorry—'

He moved forwards again and Aliena had no choice but to follow him, more fearful than she was before. He was losing control again and she would be able to do nothing to stop him if he unravelled completely...

The noise came again, a faint scrape of metal against stone and then the gentle footfalls of more than one person. Quinn's whole body tensed up. He raised his sword over his right shoulder and gripped it with both hands, ready to swing it with the full weight of his body behind it. Slowing down, he came to a stop at the right-angled turn of the dim passageway and waited, poised, ready to strike.

Aliena stood behind him, shaking.

Then he threw himself around the corner.

CHAPTER 39. QUINN'S TRUE TARGET.

'*For the love of Christ!*' hissed Quinn, halting his movement so suddenly he skidded on his heel and sat down heavily. The orb disappeared with a flash and a low buzzing noise, like a startled bee.

Erelas lowered his sword and rushed to help his friend to his feet. 'No need to be like that...' he whispered. 'Are you alright?'

'I could have *killed* you!'

'And I could have killed you – which is the more likely, by the look of you!'

Quinn ignored him and scowled at Renn instead, who was trying hard not to laugh from behind Elyan. Renn's smile vanished and he took refuge out of sight.

'Quiet, both of you,' Aliena urged. 'We must get out of here – the guard could come back this way any moment.'

'What guard?' asked Elyan.

'You must have followed him down this way – he passed us not long ago. He's the reason Quinn is...unwell.'

'I'm fine,' snapped Quinn, shrugging off Erelas' help once he was upright again.

Aliena looked at him crossly, but said no more.

'The way we have just come was clear,' Erelas said. 'We passed a door, but I sensed your orb, so we came to meet you.'

'What was that thing, anyway?' asked Aliena.

'A kind of guiding light. It gives off an energy that links to the consciousness of—'

'We need to go through that door,' said Quinn, cutting him off. 'No sense in continuing around the outside of this thing.'

Erelas stared at him. 'What is the matter with you?'

Quinn sighed. 'Nothing. Just don't ask me to use any castings for a while.' He pushed past them all and set off along the passageway towards the door, not bothering to see if anyone followed.

Erelas raised an eyebrow at Aliena, who could only shoot him a sympathetic look. He resigned himself to – possibly – finding out later what the issue was, as they all went after Quinn.

***

Just minutes later Quinn threw a hand out behind him to signal them to stop. As they listened, Quinn felt sick as he realised there was more than one person – probably guards – approaching their position. They sounded quite far off still, so he turned and whispered urgently to Erelas. 'Where the hell is the door?'

'Just there!' Erelas pointed to a dimly-lit

portion of the passage and when Quinn looked carefully, he could see the dark wooden shape, set back a few finger-finger-widths from the wall's edge.

Quinn cursed his partial blindness. 'We can make it – go!' He set off, not quite able to make out the Latin that Erelas was reciting as they went. They reached the door and Quinn opened it as fast as he could. Moving quickly through so that the others could follow, he scanned the room they had just entered. They were inside the chapel.

Last in, Erelas closed the door and they gave a collective sigh of relief – except for Quinn, who was looking around uneasily at the dimly-lit chapel.

'What were you doing?' he asked Erelas.

'Creating a diversion. Those guards are about to find an enormous rat running towards them. The sport of chasing it will keep them away from here.' Erelas had a playful grin on his face and Quinn could not help but smile. It was not long before they heard a shout from outside the door and rapidly receding footsteps.

'Erelas, we need another orb and I dare not try anything.' Quinn looked around the stark and gloomy chapel. 'Especially not in here,' he added.

Erelas raised an eyebrow. 'What does being in here have to do with anything?'

'I don't know…It's making my blood run cold. Let's get the orb and move on. Please?'

Erelas – and the others – could see that he

was distinctly uneasy about being in this room. He nodded. 'Alright. For the king, yes?'

'No.'

'What?'

'The prince.'

Erelas frowned. 'Quinn, what do you want with the prince..?'

Quinn bit his lip and looked at the others, well aware they were not going to like what he was about to say. 'I'm not going to do anything to him, except...borrow him. I cannot take the risk that the king will not grant me a pardon based on Renn's story alone. I want him to think about what he would want someone to do for his son, if he were in danger, like Renn was in danger that night.'

'You're going to hold him to ransom?' Aliena said, incredulous.

'*No!*' Quinn said, louder than he intended to. Then, his voice lowered, he said, 'I'm not going to blackmail him into giving me a pardon! He is probably going to think we are going to harm his son, but it's not going to be for that reason. I will ask him, if someone were to come across a situation where his son is in mortal danger, what would he want that person to do for him? Would he want him to ignore it and walk on by, or would he want that person to step in and do something, even if that meant—' He stopped suddenly, looking at Renn, who was standing next to Elyan looking saddened. 'I'm sorry, Renn. You understand what I am saying, don't you?'

Renn nodded. 'It's alright,' he said quietly. 'I prayed every day for someone to help me when Father beat me. You helped me. If it was not for you, I would be dead. The king should be told that…he should imagine the prince being dead.'

Nobody spoke for several moments. Aliena stared at Quinn, who was rubbing his temples. Elyan looked at the floor, uncomfortable. Erelas and Renn looked at each other, both waiting for someone to make the next move.

Finally, Quinn spoke. 'We only get *one* go at this. If we don't get the king to understand the injustice of my death sentence, then Aliena and Elyan are lost, too. Surely that makes it worthwhile?'

'Toren is nine years old, Quinn,' Aliena said gently, her soft brown eyes transmitting her concern for the path they were about to take. 'He will be terrified.'

'And I'm sorry for that. I didn't say I *liked* the idea myself. But, it's the only way. I am not going to harm him. Mattias is devoted to the boy – he will not refuse—'

'What if he does refuse?' Elyan cut in sharply. 'Will you harm him then?'

'Did I harm *you*?' Quinn snapped back. 'Even after what you did to me?'

Erelas held up both his hands. 'Alright! That's *enough* – all of you. I don't like this any more than the rest of you, but Quinn is right. We cannot risk failing, if the king – for whatever reason – has no sympathy for Renn's story. We'll do it Quinn's way. I trust him with my life and I know he will not hurt the boy.' He looked pointedly at Elyan, his silver eyes glinting in the candlelight. 'What happened with me after his dream does not count – before anyone brings that up. We're wasting time. Let's just get this done.'

CHAPTER 40. A CRISIS OF FAITH

Erelas cupped his hands and summoned the orb. It appeared at the utterance of the prince's name and hovered for a moment before moving slowly towards the main door at the other side of the chapel. Erelas followed it and Elyan moved up behind him, glaring at Quinn as he passed. Quinn met his stare, until Aliena drew alongside him, holding Renn's hand, then his eyes dropped. He was unwilling to risk meeting her gaze, feeling ashamed that he was forced to resort to such measures with a child younger than Renn, who had probably led a charmed life thus far and had never had to fear anything. But he was even more ashamed that Aliena would have to watch him do it.

He waited until there was a small gap between the group and himself, then moved forwards. But as he crossed in front of the small, stone altar, he stopped again and stared at it. Something made him shiver and suddenly he did not know if he could go through with any of this. It felt wrong. He knew it was wrong. There was a reason the others were uncomfortable with it, and that same reason gnawed at his conscience as he stood transfixed by the golden cross on the altar.

Aliena turned and saw that he had stopped.

Coming back to join him, she took his hand and stood between him and the altar. 'Come on, Quinn,' she said gently. 'Men have killed for far less honourable reasons than you did. Whatever the method we use to get you your freedom, you do deserve it.'

Quinn stayed where he was, looking into her eyes with a mixture of fear and despair that she could not understand. 'It's not that, Aliena. It's this place. It's as if something in here is reacting to my presence. Or the presence of something *in* me...'

'What do you mean, something in you?'

'It's like a form of evil. More than just Rook's memories...Erelas will tell you...before the incident in the Plane of Shadows, I would not have been capable of killing Renn's father. I don't know what I would have done that night if that had not happened to me and changed me. Renn would be dead.'

'Quinn—'

'But in the same vein, none of this would be happening to us. I tell you, something evil is in me now and I can't do anything about it. This place – this is a *holy* place...I swear it's making me feel the way I do.'

Erelas came back to join them. 'What exactly is it you are feeling?'

Quinn's eyes glinted with tears as he looked at his friend. He bit his lip and his eyes dropped to the floor for a moment. When he looked up again, Erelas could see the pain in Quinn's eyes as he spoke. 'Cold. Weak…. Almost as if I can't go any further. And heaviness around my heart – like there is no hope for me anymore. As if God won't forgive me, after all. Even if the king pardons me, what happens to me when I die? I know where I'm likely to end up…'

'You're a Soul Conductor – you know how it works, Quinn, and that is not how it works. Even the people we serve are not judged on one single act, either good or bad. One act that is deemed to be evil does not always get them condemned, any more than one single act of compassion, bravery or generosity will undo a life of violence or greed!'

'I know that…'

'You also know that as a Soul Conductor, things are different for us. We spend our lives serving the Keepers and we are rewarded accordingly. You're still a Conductor. The Archdeacon cannot take that away from you, any more than you could give it to someone else.' Before Quinn could argue that point, Erelas put his hand on his shoulder and stopped him from saying a word. 'You're feeling guilt, Quinn, if I know you as well as I think I know you. Guilt that you took a life – however justified it may have been – and guilt over everything that has happened since that night. You feel bad for Aliena and Elyan and I know you feel awful about Galen's death. Just because you're not talking about it, doesn't mean I don't know you're thinking about it. You've been doing almost nothing but think about it since it happened and it's eating away at you. But you need to see things for what they are – the results of the actions of the truly evil man in all of this.'

'I agree with Erelas, Quinn,' said Aliena. 'It was the sheriff who threatened our freedom and safety. And, if you want to look back far enough, it is the sheriff who has made such ridiculous "rules" that say we cannot help a stranger in our own homes however that stranger ended up there.'

'As for the way this place is making you feel,' said Erelas, 'it is not making you feel anything more than the chill in the air we can all feel – it may be stronger for you because you're exhausted. This place is a huge part of the fight between good and evil for the people who live in this land and being here has helped to trigger these thoughts. You're fearful of the future and nobody can blame you for that. But you also feel physically rotten because you've hardly eaten or slept properly for more days than I care to guess at and you've just had to do a casting that has taken what little energy you did have.'

Quinn tried to digest their words as they stood in front of him, wondering if he was capable of going any further. He glanced over at Elyan, who still glared at him with disapproval, and at Renn, who appeared nervous and impatient.

Aliena placed her palm on his cheek and drew his gaze back to her. Speaking a little lower than she had been, she said, 'Elyan will be alright,

Quinn. Do not worry about him, or allow him to make you feel worse than you already do.'

Quinn looked into her eyes – eyes full of warmth and compassion he had so badly craved – and put his hands on her shoulders. Pulling her closer to him gently, he said, 'Just promise me one thing – all of you. Don't let me lose control. Do whatever it takes. I know that all of our futures rest on this going right, even Erelas', just for his being here. Don't let me sentence you all to death.'

Aliena's hand slid to his neck and she pulled him to her and held him close. 'We promise,' she whispered into his ear. As his chin rested on her shoulder, Quinn closed his eyes and sighed. He wished he could stay right there and allow time to take their problems away, and turn them to dust…but he knew that was impossible. After a long while, he moved back from Aliena's embrace and took a deep breath. He brushed her cheek with his hand and then clutched Erelas' arm in thanks. 'Let's go,' he said.

Erelas lead the way again.

CHAPTER 41. TOREN

The orb guided them out of the chapel and across a small, damp courtyard, where they met no challenges from the Guardsmen patrolling along the battlements. The guards simply took no notice of the inner parts of the castle they defended, believing it to be safe.

On reaching a door on the other side, Quinn was content for Erelas to go through first this time; he was feeling more and more weary as they went on and knew he would be relying on Erelas and Elyan to protect Renn and Aliena if they were challenged. All he would be able to do is try to shield them from harm with his own body – to the death if needs be.

They were soon all through and he saw that they had entered one of the halls of the castle. The Great Hall was only used at times when Mattias was entertaining guests; this smaller, less-grand hall was where the king and his son dined when they were without visitors. The table in the centre was large, but nothing on the scale of the ones in the Great Hall. It would seat only around eight people, three on each side and one at either end. It was completely clean and empty now; the meal of the evening had already been taken. The windows had shutters across them, preventing anyone inside the courtyard or along the curtain walls from looking in. The inner wall of the dining hall was covered in rich tapestries, depicting battle scenes involving kings in splendid armour, with legions of knights following them into an epic battle with some unseen enemy. The room was lit by four small torches set into the walls at each end, although grand candelabras were stored on a large wooden cabinet at the far end, where there was also another door...

'Let's keep moving,' said Erelas, not whispering, but keeping his voice low. 'This room seems too well lit to be ignored for long.'

No sooner were the words out of his mouth, when the far door opened and the prince himself entered the room, followed by his personal servant. Moving so fast that even Erelas almost did not see it, Quinn threw himself at the door and slammed it shut, trapping them both inside.

'Erelas! The servant!'

Erelas was there in just a few long strides. He grabbed the poor young man, who had his mouth and eyes wide open in fright. Erelas had no need to hold him tight as he was so terrified he stood perfectly still, trying to comprehend what was happening. Elyan raised his eyebrows, wondering how such a spineless man had been given the job of escorting a prince in the first place.

Aliena was about to go to the boy and reassure him, but before she could move, Quinn seized hold of him, his sword drawn. Panicking that she would give their plan away, he looked sharply at her and shook his head. 'Stay there, Aliena – all of you, stay still!'

Aliena seemed to understand and stopped, but Elyan did not and angrily pointed his sword at Quinn, stepping forwards.

'I mean it, Elyan!' Quinn wrapped his free arm around Toren's shoulders and pulled him back roughly against his body. 'Don't move again!'

Aliena stepped back alongside her brother and made him lower his sword. 'Do as he says, Elyan.'

Elyan hesitated, not sure if Aliena was reading the situation in the same way that he was, but eventually he gave in.

'Erelas?' Quinn said. He didn't look around, or lessen his grip on the boy, who was visibly trembling, but too shocked to cry.

'Sleep?'

'Do it.'

Nobody else moved or spoke as the servant was gripped around the throat, half-choked into unconsciousness, then hidden under the table. Aliena's face registered her uncomfortable surprise at Erelas' violence towards the defenceless man, but she knew it had been necessary. The prince tried to see what was happening, but Quinn kept turning him away from Erelas, never taking his eyes from Elyan. Although Aliena seemed to realise that he was making sure Toren was genuinely afraid for when they faced his father, he did not trust her brother. Elyan seemed anything but relaxed, his hand gripping the hilt of the sword so tightly his knuckles were drained of their blood. His dark eyes were locked on to Quinn's and the fury they were radiating made him look unnatural, almost possessed. Quinn decided he did not want Elyan around him anymore.

'It is done. He won't be emerging from that for a good while.' Erelas came around behind Quinn and stood between him and Elyan, sensing the danger.

Quinn nodded slowly, still not taking his eyes from Elyan. 'I think someone should stay here and watch him anyway – just in case.'

Erelas hesitated, knowing full well who Quinn meant. 'We can't split the group again, Quinn. We need everyone together. We need everyone's strength on this...'

Quinn looked at Erelas and knew he was right. Elyan might be a risk, but there was greater risk in leaving him behind. They could not afford to be one swordsman down, especially with an extra child to keep under control.

'Alright. Aliena, take the boy.' He gripped Toren by the shoulder and spun him roughly around. Seeing Quinn's peculiar eyes and angry expression, the prince's jaw dropped and he tried to back away. 'Listen to me,' Quinn said, holding on to him. 'This lady will not hurt you. But if you do not do exactly as we tell you, without any mischief or any kind of noise, I will. Do you understand?'

Toren nodded as tears finally welled up in his wide, brown eyes. 'Good.' Quinn looked at the rest of the group, paying special attention to Elyan's unconcealed look of fury. 'Then it's time to meet the king.'

CHAPTER 42. A PLEA TO THE KING

Toren led them tearfully, but silently, from the dining hall, along another passageway and up a flight of stone steps. They saw no guards as they went and Quinn began to think it was a little suspicious that they had met with so little resistance. Before they reached the top of the steps he stopped the prince and everyone else halted behind them.

'Where are the guards normally posted at this hour?' he asked the boy.

Toren sniffed and said: 'There's a passage at the top. There's one at each end.'

'So they will see us coming up these steps?'

The boy nodded.

Quinn turned to Erelas. 'Can you see if they are there?'

Erelas squeezed past them and moved up the last few steps. Crouching down, he poked his head around the corner as far as he dared. Glancing quickly in both directions, he took just a moment to see what he needed to, before straightening up and turning around. 'They are there.'

'Where is your father? How far is he from here?' Quinn asked Toren.

'There's a door…to the right, on the other side of the passage. It's not far down. He's in that room. It's his study. He likes to read after dinner.'

'I can deal with the guards from here, Quinn.' Erelas said.

Quinn nodded and looked at the trembling young boy again. 'Is there likely to be anyone in the study with your father?'

Toren shook his head. 'Not at night.'

'Good. Erelas...?'

'Everybody needs to get back.' Erelas said.

Aliena took the prince back down a few steps and stood with Elyan guarding their position against anyone coming up the staircase behind them. Renn leaned against the wall in the middle of the group. Quinn stayed where he was, sword drawn, ready to react if anything went wrong.

It did not go wrong, however. With just a few words, Erelas sent forth a shock wave, then a bright light forced them all to close their eyes and turn away. The casting made no more noise than the fizzing their conjurations usually produced, but the effect on the guards was far more dramatic. They collapsed where they stood, at either end of the corridor, armour and weapons clattering to the wooden floor.

'Go!' hissed Quinn, waving everyone past him. 'Get into the room before the king has a chance to react to the noise – he may have weapons in there!'

Erelas led the way, followed by Renn, Aliena and the prince and, finally, Elyan. As Elyan passed, he would not look Quinn in the eye and Quinn clenched his fists in frustration. This was for their own good – did he not realise that? He overtook Elyan and rushed to the door, reaching it at the same time as Elyan grabbed the handle. They all thrust themselves into the room and slammed the door shut.

They heard the scrape of a heavy chair being pushed back and then the crash of it tipping over, as their eyes adjusted to the gloom of the study, lit by a single candle on the large table in the centre. Behind that candle stood King Mattias, jaw sagging, eyes almost disbelieving.

'What is the meaning of this intrusion? What do you want?' he said, in a voice that was not quite 'kingly', in Quinn's opinion. Then it changed. 'What are you doing with my son?' he shouted, then started to move around the table.

Quinn shoved the boy to the front of the group and tucked the blade of the sword under his chin. '*Don't...*'

Mattias froze. He stared from Quinn to his son, reading their eyes, trying to gauge the situation.

Quinn pushed Toren forwards another step, sword digging in to the boy's soft skin. 'We need to talk.'

The king started as he noticed Quinn's alien eyes. 'Who are you people?' he said, almost whispering the words.

'*These* people,' Quinn said, indicating Aliena and Elyan with a nod of his head, 'are just loyal citizens who are being punished for helping a stranger in danger of losing his life. That stranger was me. I'm here to plea for their protection from your Lord Sheriff, and also to ask for a pardon for myself.'

Mattias scanned Aliena and Elyan's faces, before looking back at Quinn. 'What did you do?' he asked.

This is it, thought Quinn. 'Renn, come here,' he said.

Renn shuffled forwards, looking in awe at the finely dressed man in his late forties.

'This boy,' explained Quinn, still holding on tight to the prince, 'was being beaten severely by his father. And not for the first time. When I came across them, he was close to death. I killed his father to save his life. Garin had me locked up and tortured for it and would probably have killed me eventually, had I not escaped.'

'The hole in my castle wall…that was you? You're the one with magic…?'

'If you want to call it that, yes. Erelas, here, also has gifts from God. I know it is feared among your people, but we are peaceful and we do not use it to harm others, except in extreme circumstances.'

'Like the boy's father?'

Quinn sensed some level of scorn in Mattias' voice, but ignored it and just nodded. 'What I have come to ask you to consider, Sire, is this: looking at your boy now, standing in front of you with a sword at his neck – what would you want, or expect your guards to do to me?'

'They would protect the prince with their lives, if needs be...'

'Exactly. I did for Renn what you expect others to do for your son. So, I ask you – do I deserve imprisonment, torture and execution for my actions?'

Nobody spoke. Quinn felt cold panic rising in him. He gripped the prince's shoulder and pointed his sword at Renn. 'Sire, I'm asking you if this boy's life is worth *nothing*?'

'Of course not!' the king replied indignantly. 'But let my boy go—' He stepped forwards, a hand outstretched towards the prince.

The effect on Quinn was instantaneous. 'Get back!' he yelled, pushing the sword back up under Toren's chin, making him whimper in fright. 'I don't have anything to lose – so don't think I won't!'

Mattias moved back again, his hand trembling as it was slowly lowered. Aliena was frozen to the spot, but Elyan took a step forwards. Renn took refuge behind Erelas.

'Quinn,' Erelas said gently.

'No, Erelas – he is going to listen to me, or I will use this sword before any of you can stop me!' Quinn's voice shook with emotion and the red sparks began their display in his eyes.

Erelas made no movement, deciding it was better to let Quinn say what he needed to. He only hoped Elyan would feel the same way...

'You,' Quinn said, pointing the sword at the king for a second. 'You have no idea what is going on in your precious kingdom, do you? I saw it every day. Men and women, barely able to feed and clothe themselves, afraid to appeal against the taxes and trade restrictions imposed upon them. Any that do are cut down in the most brutal ways, because this land is ruled by violence. Your guards – led by your sheriff – have this country on the brink of a rebellion that nobody is brave enough to start! Garin threatens the worst punishments for the most minor of crimes. He even intimated to me that he was going to take Aliena and keep her for his own pleasure, here at your castle, because I would not bend to his will! Do you know, Sire, that this is the kind of man you have ruling the kingdom in your name?'

Mattias looked at Aliena, who looked down. Her eyes stung with tears as she heard the truth of Quinn's desperate race to get her and her brother to safety.

Quinn lowered his voice. 'Sire, do you have any idea what it was that the sheriff wanted me to do, that I refused to do, even though he threatened Aliena, Elyan and myself?'

Mattias shook his head, looking sadly at his son, who looked as if his legs would give out at any moment.

'He wanted my abilities. More specifically, he wanted me to use my abilities for his own personal gain – to *eliminate* his enemies.'

Mattias looked up at Quinn, digesting this information.

'Yes,' Quinn nodded. 'Even *you*. Garin craves power. It seems obvious to me, an outsider, where his eventual ambitions lie. With the prince too young to rule, who do you think would hold ultimate power if you were gone?'

'The sheriff.'

'And do you think Garin will want to let your son live long enough to rule? To produce an *heir*?'

The king was unable to respond. His gaze fell on his weeping son, still held in Quinn's tight grip.

'I know I am not a perfect person, Sire, and what I am doing now will only serve to make me look worse in your eyes. But ever since I came here after being punished by my own people for the death of Renn's father, I've had my eyes opened very wide indeed to the things that go on in your kingdom – supposedly with your blessing!' Quinn ignored the king's open-mouthed, but silent protest. 'Not just deaths from the violence, not just the fear people live in, or the rules that mean everyone is afraid to help a stranger in need, or even step outside their doors after dark. I've seen that a child's life is worth nothing. I've seen your sheriff murder his own flesh and blood, simply because he was in the cell I escaped from.' Quinn watched the king's eyes widen in horror. 'That's right, Sire. Garin slit his uncle's throat and threw his body into the moat. He values nothing and nobody, except power and his own progress. That progress is being hampered by your survival and that of your son. He sought to use me to eliminate you both.'

'What is it you want me to do?' the King asked, his voice high with fear. 'You have stated your wishes as far as yourself and your friends go, but you must want more, to be telling me all of this.'

Quinn sighed, suddenly weary again. 'I don't want any more than what I have asked. I just want you to understand. I want you to take back your kingdom and free these people. Everyone wants that. My anger is a mere reflection of their feelings – feelings they are too frightened to express. Make a child's life worth something. Protect your own son from the evil Garin plans for you both.' Quinn moved the sword away and seemed about to let go of Toren's shoulder...

But before anyone could react, Elyan grabbed Quinn's sword arm and wrenched it backwards against the natural bend of his elbow, forcing him to drop the weapon with a shout of pain and let go of the prince instinctively. Then he kicked Quinn hard in the back of his knee; Quinn was twisted around as he fell heavily on to his back. In an instant the point of Elyan's sword was digging into his throat and he could do nothing but lie there, slightly winded, his right arm useless.

'Elyan! What the *hell* are you doing?' cried Aliena, not sure whether to move or keep back, but Erelas stayed her with his hand outstretched, encompassing her and Renn.

'The right thing, Aliena!' Elyan looked up at the king, who was comforting his terrified son. 'Sire, this man has committed murder and now treason! He would have killed your son – you can see it in his eyes!'

Erelas stepped forwards as far as he dared. 'That is not true, Elyan! You know that the plan was just to frighten the boy, so that his father would take our story seriously. Stop this insanity and let him go!'

'He had you fooled, Erelas – he was *never* going to just talk this out calmly. You saw that when he took the boy! I've seen that look before; he looked the same way when he caught up with me, and when he attacked the soldiers at our house. He claims the sheriff rules by violence but that is exactly what he has been doing since he arrived! He has caused all of this and, Aliena, I don't care what you think of him, everything that has happened to us has been because of him! Don't—' he warned, as she opened her mouth to argue. 'I don't want to hear it. I'm sick of your faith in this man, who has ruined our lives! I want things the way they used to be!'

Suddenly Renn stepped out from behind Aliena and knelt in front of Mattias and the prince.

'Please, Sire, let Quinn go. He would not have hurt the prince.'

Everyone stared. The king looked at Renn with pity and said: 'I'm sorry, my boy.' Looking up at the adults, he continued: 'I would have pardoned him had he not carried out this assault on my son's senses and instead come to me calmly and openly. Although he may speak many truths, this man has attacked my son in his own castle and frightened the wits out of him. I cannot allow such actions to go unpunished. The rest of you, however, will not be harmed. You can return to your homes without fear of retribution.'

Renn bowed his head in despair and Aliena began to shake in fear and anger.

'You're just afraid of the sheriff!' shouted Quinn, ignoring the pain of the sword pressing into his throat so hard a trickle of blood began to run down behind his ear, before dripping on to the floor. 'You will pay for that with your life one day, Sire! And so, too, will your *son*!'

They were all made to jump as two Guardsmen burst in. Mattias held up his hands. 'Hold!' he called. 'All is well here. This man,' he said, pointing at Quinn, still pinned down by Elyan's sword, 'is to be taken down to the dungeons to await trial for treason. The rest are free to leave unhindered and without stain on their characters. But see that they *do* leave.'

'Yes, Sire,' said one guard, pushing Elyan out of the way and hauling Quinn to his feet. 'Might as well come quietly,' he said to his prisoner. 'Nowhere to go.'

Just then the amulet at Erelas' throat began to glow. Everyone in the room was momentarily transfixed as the turquoise light brightened the room. The guard was distracted just long enough for Quinn to seize the chance and he wrestled free from his grasp. The guard gave a shout, but everyone was too slow. Quinn ripped the amulet from his friend's neck and with a few words, he was gone.

Breaking the shocked silence which had followed, Aliena sank to her knees and sobbed.

CHAPTER 43. DUTY DONE

Quinn found himself in a cold, dark dwelling that was little more than a hut with a place for a bed and a fire. The fire had gone out and the only light was the weak orange glimmer from a mere stump of a candle burning on the floor in the corner beside the bed.

On the bed, which was no more than a mattress of straw on the dirt floor, lay a woman of about seventy. She looked as if she had simply climbed into her bed and died of some unseen ailment, or maybe just old age. Her face reflected peace and her grey hair was neatly tucked under a sleeping cap. She had been cold; the single, thick woollen blanket was pulled up tightly around her shoulders and under her chin.

Kneeling down on the floor beside her, Quinn prepared to take her soul to the Plane of Shadows. He knew that, as desperate as his escape from the castle had been, he could not just leave this poor woman as she was – her soul would eventually be severed from her body naturally and she would be forever trapped in this world, lost and wandering, perhaps unable to accept that she had died. As he feared Galen was...a thought which tore at his heart. Above all else, despite the Archdeacon's sentence, he was still a Soul Conductor and he would do his duty and guide this woman to her fate in the afterlife.

He placed his hands either side of her head and took a deep breath. As he said aloud the words he knew so well, he said a silent prayer for a gentle journey for himself and a safe return – he did not know how much strength he had left...

His good eye changed from silver-grey to bright turquoise as soon as the words were out of his mouth. He kept his grip on her as he locked their energies together, but relaxed a little as he began to feel the condition of her soul. She had been a good woman, a gentle woman, who had lived a simple but relatively happy life. She would probably go on to be with God, unless there was something very dark in her past which he could not feel, but he doubted that was the case.

As he recited the second part of the incantation, the old woman's essence appeared next to him in the Plane of Shadows, leaving her body behind. Quinn now had no need to grip her head, as she stood looking past him at the barren, dusty landscape with its ominous red sky.

Blinking as she took in her surroundings, she looked confused, but not alarmed. She thought she was in a dream. The violently swirling sand and the far-off screeching of the Guardians did not seem to frighten her. The clear conscience she carried meant she expected no punishment from any quarter for anything, so she accepted everything she saw as just something new to behold.

Quinn smiled at her – something he rarely did in this place. Usually he would just wait, silent and expressionless, for the dead to realise where they were going and then release their souls. But this woman was somehow giving him back a little of his own mental strength, calming the fire in his mind that was caused by the wickedness clamped to his soul like a deadly parasite. As she looked into his eyes, he felt some of the love this woman had bestowed upon many people in her lifetime and he felt his heart lift as she smiled back at him. Paradoxically, he also felt like sobbing.

After he squeezed her hands his thanks for her gift, she slowly turned away from him and walked off, her gown fluttering wildly in the winds, but her pace was unhurried and unresisting. Quinn watched her for a while, then looked down at the amulet he had placed around his neck.

It was time to go back and forge a new plan.

CHAPTER 44. THE WRATH OF ALIENA

Erelas' mind raced as they were ejected from the castle by a guard, who said nothing to them, merely shouting instructions to other guards at the gate tower for the portcullis to be raised. Where had Quinn gone? What would he do after conducting the soul? There was no doubt in Erelas' mind that Quinn would do his duty, but what then? He could not remain in the Plane of Shadows longer than was necessary – the Guardians would surely not spare him a second time.

And what of their own fate? Were they now safe, or would Garin disregard the king's assurances that they were free to go and try to capture them again? One thing was certain: they could not stay here.

Aliena interrupted his thoughts as they reached the end of the drawbridge, by landing a slap so hard on Elyan's face that he stumbled sideways and fell to the ground. In the dark they could barely see a few feet in front of their faces, but Erelas could make out the young man's shocked expression as his sister stood over him in a fury he would have doubted she was capable of. Erelas put a hand on Renn's shoulder and drew him away a little.

'How *could* you?' she screamed. 'How could you do that to him? You know full well he was about to let the prince go and keep his word!'

Elyan could do nothing but sit in the sticky mud, churned up by countless boots, hooves and cart wheels, looking agog at the silhouette of his sister leaning over him.

'Well? *Say* something!'

'Aliena, I never trusted him, you know that!' Elyan said, his voice weak, but gathering strength as he continued. 'He was not going to let the boy go, you saw his eyes!'

'You just wanted to believe he wouldn't keep his promise! His eyes have nothing to do with it...he didn't harm you did he?' Aliena could not calm her voice. 'Perhaps he *should* have!'

That was too much for Elyan and he scrambled to his feet. 'Well you just go and find him then! He can *never* do wrong in your eyes, no matter what he does, even to a child! I refuse to be part of this now...I've got my life back and I'm going to the farm to live it. They were right about one thing – there is nothing wrong with a boring life as a farmer!' He gestured to Erelas. 'If you want to stay with *him* and get yourself in to more trouble, you're on your own!' He ran off into the darkness, the sound of his sword clanking against the armour gradually fading away from the others.

Aliena had no intention of trying to call him back.

Erelas approached her with Renn and put

his arm around her trembling shoulders. 'Do not worry, Aliena. He will just go home, cool down and wait for us, no doubt.'

'Where do you think Quinn went?' she said, taking Renn's hand, as much to comfort herself as the boy, who looked merely bemused by the whole episode.

'I will take you home and then go and find him. I think I know where he would have gone.'

'I want to go with you,' said Renn in protest.

'I do, too,' said Aliena, straightening herself up. 'I need to know he is alright.'

Erelas considered for a moment. 'But what if the king is sending guards out after him? They could be coming out of that gate at any moment.'

'Then we had better make sure we get to him first. And *don't* tell me it's dangerous, Erelas – I don't care. This is my brother's fault, no matter what his reasoning may be. Quinn does not deserve this and he needs help. Maybe only you can give him that help, I don't know. But I still want to see that he is safe.'

'But what about Renn?'

'I'm not afraid,' said Renn. 'I may not have been his friend at first, but he has been mine and I want to help, too.'

Erelas smiled and patted the boy's shoulder. 'Alright – we all go. But I cannot use an orb and we need to be careful and quiet. Otherwise, we will lead the guards straight to him.'

***

Quinn changed the words he normally recited as he left the Plane of Shadows and was relieved to find himself standing within a few feet of a dozing Cara when he opened his eyes again.

She eyed him with disinterest as he approached her, as if she had expected him all along. He smiled and patted her neck, moving in close to lean against her and share her warmth for a moment. He was truly exhausted, both physically and mentally. He felt light-headed, almost drunk, from lack of sleep and food, and would have liked nothing more than to curl up somewhere against her back and sleep the rest of the night away. But he knew he had to get as far away from Castle Rivallen as he could, and quickly.

His first – and only – plan was to go back to the cave. If the king had kept his word, the others would be free to go wherever they wished by now. He knew Erelas would look for him there first and would take care to ensure he was not followed. They would be safe there, for a while, at least. He tried not to think about whether the rest would stay with Erelas – he did not want to consider that he might never see Aliena again, or how he might react when faced with Elyan.

Whatever happened, he knew he could not go anywhere without seeing Erelas one last time. This was not going to be a repeat of his banishment from Delmoril.

He checked through the bags attached to Cara's saddle, which was right where they had left it at the foot of a very old tree, relatively sheltered from the elements. He found water, a small amount of food and a small knife that was really only good for picking stones out of Cara's feet. Not much to get by on, but get by he was determined to do. This would not be much different to his normally nomadic lifestyle, except that instead of hunting for souls that needed his help, he was now the hunted one.

Saddling Cara despondently, he tried to keep Galen's words in the forefront of his mind. There would always be hope, no matter how small, until the moment of his own death, that something could come along and change his fortunes for the better. All he had to do was hold on – and pray.

The moon began to poke out from behind the clouds as he finished fastening Cara's girth. Although Cara would follow the path back through the forest in the dark with no problems, he needed to be able to see if anyone was approaching their position, so any light was welcome. The last thing he needed, with very little energy and no weapons, was a surprise attack by heavily armed and armoured Guardsmen. Of course, the moonlight also meant they could see him. With more than a little trepidation in his heart, Quinn took hold of Cara's reins and climbed wearily onto her back. Resisting the temptation to lean forwards and doze, he forced himself to sit upright and scan his surroundings as they set off. It was going to be a long night...

CHAPTER 45. ELYAN

Despite all Quinn's good intentions, lulled by the horse's steady movement, he had begun to fall asleep by the time Cara brought him to the entrance of the cave. When she suddenly snorted in alarm and shuffled backwards, he almost fell straight over her shoulder.

'*Steady*, Cara!' he growled, trying to shake the clouds of fatigue from his mind. Pulling her up to the entrance once more, she nodded her head violently and refused to go in. 'What is it, girl?' he whispered impatiently. Cara snorted again and Quinn knew there was no sense in fighting with her further. Something within had spooked her – most likely one of Erelas' giant rats.

He slid down off her back, wincing at the ache in his knee, then hooked the reins over her saddle. With one last glance around the moonlit forest, he stepped inside, his ears straining for sounds of movement within.

He soon heard them. Very faint, but distinctive, they were the sounds of someone's lungs fighting for air through some sort of fluid. The hairs on the back of Quinn's neck bristled and his heart seemed to beat louder, sending the blood thundering through his ears until he could barely hear the noise at all.

Scanning the darkness as he crept slowly forwards, he eventually picked out a shape on the ground that was darker than the dirt around it. Frowning, he edged closer, and as his eyes adjusted to the gloom, he could just make out the moon's soft, transient glow, reflected from a smooth object in the centre of the dark shape, which rose and fell irregularly.

He raced through every thought that was beginning to form about the possibilities that lay in front of him, fighting them off, not wanting to give any of them enough time to validate themselves. All he would accept was the fact that the shape was a person, and that that person was in a bad way. As he took tentative steps forwards, further into the darkness, but closer to the truth, he could feel his panic beginning to rise, his own breaths coming almost as quickly as those of mysterious figure on the ground.

The confirmation of recognition hit him like a blast of hot air from the Plane of Shadows, as he reached the ground just inches away from the armoured figure.

Elyan.

Quinn dropped to his knees, the hot blood in his face being replaced by an icy chill that ran down his back. It was definitely Elyan. Cupping his hands in front of his own face, Quinn quickly conjured an orb. This one held position and grew. Soon the cave was lit brightly enough for him to see the damage.

'Oh, Elyan,' he whispered, his whole body sagging.

Elyan had been knifed in the ribcage, under his right armpit, where he was not protected by the armour. It was only a small wound, but a deep one; as Quinn undid the breastplate and tore at the clothes underneath, he found blood was bubbling out through the hole in the skin. There was a significant pool of it on the ground, too. Elyan could not draw in his breath properly and was slowly drowning in his own blood. There was absolutely nothing Quinn could do for him, even if he had been in possession of untainted supernatural skills.

Quinn leaned forwards over his face and saw that he was still fighting to stay awake. His eyelids twitched and opened a little way, before becoming heavy again and closing. His skin was an eerie grey, even in the strange light of the blue flame. Quinn knew he did not have long.

'Elyan,' he said gently, not wanting to startle the young man.

Elyan's eyes opened and he searched for a moment before finding Quinn's unmatched eyes gazing down on him. 'Quinn...'

'Who did this to you?' Quinn asked, already knowing the answer.

'The sheriff,' Elyan whispered, before the froth of blood in his throat caught him out and made him cough involuntarily. The struggle for breath was increased tenfold and Quinn thought for a moment that it was all going to be over right then. But soon Elyan regained control and looked up at him again. 'He said...he said...he...' he began, then swallowed. 'Forgive me, Quinn...he came to the house...made me tell him where you might go...made me show him the way...but I never thought you'd really come back here. Ask Aliena to forgive me.'

'You stood up for what you believed, Elyan...there is nothing to forgive. But where is Aliena?'

Elyan began to shake his head. 'Don't go back to the castle. It's a *trap*...'

'What is a trap? What is he going to do? Is she there?'

Elyan coughed again, spraying blood over Quinn's face and neck. This time he could not fight back control and with his eyes wide, he grasped the air with his hand. Quinn took it and held it tight. Elyan fought to get a few more words out, but there was no air left to make any more sound with and Quinn could not read his lips. He could only look on, tears viciously stinging his eyes, as the fight finally went out of Aliena's younger brother. His eyes closed, the fingers lost their grip and the arm became heavy. The lungs fought for air no more, for he was gone.

Quinn remained still for a while, staring at Elyan's body, holding his hand, until the flame burned itself out and he was left in darkness once more. He could not believe this had happened.

Why had Garin so openly targeted Elyan, when it was Quinn he wanted his revenge on? What scared him most was that he did not know where Aliena was, and could only hope that Elyan's failure to mention her meant that she was safe back at the farm.

The amulet began to glow. Quinn felt sick. He did not think he could cope with conducting Elyan's soul – but he knew he had to, or he would be trapped here, like Galen. If that happened, he would never be able to forgive himself, and he could not bear to think of what it would do to Aliena.

Aliena. At the thought of how her heart would be torn in two by the loss of her brother, Quinn finally broke, letting go of Elyan and silently weeping with his hands over his face, as if in some way he could block out the horror just by not being able to see the proof of it any more.

A soft whinny from Cara brought him out of his thoughts and he struggled to get to his feet, his legs shaking and weak. As he stumbled to the cave entrance in the dark, fighting to see through stinging, wet eyes, he had an idea...

Cara nuzzled his chest, understanding in her own way what had happened and Quinn was grateful for her company. He was reminded again what a precious, priceless animal his mare was and he was glad that she would be with him on his future travels – assuming he had a future at all.

'Cara, we have a job to do, my dear friend.

You need to be careful, but quick.'

Cara nodded, nudging him. Quinn patted her neck and, taking hold of her bridle, led her into the cave. This time she did not resist and stepped carefully in, until Quinn signalled her to stop, a few feet from Elyan. There she waited patiently, while Quinn created another orb of light.

Swallowing bile and holding back the tide of grief through his sense of duty, Quinn sighed and got down to the task before him. He carefully removed the armour from Elyan's body and placed it to one side, feeling bitter that it had not protected him at all in the end. Then came the difficult part.

'Cara....'

The horse took small steps forwards, treading very carefully. When she was close enough, Quinn stood up and went to her side, rubbing her muzzle gently.

'You're going to be carrying a precious load, now, Cara. I know you won't let him fall.'

Cara lowered her head in acknowledgement of her companion's wishes. She bent one foreleg, resting her weight on the knee, before following with the other and then lowering her rear. Leaning slightly to one side, she waited, breathing softly, keeping as still as she could.

Quinn returned to Elyan, crouched down and gently lifted his head. He slid his arm under Elyan's neck and shoulders and pulled his body up almost into a sitting position. With his other arm he lifted Elyan's legs under his knees and hoisted him up off the ground. Cradling him carefully, he turned to Cara and, with an irrational fear of damaging him further, managed to place him upon her back, a leg either side, as if he was going to ride her himself. Breathing a sigh of relief that the first part was done without incident, he supported Elyan's upper body while swinging his own leg over Cara's back and sitting behind him.

With his feet safely in the stirrups, he pulled Elyan back, allowing him to rest against his chest. Linking his arms around the front of Elyan's blood-soaked shirt, he took a deep breath.

'Up, Cara. Slowly...'

Cara answered with a gentle snort and heaved herself straight, before carefully getting to her feet. Quinn held on tight as he was tipped backwards, then forwards, as she straightened herself and positioned her feet securely.

'Well done, Cara,' he said. Then, balancing Elyan against his body, with his head resting against one shoulder, Quinn cupped his hands as close to his face as he could and whispered in Latin the words he needed to summon the orb. It immediately appeared, dancing in front of Cara's ears. Quinn placed one arm around Elyan's torso and, with the other hand around his forehead, held him still against the dip of his shoulder. His heart felt crushed as he looked at Elyan's closed eyes and the blood that had stained his mouth, chin and neck. He looked so much younger now, as if he were no more than a child. He also looked peaceful, but Quinn knew that was not the case just yet – and they were running out of time to get him where he needed to be.

'Follow the light, Cara. Quickly, but smoothly. We need our friend's help.'

Cara nodded and turned, watching her step as she made her way out of the cave. Once on the moonlit track, she gradually increased speed, until she was smoothly cantering along, Quinn gripping her sides with his legs and trusting her to not unseat them both. He prayed there would be nobody on the track but Erelas, or he did not know what would become of them all.

CHAPTER 46. INNOCENCE

Terrified that the amulet would stop glowing before they found Erelas, Quinn was greatly relieved when the orb began to slow and Cara matched its pace. As she came to a standstill at the edge of a small clearing, his eyes scanned the trees for sight of his friend. The orb helped to light the clearing and soon he spotted cautious movement among the low-hanging branches.

His relief was short-lived, however, and his stomach turned cold as Erelas emerged into the clearing with Aliena and Renn. He felt suddenly dizzy and had no idea what to do. He had not even considered that she might still be with Erelas. As Cara snorted her greeting, Quinn could do nothing but stare helplessly as they stepped closer.

He watched as the relief on their faces turned to confusion, then to disbelief and horror. Aliena seemed to sink lower as she came closer, until finally Erelas had to catch her as her legs failed her completely. Her breathing was panicked, her eyes wide and staring and her mouth was unable to form any words. Erelas supported her as they reached the horse, leaving Renn standing transfixed and clearly frightened.

'Quinn..?' Erelas whispered.

Quinn tore his eyes from Aliena and looked

at Erelas, shaking his head slowly. 'Erelas, you *have* to help me – I can't do it...' He carefully took his arm from around Elyan's body and took the glowing amulet from his pocket. Holding it out to Erelas, he said, '*Please*, before it's too late...'

Erelas took the amulet and looped it over his head. Gently taking Elyan by the arm, he pulled the young man's body towards him, taking the other arm and his weight as he slid from Cara's back. Lifting his legs down, careful not to bump or drag him, he lowered his body to the floor. Quinn swung his leg over and dismounted, almost slumping to the ground as his weak legs struggled to hold him upright. By the time he steadied himself and turned, Erelas had laid Elyan on the ground and Aliena had fallen to her knees beside her brother's head. She was trembling, her eyes full of tears that her unblinking eyes would not send on their way. She held out a shaking hand and gently brushed some hair from Elyan's eyes, assessing the damage to the rest of him as she did so.

Erelas looked up at Quinn, who stood, swaying slightly, staring at Aliena. 'What happened?'

'I don't know – not much, anyway.' Quinn looked at Erelas, his eyes pleading. 'There was nothing I could do for him, Erelas. He tried to tell me something about a trap and then—'

Quinn had no time to defend himself as Aliena jumped up and launched herself at him, swinging her arm and landing the back of her hand so hard across his face that he went down hard, the back of his head smacking against the impacted dirt of the track. Dazed, he just lay there, swallowing blood and blinking back the tears that stung his eyes.

Erelas scrambled to his feet and grabbed hold of Aliena's arms before she could attack Quinn again.

'*Liar*!' she screamed at Quinn, careless of whether any guards were close enough to hear her.

Erelas spun her round firmly. 'Aliena, *stop*!' he said. 'I don't believe for a moment Quinn is responsible for this! But for Elyan's sake, you *must* stop this now! You understand what we do, and his soul needs to be conducted before it is too late. Please,' he said, softening his tone a little. 'There's nothing you can do for him except stay calm and let me do this for him. Look after Renn – he's terrified and needs you!'

Aliena looked at the young boy, still standing in the same place, crying silently and trembling all over. Then she looked back at Erelas, fury lighting up her eyes, but did not fight to get away from him. 'You would stand by your friend no matter *what* he has done!'

Erelas frowned at her and his tone sharpened. 'I do not believe he would have asked me to do this if he was lying. He knows I will hear the truth from *Elyan* myself! You *will* leave Quinn alone – do you understand me?'

Aliena stared defiantly for a moment and then her body began to relax a little. Erelas let her go gradually and when she was free of him, she simply sat down beside her brother and sobbed as her heart broke into a thousand pieces.

Erelas walked over to Renn and crouched down in front of him. 'I'll be back soon, Renn. Please don't be scared – everything will be alright. Come and sit on Cara until I get back.' He led the boy to the horse and Renn did not resist as he was helped up into the saddle and wrapped in Erelas' cloak. Erelas patted the horse, who stood perfectly still, unsure of what to do except stay close to Quinn.

Walking back to Elyan, he knelt down beside him, opposite Aliena, then placed his hands on either side of his head. Reciting the necessary words, in just a few moments he vanished, making Aliena jump. She lowered her head until it was touching her brother's chest and cried quietly, her shoulders shaking without restraint.

Quinn stayed where he was, feeling so wretched that he did not care if he never stood up again. Erelas was taking care of Elyan's soul. That was good enough for him.

CHAPTER 47. COMFORT

When his head began to clear a little, Quinn sat up. He had no idea what to do except sit where he was and say nothing to Aliena; he thought the chances of being hit again were very high if he so much as opened his sore and bleeding mouth.

He understood the accusation all too clearly. Elyan had betrayed him for a second time and forced him into fleeing from the castle once again – of course he had been extremely angry with the boy, and the knowledge that he could and would kill given the 'right' reasoning, probably did much to solidify his guilt in her eyes.

But he would never have killed Elyan and the fact Aliena thought him guilty of it crushed him. Much of his anger had been generated by Rook's 'presence' in him. It had never been Quinn's place – or desire – to punish the boy for having the courage to stand up for what he believed. It did not matter that Elyan had been wrong about a number of things and wrong to carry out some of the things he had done. What mattered to Quinn was the intention behind those actions. Each time he had acted to protect another person – Aliena, Erelas, Toren. Of course, Quinn was angry that all of those actions had been against him, but not all had been unjustified.

He watched as Cara bent her head to nibble at some thin grass in the clearing. Her movement made Renn anxious and he held on tight to the front of the saddle. He had stopped crying now, but was obviously too scared to say or do anything. Quinn felt a stinging empathy for the boy. He had lost his mother at a young age, endured a life of violence at the hands of his father and had then been thrust into this new world that seemed to be punctuated with just as much violence. Quinn imagined Renn must be very confused, when people who were supposed to be friends kept lashing out at each other. They must have proved to be a big disappointment. He hoped that he would be able to make it up to him some day...

He looked over at Aliena, desperate to comfort her, but not daring to disturb her. She would hate him until Erelas came back and validated his story. Even then, he wasn't sure.

He knew he would not hold it against her when it was all sorted out. She, too, like her brother, was only reacting to what she believed had taken place based on the evidence she had seen. And she was in shock, grieving and could not be expected to think with any kind of clarity – or to listen to Erelas, who was, after all, a relative stranger to her and Quinn's oldest friend and obvious ally.

He would just want it forgotten about and never mentioned again. He did not want to remember the look in her eyes as she had approached Cara and seen her brother's lifeless body in his arms. Inside, though, he knew it would haunt him regardless.

Suddenly Quinn turned on to his hands and knees and crawled to the edge of the clearing. Having eaten very little that he could remember for a long time, he threw up the almost pure blood that he'd just swallowed. Dry-retching for what seemed like an eternity, he finally slumped down against the trunk of the nearest tree, drew his knees up and rested his head back against the bark, closing his eyes. Everything hurt and he was so tired he just wanted to remain there and sleep forever, but he knew he could not. Erelas would be back soon and they would need to decide what to do next, starting with what should happen to Elyan's body.

He felt a hand rest on his knee with the lightest of touches and his eyes fought their way open. Crouching down in front of him, Aliena held out a clean, white strip of cloth to him. Her eyes were red and her cheeks still wet with tears, but she no longer had anger on her face – just a deep, incurable sadness.

'You're still bleeding,' she said, holding the cloth closer.

Quinn took the cloth and nodded his thanks. Touching it to his face, he drew it away again and looked at the spreading stain he had transferred to it.

Shaking her head, Aliena held out her hand and shuffled closer to him. 'Here, let me,' she said.

She took the cloth from him and gently tilted his head to one side as she wiped at the blood that was coming from both his nose and his upper lip. 'You look very ill, Quinn. I am sorry I did this to you. It's the *last* thing you need.'

Quinn tried to look at her, but she held him still and he did not persist. Perhaps she was not quite ready to call a complete truce just yet. 'I'll be alright,' was all he could say, not wanting sympathy when Elyan was dead.

'You always say that,' said Aliena, folding the cloth to present a clean side and starting again. This time she put pressure on the cut on Quinn's mouth and he winced. 'But I seem to end up looking after you an awful lot,' she added.

Quinn stayed quiet and let her work. He did not want to end up saying the wrong thing and ruining the progress they seemed to be making.

'There,' she said finally. 'That's the best I can do for now.' She released her gentle hold on him.

'Thank you,' Quinn said, looking around at her.

'Quinn…' she began, but then hesitated and looked down at the blood-stained cloth still in her hands.

He waited, fear clutching his stomach again.

'I know you didn't kill my brother,' she said finally. She looked at Quinn's eyes, moist with tiredness and the threat of tears he would not let fall, then took his hand. 'I realise now that this would be exactly the kind of thing Garin would do, to get revenge on you, or even on me and Elyan for getting away from him. Or simply just to draw you back to the castle.'

Quinn swallowed hard, unable to speak.

'I knew I had to say something before Erelas got back, because I wanted you to know that my faith in you has not changed – I was just blinded for a moment, by the shock, I suppose...'

'You don't need to explain, Aliena. I understand how it looked.'

She looked at him for several moments and then asked: 'Did he say anything else, apart from what you already mentioned?'

Quinn nodded, looking down. 'Garin went to the house. He forced Elyan to take him to the cave to find me. Elyan asked me to forgive him, then he asked me to ask you to forgive him, too...'

'Oh, Elyan!' she gasped, looking over at his body. She looked back at Quinn, fresh tears spilling over and running down her face. 'I'm glad he wasn't alone at the end. I am glad you were there for him.'

Quinn gripped her hand firmly and pulled her close to him. Burying her face in his chest, she was overtaken by grief again and did not resist when Quinn put his arm around her shoulders and held her tight. She took comfort from the beat of his heart and the rise and fall of his chest as he breathed, as her tears fell afresh.

Hearing the sound of light footsteps, Quinn

looked up and saw Renn, who stopped when he knew he had been seen. He stood, looking unsure of what to do next, tears trickling down his pale face.

Quinn held out his free hand and beckoned him. Renn hesitated, then began to move towards them again. Aliena looked up as she, too, heard his approach and straightened herself up a little, making room for the boy in between her knees and Quinn's legs. Quinn straightened his legs out in front of him as Renn took Aliena's outstretched hand. She guided him down and he turned as he sat, settling against her and Quinn. Resting his head on Quinn's chest, he let the tears fall freely as Aliena wrapped her arm around him, tucking in the cloak.

There they stayed, united in their grief and fears, until Erelas reappeared.

CHAPTER 48. GARIN'S GAMBLE

Renn sat up as Erelas approached the three of them, his movement weighed down by the emotional and physical effects of the task he had just performed. 'It's alright,' the boy said, smiling a little. 'They are friends now.'

Aliena also straightened up expectantly, but Erelas was looking at Quinn and frowning. Turning to see what he was concerned by, she realised that Quinn's head had fallen back against the tree again and he had passed out. 'Oh, no...' she breathed, as she moved out of the way and let Erelas crouch down beside him.

Erelas supported Quinn's head with one hand as he gently opened an eyelid with the thumb of the other. 'He will be alright,' he said after looking into them both carefully. 'He is just exhausted and has neglected himself for far too long. I can help him, but he must not be moved tonight. He must be allowed to rest.' Moving him very gently, he laid him down on his side on the soft, moss covered ground at the base of the tree.

Renn took off Erelas' cloak and handed it to him. Erelas smiled his thanks and folded the cloak, placing it under Quinn's head. Aliena went to Cara and removed her saddle, retrieving the blanket underneath. She placed it over Quinn and sat down beside his head, listening to his slow and steady breathing. Renn joined her, settling down to watch Erelas work on restoring his friend's health once more.

'Erelas,' said Aliena in a hushed voice when he was finished. 'We cannot stay here all night. We are exposed. What if the guards come this way?'

'Quinn cannot be disturbed now. I have limited influence on him without more help from potions that I don't have with me – they are in Delmoril. But try not to worry. They will not find us. I can place a natural barrier with branches and such around this clearing, much like the one I created for the cave. It will force them on to a false path and they will pass right around us. It's too dark for them to be any the wiser. They shouldn't hear us, either.'

'Will he *really* be alright?' asked Renn.

Erelas placed a hand on the young boy's shoulder. 'He will be fine by morning, you'll see. He has just had so much to deal with for a long time. He ran out of strength. He'll soon get it back.'

Renn nodded in understanding, then lay himself down beside Quinn, preparing to remain at his side for the night.

'You should rest too, Aliena,' said Erelas. 'I will keep watch.'

'I need to hear what happened first, Erelas. *Please...*'

Erelas saw both the plea and the determination in her face and he sighed, moving away from

Quinn's side. 'Give me a few moments. I'll hide us all first.'

***

'Remember what Elyan had said outside the castle about going back to the farm?' Erelas asked Aliena, as they sat by a small fire he had made for them near to where Quinn and Renn lay sleeping.

Aliena nodded.

'The sheriff overheard that from the top of the gatehouse. Elyan said that Garin had told him that he should not have shouted it out for all the world to hear. When Elyan got back to the cottage, the sheriff and his guards were waiting inside for him. He didn't stand a chance.'

Aliena's gaze dropped to her lap, as she tried to keep from weeping again.

'Elyan told me that once he'd led them to the cave, Garin had given him two reasons why he was going to be killed,' Erelas continued. 'One, because he didn't like the fact that the king had let you both go, and two, because he knew that Quinn would be outraged and come back to find him at Castle Rivallen to get his own revenge. The sheriff wants Quinn on his territory, so that he can trap him there and kill him.'

'Why didn't he just kill Elyan at home?' Aliena asked.

'Because he was counting on us thinking that *Quinn* had murdered him, so that he would be alone when he went to the castle. Alone and without help.'

'He almost got his way,' Aliena said, her head dropping again.

'No, he didn't. You didn't really believe he had done it, or you would have needed my proof to change your mind.'

'It was just a flash of madness. It was horrible...poor Quinn.'

'He will be alright. He's probably already let it go.' Erelas took her hand. 'Aliena, there is one more thing Elyan said. He said that he knows you will hide how you feel about your last words to each other being in anger.'

Aliena's eyes spilled over again and she bit her lip.

'He told me to ask you to forget that. He said one small bad memory should not take the place of a thousand good ones. He will carry all of those with him, always. *You* must, too.'

Aliena broke down again, and Erelas held her close, until she was all cried out.

'You should sleep now, Aliena,' Erelas said, as her tears subsided. 'No doubt we will all need our strength for whatever tomorrow may bring...'

'Erelas, can I ask you to do something for me – for Elyan? And for Quinn, too?'

'If I can do it, I will. What is it?'

Aliena looked over at Elyan's body. 'We can't just leave him there. I know he is not there now. I know he is at peace. But he should be buried. I don't think Quinn will be able to cope with that task – and I'm not sure I have the strength, either.'

'I will take care of him,' said Erelas. 'I will bury him here and mark the spot. I'll set a stone on top, so that you can come back, if you wish...'

'Thank you. Even though I know he is gone, it will be of some comfort to have a place I can come to, to talk to him again...' She covered her face with her hands, but could not cry anymore.

Erelas kissed her forehead. 'Get some rest, now. When you wake, it will all be done.'

CHAPTER 49. NON-DISCUSSION

'You know that I *will* go to the castle,' Quinn said, leaning back against the tree he had passed out against the night before. He rubbed his eyes with his fingertips and drew his knees up. He still felt weak in body and mind, but Erelas had done well and he felt he had enough strength to at least make plans and prepare for their next move. That was if he could get past the burning grief, anger and guilt that had churned through his veins like a malevolent river. He knew the only thing that would lessen those feelings would be to dispense justice, hard and fast.

'Yes, I know that. Elyan knew it too,' said Erelas, pacing up and down between Quinn and the fire.

'Why, Quinn?' said Aliena, who was stood staring into the flames. 'Why give Garin what he wants? You should leave, while you have an advantage – there will not be many guards in these parts, with Garin waiting for you at the—'

'And what would that achieve, Aliena?' Quinn said, frowning. 'I go on my way with Cara, Erelas goes back to his life as a Conductor, and what happens to you and Renn? When the sheriff realises I'm long gone, who is left to pay for it?'

Aliena fell silent.

'We could run away, too!' said Renn, as if it would be an adventure.

'That's no kind of life to lead for someone as young as you, Renn,' said Erelas. 'You've had to grow up fast, and you've been exceptionally brave, but you would not want to be constantly in fear of capture, while not having a bed to sleep in, or a hot meal inside you.'

'But you live like that, don't you?'

'No – it's not the same. Conductors do live their lives travelling around almost all of the time, but we are generally relaxed and happy; we're not being chased around by people who want to hurt us. And we can provide for ourselves and go home to a bed when we need to.'

Renn looked disappointed. 'Then what are we going to do?'

'I'm going to remove the problem,' said Quinn, standing up.

'Quinn, you don't know that killing the sheriff *will* remove the problem,' said Aliena. 'How do you know that whoever Mattias puts in his place won't be just as bad? And besides that, killing him will be another crime against your name that the king will want to punish you for!'

'Punish *me*, yes. Not you and Renn. You'd be safe. You already have the king's word on that. I'll take my chances on a new sheriff. I can't allow this one to get away with what he's done.' He walked over and started to scratch Cara's cheek. 'I'm going – and it's not up for discussion.'

Aliena exhaled sharply, but said nothing.

'You will need help – and that's not up for discussion, either,' said Erelas.

'I was counting on your help, my friend.' Quinn looked at Erelas, his expression softening for a moment.

'And what about *us*?' asked Aliena.

'You stay here,' said Quinn, studying a smear of mud on the mare's neck.

'Don't tell me – that's not up for discussion?' Her tone made him look up, and her face said it all.

But Quinn would not be swayed. 'It's not going to be like before, Aliena. When we went to the castle last night, nobody knew we were coming. Now, *everyone* is going to be waiting for us – or at least for me. It's too dangerous for you and Renn. It's not safe for you at the farm, either. You have to stay *here*.'

Aliena knew she could not argue with his logic, but she decided that did not mean she had to like it. She turned back to the flames without replying.

'So...' Erelas said, stopping his pacing and joining Quinn at Cara's side. 'Do you have any idea how we are going to do this? How are we going to even get in this time?'

'I doubt it would be wise to use either way in that we used last night. I'm still thinking about that.'

'I could try making an opening in the wall?'

'Well, you would have more luck than I

would. I'm not trying that one again.'

'When are we going?' Erelas asked, ignoring Quinn's self-reproach.

'As soon as it's dark. And properly dark, this time. He's probably been waiting for me since...' Quinn stopped, glancing at Aliena, but she did not look around. 'So the cover will give us a little help, and we will need all the help we can get.'

'You mean as soon as it's dark, *tonight*?' Erelas said. 'Quinn, I don't think you're strong enough yet.'

'If we leave it any longer, Garin will think I'm not taking the bait and he will have everyone out looking for me. I would have gone last night—'

'Yes, well...last night you'd have fallen off Cara before you even got out of the forest. Tonight you might stay in the saddle until you reach the gate tower.'

'Erelas...'

'You aren't at full strength, Quinn. We are short of decent weapons. We only have my sword and Aliena's knife. There will be only two of us against who knows how many Guardsmen and, although I hate to rub salt in the wound, your abilities are hardly reliable. Not only do they go wrong a lot of the time, you are wiped out just from attempting it.'

'I know that—'

'You get one chance at this!'

'I know that, too!' Quinn felt his rage building up, an outward reflection of his inner disgust at his weaknesses. He fought to control it. None of it was the fault of his friend.

'Then why not wait until the guards do start looking for you? You can track down the sheriff and get him when he's got far less support behind him.'

'Because it might not give us much of an advantage. What do Aliena and Renn do in the meantime? Sit in this clearing with us, while we drive each other mad arguing about whether it's time to go or not?'

'Beats watching you fall off your horse.'

Cara snorted and Renn laughed, making Aliena look around, drawn from her reverie. Erelas raised his eyebrow at Quinn, stifling a smile, but Quinn just shook his head and turned away, going to Cara's saddle and retrieving the knife for her feet.

'I'm going tonight, Erelas. Preferably with you, but alone if I must.'

Erelas sighed. 'By *God*, you're stubborn. Alright. Tonight it is, then. But at least let me go back to Delmoril for your sword. You'll need its power.'

Quinn looked up sharply as he returned to Cara. 'Won't that raise a few questions? Nobody is supposed to think you are doing anything other than travelling around, conducting. If the Archdeacon finds out you are helping me—'

'He won't. Anwenn will help me get it without being discovered. Besides, they didn't care that I stole your horse...'

Quinn finally showed a hint of a smile. 'I've been meaning to talk to you about that, too.' He thought for a moment and then nodded. 'Alright. But be careful. I wouldn't trust any of those scholars, either. Not one of them spoke up for me, even though half of Delmoril was on my side.' He sighed as the memory weighed him down further. 'I'm sorry…that's all irrelevant now.'

'More than half, Quinn,' Erelas said, patting him on the shoulder. 'I will be careful. But I need to steal your horse again.'

'Cara,' Quinn said to the mare. 'Make sure he falls off…'

CHAPTER 50. GOOD NEWS

Cara thundered into the clearing and skidded to a halt in the centre, sweating and snorting from exertion and swishing her long, black tail. Impatient for Erelas to dismount and take off her saddle, she shifted her weight between her feet, scuffing up dry bark and twigs among the carpet of decaying leaves.

Renn had been dozing, sitting back against Aliena, who was leaning against a tree, but they both looked up and smiled at the travellers' return. Quinn had been sitting alone, deep in thought, but had heard Cara's approach and was standing expectantly by the time they came into view. Aliena raised an eyebrow as she noticed him digging his nails into his palms, the muscles of his jaw tensing.

Erelas sprang from Cara's back and the horse stepped forward to nuzzle Quinn.

'I have some news for you, my friend,' Erelas said, smiling gently.

Quinn raised an eyebrow – he could not imagine how news for him from Delmoril could possibly be something to smile about. 'What is it?'

'Come and sit down,' Erelas said. 'Aliena, would you mind seeing to Cara, please?'

'Of course,' Aliena said, happy for something to do at last. She settled Renn back down on the mossy woodland floor and left him to sleep. All the excitement had worn the poor child out.

While she tended to Cara's needs, Erelas took Quinn to the edge of the clearing and they sat down, backs against a wide oak tree. Quinn squinted a little as the low sun of the autumn morning fought its way through the reduced foliage. He also felt worn out and was secretly glad that they still had the afternoon to rest before returning to the castle that night.

'I saw Anwenn.'

'I assumed you would...'

'Well, there was no guarantee she was going to be there.'

'True. What happened? Are you two still—?'

'Oh, my news has nothing to do with me and her,' Erelas said, flushing a little. He did not like talking about his private life, even with his best friend.

'Erelas, the suspense is killing me.'

'It's about Galen.'

Quinn sat bolt upright and stared at Erelas. 'What did you say?'

'Let me start from the beginning. When I went to get your sword I managed to sneak in unseen by anyone and found Anwenn. She told me the Archdeacon was in a meeting with the scholars, so I relaxed a bit, and, knowing we weren't going to the castle until tonight, I thought I'd stay and explain to her what was happening with the sheriff – I know you trust her as much as I do.'

Quinn nodded, trying to remain patient. 'Anyway, she told me that on the day of your escape, she was called to conduct a man who had been killed at Castle Rivallen. She said that as she arrived, she saw someone running from the castle near the spot where she found the body. She said she thought it looked like you, but she couldn't be sure; she was too far away and thought perhaps it was her imagination. It wasn't until I told her how I'd caught up with you, she realised it must have been you…and then *I* realised the dead man must have been Galen.'

Quinn hardly dared hope…

'Galen *was* conducted, Quinn. I know you felt awful about leaving him like that, but you really had no choice. I'm very glad to be able to say that he was conducted and Anwenn is certain that he went to reward, not punishment.'

Quinn stared at Erelas' smile, unable to think of anything to say, doubtful that any words would have come out of his mouth in any case. His stomach hurt as if he had been thumped and his heart ached, but somehow he knew it was a feeling of total elation, manifesting itself in an odd way. It was completely overwhelming and he knew that Erelas understood when he simply touched his arm and got up, leaving him to digest the news.

He realised at that moment just how much the manner of Galen's death, and his inability to help his new friend's soul afterwards, had really affected him. All his life he had seen injustices, from the minor to the serious, but none had left such a feeling of anger, emptiness, guilt and utter helplessness as Galen's murder by his own nephew had. At that moment, he felt something close to joy – the closest he could feel under the circumstances – that Garin had not *won*.

Garin was a wicked and ungodly man. If he had any beliefs about God and the afterlife, he certainly did not let them affect his ambition or his policies. He had no human decency left, and Quinn felt sure that he would be feeling proud of sending his uncle to his death, to some sort of oblivion, or maybe in his own delusion, Garin believed Galen was destined for Hell.

Quinn had known right from the first time he had met Galen that his was a soul that belonged in Paradise. The thought of that compassionate, brave and gentle man ending up stranded in this world – confused, unable to communicate or reach out, unable to grasp the full extent of what had happened to him, or comprehend that this was where he would stay for all eternity – had wrenched Quinn's heart every day since his death.

Now he knew that Galen had passed over into eternal peace. Now, no matter how long Garin lived, Quinn knew that Galen's spiritual reward in the afterlife was in itself a kind of justice.

He drew in a deep shuddering breath, and only then noticed the tears streaming down his face. He had not blinked for a long time, and now he did, his eyes stung. He cupped his face in his hands and sobbed silently, grief and relief finally washing over him in equal measure.

As he wept for his friend, he said a silent prayer of thanks.

Then, finally, he said goodbye.

CHAPTER 51. BROTHERHOOD

Quinn had been silent and pensive for a long while after they had left the clearing, but suddenly he stopped leading Cara and looked at Erelas in the last of the twilight.

'Erelas,' he said. 'Are you alright with the knowledge that I am going to kill the sheriff?'

Erelas turned back, looking puzzled. 'What do you mean?'

'We're forbidden from taking lives. We're not even taught how to do it. If it were not for this...*evil*...inside of me, I would not have been able to do it. You haven't said anything about what I'm planning to do. Neither has Aliena, but she has lived in this chaos all her life and knows it's the only way to get justice for Elyan. I just wondered what your feelings are...'

'I'm surprised you didn't work that out from the fact that I'm going with you.'

'But does it not bother you? It's against everything we've been taught and, although I can blame my feelings on what happened to me, and on my desire to get justice and rid these people of this tyrant, it's not the same for you. It must feel sometimes as if you're watching all of this unfold from the outside, with no say in any of it. I don't want you to feel that way. You have every right to voice your opinion. I don't want you to feel uncomfortable with what I'm doing.'

'Quinn, we both know that if I voiced an opinion against this plan, you'd still do it anyway,' Erelas said with a wry smile. 'But as it happens, I'm *not* uncomfortable with it. I've given it a lot of thought today and I know there is no other way to guarantee the safety of these people, not just Aliena and Renn. You're going to be removing an evil from Rivallen that Rivallen does not seem to be able to remove for itself. It's not as if you are going around killing innocent people for no good reason. I want to see justice done too, and I want you all to have your lives back, even if your life has to continue here in Rivallen instead of in Delmoril.'

'If the Archdeacon ever finds out...'

'I don't see how he will. He's never been seen in Rivallen since that night with the Saloreans and nobody seems to know where he goes when he's not in Delmoril. Anwenn wouldn't breathe a word of anything I shared with her.'

Quinn conceded the point with a nod and then sighed. 'I wonder if I'll ever be able to relax when all of this is over. I'm finding it very hard to see a future for myself here. What can I possibly do among these people except look after their horses? And drag myself into their wars...' He laughed scornfully. 'I think I'm more afraid of *that* than I am of going through with this insane plan.'

'It will work out, Quinn. I have faith in you and in the gifts we were given. Even—' he added quickly, as Quinn was about to argue, '—even if yours are a little...*altered*. You will master them in time, I'm sure.'

'Just be careful, Erelas. Do not make yourself well-known here. It's enough that the king already knows about you, knows your face – if it ever gets out that you were involved in this, you'll be banished too. And that would break Anwenn's heart, as well as make me feel terrible for you. You don't want this life.'

'You're missing the good points about this life, Quinn.' Erelas smiled.

'Oh? What might they be?'

'Aliena, for one. I think you've been blinkered by everything that has happened here, my friend. That lady loves you.'

Quinn raised his eyebrow. 'Don't be ridiculous. She punched me in the face. That's hardly the way you treat someone you love.'

'I'm not so sure about that. She did that to Elyan, too.'

Quinn frowned, unsure if Erelas was being serious or just teasing him. 'Let's just concentrate on the task ahead, shall we?' he said, ignoring the grin spreading across his friend's face and the sudden hotness of his own.

'Stop *worrying*, will you? And stop worrying about me, most of all. I'm in this because I want to be. I can't let you get in to trouble all by yourself, can I? It goes against tradition.'

Quinn couldn't help laughing at that and

felt better. 'I couldn't do it without you, Erelas. I couldn't have done any of it without you.'

'I'm not sure I agree with that. You escaped the cells without me. But what else would I do? You're as good as a brother to me. Now, let's pick up the pace a bit, shall we? It's almost dark and we still have to go through this crazy plan one more time.' Erelas patted Quinn's arm and moved off.

'You'd steal my horse, that's what you'd do...' Quinn muttered after him, and smiled at Erelas' snort of amusement.

CHAPTER 52. TAKING THE BAIT

The air had a distinctly autumnal feel to it as they neared the castle. There was a breeze in the air that crept beneath Quinn's collar, cooling the sweat of anxiety on his skin and making him shiver. Erelas rubbed his arms periodically as they walked, guided by Cara, down the gently sloping land that would lead them to the moat.

The moonlight was weaker than the night before, a thin haze hampering its influence on the landscape and making their progress slower and more cautious than they had anticipated. Quinn had wanted to get to the relative cover afforded by the imposing castle walls as fast as possible, but now they were forced to walk carefully over the rock-strewn ground, with Cara picking out the safest path.

Neither man spoke as they went. They had been silent since leaving the forest, in case their voices carried and alerted the castle to their approach. They had already agreed upon where they were going to try to gain entry to the castle this time – they would find the narrow crossing Quinn had used before and then Erelas would use his abilities to get them in right there – through its wall. The ledge joined the castle almost at the point where a tower rose up, and they decided that would be the best place to force their way in as it was away from the postern gate, which they guessed would be heavily guarded this time, and out of sight of the battlements on the tops of the walls. They expected to end up in some kind of lower level store-room – if they were lucky – or the waste pit from a garderobe if they were not. If this plan failed, they would simply have to use the postern gate again and Erelas would use his skills to safely subdue the guards.

Once they were in, they would use an orb to lead them to Garin, dealing with guards along the way. The plan became a little thin at that point, but there were no guarantees here. They would have to think and act fast, whatever was in store for them…

Quinn was glad Erelas had offered to go back for his sword, but it would be hard to use such a weapon without lethal results. It, like all swords forged in Delmoril, could be wielded with powerful energy channelled from its owner. It could transfer searing heat down the blade of another sword, forcing the bearer to let go and, if knocked from a Conductor's grip, could be 'called' back into their hand with just one word. They could not be wielded by anyone but a Conductor, instantly rendering anyone attempting to do so unconscious for several hours. With two such swords, Quinn knew they started with a great advantage.

But, as with many things, it was a mixed blessing. Since the sword drew its power from the Conductors themselves, they could not use its special qualities for any length of time without wearing the bearer out. They would have mere moments to get past each guard and give themselves a chance to recover, or they would just have to fight with it as if it were any sword forged in Rivallen. Quinn did not think this would be a problem, but Erelas worried about how it would react to Quinn's altered powers, if they *did* need to use them. If a simple casting could, and did, go wrong, leaving him on his knees, what might a sword of Delmoril do to him and others when mingled with his flawed energies? He also doubted Quinn had recovered enough to best a guard without the advantage of the sword's special qualities...let alone several of them at once. He wished they could have waited at least one more day, but there had been no talking Quinn around.

There was nothing for it but to go ahead with the plan and worry about problems if they arose, adjusting the plan as they went, if necessary. But it did not stop their minds racing with every step they took towards the looming shadow that was the castle.

They left Cara as close to the castle as they dared and continued without her. She would wait for them in silence, until they returned, ready to spirit them back to the forest and relative safety. With her coat as black as a moonless night, she would not be seen against the silhouette of the bank of earth on this side of the castle and was too well trained to give away her own position by making a sound. Quinn had kissed her muzzle and she had nudged him gently, before he reluctantly left her comforting presence.

They swiftly made their way down to the edge of the moat and the cover of the reeds. Crouching low, hands on the hilts of their swords, they listened carefully for the positions of the guards on the ramparts high above them. In the darkness, Quinn tapped Erelas' arm twice and Erelas tapped Quinn's arm twice: they could both hear two guards. For a few long moments they waited, listening to see how long it took for the guards to make their passes and reach their respective ends of the rampart. Once they worked out their own position in relation to the guards', they made a move. Quinn led the way, knowing exactly where the crossing was. They moved without a sound, keeping low, careful to keep their weapons from bumping or scraping against anything. He gave a short whistle between his teeth, as the signal for Erelas to stop when he had reached the crossing; if he had been heard from above, which was very unlikely from that height, the guards would just believe it had been a night-foraging bird.

They waited again, checking the guards' routine pacing had not altered, before making their way across the moat.

They were now on even more dangerous ground. Quinn had warned Erelas that the ledge had been very slippery. Even the knowledge that they did not have to move along it very far before reaching the tower did not erase the fear of losing their footing while they forced an opening in the tower. Erelas could not guarantee that the casting would be completely invisible or noiseless, either, so once they had made their entrance they would need to move fast. Worse still, if they had picked the wrong spot in the tower wall, they would have to move along and do it all over again. There was so much scope for it to all go horribly wrong.

Quinn slowly drew his sword and stood still, hardly daring to breathe, as Erelas approached the wall and spread his hands in front of him in the darkness. This was it. The biggest battle of their lives was about to begin.

***

The orb glowed with alarming brightness as they looked around the small food store. Erelas pondered trying to hide the hole he had created as its light hovered near the low door, and Quinn strained to hear any noise from the corridor outside.

'He's close,' he whispered. 'I can sense him...'

'Isn't that a bit of a coincidence?' asked Erelas, joining his friend at the door, sword drawn.

'Maybe, but I'm not complaining. The less we have to run around this castle, the better it will be for everyone.'

Both listening for a few seconds more, they nodded simultaneously and Quinn reached for the door handle. Opening it as quietly as he could, he listened again, staying back so that the orb's light would not show along the passageway. Erelas carefully peered out, looking both ways and keeping low. Seeing the way was clear for them, he drew his head back in and gave Quinn another nod. They left the store together, closing the door behind them.

The orb moved to their right and Quinn realised that it was taking them in the direction of the cells. It was not a place he had any desire to see again, but the thought of Galen seemed to fire up a furnace in his heart. He grew impatient to have his own brand of revenge. His pace changed to match his sudden energy and Erelas was almost left behind. His senses were becoming sharper as the adrenaline and anger coursed through his body. His skin tingled with anticipation and he marched along the cold passage, guided only by the orb.

Erelas accelerated to catch up with him, and caught his arm. '*Wait*, Quinn!' he whispered with urgency.

Quinn looked at him, and Erelas could see by the light of the orb that the red sparks were starting to appear. Eyes wide, Erelas stood in front of him, blocking his path. 'Slow down...you need me in front, remember?'

Quinn stared for a moment, not seeming to understand. Then the realisation came upon him –

they needed Erelas' skills to clear their way. Leaning on his back foot, he placed a hand on Erelas' arm. 'Sorry. It's this place. This is taking us to the dungeon tower. I got angry thinking of Galen.'

'You need to stay focused.'

Quinn nodded and took a deep breath. He gestured for Erelas to lead the way and glanced behind them as they set off again. The orb slowed, no longer pushed by Quinn's impatient stride.

It was not long before Erelas threw his hand out and signalled for Quinn to stop. They stood and listened for a few moments.

A chilly draught blew down the passage, bringing with it the unmistakable sound of a child crying. Within moments, it was followed by a gruff voice. 'Quiet!' the unseen man said, but the child still cried. It was the sound of a grief too potent to be brought under control so easily. Erelas and Quinn were concerned that a child should be in this gloomy, cold and unclean section of the castle at all…

Moving cautiously forwards, Erelas began to whisper the words of the casting he had used the last time they were at the castle, pinned down by guards. The shock wave and flash of light pulsed out from his hand, travelling at a speed that made it almost impossible to track with their eyes. A moment after it vanished around a corner, the clatter of an armour-clad body falling to the ground reached their ears.

Erelas and Quinn rushed forwards, racing

around the corner to where a weak torch on the wall barely lit up the area. The unconscious guard lay sprawled in front of the iron gate of a single cell. To the left of the guard was a closed door and Quinn knew it led upwards, to more cells. One of those cells was the one he and Galen had been in and he wondered if it still had the hole in the wall. Other parts of the castle could also be reached through the door – he remembered that from when he had been marched along it with an arrowhead sticking in his shoulder.

Erelas was looking in through the iron gate as Quinn was lost in his thoughts. '*Quinn!*' he whispered, a panicked edge to his voice.

Quinn followed Erelas' gaze. Locked in the tiny, dark cell, wearing filthy, wet clothes, sat Toren, Prince of Rivallen, who had stopped crying in surprise at the guard's collapse. When he recognised the two men, the only heir to the throne scrambled to his feet and rushed to the gate. His small hands grasped the cruel bars tightly, but the rest of his body shook with cold and fright.

'*Please*, you have to help us!' he cried.

Erelas put a finger to his lips. '*Shh*! It's alright now. What is going on?'

'The sheriff has taken Father somewhere! He said he's going to *kill* him...' Toren said, his voice a little lower. He pointed at Quinn and said, 'And *you* are going to get the blame!'

The Conductors looked at each other in horror. Neither of them expected anything like this.

It occurred to Quinn that they had been so focused on getting to Garin, they had not given any thought to the king's whereabouts. They had not planned to have anything to say to him until after their task had been done.

'Erelas, he cannot stay here. Take him some place safe, here in the castle. I will find Garin with the orb and come and find you when it is safe for the boy.'

'You cannot go *alone*, Quinn!' Erelas no longer worried about the level of his voice. 'It's what he wants – you, against him and his guards!'

'Erelas, listen to me,' Quinn said, trying to keep calm himself, when a fury was building inside him. 'There is more at stake here now than just getting rid of the sheriff. Mattias is in danger, and so is his heir. You *must* keep him safe, no matter what. Can you imagine what will happen to the people of this land if Garin takes the throne for himself? Who will stand against him then? We must protect the *kingdom*!'

Erelas stared, paralysed and desperate to find a way to avoid letting Quinn go on without him. This was nothing like any of the scenarios they had envisaged. But he knew Quinn was right. All would be lost if Garin took power...

'Please, Erelas. Take the prince somewhere and hide him. I will come and find you as soon as I can.'

'Just be *careful*, Quinn. Garin will have you exactly where he wants you.'

'And he'll be exactly where I want him. I only need him in the same room.'

'Will you save my father?' asked Toren. His dirty face was moistened by fresh tears as Erelas unlocked the gate with the guard's keys.

Quinn bent down until he was at eye level with the boy as he emerged from the cell. Placing a hand gently on each arm, he said, 'I swear I will do *everything* I can for him. Go with Erelas...you will be safe.' He stood back a little way as Erelas opened the door and checked the passage outside it for more guards. When he saw the way ahead was clear, he ushered the prince through it, glancing one last time at his friend. His eyes pleaded with Quinn again.

Quinn whispered: 'It will be alright, Erelas.'

Erelas gave a slight nod in unconvinced agreement and was then gone, heading away from the dungeon tower.

After listening for a moment or two, Quinn moved out of the door and into the same passage. But the orb, instead of following Erelas, moved upwards and to the right, towards the stone staircase that led to the cells above. The last place Quinn wanted to see again.

With his sword tightly gripped in his right hand, he began to climb the steps.

CHAPTER 53. ASSASSIN

As Quinn climbed the steep staircase, his mind went through a momentary wash of panic. He had no idea what he was facing, or what exactly he would do. He also had no time to think it over.

Galen and Elyan, he thought. *Just think of them and that will get me through.*

He saw a dim, orange light from above and slowed his ascent, listening. He could hear nothing, which was in itself suspicious. Where were the guards? He wondered grimly if Garin somehow knew that he had arrived and was waiting quietly for Quinn to come for him.

As he neared the top, he heard the soft whimper of a man, the quivering weakness of the voice clearly from one who was very afraid indeed. Mattias. Quinn squeezed his eyes shut in a swift prayer and then pressed on, gathering the fire in his heart and reminding himself of all that had happened to him at the hands of the sheriff. As the vision of Elyan's dying eyes flashed through his mind, he felt the heat of his anger rising up and it urged him over the top step and into the light of a single torch. In front of him was the cell, the gate wide open, but it was empty, save for a scampering rat which squeaked in alarm before reaching the safety of a small hole in the damp stonework.

'I am up here, Quinn,' came the deep, leering voice of Garin.

Quinn slowly turned and saw the next flight of steps that would lead him up to his old cell. He felt suddenly sick, but he allowed the anger in his soul to push that feeling aside and, with his sword raised and pointed forwards, he began the climb to whatever future awaited him.

As he climbed the last step and peered around into the cell, the breeze from the hole in the wall hit his face. He saw, in the stuttering light of the torch, the elegantly-robed king standing in front of Garin, who was dressed as ever in his appropriate black clothes and boots. Still pointing the sword straight at the sheriff, Quinn assessed the scene before him.

Garin had one arm around the king's shoulders and, being the taller man, was having no difficulty holding on to him, while keeping his gleaming, gold-handled dagger at his throat. Mattias had stopped making any noise as soon as Garin had called Quinn up and now stared, terrified, at Quinn, his brown eyes begging for help. Quinn did not react to him and looked directly at Garin, whose self-satisfied sneer brought Quinn's anger to the point of erupting at any moment. He gripped his sword with both hands and held it in front of his body, fighting to control the rage that made him shake. He had to get the king to safety first...

'Good to see you again, Quinn!' declared

Garin, a smirk giving his face a crazed aspect. 'I was beginning to think you had lost interest in – what was it – "personally escorting" me to Hell?'

'The trouble is, Garin, in Hell you would still *exist*. I think I'll let the Guardians destroy you, instead.' Quinn's voice was low and steady, despite how his body felt.

'The Guardians? And what are *they*, exactly?'

'Something beyond even your ideas of what evil is. Let the king go.'

'Oh, I'm afraid I can't do that. You and the king feature very prominently in my plans. You are going to kill the king. At least, that's what everyone will *think*. With him dead and the prince too young to rule…as High Sheriff, the task naturally falls to me to rule as regent.'

'What then?' asked Quinn, taking a step sideways, further into the cell. He was now only a few feet from the sheriff, but with no clear target to aim for, he held the sword still. 'You kill the prince?'

The sheriff feigned thoughtfulness before he replied. 'That's a good idea. The poor, traumatised child is *bound* to come out with all sorts of crazy tales about how his dear father died. Best to deal with him now, while I can have you blamed for that, as well.'

Mattias tried to struggle, but was held fast. 'You leave my son alone, or *God help me*—'

'God is not helping you much so far, is

he?' Before Quinn had any chance to react, Garin slashed wildly with the dagger and opened the king's throat. Blood flew into Quinn's eyes, but he wiped them quickly with one hand, keeping the sword raised to protect himself, as Garin dropped the king's body to the floor with a look of distaste and stepped over it.

With just the sword's length between them, they stared at one another, Quinn in shock, Garin in unconcealed pleasure at the reaction he had provoked.

'There,' he said mildly. 'The wicked deed is done. Quinn, the traitor – and now the king's assassin – has sealed his fate. How does it feel?' Without waiting for an answer, he shouted, '*Guards*!'

Quinn felt himself being grabbed by the arms and hauled backwards. He thought they must have appeared from the dark corner behind him, where Galen used to sit...Quinn had forgotten how big this cell was.

Fighting back with all the rage he could muster, he threw his sword arm forwards, dislodging the grip the guard had on it. Spinning wildly, he swung his weapon, making contact with the other guard's arm, just above the elbow. The guard screamed as his arm was severed and he staggered back against the wall and collapsed. Quinn quickly turned his attention to the first guard, who had recovered his wits and drawn his own weapon. As the guard swung, Quinn gripped the blunt section of the blade of his sword and pushed it forwards with both hands, meeting the attack face-on. The blades clashed and instantly Quinn's sword began to glow bright orange, intense heat being conducted across to the guard's blade. The guard yelped in surprise as the handle burned and he dropped the sword, stepping back, unsure of what his next move should be.

Quinn felt suddenly very dizzy, the effect of using his energy through the sword rendering him weak and making him lose his coordination. The tiny side-step he made to correct his balance was not missed by the sheriff and before Quinn could properly right himself and get into a defensive position, Garin seized him by his right arm. Quinn saw a glint of light reflected from the blade of the dagger and a searing pain, as his wrist was sliced into, forcing him to drop his sword. He let out a shout of pain and tried to wrench himself away, but Garin was prepared. He viciously kicked Quinn in the side of his right knee and Quinn went down, holding his breath at the shock of the intense pain it caused him. Landing on his front on the dusty floor, he could only lie there and watch the blood oozing from his wrist, as the sheriff knelt down on his back and held the blade to the side of his throat.

'Now you have provided more proof to help me convince the people that you're a violent murderer, shall we get down to the business of your death?' Garin said, his perpetually mocking tone rankling every nerve of Quinn's.

Red sparks began to dance in Quinn's eyes

and he welcomed the rush of rage that began to wash over him. Waiting patiently for the sheriff's next move, he gathered his thoughts and fought to control it – he did not have much time, but he did not have much strength left, either. He would need to pick his moment with care, not passion...

CHAPTER 54. TORTURE

Erelas had ushered Toren along two poorly-lit passages, unsure of where he was supposed to go. The prince seemed to decide for him after the first passage, picking up his pace and appearing be less scared. Erelas ended up following rather than guiding him.

Eventually they came to a door that the prince gestured towards. Listening for any signs of life on the other side, Erelas opened it outwards and found that they were in the corner of the courtyard that contained the stables. Looking around for guards, but finding none, Erelas decided that they should make a break for one of the stalls.

Once in, Toren immediately ran to the far corner and forced himself into it as far as he was able, pulling up clean straw in an attempt to hide himself further. Erelas had to stay in the shadows behind the black mare, who did not seem alarmed by their sudden intrusion.

There they waited, and while the boy was content to stay where he was, in the dark, warm stable with any view of him obscured by a large horse, Erelas felt restless. Every fibre in him felt it was wrong to have left Quinn to face the sheriff alone – even though Quinn had been right about the future of the kingdom. There was nothing he could do except wait for Quinn to do what he had to do and then come and find them.

Unless...

Erelas crept to the back of the stall and crouched down in front of the boy. 'You trust me, don't you?' he whispered.

The prince nodded. 'I need to go and help my friend to help your father. I need you to stay *right here*. No matter what you see or hear from anywhere or anyone, *do not* leave this stall. We don't know who we can trust right now, so right now we trust *nobody* but each other. Do you understand?'

Toren nodded again.

'Good. This mare will look after you; she's a kind horse. Quinn has one just like her.' Erelas smiled. 'Stay here, remember. And not a sound. You've been *really* brave so far – can you keep it up for me?'

The boy nodded a third time.

'I will be back for you, I swear to our Holy Father.'

***

Two more guards arrived and Garin stood up, making way for them to drag the prisoner to his feet.

Quinn's knee seared with pain and he knew walking anywhere was now out of the question, let alone running. He was trapped again, in the same cell as before, at the mercy of the sheriff once more. As the guards held him upright and Garin slowly walked around him, smiling in his ugly, sinister way, Quinn could do nothing but drip blood on the floor and pray that Erelas and Toren were safe. There was only one thing left to do now...

'Chain him up!' Garin barked, making Quinn flinch.

He did nothing to resist them as they fastened the chains to his wrists, not bothering with the chains for his legs. They knew he was in no state to go anywhere now. One of them cut off Quinn's shirt and threw it to the floor and Quinn noticed how much colder the breeze had become.

'Now, leave us,' Garin said. Gesturing to the injured guard with a disgusted grimace on his face, he added: 'And take *that* with you.'

The guards obeyed and the unconscious guard was dragged between two of them out of the door and down the stairs, leaving the bloody severed arm on the floor. The fourth guard followed, cradling his burned hand in the crook of his elbow.

Quinn was now hanging, helpless, with his arms raised up, the cuff biting into his slashed wrist and blood trickling back down his arm all the way to his waist. He felt weakened, but his fire was still rising and he was almost ready.

'How was Aliena, considering you murdered her brother?'

The question caught Quinn off guard and he snapped his mouth shut to avoid saying the wrong thing. His eyes stung and Garin frowned.

'Oh! I see that is a topic you don't really wish to talk about! Did she cry? Did she try to kill you? He laughed. 'Perhaps when tonight is over I will go and pay her a visit. Offer my *condolences* for her loss.'

Quinn fought desperately to control the rage inside him, knowing the sheriff was deliberately goading him into losing his temper. He could not guess at why Garin would want that. Did he want a demonstration of Quinn's power? Was it a way to weaken him further before he was finally killed? Whatever the reason, he could not allow it to happen. He needed the right moment and enough time to say what he needed to say, before he brought everything to an end once and for all.

Garin walked up to him, standing so close that Quinn could smell his foul breath again. He ran the tip of the knife down Quinn's throat and down his chest, stopping over Quinn's heart. Slowly raising the handle so that it was ready to be plunged straight in, he looked into Quinn's eyes for a moment, then laughed again. 'No – that would be *far* too quick for you.' His expression changed to one of undisguised malice. He moved the knife down further, increasing the pressure until the point broke Quinn's skin and drew a thin line of blood.

Quinn gritted his teeth, praying that whatever Garin did, it would not injure him so much that he was too weak to do what he needed to do. The knife was now directly under the last rib on his left side. He held his breath, not taking his eyes from the sparkling malevolence that was radiating out from Garin's own. He knew that this man had to be destroyed; evil of this magnitude must not be allowed to continue living in this world. He just needed the right amount of time and space – he needed the man to move.

Garin flicked an eyebrow up, as if he was wondering why Quinn had nothing to say, preferring to simply glare at him in defiance. Then he gave a little shrug and pushed against the knife. Slowly, agonisingly slowly, the knife sank deeper into Quinn's flesh, until he could not help but scream in pain and rage. Then it became so unbearable that his voice seemed to be cut off completely and he could no longer breathe. His wide eyes flashed with blue and red sparks as Garin stared, fascinated, clearly drawing pleasure from Quinn's suffering.

Suddenly Quinn retched, the spasm throwing blood up into his mouth and even out of his nose. He could not help but cough, spraying the blood over the sheriff's face. Then he tried to catch his breath, but only managed tiny snatches of precious air, the pain just too great for any significant movement.

Garin seemed undisturbed by the blood on his face. Still staring at Quinn's glowing eyes, he gave one final push on the knife, making him cry out again, before letting go and backing away, leaving the weapon buried in his flesh, right up to the hilt. He walked slowly around the cell, making his way towards the body of the king.

Through the fog of pain and anger, Quinn knew he had to carry out his plan right now – he would have just enough time to say what he needed to before the sheriff had a chance to rush back over to him and stab him in the heart.

It was time to finish it.

CHAPTER 55. SACRIFICE

Erelas sneaked back through the courtyard door and heard a scream that turned his blood to ice as he closed it behind him. Gripped with panic, he moved as quickly and as quietly as he could down the long passage. He paused to listen at the bottom of the first flight of steps. Hearing nothing further, he began to climb...

He had taken only two steps when there was a huge explosion from somewhere above him. A blinding flash of orange destroyed the shadows for an instant and he was thrown backwards by the shock wave travelling down through the narrow, winding staircase. He picked himself up, dazed, deafened and with a high-pitched ringing in his ears. The air was thick with dust and smoke, and it took him some time to stop coughing enough to move further. The torch had been blown out and he could not even see his hand in front of his face.

Long, icy talons of fear gripped his stomach and relentlessly squeezed the hope out of him, as he realised what the magnitude of the explosion must have been like to anyone caught in the same room. He staggered as he felt for the wall, desperately trying to call up an orb, but it would not come.

As soon as he found the steps, as fast as his shock-weakened legs would take him, he began to climb through the darkness, terrified of what he might find when he reached the source of the blast.

Oh, Quinn, he thought. *What have you done?*

***

Erelas reached the scene of the blast, coughing more dust from his lungs. It was still impossible to see anything and he had had to feel his way up the steps until he started falling over blocks of stone that should not have been there. He knew he'd reached the right level.

'*Quinn!*' he shouted, then coughed again.

No reply.

Again Erelas tried to summon an orb, but something was stopping him from using his power. He prayed it was just the shock of the blast and that he would not be affected for long. Quinn might need it.

He heard footsteps approaching from behind him on the staircase and, as he turned, light became visible. In a few moments, a guard appeared, carrying a torch. He did not see Erelas until it was too late. The guard cried out in surprise as Erelas simultaneously snatched the torch from him and hit him in the face with the hilt of his sword.

'Thank you!' he called, as the stunned guard tumbled back down the staircase. He did not get up again.

Erelas knew he had to be quick. More guards – many more – would soon make their way here. He had to find Quinn and try to get him to safety before they were overrun.

The torch did its best through the thick dust and lingering smoke, but it still took Erelas a while to get his bearings. Almost all of the outer part of the tower wall had collapsed into the cell and some of the roof had come down with it. Tiles, stones and timbers littered the floor, slowly being covered by the fine dust. The breeze was doing a poor job of clearing it and seemed to just stir up more as Erelas looked around desperately for his friend.

The centre part of the broken section had the largest pile of rubble and Erelas gasped as he saw a bloodied hand sticking out from the bottom of it. The dread lasted only a moment, as he looked closer and saw an expensive ring and the cuff of a black sleeve. Garin. Pushing a timber away from the sheriff's face, he was met with a grimly disfigured corpse: his skull had been crushed and the pressure inside had caused one of his black eyes to protrude alarmingly from its socket. His lips were split and bloody, his teeth were snapped and more blood and matter plopped into the rubble under him. Erelas turned away, both satisfied and disgusted, then kept looking for the only man who mattered to him.

Moving around to one side, he spotted some thick chains that had broken free of the wall they had been attached to and were strewn over and under more stones and timbers. He saw all the blood and knew, bile rising in his throat.

Propping the torch against some rubble, he bent down and placed his sword on the floor. Gently moving some of the stones and one large timber, he found what he was both looking for and dreading to find.

'Quinn...' he said, fear tightening his throat as he hurriedly cleared more of the debris. 'Oh, don't you *dare* have the nerve to be dead!'

The majority of the blood was seeping from a wound around a short dagger, which was stuck in Quinn's side, just under his ribcage. His wrist was also bleeding; his arm – still in the chains – was stretched over his head and the blood was soaking into his hair. His hands bore scorch marks, a sign to Erelas that whatever had happened here, it was down to Quinn's flawed energies. All over his body there were scratches and bruises from the rubble of the fallen tower landing on him. His breathing came in rapid, shallow gasps, interspersed by attempts to hold it in to avoid the pain it gave him. As he felt Erelas' movements beside him, he dared to move his head and Erelas saw the blood coming from the other side of it, where he had fallen on to the sharp corner of a piece of shattered stone.

It looked utterly hopeless to Erelas – and Quinn seemed to know it, too. He lifted his arm from behind his head, groaning softly, and then reached for Erelas' hand. As Erelas took it, he tightened his grip to stop it from slipping, as covered in blood as it was.

'The prince...' Quinn whispered.

'Safe. Hidden.' Erelas tried to keep the emotion from his voice. 'What happened?'

'He is the king now. Tell him I'm sorry. There was nothing I could do.'

Erelas frowned, gritting his teeth and breathing in through his nose to fight back the tears. 'What *did* you do?'

'Removed the problem...' Quinn closed his eyes and took a shuddering breath against his pain.

'But – like *this*?'

'No choice,' Quinn said, moving his arm and indicating the chains. 'I managed to cast when he had stepped away from me, but he'd already stabbed me.' Quinn swallowed, trying not to cough.

'And then what happened?'

Quinn looked at his friend, tears stinging his eyes. 'I'm not sure...the rage must have affected the energy, I think. The chains broke and the next thing I know there was the explosion...it came from me. I don't know how...I thought I was weak.'

'Alright, don't worry about it now...' Erelas ran out of words as Quinn closed his eyes again, exhausted. He did not know what to do. The guards would be on them in moments and he had no power to stop them. He would not be able to fight them all, either – even if he had wanted to let go of Quinn's hand.

His mind did not want to accept what his eyes could clearly see, but he was suddenly forced to when his amulet began to glow. It could have easily been for the king or the sheriff, but Quinn's fate was the only one on Erelas' mind at that moment. At his sharp intake of breath, Quinn opened his eyes and saw it too. He frowned, looking at Erelas, then gripped his hand tighter.

'Erelas...I'm alright with it,' he said, speaking slowly and resting often to catch his breath. 'I did what I came to do; Garin is gone, Aliena is safe...I've got justice for Elyan and Galen. The prince – and Renn – will be safe now, too. So I'm alright with it. I need *you* to be, too...'

Erelas took a moment to grasp what he was saying and a wave of despair passed over his face. He shook his head, blinking hard, once, twice – desperate to not break down. 'I...I can't...' he said, his voice barely functioning. 'This is not *right* –'

'I am torn, Erelas, between not wanting to put you through it and not wanting it to be anyone else – if there *were* anyone else.'

Erelas could not stop the tears from falling any longer and bowed his head.

'At least we get to say goodbye this time...' Quinn whispered after a few moments.

Erelas looked up and saw that Quinn was fading. Completely incapable of saying anything or doing anything, he could only watch helplessly, his heart feeling as if it were being crushed, as the body his friend of so many years slowly gave up the fight they both knew he could not win. With a slight smile that seemed partly apologetic and partly reassuring, Quinn's eyes slowly closed and a single tear escaped to trickle slowly across his temple. His hand lost all its grip. He was gone.

But Erelas held on, his breath trapped inside his lungs for fear his heart might burst. He was not about to give up just yet. He reached into his tunic and pulled out the page he had torn from a book and kept hidden there since his return from Delmoril. Still gripping Quinn's lifeless hand, the congealing blood now sticking them together, he flapped the folded paper open and held it in front of his face, close enough to be able to read the spidery script in the dim glow of the torch.

The approach of guards up the staircase forced him to look away before he could begin and in a panic he looked towards the sound. He did not pick up his sword – there would be no sense in trying to fight them off alone.

Two guards appeared, both with torches. They took in the scene of devastation before them, swords drawn, but made no move towards Erelas and Quinn. Erelas held his breath again as they moved to the pile of rubble and the body which lay under it. One of the guards bent and placed his sword on the floor. Using both hands, he moved more of the stones to one side, exposing the disfigured and bloodied face of the sheriff further. Retrieving his sword, he stood up and turned, looking at Erelas, who felt sick with fear. He did not have time for this...

'Who did this?' the guard asked quietly.

Erelas looked at Quinn. 'Someone who has paid for it already.'

The guard came closer. Erelas tensed.

'Have no fear of me,' the guard said. 'I am loyal only to the crown. The other guards have told me the sheriff has murdered the king. Since Mattias was a weak ruler and allowed Garin free rein, we – in our *own* weakness – were forced to obey his orders. Indeed, many of my men have suffered, even been killed, for attempting to do otherwise. But *this*...' The guard gestured to the sheriff's body. 'This frees us from that threat.'

Erelas looked up at the guard. 'You have no quarrel with us? My friend was trying to protect the prince and someone very dear to him...' Erelas did not think he could go on without breaking down again, so he fell silent.

'None. Is there something you need us to do?'

'Yes. I need you to *leave*. I'm sorry – I cannot explain. I need to do something and it is unwise for you to remain.'

'You're the people with magic, aren't you?' The guard's tone was one of curiosity, not suspicion or fear.

Erelas nodded. There was no sense in lying to them.

The guard looked at his comrade and then back at Erelas. 'We can do that. The king is beyond our help and the sheriff can rot there, for all we care. Do what you need to do. We will go and summon the remaining guard. We need to locate the prince.'

'Toren is safely hidden. I will take you to him when I have done what I need to do here. Will you trust me?'

The guard nodded again. 'Very well. We will wait in the courtyard for you.'

Erelas bowed his head in gratitude and the guards left.

Erelas took a moment to gather his courage again and then looked down at the paper. Praying hard that his power would work this time, before it was too late, he began to read aloud...

CHAPTER 56. A PRECIOUS SOUL

'Erelas.'

He jumped as if he had been zapped by his own energy. There had been no sign that the casting had worked; no flash of light, no fizz, no feeling in his veins. The Keeper was simply, suddenly, just there.

Erelas finally let go of Quinn's hand and stood up. After bowing in respect, he looked up as the Keeper stepped closer to him. The Keeper looked at Quinn and under the hood of his robes, Erelas could see the shock and sadness in his face.

'What happened here?' the Keeper asked in no more than a whisper.

Erelas swallowed. He had planned what he would say while travelling back from Delmoril – the inescapable fear that this very thing would need to be done never far from his thoughts since they had decided to go to the castle – but now, his words failed him and all he could do was stare at the Keeper.

The Keeper looked around, trying to understand. 'Who killed the king?'

'The sheriff, my lord.'

'And the sheriff?'

Erelas bit his lip. 'That was Quinn.'

'Where is the prince?'

'I hid him in the stables. He is safe.' Erelas swallowed again, then said: 'I *know* this looks bad for Quinn, my lord. I know he has taken another life – but he has saved *countless* others in doing so. The prince, Aliena, Renn. People in this kingdom no longer have to live in fear—'

'It is not Quinn's place to decide who should rule over this kingdom, Erelas.'

'I know that, my lord. That's not why this happened. Garin murdered the king and would have killed the prince too. He was locked in a cell on the lower levels. Garin wanted the throne for himself, with nobody to challenge him—'

The Keeper raised a hand and Erelas fell silent. 'I know why you have summoned me, Erelas. What I want to know, are the real reasons this has taken place – from Quinn's point of view.'

'My lord..?'

'Quinn is neither a political person, nor an ambitious one, and I am quite sure he did not have the future of the kingdom at the forefront of his mind...'

Erelas frowned, glancing down at Quinn's face – the face he had known for so long, but had never seen like this – helpless, lifeless...heartbreaking. 'The sheriff killed Aliena's brother and threatened her freedom and her safety. Quinn wanted to protect her and get justice for Elyan. When we arrived we found the prince was being held in a cell and Quinn came up here to try to rescue the king from the sheriff. It was *life* he was trying to protect, my lord.'

The Keeper nodded solemnly.

'Will you restore him?' Erelas looked almost taken aback by his own bold words and added quickly: 'I'm sorry, my lord, but you said you knew why I had summoned you. Quinn doesn't *deserve* to die. I had it all planned in my head: how I was going to plead for you to save him...' Erelas could barely speak anymore and the tears began to sting his eyes again. 'But the words just won't come.'

'They do not need to, Erelas.' The Keeper touched him on the shoulder. 'I can feel the plea in your heart. I will save him, if *God* wills it.'

Erelas lost the strength in his knees and slumped to the floor, bowing low in gratitude as the tears ran freely.

'Erelas, it seems as if the evil that was passed to Quinn has made his own power work against him, weakening him. He can no longer control it. Before the incident in the Plane of Shadows, this would not have happened. He was too strong and too skilled. One day he will be that way again.' The Keeper bent down in front of Quinn and looked into Erelas' silver eyes. 'Had he taken a life for selfish means, or for political gain, then I would not be able to intervene, and my own hopes for him would have been dashed. But sacrificing one's own life for the love of others is entirely different. It means that essentially, he is still the same Quinn. And because of that, he shall be restored.'

Erelas looked up, confused. 'Hopes? I do not understand, My lord. Is that what you meant when you told Quinn he was special?'

The Keeper paused thoughtfully. 'Something is happening in this world. Souls are being destroyed and we do not know how. It has been going on for some time and we have been powerless to act. But ever since Quinn was spared by the Guardians, we have known that something is different about him. As you know, Keepers never normally intervene in the lives of Conductors, but never before has a Guardian spared one of you – that is why we sent him home. God decided he should live then, I'm sure he wills the same now. His differences could aid us in our quest to discover the cause of all those souls being lost. He may be the solution. A solution which lives in his ability to take lives in the manner he does. We fear the foe we seek is no ordinary human...'

'But it has cost him his life – how can he possibly do it again?'

'He can be helped to control this new thread of power, in time. He must *unlearn* much of what he has learned as a Conductor. It will take time. Time which I will restore to him, if I am permitted. And not simply because we need him for our own purposes,' the Keeper added quickly, noticing the flash of emotion cross Erelas' face. 'As I said before...'

'"Some souls are too precious to be lost," '

finished Erelas. 'All I know is that the world is a far worse place without him in it.'

'That is why you rarely return to Delmoril?'

Erelas nodded, surprised that he, too, seemed to be being watched by the Keepers. 'I will continue to work, as before. But it is not *home* anymore, not without Quinn there.'

'I am sorry he was banished. But discipline must be maintained among Conductors. Sin must *never* be ignored.'

'Will he be punished for whatever actions he carries out on your behalf?'

'We transcend the laws of Man *and* the laws of the Archdeacon. He will operate above those, under our authority. *This* is the will of God. Quinn will become a soldier of Christ, in a way. Have no fear, Erelas.'

Erelas nodded, greatly relieved.

The Keeper stood up. 'Will you wait at the bottom of the tower?'

'Of course, my lord. And thank you…although that word seems so inadequate.'

'I can feel your soul, Erelas. No words are needed. Go in peace.' The Keeper placed his hand on Erelas' bowed head.

Erelas stood up and took one last look at the way Quinn was, wanting never to forget where his friend had forced himself to go for the sake of others, and then left the devastated tower.

CHAPTER 57. A NEW QUEST

Quinn's return to life was no gentle transition. It began with a violent gasp for air, followed by terrible, painful coughing that sprayed blood and made his throat feel as if it would tear open. He could not draw in his breath for what seemed like an age and neither could he open his eyes, as they stung with dust, blood and tears.

He felt a hand on his arm and tried to calm himself, even though he could not understand what was happening. He *knew* he had died; he had seen enough death in his life to know when it was inescapable. But this was not the Plane of Shadows, he was certain of that – and something told him that Erelas was not there. Panic gripped him as he wondered if he was already in eternal punishment...

Finally he was able to see a little and was shocked to discover he was still in the dark, dusty tower. A single point of light was somewhere behind him, but his head was in far too much pain to contemplate the slightest movement now that the coughing had subsided. He tried to see who was touching him, but they did not move and remained just outside his field of vision.

Pain began to grow all through his body, building up like a wave that did not seem to want to break, and at last he could not help but cry out. Then the hand touched his face and somehow he knew he would be alright and that he was safe. He tried to relax and after a few moments, the hand left him and the figure it belonged to moved into view. As he fought to accept the pain, he could barely believe who stood in front of him, holding the dagger that had been embedded in his flesh.

'Your eyes do not deceive you, Quinn. Please, do not be alarmed. I was summoned here to restore you.' The Keeper held out his free hand and when Quinn's shaking fingers grasped it, helped him to sit up.

Quinn could not avoid giving voice to his agony as he struggled to remain sitting upright and, as the Keeper put down the dagger and removed his cloak, he leaned away and vomited blood onto the stones he had just been laying on. The Keeper paused, waiting for Quinn to catch his breath again, then placed the heavy, black cloak over his trembling shoulders. Quinn bent his good leg and drew the foot under the thigh of the other one, regaining some balance. His sliced wrist lay limply on his thigh, while his scorched hand held the cloak around him. Wincing at the pain in his head, closed his eyes and waited. He knew the Keeper would explain in his own good time, and besides, trying to get even one question out was too difficult, let alone the dozens that where racing around in the fog of his mind.

'I must not remain here long,' said the

Keeper. 'But you must *listen* to me, Quinn – this is very important.'

Quinn opened his eyes and looked at the Keeper, who was crouching down in front of him. The look of concern on the Keeper's face made Quinn force himself to concentrate and ignore the pain and emotion he was feeling.

'I told you before that some souls are too precious to be lost. It alarms me that your *own* power is the cause of my being summoned. But you *are* special, Quinn. You *can* overcome these problems in time and we will help you to do so. You will become strong again – indeed, we are counting on it – and you. We know you sacrificed your life to protect others. That reassures us that you are the right person to take on what we need to ask of you – when you are strong again.'

'What is that, my lord?'

'There is an evil in this world. An evil far greater than you have faced this night.'

Quinn frowned, unable to grasp what the Keeper was trying to tell him.

'Something is destroying souls before they reach us. Recently, souls have been asking to be taken to members of their families when they reach us...to people who are not in the afterlife waiting for them, as they expect. It has been going on for some time, but it is only through *your* experiences that we have worked out how it may be happening – we believe a Conductor may be responsible...' The Keeper did not react to Quinn's expression of shock and disbelief. 'We cannot remain here long enough to find out where the evil lies – as you know, our bodies are not meant for this realm. We need you to discover who it is and put a stop to it. Another Conductor is clearly capable of taking a life, as you are. But we've been watching you long enough to already be certain of your innocence. Also, you were honourable enough to at least conduct the soul of Renn's father – these souls are being destroyed altogether. But...that does mean *you* are our only hope of stopping the one responsible.' The Keeper paused, allowing Quinn to try to take it all in. 'I know you are confused and I am sorry for that. But I have faith in you.'

'Because I'm the only Conductor on your side flawed enough to kill people,' Quinn said bitterly. He regretted his tone instantly, but the Keeper seemed to let it go.

'We knew something was different about you when the Guardians spared your life, Quinn. Your ability to kill was not apparent then. I am sorry I did not mention it when we last met, but it was not the appropriate time. You needed to deal with those events first. I was due to come to see you at the solstice – but I'm here now, thanks to Erelas.' The Keeper paused again. Quinn was tiring rapidly. 'You will come to terms with it all in time, Quinn, and not view it as a burden. For now, rest and heal yourself. I can only do so much for you.'

Quinn nodded. 'And I accept the gift gratefully, my lord. It is infinitely better than…' Unable to finish the sentence, Quinn merely looked into the Keeper's eyes.

The Keeper smiled and stood up. 'I don't think you will ever end up there, Quinn. Now – let me help you to the courtyard. Your friend is waiting.' 'Keeper…by summoning you, isn't Erelas going to be in trouble with the Archdeacon?'

'I do not think Erelas has any concerns about that, Quinn. In fact, I think he would willingly join you in your exile. He did the right thing to summon me, but there would be no sense in wasting energy convincing the Archdeacon of that. As far as I am concerned, he does not need to find out. Both of you have leave to summon me whenever you wish. Sadly, we cannot see much of what goes on here for ourselves. Expect me to visit regularly. I will keep an eye on you as best as I can.' The Keeper smiled again and held out his hand.

Vowing to accept the pain, no matter how bad, Quinn took it.

CHAPTER 58. TEARS OF REGRET

By the time they reached the courtyard Quinn had used up what little energy he'd had. He could not bear any weight on his injured leg and the other began to give out. Erelas rushed to help the Keeper lower him to the ground against a wall, his eyes wide at the Keeper's appearance in this very public setting.

Most of the castle's servants and all of the guards were gathered there, awaiting news of the prince. Erelas had refused to go and retrieve him until Quinn had returned, and there now seemed to be a collective sigh of relief that they would not have to wait much longer.

As Quinn was gently unwrapped from the Keeper's cloak and covered in warm blankets brought by a maid, the Keeper touched Erelas' arm.

'I must leave, now. He understands as much as he is expected to at this point. Summon me again when he has sufficiently recovered to hear more about what I have told him.'

Erelas bowed low and then looked up, his face a reflection of his relief. 'Thank you again, my lord.'

The Keeper bowed his head and disappeared back into the tower doorway, to keep the manner of his leaving hidden from the people.

Most were so eager to see the prince safe and well, they would forget the Keeper was ever there, let alone wonder where he had gone after entering the shattered tower.

Erelas bent down in front of Quinn and peered at him in the dim light. 'We need to get you to a warm bed and get you looked after.'

Quinn shook his head. 'Aliena and Renn are still out there with Cara...'

'They will be alright, Quinn. They cannot be found, even if there were any left who would want to harm them. They are perfectly safe until we can get you comfortable. And don't even *think* of arguing with me.'

Quinn gave up immediately, evidence of his precarious state. 'What is happening here?' he asked, shivering again.

'Apart from everyone wondering how you destroyed half of Castle Rivallen single-handed? The captain of the guard is going to address everyone once the prince has been told of the king's death. I will go and tell him shortly and bring him out. He will then be in the care of the captain and his personal servants, along with the captain's most trusted guards.'

'How do we know any of them can be trusted?' Quinn said weakly.

Erelas paused. 'We don't. But that is a risk that has to be taken. The kingdom is not our responsibility. I trust the captain. He was upstairs with me before I summoned the Keeper.'

Quinn looked at his friend with exhausted eyes and gave him a grateful smile. 'That took some nerve, Erelas.'

'My knees are still shaking. But no matter – it worked – we have you back.' Erelas bit back his emotions with some difficulty. 'Now, come on...you're going to a castle bedchamber, like it or not.'

'Vagrant to castle guest in such a short time. Even the Archdeacon would have to be impressed by that...'

***

Try as he might, Quinn could not stay awake to await the arrival of Aliena at the castle. He had even tried to focus his thoughts on the Keeper's revelations, but the pain and the physical and mental exhaustion overtook him within minutes of being settled into a large bed with heavy covers and thick pillows. He was not comfortable, by any means, and he was utterly filthy, but he was at least warm and could relax, knowing he was safe and would recover – in time.

Consequently, Aliena was able to sit with him for a long while before he awoke and found her there, which gave her a chance to weep as much as she needed to without him seeing her do so. She cried for him, and for the sacrifice he had made for her and for Elyan. She cried for Elyan and for the fact he would never know what Quinn had done for him. She cried as she wished the two of them could have been friends. She cried with her head on his chest, the steady rhythm of his heart reassuring her that he was strong enough to pull through and would not be lost to her again...

The realisation that she loved Quinn had been slow in coming. They had been thrown together by chance. Her desire to help those in need and his helplessness at the time had meant that theirs was a friendship that may never have happened under different circumstances – with him being a Soul Conductor, they would probably have never met at all.

But meet they had, and, being in close proximity to one another for several days with Quinn unable to leave, meant they had had a lot of time to talk. Although she had learned very little about him in real terms until his arrest at the farm, she had gleaned a considerable amount about his personality from their conversations and knew that he was a man of courage and honour and compassion. He had a dry sense of humour that appealed to her. He had an interest in many things, and their conversations, when he'd regained some strength, were lengthy and varied. She had enjoyed his company more than she realised.

The revelations of Elyan had shocked her to the core and everything that had happened since had forced her to re-evaluate him – but she knew now that even all of that had not changed her opinion of him. He was still a brave man who cared deeply for the safety of others and now, as she sat by his bed and looked at the blood, dirt and bruising that almost completely covered him, she knew that he would do anything – including die – to protect those he cared about.

She was only sorry that she had not realised the strength of her feelings for him and consequently had not told him how she felt before he had returned to the castle. She knew he was safe now, but the thought of losing him, without him ever knowing what he meant to her, made fresh tears spill from her tired eyes.

Erelas entered the room and she tried to wipe the tears away before he saw them, but he placed a comforting arm around her shoulder. She stood up and turned, and he held her close as she sobbed afresh.

'Is there nothing we can do to help him?' she asked finally, stepping away from his embrace.

Erelas shook his head solemnly. 'His injuries are severe, even the Keepers are limited in skills for such trauma in full-grown men. I can help him sleep and ease his pain a little, but what he needs most of all is time.'

'How long will he be like this?'

'Difficult to say. He should be healed from most of the injuries within a month, but I fear that knee is going to take much longer to recover.'

'Then how is he supposed to prepare for this task he's been set to?' Erelas had trusted her with the Keeper's disclosure, knowing Quinn would need every bit of support when the time came.

'With *patience*, Aliena. As must we.'

Aliena pursed her lips and Erelas knew what she was thinking. He touched her arm gently. 'There *is* nobody else.'

CHAPTER 59. ADJUSTMENT

It was dawn when Quinn finally awoke to a watery sunlight coming through the castle windows, making his eyes hurt. As he turned his head away, he saw Aliena looking at him, relief and concern in equal measure upon her tear-stained and tired face.

He was in far too much pain to manage to smile, but she saw the flicker of relief in his eyes as she took his hand gently in hers and kissed it.

'Before you ask,' she said, 'Renn is fine, and Cara is being bossy down at the royal stables. Renn is with the prince – he seems to be a great comfort to him at the moment.'

'He knows, then?' Quinn said weakly.

Aliena nodded. 'He didn't seem all that surprised. He heard the explosion. He knew you would not have set off anything like that if his father had still been alive in there. Poor child. But the captain of the guards is looking after him personally, with several other guards in attendance, along with his servant, a maid and Renn. The rest of the guard are busy rounding up the sheriff's few supporters. There will be some executions in the coming days, I think.'

'So the killing doesn't stop...' Quinn said, wincing as pain travelled around his awakening body.

'Shh. Don't worry about that now. I shouldn't have mentioned it. Just get better.'

'I'll be alright, Aliena.'

'I know. But I still end up looking after you, don't I?'

'Maybe I enjoy it.' Aliena feigned shock and then smiled. 'I may have to change that, then. I'll make you a really foul-tasting draught.'

Quinn finally managed a slight smile. 'Where is Erelas?'

'Delmoril.' At his look of puzzlement, Aliena quickly added: 'To see Anwenn. He is going to tell her that he will not be returning to Delmoril for a while. He told me to tell you that he isn't going to disclose any of what the Keeper spoke of. If a Conductor is involved...'

Quinn looked surprised. 'I thought he trusted Anwenn. They are getting *married*...'

Aliena shook her head. 'He is going to call it off, for now, at least. He doesn't know what reason he is going to give – he said he would think of something on the way, but he feels it would be wrong to go ahead with the wedding and then abandon her – and he absolutely will not abandon you.'

Quinn sighed and his eyes closed. Feeling her warm palm on his cheek, he opened them again and she saw the guilt in his eyes. 'This is not right, Aliena,' he said. 'So many lives have been torn apart already. He loves Anwenn and she loves him. They should not have to suffer...'

'Quinn, ask yourself where you would be if it Erelas was tasked with solving this...this "problem"?'

'Right by his side.'

'There you are, then. Let him be where he wants to be. You need him.'

He looked into her eyes for a moment longer, and then nodded slowly, before exhaustion took over and he sank back into a fitful doze.

***

'The dreams are the key.' Quinn winced as he shifted position, his knee the only part of him which still gave him severe pain three weeks after the events in the tower. 'I need something that can help me open them up further, get deeper into the memories of that man. He was working for someone – bringing them people, to be killed, I suspect. It's not much of a leap to conclude that this person and the one the Keeper spoke of are one and the same.'

'I'm not happy with that idea, Quinn,' said Erelas, pacing around the dimly-lit room of Aliena's farm. 'All through your recovery those dreams have plagued you, even interfered with your healing. I don't like to imagine what delving deeper into them might do to you.'

'I have no other ideas, Erelas. None of us do. The Keeper has made it clear he cannot help us more than he has already. They are unable to remain here for long enough to follow up on any clues and all they have given us are the names of people who have gone missing. It's down to us.'

'At least you're finally saying "us", instead of just you,' Aliena said, passing Quinn a bowl of steaming potage.

He gave her a wry smile as the three of them settled down to their meal.

The winter had drawn in and it was a hard one; the fire in the hearth and the hot food took the edge off the chill that permanently seeped through the little cottage, and Quinn was glad of both. Erelas had tried to persuade him to stay at Castle Rivallen, where he would have been more comfortable, but he had felt out of place and under too much scrutiny there. He was a curiosity, eyed with suspicion by some, outright fear by others and, worst of all, with a hint of reproach by the young King. The last thing Quinn needed on his long journey to health was a daily reminder that he had failed to protect the boy's father...

In the end, Aliena had consented to bring him back to her farm. She had not been back herself since before Elyan's death, and it had been a traumatic few days for her. But she had rallied, and set about caring for Quinn once more, with Erelas on hand to help run the farm and keep food on the table and logs on the fire.

Erelas himself had needed their support, too. He had returned from Delmoril in a crisis: things with Anwenn had gone disastrously wrong. He had been honest with her about spending time with Quinn, but would not reveal where they were going, or what they were doing next – not really knowing himself – and she had reacted badly. She had not ended their relationship completely, but said that she did not know whether it could continue when he returned if he could not be completely truthful with her. She admitted she resented Erelas choosing Quinn over her and he had snapped and accused her of behaving like a child. Quinn was lying in the castle at that time, his body a mass of pain and his mind filled with trauma, and she had resorted to immature ultimatums. He had reduced her to tears and returned to Quinn and Aliena under a dark cloud of churning emotions, unable to talk about it for several days. He eventually told Quinn that he couldn't see how they could ever be what they once had been, and that if their relationship had died, he would never return to Delmoril.

The farm kept him busy, kept him from brooding, but the others knew he was distraught – he and Anwenn had known each other for most of their lives and had been betrothed for more than three years. Their lives had been intertwined like threads in a tapestry and it was obvious he could not cope with it falling apart.

At least, with Quinn and Aliena there, and much to keep his thoughts occupied, Erelas could partially convince himself he had a new home at the farm.

It wasn't home to Quinn. He wasn't sure where that was anymore, but at least here he felt safe and he had the two people who mattered most to him alongside him on his new path.

Erelas finished eating first and as he set his bowl down, he said: 'So...do you have any idea *how* you are going to get deeper into the memories?'

Quinn shook his head. 'Not yet. I was hoping I would gradually see more and that was the case at first. But now I just seem to be in a rut with them. It's the same events, over and over.'

'I have an idea,' Aliena said. The men waited for her to continue. 'There's a woman. She lives in Kilora now, but she's from Rivallen, way over on the western side. I don't know how much of it is true, but it was said that she knew things she had never been told. People's *feelings*. They say she tames wolves because she can communicate with them somehow. Some people say it's nonsense, but others are really afraid of her, calling her a witch. That's why she left Rivallen. I was interested in her story because, as I said to you in the past, Quinn, I have to be careful that someone doesn't decide that I am practising some kind of witchcraft. But I could never find more out than just rumours. It may not be much of an idea if she turns out to be just a crazy old lady, but it's worth finding out, isn't it?'

Erelas shuddered. 'Wolves,' he muttered. 'I hate wolves.'

'Erelas was chased by a wolf pup when he was a mere pup himself,' Quinn explained, a glint in his eye. 'He's never forgiven the entire species...'

'It wasn't the chase that bothered me! Those teeth were damned sharp!'

'You shouldn't have allowed yourself to be caught, Erelas. Too much good living, was it?'

'If you weren't already in pain, I'd inflict some on you for that,' Erelas said, a grin escaping as he stood up and placed more logs on the fire.

'Children, children,' laughed Aliena. 'It's time we got on with the day. Erelas, I will go to market this morning, since Quinn wants to try walking around a bit again. God knows I can't hold him up if he falls, so he needs you.'

'Too much good living, Quinn?' Erelas teased.

Quinn's mouth dropped open in mock offence and he laughed. It was a sound his companions had longed to hear, and they prepared for their day with a little more hope.

CHAPTER 60. THE SOLITUDE OF SELF-REPROACH

In spite of those precious moments, two months after he had faced the sheriff, Quinn still felt tormented inside. He felt as if he had made very little progress and was far from ready to take on any kind of task for the Keepers who had such faith in him.

Physically, he was recovering reasonably well, although his knee still caused him considerable pain after a hard day's training, or too long in the saddle. He had begun training as soon as he was able to walk again and Erelas was there to help and encourage him. It had been slow going at first, but his natural strength soon returned and helped him to hone his sword skills again. He even felt confident he could defend himself without a weapon.

His abilities – or his magic, as even Aliena insisted on calling it, so gradually he learned to see it less and less as a derogatory term – were taking far longer to master. Small successes were punctuated by failures which were dramatic and often dangerous, although he had managed to avoid injuring anyone so far. Every failure knocked his confidence, and it would take Erelas a lot of effort and patience to coax him back into trying again.

But it was in his mind that he was least prepared for what was to come.

He very rarely laughed, even with Erelas, who still tried to raise his friend's spirits every day, despite having his own troubles. He did his best to be himself, and Quinn did his best to respond to his earnest efforts, but it seemed as if they were both acting.

Although Quinn did love Aliena and knew she loved him, he did not allow their relationship to develop, for fear of what might happen to them all. He could not explain his feelings to her, but, even though he knew she was hurt by his lack of outward affection towards her, she did not criticise him for it. She was there when he needed her and gave him space when he did not. He felt pangs of guilt over it, but could not do anything to change how he felt about their future.

He missed his parents terribly – the memories of his father's rejection of him did nothing but compound his feelings of self-loathing and undermine his confidence. He also felt the oppressive clouds of the Keeper's hopes, and could not shake the feeling of dread at what sort of a future he was destined to have – and lead others in to – with such high expectations placed upon him. Added to all that was the fact that someone wanted him dead, and he still had no idea who. He spent his days trying to shake off the feeling of impending doom, but could never really manage it. He ended up avoiding everyone and everything as much as he could. Even his friends.

The castle chapel had become his hiding place, his sanctuary. Every time they visited Renn he would spend a long time there alone, trying to reconcile the many facets of his new life with God. It was no longer a place that frightened him because it somehow 'knew' that evil resided inside his soul. It was now the only place where he could remind himself that, ultimately, it was not his fight, but God's and that he was just a warrior for good in this evil-infested land. Sometimes it worked and he would leave the dark, smoky room with renewed purpose, prepared to face whatever might come along.

But not today.

Today he just wanted to walk away and let the Keepers find someone else to pin their hopes on. He could not help asking himself, or the others, why it had to be *him*. He knew Galen would have accused him of behaving like a sulky child, but he still could not come to terms with this burden of fate that had been placed on his shoulders. He had not asked to be special and certainly did not feel precious. Much of what he did see in himself was not the stuff of heroism. He could not accept the Keeper's words, telling him he was something more than all the rest. He was sure the Archdeacon would not accept them, either. He was just a disgraced Soul Conductor, disowned by his own parents and banished from his home for taking the life of a man. Then someone had tried to murder him. Then he had taken another life, that of the sheriff. And now the Keepers wanted him to do it again, if that was what it would take to stop this unknown destroyer of innocents. It was all too much.

Quinn jumped as the chapel door latch was lifted noisily and the heavy wooden door swung open.

'Sorry,' whispered Erelas, coming in and closing the door behind him. 'I was worried. You've been in here *hours*.'

'I'm sorry, Erelas – I didn't realise...'

'It's alright. Everything is ready. It's time to go.'

Quinn took a deep breath and stood up slowly, his knee stiff from sitting still for so long. 'Where is Aliena?'

'In the courtyard with Toren and Renn.'

Quinn reached Erelas and smiled resolutely. 'Let's get this over with, then.'

CHAPTER 61. A PROMISE MADE

Aliena stood frozen to the spot and stared hard at Quinn.

'Don't look at me that way, Aliena,' Quinn said, his eyes dropping to the dusting of snow at their feet. 'I *have* to do this. I didn't tell you before, because to be perfectly honest, I don't want to do this and I couldn't risk you managing to talk me out of it. You've spent a lot of time in the past few weeks telling us how dangerous Kilora is, even though it was your idea in the first place!' At her continued silence, he looked at her again and saw that her stare had become misted with tears, her face flushed with the effort of holding them and her anger at bay. 'I'm sorry...'

'I'm *scared* for you, for both of you. Kilorans hate strangers in their territory – surely even Conductors know that?'

'Then why would you suggest something you don't want me to do? I see no other way to make sense of these memories, and there is no way to reach this woman without going there ourselves...'

Aliena looked over at Erelas, who stood a little distance away, talking to Renn and holding Cara and the new horse, Einna. 'I wish I had never mentioned it, now! I found out more about the place since that day, but when you never mentioned it again, I assumed you had no plans to go there. It seems I was mistaken. *Erelas* knew all this time, I suppose!'

Quinn suddenly grabbed her by the arms, holding her firmly, but without hurting her. '*Listen to me!*' he said, a flash of anger in his eyes.

Aliena looked up at him, alarmed but not frightened – there were no red sparks, just a glint of turquoise light in the silver iris of his left eye. Erelas, Renn and the prince all turned, startled, but none of them wanted to interfere.

'Do you *still* not understand, after all you have seen since you met me, that you cannot be involved in everything? Can you not see that I am trying to protect you, as much as anyone else in this kingdom? Everyone knows where I live now, including half of Delmoril. What if someone were to start questioning you about where we have gone – someone connected to whatever is happening to those lost souls? *Why* do you have to question my decisions?'

'Because,' said Aliena, the tears spilling over at last. '*I* value your life a sight more than you do!'

It was Quinn's turn to stare.

'Why do you still believe you deserve *punishment*, Quinn? You have healed. You have taken every bit of pain, every hard training session, every knock-back – and yet still you walk around as if it wasn't enough suffering for you! You don't allow yourself to be happy, or to be loved. You hate yourself! What good are you going to be protecting anyone else when you place no value on your *own* life?'

'What if I'm not meant to be happy, Aliena? What if this is how it is meant to be for me from now on? I haven't chosen this path for myself, the Keepers have. They are not what I would call "happy" in their existence! I know I am not one of them, but neither am I one of you! I'm not even a proper Conductor anymore, I'm an outcast, a rogue, someone even my own parents won't speak to! As a chance to claw back something worthwhile out of it all I have something that I have to do, whether I like it or not – which I *don't* – something unknown for the most part. It *feels* like another punishment for my sins. So what right do I have to be happy until it's all over?'

Aliena sighed. 'Do you honestly believe that you were chosen by the Keepers because you have never known happiness, or don't appreciate happiness, or crave happiness? They need you to remember what it is you'll be fighting for. You said yourself, the Keeper had to be reassured that you were still the kind of person they believed you to be, even after everything that had happened to you. You're the one denying yourself a little light in the darkness, Quinn. I have tried to keep showing you that light, as has Erelas. *Still* you push it away. And now you're pushing *me* away.'

Quinn was stung, knowing he was hurting the people he cared for most. He let go of Aliena and stood, looking dejected, and her expression softened in response.

'I know...' she said, taking his hands again. 'I know you have to go, and I know deep down that I can't go with you. You've made that clear. Part of me is glad to not be going. It's not knowing if you're safe that will tear me apart. But I understand why you're going, I really do. That doesn't mean I have to like it.' She sighed as Quinn dropped his gaze from hers. 'Just promise me one thing.'

'What's that?'

Aliena placed her hand on his face and leaned in, kissing him on the lips. It was a long lingering kiss that carried with it all the emotion, the heartbreak and the passion she had held back over the last two months. When she finally pulled away from him, she wiped away a stray tear and said, 'That when you return, you will bring *that* back with you.' Then she turned and walked away towards the main hall, the boys following along behind.

Erelas mounted his horse and silently led Cara over to where Quinn remained, allowing her to nudge his friend from his daze. As Quinn climbed into the saddle, he watched Aliena go through the doors and disappear from view. He felt stunned, his own heart feeling crushed, but knowing deep in his soul that he would keep that promise.

CHAPTER 62. EINNA

'Are you sure about this, Quinn?'

'No. Are you?'

Erelas shook his head as he tried to make his new horse walk in a straight line. The young, chestnut mare was being skittish, and clearly Cara's calm example was not sinking in. He suspected Einna was going to be a real challenge on this long trek... 'I can only go on what I found out by digging in priory records. This woman lives in exile, but I take that to mean that she is good at what she does.'

'Or...it could just be that the church is doing its usual thing and condemning anyone who doesn't follow their teachings.'

'You cynic...' said Erelas light-heartedly.

Quinn smiled. 'Hey, *you're* not sure about this either.'

'I think the journey worries me more than what the woman turns out to be like. Nobody from Delmoril goes to Kilora, and we already know what the Conductors who live in the kingdom will think of us being there. Some of the stories are true...I think we're mad.'

'I think we should just take things as we find them when we get there.'

Erelas could not answer as Einna started to

spin in circles. Quinn smirked and pulled Cara up, waiting for his friend to regain control. Eventually, he managed to get the horse pointing in the right direction and looked at Quinn, exasperated. 'I swear this horse chose me because she wanted to have some fun with me.'

'She's young. Give her time.'

'I think we should stop for a while.'

Quinn nodded and dismounted, careful to not jar his knee. Gathering his pack from the saddle, he suddenly found he was very hungry and they had not brought much with them. 'I hope there's a river nearby,' he said. 'I need a proper supper.'

'You've been spoiled. Next you'll be wanting wine.'

'Don't blame me. Aliena still insists I'm too skinny. I keep telling her I've always been this way. All of us have.'

'Ahh she can't help it,' Erelas said as he tethered Einna close to where Cara stood, grazing freely. 'She loves you. And you love her, so don't complain.'

Quinn's expression fell into one of sadness. 'I'm not sure she does.' 'Don't be ridiculous. She's just afraid for you, and worrying about you. You two will be together when all this is over, trust me on that. You know, you'll have set a precedent.'

'How so?'

'No Soul Conductor has ever partnered someone who isn't also a Soul Conductor. The

Archdeacon would spit.' 'In that case, let's make sure he hears about it someday.'

***

As soon as they entered the kingdom of Kilora, they heard the wolves.

They had travelled for three days across Rivallen to the border, resting only when the horses needed to, pushing themselves as much as they could. Neither of them wanted this journey to take any longer than was necessary.

The boundary between Kilora and Rivallen was a wide, dry river-bed at least three miles across. The surrounding strip of land on both sides was forested, and as they looked across the deep scar on the landscape, they could see snow-capped mountains in the distance. Their destination lay beyond those peaks.

The wolves started to howl mournfully as soon as they set foot on the sandy river-bed. Einna reared up, and even Cara snorted and threw her head up, the whites of her eyes showing. Erelas managed to stay on Einna, but she would not move forwards until Cara had settled down and led the way.

Quinn was lost in thought again by the time they reached the far side of the river-bed. The wolves were still howling, but aside from exchanging looks with Erelas while the horses were playing up, he seemed to have taken little notice of them.

'Are you alright?' asked Erelas, as they stood the horses side by side and surveyed the forest in front of them.

Quinn nodded. 'I was just thinking: this is worse than when I was dumped in Rivallen the day I was banished. At least I knew something of the land and its people. We know nothing of Kilora. Thanks to their hostile and violent ways, nobody knows much at all, except that they *are* hostile and violent. Those wolves do not seem to indicate a very welcoming reception for us.'

'What happened to taking things as we find them?'

'I'm more worried about what finds us...' Quinn pointed at the mountains. 'We have to go right around those – it's going to take at least two weeks to get to where Alara is rumoured to live. And I stress the word rumoured. It could take us far longer than that to find her.'

'Well, you needed a holiday... Cooped up in all that luxury. Who wouldn't crave a bit of mud, sweat and whatever the elements throw at us after all that splendour?' Erelas grinned as Quinn turned to him, and Quinn could not help smiling.

'I know, maybe I'm worrying over nothing. We probably won't meet a single soul in all that time. It looks as if nobody lives here at all.'

'Except the wolves.'

'Except the wolves. I don't think I ever told you I saw one the day I was banished. I'm thinking now that maybe it wasn't just a fatigue-induced hallucination.' Quinn drew his sword from its sheath, making Einna step back, while Cara took no notice. 'Let's find out if they're friendly. Maybe they belong to Alara.'

'A legendary witch, with the power to explore a man's subconscious mind, who keeps a pack of wolves as pets. That's a comforting thought. Thanks, Quinn.'

As Cara walked confidently forwards and Einna shuffled along sideways behind her, Quinn tried to relax and focus on the here and now. They could do this. They would find the alleged sorceress who lived in hiding and persuade her to help Quinn access the memories left behind in his mind.

After that…only God knew.

CHAPTER 63. A PACT WITH THE PACK

Erelas drew his sword, careful not to make a sound, and stood by the horses, slowly untethering them from the low branch of a tree without taking his eyes off Quinn. Einna was not making it easy for him to quietly make them ready for an escape; she was pulling back on her reins, breathing hard, her eyes wide with fear. But Cara stood calmly watching. She trusted her master.

Quinn stood just inside the tree-line, watching the pack advance yard by yard. The peace was almost tangible; there was no hint of a breeze as the fat flakes of snow floated to the ground in the blue-grey light of the waking day. His sword was already in his hand, although his arm was relaxed at a slight angle to his body and the tip of the blade pointed downwards. He stared hard at the huge, black leader of the dozen-strong wolf-pack, as the beasts halted just outside of the forest, where the land was gently sloping up towards a more sparsely wooded area. Then he moved the sword around behind his back, his movement casual, his stare unbroken.

'What are you doing?' whispered Erelas urgently.

Quinn made no reply. The animal looked

back at him, its vivid blue eyes standing out against its dark fur. For several moments they eyed each other silently, as the snow continued to fall around them. Then Quinn said quietly: 'Peace, brothers.'

Erelas raised a cynical eyebrow. He knew that most encounters with wolves ended in serious damage being done to one or both parties. Even their powers rarely worked against the hostile ones, and only then if the wolf was already injured or weak. And this huge male was neither.

But once again, Quinn surprised his friend. The pack leader lowered his head and padded forwards, his tail gently signalling agreement to Quinn's proposal. Quinn drove the blade of his sword into the sodden ground and crouched down as the wolf approached. Erelas held his breath and stayed where he was, still holding the horses, who seemed to understand the situation better than he, for they both now stood still and watched, ears pricked.

'We mean no harm to you,' Quinn said, slowly extending his hand. The wolf reached him, while his companions held back outside the forest. He bowed his head still further and placed his muzzle under Quinn's outstretched hand. Quinn smiled and lightly scratched the wolf's head, before rubbing his ear and then standing up.

The wolf walked around Quinn and approached Erelas, who had been watching openmouthed. Trying to hide his alarm, Erelas remained still as the wolf reached him. The animal sniffed at him briefly, then licked his hand, which had sunk to his side in disbelief, still holding the sword. As the wolf walked away, Erelas glanced at Cara, who shook her head as if in disgust at Erelas' lack of faith in her master.

The wolf re-joined his pack and they turned away from the forest. As they began to move off, the leader let out a mournful, but beautiful howl. As the others joined in, Quinn smiled and bowed his head to them.

Erelas joined him at the tree-line.

'They will not harm us,' said Quinn.

'You know, it's lucky I'm not the jealous type,' said Erelas, watching the wolves leave. 'How did you do that?'

'He could sense my power is dangerous, Erelas, even if I don't mean them any harm. There was no skill on my part in bringing about that truce – he just knows I could wipe them all out.' He retrieved his sword from the ground and walked towards Cara. 'I wouldn't be jealous of *that*.'

***

Some hours later, Quinn pulled Cara up and got down from the saddle, again careful not to drop to the floor and jolt his knee. Even so, the sudden change of position and the weight it had to bear caused him to inhale sharply in pain and he limped as he led Cara to the stream in front of them. As she drank they were joined by Erelas, who dismounted, careful not to let go of Einna's reins as the young horse made to step into the water.

'Are you alright?' Erelas asked, despite already knowing the answer. He knew Quinn's leg still gave him severe trouble, even though it had been almost three months since the injury Garin had inflicted upon it.

'I just want to stretch my legs a little,' Quinn said, bending to fill his water skin. 'Too long in the saddle and my knee feels like it's going to pop out of place.'

Erelas winced in sympathy. 'We can rest here a while...'

Quinn shook his head. 'I'd rather we pressed on. There's no shelter for miles around…It would be best if we aren't stuck out in the open when night falls. I'll be fine walking for a while.' He smiled as he saw Erelas' unconvinced look. 'Stop fussing.'

'Someone has to!' said Erelas, retrieving his own water skin from the packs tied to Einna's saddle. 'You'd keep going on one leg through a blizzard if I wasn't here to give you disapproving stares.'

Quinn laughed. 'I promise to stop if it gets too much, Erelas. I would just rather not have the horses out in the open overnight. It's cold enough in the forest.'

'What we need is a cave. This land is too flat; I think those mountains are a mirage…'

'How so?'

'Well, we never seem to get any closer to them.'

'We've only been in Kilora for four days, Erelas. By those charts you showed me, we've got at least another couple of days before we get near them.'

'Then let's at least pray there is no more snow...'

***

There was more snow, which continued into the following day. Rising early, they had covered as much ground as Quinn could cope with, stopping frequently to ease the stiffness in his knee.

But as the afternoon wore on and the light grew dim, Quinn finally had to admit that he could go no further. 'This is a bad place to stop for the night,' he said, exasperated. 'These trees won't provide much shelter.'

'We'll manage,' said Erelas, taking off Einna's saddle. 'It's better than *no* trees, and at least there are dry patches of ground to sit on. As long as we don't fall over the cliff in the dark.' He pointed to the right, where a sheer drop led to a deep and wide river some hundred feet below. 'Don't worry about it, Quinn. We've made good progress and we can't be far, now. It's more important that you rest that knee, otherwise we'll be going nowhere at all tomorrow.' He placed the saddle on the ground and moved over to take hold of Cara. 'Let me see to her. Go and sit down before you fall down.'

'I'm sure it's the cold and damp. It seemed easier to keep going yesterday.'

'Maybe, or maybe even *your* stubbornness has its limits.'

Cara nudged him hard and Quinn laughed. 'You have to watch what you say around Cara these days, you know. She's very protective.'

As Quinn would have refused help from Erelas' healing ability, Erelas did not bother to offer it and just left him to rest while he made the horses comfortable. As far as Quinn was concerned, despite Aliena's outburst to the contrary, he deserved his pain. He became frustrated with himself regularly, especially at times like this when it was hampering their progress, but he would not give in. And Erelas would not push it.

They both hoped a good night's rest would be enough.

CHAPTER 64. DAWN ATTACK

The attack came just as the first shades of dawn began to steal over the horizon.

Cara was the first to react, her keen hearing picking up the soft sound of feet crushing the virgin snow. She gave a soft whinny and turned to face the unknown intruder to their camp. The noise stopped, but Cara stared, ears twitching, straining to see in the weak light.

Erelas awoke with a jolt and sprang to his feet. Glancing at Quinn, he decided not to wake him unless he had to. He silently drew his sword and crept past him towards Cara and Einna. Einna was now looking in the same direction as her companion, but more fearfully, fidgeting and swishing her tail up and down, thus drowning out any sound they might have heard from the intruder.

He closed his eyes and tried to 'feel' their surroundings with his mind. He could not be certain, but he thought he could sense the presence of a power other than his own and Quinn's, and he could not decide if that was good or dangerous – a Soul Conductor from their own land would have been harmless, of course, but they never ventured here. A Soul Conductor from Salorea would be a different matter altogether...

He heard Quinn stir behind him. He looked

around and saw his friend getting to his feet, stiff from the cold and still plainly exhausted. He could not read his expression in the gloom, but he was sure that Quinn was probably too tired to grasp what was going on. Erelas was torn. He wanted to stay close to where the noise had come from, but also wanted to warn Quinn of the potential danger.

Einna forced the issue for him. Her newness to the role of Conductor's companion and the dangers it often brought made her react much more than Cara would have – a sudden noise that Erelas did not hear startled her into pulling back violently on her tether. Erelas ran forwards and grabbed hold of her before she could bolt.

At that moment, as Quinn strained to see what was happening, someone moved in close behind him, and in an instant, he felt something tighten around his throat. He had been caught completely off guard and suddenly he was being strangled. He could not cry out, as the pressure increased and he staggered backwards, pulled by the strength of the person who was plainly trying to kill him. He raised his hands, desperately trying to get a hold on what felt like a leather strap crushing his throat, but it was too tight and his fingers slid off repeatedly.

Wide-eyed and feeling panic and rage building up in equal measure, Quinn tried to see where he was and where Erelas was. He saw in the dim light the shapes of the horses, one shifting uneasily, the other spinning around wildly, and he glimpsed his friend trying to regain control of Einna. He could see no other person around their resting place. He knew that if he did not beat this attacker, Erelas would die right after him.

Remembering where they were, Quinn had an idea and suddenly embraced the rage building inside him, forcing the panic back down as his lungs began to burn. Gathering what strength he could and ignoring the ache in his knee, he pushed himself back into his assailant as hard as he could. He met strong resistance, but his tendency towards absolute fury became his advantage and soon the figure was forced to step backwards. Once, twice, then further and further he was pushed. But his grip on the strap never lessened and Quinn began to wonder if he had misjudged the distance to his intended destination. Would he lose consciousness before he could reach it? He heard a faint shout from in front of him and guessed that Erelas had realised what was happening. Desperation gave Quinn extra strength and he pushed harder, not wanting Erelas to get involved.

He almost stumbled as at last the lack of oxygen to his brain began to tell on him. His vision blurred and the burning in his throat made him want to scream, which he could only do in his mind. He threw his head back suddenly, but his attacker's face was too far away from him and he made no contact. As he began to fear that he was not going to win this battle and that he and Erelas were both doomed, he at last felt what he had been aiming for.

His whole upper body was wrenched backwards and his attacker let out a cry of surprise as he instantly tried to push Quinn forwards. But the reaction gave Quinn hope, and he was just too strong. He gave one last push, forced to use the heel of his weaker leg to gain grip on the snowy rubble beneath them, but it was enough. They fell backwards as the last of his strength was used and his vision failed. The last thing he heard was a scream behind him and he felt the sensation of air rushing past him as he sank into blackness and silence.

CHAPTER 65. CARA TAKES OVER

'*Quinn!*'

The void of silence was oppressive as Erelas dropped to his knees and looked desperately over the edge of the precipice. He knew that even in daylight he would not have been able to see his friend; the drop was too far and the river too fast-flowing. Not only was Quinn gone, he was certainly dead, too.

Erelas seemed to suddenly lose all his strength and toppled sideways, not caring that his head was hanging over the edge. His breath had been squeezed out of him and his heart felt as if it was collapsing in on itself. How could this have happened, after all that the Keeper had said about Quinn's strength and importance? How could he be dead *now*, after everything he'd gone through and all the Keeper had done to keep him alive?

Erelas was not sure he even knew what had happened. He had only been able to see Quinn struggling with a dark, tall figure and before he could get any closer to see what was going on, they had both gone over the edge of the cliff. There had been no time to understand anything, let alone do anything.

He let out an anguished yell into the breaking dawn. Then his breath came shuddering back and he squeezed his eyes shut. He did not know what to do now, and he could not seem to focus his mind at all. '*Damn you to Hell*!' he cursed at nobody in particular, rolling back over and scrambling up on to shaky legs.

He looked over the cliff and called Quinn's name once more, but heard and saw nothing but the dark ribbon of water beginning to come into view in the growing light.

Hearing movement behind him, he spun round and there was Cara, approaching him slowly, flicking her tail, her ears rotating this way and that. Erelas looked past her, but there was no sign of Einna. 'Shit,' he muttered. His shoulders slumped and he looked heavenward in despair. Cara nudged him and stamped a hoof on the ground, making deep depressions in the already disturbed snow. Erelas felt bad for her and put his palm on her muzzle.

Frowning, he put his hand under his thick cloak and linen shirt and pulled out the amulet that was hung around his neck on a thin silver chain. It was vibrating intermittently, and its turquoise glow was almost imperceptible. 'What the...' he breathed. He felt sick as the memory of the night in the devastated tower of King Mattias' castle came flooding back to him. He could not conduct his friend's soul then, and he knew he could not do it now. But why was the amulet so weak?

He looked at Cara, who looked blankly back at him.

'The Keeper!' he said suddenly, making the horse lift her head sharply, knocking him back a step. 'Sorry, Cara. Stay there.'

Erelas walked back to where their small camp fire had died in the dark hours before dawn. Gazing around the poor attempt at shelter they had made, he dropped the amulet back under his shirt and whispered the Latin he had memorised since the Keeper had given them permission to summon him whenever they needed him.

Nothing happened. The Keeper never appeared with a flourish, or even with the slightest noise or flash of light, but Erelas did not see the hooded and cloaked figure standing before him as he had on the other occasions. He repeated the words, and waited. Still nothing.

'*No!*'

He turned to face Cara, who was fidgeting on the spot. Biting his lip hard and wringing his hands together, he knew what he had to do. He fetched Cara's blanket, saddle and bridle and carried them to where she stood. Einna's was left on the ground at the foot of the tree they had been resting under. There was no point in trying to carry that around on the off-chance they would find her. He prepared Cara and grabbed Quinn's sword, attaching it to the saddle. Cara stamped her feet in anticipation, knowing they were going to search for her master. As Erelas leaped on to her back, she whinnied and wheeled around, and he had no need to urge her forwards.

As Cara cantered smoothly along the edge of the cliff, Erelas looked out for a place where they could trek down to the river below. And the amulet stopped vibrating.

***

The snow had begun to fall again before they were half-way to the valley below, which had been carved out of the cliffs by the violent flow of the deep river. The wind had also picked up, blowing icy flakes into their faces and making it difficult for Cara to keep up the pace she had begun the descent with. She was forced to slow to an unsteady trot, picking her way through the deep snow with care now that she could not so easily see obstacles in front of her.

The daylight was brighter now, at least, but Erelas sensed that this snowstorm was here to stay. They needed to find Quinn fast.

As they had cantered along the top of the cliff, the amulet stopped vibrating, sending him into a momentary panic so severe, he almost fell off Cara as he lost concentration on keeping his balance. She slowed a little, letting him compose himself, before picking up her pace again.

Something about her made Erelas start to believe Quinn was not dead. She was eager, her movements smooth and not those of a horse who believed her master was lost forever. Conductor's horses were blessed with heightened senses and, although they could not communicate in any sophisticated manner, their behaviour was often enough of a clue as to what was going on in their heads. Cara was too energetic and she did not seem to be mourning Quinn's loss at all.

The muted call of the amulet must have been for someone else – Quinn's attacker?

These thoughts and the snowstorm made him realise that Quinn had to be found – fast. If he was still alive, he would be wet and freezing to death and there was no telling what the fall would have done to him. Erelas wondered whether the Keeper would have been able to bring him back a second time, even if he had come when he had been summoned…

The Keeper's failure to appear alarmed Erelas. Did the words no longer work, or had the Keeper simply refused to respond? Was there something wrong with his own ability? It had worked a few days previously, when he had healed a small scratch on Einna's leg. Why not now?

As they made their way to the valley floor, Erelas turned his focus back to finding Quinn – everything else would have to be worked out later.

It was hard to see too far in front of them with the swirling snow all around them, but eventually Erelas was able to hear the rush of the water as it sped its relentless way towards some distant and unknown destination. His heart leaped in expectation as the dark river came into view some long minutes later. He tried to suppress it – he knew that Quinn could have been carried a long way by the swift current, and it could be a long while before they managed to find him.

They finally reached the banks of the river and he pulled Cara up so he could try to get his bearings. They had travelled up-river, and along the cliff-edge before they were able to travel in the right direction down the sloping path to the valley floor. Now he could not see where they were in relation to the point at which Quinn had fallen.

Erelas created a small, bright blue orb in his outstretched palm and, for one hopeful second, it hovered just above it. But instead of rising up in front of him and moving off, the orb suddenly fizzled out, popping as it met with the skin on Erelas' hand.

Erelas sighed in anxious exasperation. Was his power really not working, or could the orb not find Quinn because he was dead, after all?

Cara moved off suddenly, catching him off guard, and he tried to pull her up as he regained his balance in the saddle, but she would not stop, and instead increased the length of her stride until she was again in a tentative trot.

'Cara,' he said quietly. 'Wait...'

She ignored him, breaking into a canter as he leaned forwards to adjust his balance on the moderate slope they were now travelling up. He frowned, wondering if she knew something he did not. Within moments she broke into a gallop and he had no choice but to let her have her head and go where she wanted. Quinn could have stopped her. He could not. He was not her master.

CHAPTER 66. IMMERSION

Quinn felt very cold, but he knew he was wrapped in something warm. No – not wrapped. *Immersed.* He could not open his eyes, but he could sense a flickering light close by, and the strong smells of various herbs burning somewhere near him.

As he concentrated more, he could feel he was bathed in a warm liquid which seemed to cover everything except a narrow strip of his bare skin down his left side; he had been stripped of everything but his undergarments. He was lying with the right side of his body and face resting against something hard, but not flat. He was completely confused; he remembered what he had done on the cliff-top, but knew he was no longer outside in freezing weather where he had expected to wake up – not that he had expected to wake up at all, which puzzled him further.

He sank a little and the surface of the liquid tickled his skin as it rose up his face. He had no strength to stop himself, and suddenly there was warm water in his mouth. He coughed, causing agonising pain in his throat and chest. A strong, yet gentle hand on the back of his neck lifted and turned his head clear of the water. He still could not open his eyes, so the question of who that hand might belong to further compounded his thoughts.

Nothing was said to him as he managed to control his breathing again, so he took the opportunity to sense what state his body was in. Apart from feeling chilled to the core, he could feel a deep ache in the middle of his back, and his left shoulder pulsed with sharp pains. His head hurt, but that was nothing compared to the burning in his lungs, or the pain down his throat and the rawness of the skin around it.

Finally, he managed to force his eyelids up and blinked several times. Both eyes were stinging and began to water profusely and it was a while before the one that still worked was able to focus on anything.

A dark shape loomed large above him and it seemed an age before he could bring the figure into focus. When he realised it was a man, he panicked, not really understanding why. Perhaps some primal instinct in him awoke at the size of the figure leaning over him, but he fought to sit up, failed to get any grip with his feet or hands, and merely managed to thrash the water about, hurting himself in the process.

'You'd better come, he's awake and fighting!' the man called out to some unseen companion.

A young woman appeared, her fair hair glinting with the reflection of the candlelight. Her face did not betray any concern, only a serenity that seemed to calm him and he gave up trying to move. As he slid back down in the water, she placed her hand at the back of his head and the man drew away, moving out of sight – but not before Quinn noticed that one of his arms was missing, severed at a point just above the elbow...

The woman smiled as she moved his wet hair away from his right eye with a fingertip. 'You're safe here,' she said, her voice gentle and unhurried. 'Lie still. We'll get you out of there soon.'

Quinn coughed again, not taking his eyes from hers; they were a piercing green and sparkled with natural energy, totally unlike the energy that danced around in his when he performed a casting. They were incredibly captivating. It was not until she raised an eyebrow at him that he realised how long he had been staring at her and he blinked and coughed again, before gathering up the strength to speak.

'Who are you?' he said, the words no more than a painful whisper.

She smiled. 'The one you have been seeking.' She ran a finger along his eyebrow. 'Sleep now. You will feel better when you wake...'

He did not want to sleep, but a strange warmth spread through him and in seconds he closed his eyes and drifted back into painless silence.

CHAPTER 67. ALARA

The next time he woke he was lying flat on his back on a warm, soft bed. It was dark – just as gloomy as it had been before, with only the orange flicker of a few candles to light his immediate surroundings. His eyes were still sore, and everything else hurt just as before, too, so he spent a few moments just blinking and not daring to move. Then he turned his head a little, ignoring the increasing pain in his throat, to try to get a better sense of where in the world he was.

He felt as if he were in the centre of a vast room; the walls were not visible, nor could he see any light that might have come from a distant doorway or window. There was a small table at his bedside, with one tiny candle burning on it. Several small bottles and a little wooden bowl were placed around it. A chair was by the bed, but there seemed to be nobody around him this time.

A sudden spasm in his back sent a shock of pain up through his spine and he could not help but cry out. The sound had been no more than a hoarse groan, but the man he'd seen before appeared beside the bed. He moved the chair out of the way and bent over Quinn. The stump of the man's arm was clearly visible now. As he looked up at his face, something flickered in his eyes that

Quinn did not understand it. Had it been...shame?

The man looked away quickly and seemed to take a moment to clear the expression from his face before turning back. He was frowning now, but without malice. 'Lie still...'

Quinn clenched his jaw until the pain eased a little. 'Where am I?'

The man did not answer and Quinn became uneasy. 'Who are you?' Still no answer, although Quinn could have sworn he saw that flash of embarrassment in the man's eyes again.

'His name is Samien,' said the woman's voice. Quinn turned his head towards the sound and she came into view, looking more beautiful than he remembered. 'He is my friend. You have nothing to fear from him.'

Quinn looked at Samien, who refused to meet his gaze and backed away. He then turned around and disappeared into the darkness.

'How are you feeling now?' asked the woman.

'You said you are the one I have been seeking...'

She smiled. 'I am Alara.'

Quinn raised an eyebrow.

Alara smiled. 'I know. Everyone expects me to be a gnarled old hag, but I'm only twenty.'

'It's not that,' Quinn said. 'Well...it is that, partly. When I was told about you they said you were old.' He looked uncomfortable. 'I'm sorry.'

'Don't be. I am used to it. It is part of the

reason I have been condemned by the church. They see my youthful looks as the result of witchcraft, rather than the actual age of my body.'

'How did you know I was seeking you?'

'The wolves.'

Quinn frowned, not following.

'The wolves and Samien, I should say,' Alara said, but that did nothing to ease Quinn's confusion. 'The wolves told us of your presence – you and your friend. And Samien—'

'*Erelas*!' Quinn tried to sit up, before the pain shot through his back again. Alara stayed him with her hand.

'Easy...your friend will join us soon.' When he began to cough, Alara reached for the small bowl on the table. 'Drink this – it will help your throat.'

He drank the cool, sweet-tasting liquid, and as he handed her the empty bowl, he cleared his throat and said: 'I'm sorry, I don't understand. Where *is* Erelas?'

'Just relax and I will explain. The fact you have been looking for me means you have heard something of my...reputation?'

Quinn nodded, sinking back into the pillow and wondering if the drink was making him sleepy again.

'One of my abilities is that of looking into the minds of others. Not just the minds of people, but animals, too. I am condemned as a witch in so many places. I need the wolves to look out for me and warn me of any newcomers to the area. In return, I give them shelter when they need it. They came to tell me of your arrival in Kilora two days ago. They heard you discussing me with your friend. When I relayed the description they gave me to Samien, he recognised you straight away.'

'He recognised me?'

'When the wolves then found you on the bank of the river, barely alive,' Alara went on, ignoring his surprise, 'I asked them to find your companion. They tell me he is making his way along the river on one of the horses. Samien will head out to meet him at dawn – it is too dark now, and no doubt your friend will be resting for the night soon. The river is still some miles from here.'

'Only *one* of the horses?' Quinn felt sick. He could not bear the thought of losing Cara.

'I am sorry. The wolves do not know at this point what has happened to the other one.'

He tried not to let despair envelop him – he was tired of always feeling life would never get any better. He pushed Cara from his mind for now. There was no sense in grieving for her when there was still hope that she was not lost for good. 'What did you mean…Samien recognised me?'

'Did you notice his arm?'

Quinn nodded.

Alara placed a hand on his. 'It was you who severed that arm. Samien was a guard. He was in the tower the night the king was murdered. Fearing the sheriff's rule, he got himself crudely patched up, stole a horse and fled Rivallen that same night. The wolves found him close to death, not far from the border several days later.' She paused as Quinn tried to digest this new information. With a reassuring smile, she said: 'That is why you need not fear him, Quinn. Samien fears *you.*'

Anger filled Quinn's mind as he remembered the guards holding him, ready for the sheriff to begin his torture. Fighting free of them and inflicting the terrible injury on Samien had not prevented that torture, or what followed, and he was still bitter about what he had gone through that night. 'So he should if he was loyal to Garin,' Quinn said quietly.

'He wasn't. As I said, he fled Rivallen in fear of what would happen when Garin took power. He thought the explosion had killed *you*, not Garin.'

Quinn said nothing, finding it hard to forgive Samien just because he had been afraid of what the sheriff might do to a one-armed guard who had failed him.

'Rest for a while, Quinn. Your friend will be with us in the morning – have no fear. Samien has no wish to harm anyone, least of all people who could kill him in a heartbeat.'

He flinched at the memory of the murder he had committed several months previously – the point at which his life had spiralled into a disaster.

Alara had not missed the effect her words had on him. 'I am sorry,' she said. 'I did not mean to sound harsh. I just meant that Samien recognises the power you possess and respects it. And he knows your companion has the same power, too.'

Quinn shook his head. 'Erelas is *not* the same as me. Erelas is a better person. He would only harm someone in self-defence.'

'From what I heard, you only harmed someone in defence of another. Is that not worthy of the same respect?'

He looked at her sharply. 'You don't understand. I am not supposed to be this way! I am *flawed*. Erelas is the kind of person I should be and deserves more respect than I have ever given him.'

'Quinn...' Alara paused, not sure how to respond to his frustrated outburst.

'Please,' Quinn said wearily. 'I don't want to talk about it.'

Alara patted his hand again and stood up. 'As you wish,' she said, with no hint of offence or resentment. 'Rest now. The drink I gave you will help.'

As she walked away, he closed his eyes and remembered what his old friend Galen had told him about sulking, and about hanging on to hope, no matter what. But he could not shake off the shame he felt and fell asleep thinking bitter thoughts about all that had befallen him since the day Rook had tried to take over his mind and body. He prayed he had come to the right place for help, but right now his confidence in Alara was waning. If she could not understand what he had gone through and was still going through, how could she be of any use to him?

CHAPTER 68. DOOMED PASSION

He walked slowly down the middle of the gloomy tavern and watched himself pick up one of the filthy, inefficient lamps from a small, round and now sticky table. Crossing diagonally to the second table, he heard the familiar drip-drip, before the woman's dead body became visible in the dim, flickering light. Her dead eyes stared out at nothing in particular, and her neck was still a sickening contrast of red blood and white skin.

Hearing the laughter that came from him, but was not his, his eyes switched focus, down through the long room, taking in more mutilated bodies; the old man, the two middle-aged women, the old woman sitting with the younger one and the youth, who lay on the floor.

Quinn could feel the same fear in his mind as always, but still the laughter went on, as he saw hands that were not really his wipe the blade of a knife onto the front of a tunic that was not really his.

He stopped at the hearth for a few moments and turned, surveyed the carnage and then moved back the way he had come, more quickly this time, and with a purpose that, again, was not his own. The smell was as terrible as ever, but this body he was in did not seem to care.

He was once again taken on the same journey, up the ancient stairway to the bedroom door, where he witnessed the body's dirty, blood-spattered boot smash into it again.

The terrified young man was there again, bound and gagged as before, and it was always at this point that Quinn was even more certain that this was no dream. This was real.

'Shh,' the intruder in his mind said to the young man at his panicked cries. 'That won't do you any good now, will it?'

Quinn was again able to pick out 'please,' and 'no,' from the man's muffled response. Then he seemed to give up hope and looked down.

'That's it, lad – give up. It's easier that way. He likes 'em quiet. Helps him to get ready for his "moment", as he calls it.' Quinn saw himself draw the finger across his own neck and then the inhuman laughter began. Quinn felt chilled to his very soul.

As always, the young man vomited and it sprayed out of his nose and through gaps between the gag and his lips, dribbling down his chin. He choked, mortal fear in his eyes as his lungs fought against the liquid he had no choice but to inhale. His face grew red and his eyes bulged. This never got any easier for Quinn to watch, and he felt the same horror as he saw himself take one long step forwards and kick the young man straight in the face. The man's head slammed into the floor and he lay there, convulsing. It did not last long and, when it stopped, the dark stain grew at his crotch and spread to the wooden floor.

'Damn it all! Now I've got to go and find another one!'

Quinn watched himself go back out the door and down the staircase, straight through the tavern and out into the street. It was night-time, and there were very few people about, but he heard voices coming from an alleyway, just a few paces to his right. The body he was in turned and walked to the alley and Quinn saw a man and a woman half-way down it. The voice that was not his grunted in satisfaction when he saw what the couple were up to.

The woman's long dress had been pulled up around her hips and the man stood between them, his hose untied but not pulled down. He supported the woman by her buttocks as he thrust into her urgently, breathing heavily on to the woman's exposed shoulder. She looked skywards, groaning in pleasure as her lover's pace grew and he thrust harder.

Quinn could do nothing as the memory of this evil man's mind took him where he had not been before. He knew what was going to happen, but to see it as if he himself were doing the wicked deed was more than he could bear. Try as he might, there was no escaping this visual torture, and as he got closer to the unsuspecting lovers, he wondered how long he could stay sane.

The couple were oblivious to Rook's approach and Quinn found himself saying futile prayers in his mind for the body he was in to make some noise, to stumble, cough, anything that would alert them. But they were reaching the climax of their ecstasy now and would not have noticed a horse galloping by. It was hopeless. They were doomed. Their souls had been ripped from their bodies months before, maybe even longer…this was a vision into the past.

Quinn felt his right hand grip the cool leather covering on the handle of a dagger as he came within feet of the couple. As he reached them, he stood directly behind the man, who was now groaning loudly, but almost drowned out by the woman's cries as she squeezed her eyes shut and clung to him, pulling him deeper into her. Quinn was powerless as his left hand was raised and brought down on the man's left shoulder, while his right hand flicked between the couples throats. The dagger sliced open the man's neck and he made a strange gurgling sound as warm blood shot over the half-exposed breasts of his lover. His whole body went rigid and he was unable to break free from his final embrace.

The woman cried out in surprise, her head snapping down and her eyes opening, as she felt the hot sticky blood invade her clothes and spray on to her face. She took in what was happening in an instant and screamed, the sound exploding in Quinn's tortured mind.

CHAPTER 69. MAYNARD

While Quinn was being tortured in his sleep, Erelas faced a different kind of torment.

Cara had galloped for several miles before she finally slowed down, unable to pass at speed through the thick forest they found themselves in. They were nowhere near the river now, and Erelas was convinced they were getting further away from wherever Quinn had to be lying, close to death, if not dead already. He had tried in vain to pull Cara up and check her steady march into unknown territory, but she was too strong for him. She had even threatened to throw him off twice; he just had to sit tight until she either reached where she wanted to be, or ran out of steam. In the end she had refused to stop for the entire day and he was exhausted, hungry and out of water. And all the while his orbs refused to work.

She finally came to a halt as the daylight faded to the point of being unable to see where they were going. Erelas slid off the saddle and slumped to the ground, his legs refusing to hold him up. His knees thumped hard into the solid forest floor under the snow and he cursed out loud, trying not to feel angry with Quinn's loyal mare.

'Don't move,' a deep, male voice said.

Erelas froze as he felt the blade of a longsword pressed into his throat. He tried to look sideways to see who was holding the weapon but, unable to move his head, all he could make out in the fading light was the dark shape of a tall man.

'Where is your friend?' the man asked, not moving the blade from Erelas' skin.

'Dead,' said Erelas flatly, his anger rising.

'What are you doing here?' The man's voice was calm and confident. 'You're the intruders from Rivallen, are you not?'

'I'm looking for my horse. She bolted when my friend was killed.'

'That is not what I meant, stranger.'

Erelas sighed. 'We came here to find someone we thought might be able to help my friend with something. He's now dead, so I just want to find my horse and go home.' He hoped he sounded convincing, but doubted it; he had never been good at lying.

The man stayed silent, but moved in front of Erelas, the tip of the sword never more than a finger's length from Erelas' neck. As he moved, Erelas dared to look up at him, trying to work out whether he was a Kiloran – fully human – or a Salorean, and therefore a Conductor.

The man was dressed in black leather with glossy, black armour over it and a dark purple cloak covered the whole. His hood was up against the still falling snow, and Erelas had trouble picking out many details about his face, but there was no mistaking those silver-grey eyes – Salorean.

Erelas' heart sank and he looked back at the floor. Kilorans might be a volatile race, but they had no powers, unlike Saloreans, who were almost indiscriminate with theirs...

'Do you fear me?'

A wave of indignation swept over Erelas at the mocking tone he gleaned from the Salorean's voice. 'Hardly a fair question to ask a man with a sword at his throat,' he snapped.

The man lowered the sword and took a step back. 'You may stand up.'

Erelas stood slowly, his knees screaming in protest. As he rose, he glanced around at Cara, who had moved back a little way, but stood calmly watching the stranger as the stranger watched Erelas.

'What is your name?'

'Erelas.'

'And your friend's?'

Erelas raised an eyebrow. 'What does *that* matter if he's dead?' he replied, trying to still hold on to hope even as he worked on convincing the stranger that Quinn was not worth looking for.

'His *name*,' the man insisted, raising the sword a little way.

Erelas stared at him contemptuously. 'Quinn.'

'So...the rumours *are* true.'

Erelas frowned. 'What rumours?'

'Your friend is well known in Kilora. You don't play such a large part in the affairs of a kingdom and not have your name spread far and wide. We know about him and we heard he was here. He's easy to spot, apparently, with his different-coloured eyes. You two need to work on your stealth skills.'

Erelas ignored the jibe. 'Well he's dead now. Killed by one of *you*, probably,' He said, deciding to push his luck a little. 'We know about you Saloreans, too.'

'Is that so?' the man said, unmoved by Erelas' attempt at insolence.

Erelas fell silent. This was getting him nowhere. He stared as the man slowly moved around him towards Cara, keeping the sword poised towards Erelas.

'Beautiful animal,' the man said as he reached the horse and ran a hand down the black coat along her neck. White, frothy sweat steamed from her body and she breathed heavily, but she showed no sign of fear. 'You say you are looking for your horse – I take it this lovely creature is Quinn's?'

'Yes. I'd be careful if I were you.'

'I know about the horses of Delmoril and their loyalty. It's something we Saloreans envy. I won't be attempting anything untoward with her, I assure you.'

Cara nodded as if in approval, but this time Erelas was not amused by her interactions. 'What do you want?' he asked sharply.

'I wanted to warn you. To give you and your

friend a chance to leave before anything happened to you, but it seems I did not reach you in time. I am sorry for that.'

Erelas looked doubtful. 'And why would you do that? You did not deny that it could have been a Salorean who attacked us.'

'It was almost certainly a Salorean. Kilorans avoid these forests because of the wolves. However, that is not to say that all Saloreans wish you harm. I could have slit your throat in a heartbeat just now, but I did not. I brandish my sword because I simply do not wish you to attack *me*.'

'But why would you go against your own people and warn us away from Kilora?'

'Because I'm sick of the fighting we already face daily, without *your* kind bringing down more on us. Soul Conductors from Delmoril are supposed to know they are not to cross the border. Most Saloreans will attack you on sight – which, I am guessing, is what must have happened to Quinn. They may even see your presence here as an act of defiance and seek revenge on your people.'

Erelas could not help giving the man a scornful look. 'What are your people hiding?'

The man ignored the question. 'I don't warn you for your sake, but for the sake of myself and my own family. *Leave* Kilora. Take your friend's horse and go. Your horse is probably lost to the wolves by now.'

Erelas said nothing. During the long pause,

they stared steadily at one another, until the Salorean spoke again. 'Where is his body?'

'I don't know.' Erelas said, feeling sick at the thought of never finding Quinn, whatever state he was in. 'He fell over a cliff into the river. I was trying to find him as well as my horse,' he admitted. 'Cara had her own ideas and I ended up here. God knows why.'

The Salorean patted Cara's neck. 'She has brought you closer to the border with Rivallen. She knows you are not meant to be here.'

Erelas stared, trying to hide his dismay. If that were true, he was even further from where he had lost Quinn, and the chances of finding him alive now would be remote. Why would Cara do such a thing? He swallowed hard and looked away.

'I am sorry,' said the man. 'I know you do not believe that I am, but it's true. We were impressed with Quinn's courage, and what he did for the people of Rivallen. He has become something of a legend among the younger Conductors here.'

Erelas scoffed. 'No doubt his ability to kill was the most impressive.'

The Salorean took a step towards Erelas, straightening his frame until Erelas had to look up to meet his gaze. 'Saloreans already have *that* ability. It doesn't matter what methods we use. You should be careful of trying to insult us.'

Erelas was too tired, too cold and too upset to feel threatened anymore and he turned and walked back to Cara. He grabbed her reins and turned her head away from the Salorean, thankful that she did not resist. As he mounted the fidgeting horse, he looked over at the man and said: 'You have warned me. I am grateful for that. But if you are truly sorry, you will at least allow me to find his body and take him home.'

'It makes no difference what my personal feelings are about Quinn's death. Even if I let you continue your search, other Saloreans will find you. After all, where is the Salorean who attacked him? They will be searching for him, as well.'

'Dead, I hope,' Erelas snapped. 'But your people cannot get revenge on someone who is dead, too. I'm grateful for the warning. However, that does not mean I will heed it. I am not going back to Delmoril without him.'

'I thought Quinn was banished from there?'

'He's *still* a Soul Conductor!' Erelas shouted. 'He at least has the right to be *properly* laid to rest in Delmoril.' The man did not respond, and Erelas knew he was in agreement. 'If you truly wish me no harm, you will let me continue my search. The risk is mine to take.'

The Salorean looked at Erelas for a few moments, studying his face. Then, he said: 'Very well. I am to report back any sighting of you to my people. I will tell them I have seen you heading towards the border. But if you do not find your friend in three days, turn back and go home. No good will come from you lingering for longer than that.'

Erelas looked at the Salorean, his eyes steadily searching for any sign of deceit. Finding none, he said: 'Thank you.'

The Salorean nodded and made to turn away from them, but Erelas stopped him with a question. 'Would you give me your name?'

'Why do you want to know that?'

'So that when I bury my friend, I can tell the people who loved him who it was that helped me to get him home. That is all.'

The Salorean's expression changed from suspicion to respect. 'Maynard. Now, go in peace, Erelas. I wish you luck. You will need it.' In a few long strides, he vanished as silently as he had come.

Erelas sat perfectly still on Cara's back as the few snowflakes that could penetrate the forest floated lazily around them in the growing darkness. He knew he would never return to Delmoril without Quinn. To hell with the three days.

CHAPTER 70. SAMIEN'S TALE

Quinn ignored the agony in his back, and his near-nakedness, and half-fell from the low bed, desperately searching his surroundings for what he needed in the faint light. In the end, all he could do was follow the cold air until he stumbled through the narrow entrance to the cave and into the freezing night. Collapsing to his knees, he threw up violently, struggling to catch his breath through the pain it caused his throat. With his hands in the snow, he coughed and swallowed, gulping in air in between, as his eyes watered and blurred his vision.

'Breathe through your nose,' Samien said, making him jump. 'Sorry...' he added quickly, placing a sheepskin cover over Quinn's shaking body.

Quinn shook his head dismissively, without turning around. He then sat down heavily, not caring that his undergarments were getting wet as his body heat melted the snow.

'The cold air will irritate your throat less if you breathe through your nose,' Samien said, crouching down in front of Quinn, who blinked and tried to focus on him.

Samien smiled a little awkwardly and Quinn felt guilty. The man was obviously finding it just as difficult to be around him. He had never been comfortable with the idea of people being afraid of him, ever since he had been forced to frighten Aliena's brother to get him to safety – before that, Renn was terrified of him. He was not surprised Samien feared him...Quinn had savagely taken his arm and his livelihood and forced him into exile.

When he was able to speak, he looked at Samien. 'Did you leave a family in Rivallen?'

Samien seemed surprised by the question and cocked his head slightly, studying Quinn's face. 'I was not married and I have no children,' he said. 'But I miss my parents and my brother.'

'I am sorry.'

'Don't be, please. I deserved what you gave me. And now I know what happened after I left, I could go back to them. The guards who helped me flee would testify that I was against the sheriff's ways.' Samien hung his head in shame. 'I was just too cowardly to do anything about it. I am sorry for what he did to you.'

'There was nothing you could have done. It would have taken more than just one man to stand up against that evil.'

'But you did it?' Samien said, looking up again.

'I had an advantage over him. And it got me killed.'

'What?'

Quinn realised he had said too much, but was saved from explaining by Alara's arrival at the cave entrance.

'What are you doing out here? You'll freeze…again!' she said, then looked accusingly at Samien for allowing it.

Samien held out his good arm and Quinn took it, accepting help in standing up on his unsteady legs.

Alara made him a hot drink, while Samien helped him into dry clothes, leaving off his undergarments, until they, too, were dry. He did not feel cold, but he ached all over and was glad when Alara told him the drink would ease his pain. All the same, he still winced when he swallowed it.

'What made you sick?' Alara asked. 'It would not have been anything I gave you…' She seemed worried and he wondered if she was also afraid of him.

'No,' he said. It was nothing you gave me. It was something I *saw*.'

Alara looked puzzled.

'It's the reason I came to Kilora in the first place. I sought you out because I need your help. I have visions. Not dreams, but *memories* that belonged to someone else.' When she didn't react with scorn or shock, he continued. 'They are trapped in my mind, and although they seem to be gradually revealing themselves, I need them…unlocked, so I can understand the things that have happened since they were forced upon me. One attempt has been made on my life already, I believe *because* I possess these memories. I need to understand why they tried to kill me. Maybe the answer to that lies within them. Do you think you can help?'

Alara sat down on the side of the bed, slightly surprised at Quinn's request. 'I don't know. I can read the thoughts of a person or animal while they are awake. I'm not sure if I can read memories…especially if they are not your own…'

Quinn slumped in the bed and Alara placed her hand on his arm. 'I am sorry. I need to give this some thought. It's not just the fact that it may not be possible…If it is possible, it could be very dangerous for you – for your state of mind. Do you understand?'

He nodded, trying to hide the fear that this whole journey had been for nothing. He wished Erelas was there to share some of his ever-present optimism and encourage him to not give up…

CHAPTER 71. CORVUS

Cara sensed Erelas' anger and allowed him to push her on until he was a comfortable distance from where they had encountered Maynard. The pace had been no more than a careful walk, and once darkness had fallen completely, he had to dismount and lead her, but she did not resist. He was taking them back along the route of Cara's senseless flight, and Erelas knew that it would take them at least half of the next day to get back to the river.

He tried not to be cross with Cara. She would have wanted to find Quinn as much as he did and he suspected some trickery might have been involved in her sudden urge to run deep into the forest. And she could not explain it to him, so he was forced to give her the benefit of the doubt. But the loss of time made him almost frantic and as the snow became heavier, he despaired of finding Quinn at all, let alone alive.

Eventually he was so thirsty he drank snow that he melted in his hands, managing to give some to Cara, too. They found a patch of ground that was free of it and suitable to rest on for the night.

As he was scraping out a shallow depression in the dry earth to lie on, a flap of wings startled them both. Cara snorted crossly as she looked towards the lowest branch of the tree they were to shelter under. Erelas followed the sound and saw a raven. It was clearly agitated, and at first Erelas thought it wanted them to go away. But then it suddenly flew from the branch and perched on his arm, bobbing its head up and down and screeching somewhat weakly at him. He raised an eyebrow and tried to place it back on to the branch, but it dug its talons into the vambrace on his right arm. As he stretched out his left hand to coax it off his arm, it lashed out with one foot and slashed its talons across his palm. He flinched so violently, shouting at the sharp pain, the bird fell off his arm and landed heavily on the ground.

Erelas nursed his injured hand under his right arm, glaring at the bird. '*Bastard!*' he hissed. The bird shook itself and flew back to the branch, where it began its dance once more. '*Go away!*' he shouted at it, but the raven would not leave.

He sighed in annoyance at it and then turned away. He fetched some snow and cleaned the scratches as best he could, but he had nothing with which to bind them. As he shook off the excess water, he glanced back at the tree. The raven was gone.

***

He was woken abruptly at first light by Cara scrambling to her feet; he was shoved unceremoniously sideways, his head impacting the frost-hardened ground, making him curse as he struggled to sit up. He blinked hard and twisted around to see what Cara was doing.

She stood a few feet from him. She had been startled, but not frightened by something… She stared and snorted, stamping a hoof and flicking her tail. Erelas turned back to look in the direction of her gaze and there, standing perfectly still in the serene light, was the black wolf.

Erelas scrambled to his feet in such a hurry he lost his balance and landed on his sore knees again. When he managed to stand, he straightened his clothes, never taking his eyes from the animal. Its face was gentle enough, and Erelas reminded himself of the lick it had given his hand when Quinn had called the truce between them. He tried to relax and stopped fidgeting.

'Peace to you,' he said quietly, then bowed his head in respect.

The wolf walked over to him and he held his breath as, again, it gently licked the hand that hung limply by his side. It turned away and walked a few paces before turning its head and looking at him.

Before Erelas had a chance to think about it, Cara started to follow the wolf.

'Cara!' he whispered. She ignored him. 'Cara – *wait*…your saddle!'

Cara carried on walking, careful to not get too close to the wolf, who also seemed unwilling to wait while Erelas gathered up their things. He snatched the saddle from against the tree, muttering under his breath, and grabbed the blanket from the ground. Running after them, the blanket trailing in the snow and between his boots, he stumbled several times before he caught up and forced Cara to stop. The wolf stopped and waited while Erelas prepared Cara. He mounted and they moved off together, heading north, towards the river…

CHAPTER 72. THE WOLVES GIVE HOPE

Quinn sat outside the cave, fully dressed this time and wearing a thick cloak of Samien's. The snow had stopped, but the morning remained overcast. He was worried about what kind of night Erelas would have spent in the forest with nowhere to shelter, probably exhausted from searching for him. Did Erelas believe he was dead? Would he give up and turn back for the border, thus missing the place Samien was hoping to find him?

'It won't be long now, Quinn. Don't worry yourself.'

Quinn looked around as Alara joined him on the huge boulder outside the cave entrance. She held two wooden cups of steaming liquid and handed one to him as she sat down. He took it gratefully, his throat stinging from the cool air. After swallowing a little and wincing, he changed his mind and held it between his palms to warm them up.

'Samien will find him.'

'How can you be so sure?' Quinn asked quietly, his voice still weak.

'Because I sent Amis to meet your friend and lead him to Samien.'

'Amis?'

'The leader of the wolves.'

'Oh, Erelas will *love* that,' Quinn said, with just the ghost of a smile.

'What do you mean?'

'They have met before. Erelas has a great deal of courage, but I think it almost failed him that day. He's never been fond of wolves. He looked like he thought I'd given Amis permission to have him for breakfast.'

Alara laughed. 'Amis is a gentle creature. He will defend the pack to the death, but he would never harm anyone who doesn't wish to hurt him or his family. It took me a long time to trust him. I remember what the wolves of Rivallen were like.' Alara looked into the distance. 'They took my cousin.'

'I am sorry,' Quinn said, placing a warmed palm on the back of her hand. Alara gave him a faint smile.

'Thank you,' she said. 'It was so long ago, I barely remember him. He was eight, I was seven. I wasn't with him when it happened, but I remember my aunt's tears and my uncle's fury. He left to hunt down the pack and didn't come back until he'd slaughtered them all. It took two years, but he did it. It turned him into a bitter old man and he died soon after. Such a waste all round.'

Quinn said nothing. He could not argue for the nature of a beast when her family had suffered so much. He left his hand where it was and looked into her sad green eyes.

She smiled again as she looked back at him. 'I eventually learned there are good wolves as well as bad,' she said. 'Just as there are good and bad people.'

'I saw a wolf, in Rivallen. At least, I think I did. I may have been hallucinating from exhaustion. Aliena said there are no more wolves there.'

'When?'

'The day of my banishment. Several months ago, now. I had taken shelter in a barn and it was in the doorway, just staring at me. It looked much like Amis, actually, but with amber eyes, not blue.'

'Ryia. She's the Alpha female of the pack. She often strays into Rivallen, I don't really know why. She can be gone for months. Was she there the next morning? She will often sleep in barns if there is no livestock in them.'

Quinn shook his head. I didn't see her. But then, I was—' Suddenly he stopped and stared at Alara, his eyes widening, inhaling sharply as the possibility hit him like a thump to the ribs.

'What is it?'

'Could you…I mean, is she here?'

'I'm sure she is close by. Why?'

'Would you be able to *ask* her something for me?'

'I can try. She is not as forthcoming as Amis and tends to avoid being with us as much as possible. What is it you need to know?'

Quinn felt his body tremble as hope stirred within him. 'I need to know if she *was* there the next morning. I was *shot* in that barn. With a poisoned arrow. I need to know if she saw it happen. I need to know who did it...' As he finished, he caught his breath, startled at the effect the idea had on him – the idea that with just a simple question he might find out who had tried to murder him. It was a heady notion and his skin crawled with the chill it gave him.

Alara squeezed his hand. 'I understand. I will seek her out and try to get the answers you need.'

He was prevented from answering by the sound of a horse approaching rapidly from the path that led up a slope away from the partially hidden entrance and into the forest. He jumped to his feet, dropping the cup, and glanced apologetically at Alara. She smiled, dismissing the matter, then caught his elbow as he struggled to gain his balance.

'Steady,' she said.

The horse whinnied loudly while still out of sight. Quinn's stomach seemed to leap as hope returned – he'd know that voice anywhere. He could not help but smile as the beautiful black mare appeared, white sweat on her coat where the reins had rubbed it into a froth. On her back, weary from his ordeal, but smiling broadly at the sight of Quinn – alive, safe – was Erelas.

Alara let him go as he carefully stepped forwards and put a hand briefly on Cara's nose. She understood. Erelas slid down from the saddle and they embraced each other, neither saying a word for several long moments. The relief between them was almost tangible.

Alara smiled, while Cara nodded her head in approval.

CHAPTER 73. THE ARCHER

After settling Cara down, listening to the story of Quinn's miraculous survival and relaying his tale of the encounter with Maynard, Erelas felt exhausted. Alara made him a bed to sleep on. Within moments of lying down and covering himself with thick blankets, he was fast asleep.

Quinn looked up at Alara as she rejoined him and Samien around the fire. 'One thing I don't understand...' he said, his damaged throat still affecting his voice. 'We know outsiders are not supposed to come here. How is it you two are permitted to stay?'

'I was given permission by the Saloreans; by Maynard, specifically. I pose no threat to them, as I am essentially a refugee. I simply wish to live without fear and have no desire to meddle in the affairs of this kingdom or its people.' She shrugged. 'Maybe he just pitied me. They're not all bad, just like the wolves. When the wolves brought me to where Samien lay hurt, I got a message to Maynard and he granted me permission to bring him here and tend to his wound. When he had recovered, Maynard allowed him to remain in Kilora – as long as he stays with me.'

'*We* have no wish to interfere with the people of this land, either. We came to find you, that is all,' Quinn said, defensively. 'I can't go on living like this... And we have no intention of remaining longer than necessary.'

'I agree,' said Alara. 'And I *am* surprised by the severity of their reaction – that they would try to kill you. When I arrived they were going to escort me back over the border until I begged them to grant me refuge...I can only assume it is because you are Conductors and we are not, so you pose more of a threat...I really don't know.' She stood up, smoothing her skirts down. 'I will seek out Ryia now the others have returned. I will be as quick as I can,' she added, placing a reassuring hand on Quinn's shoulder as she passed him.

Quinn nodded in gratitude and stared into the flames, attempting to focus on them rather than the turmoil that was in his mind.

Ryia padded into the cave just as Quinn's eyelids became heavy from staring into the fire for so long. When he heard Alara's soft footfalls he looked up and started at the sight of the huge black wolf approaching him with her great lolling tongue hanging between jagged rows of ferocious-looking teeth. As his mind recalled why she was here, he relaxed and straightened himself, trying to look calmer than he felt. He was more afraid of the answers she might give than of the wolf herself. He stole a quick glance at where Erelas was still sleeping deeply, before he looked up expectantly at Alara.

'I thought you should hear this with Ryia

present,' she said, sitting back down beside him. The wolf stood in front of them, eyeing Quinn with suspicion, or so Quinn told himself. He said nothing, but his nerves prickled at the tone in her voice.

'Ryia *did* rest outside the barn that night, not wanting to attract attention if she was seen by the animal inside. She heard the approach of the woman who lived there and was about to leave, when she saw another figure approaching. He was clad in a long hooded cloak and carried a bow. Ryia was nervous, wondering if she herself was the target. When the figure moved towards the barn, she knew she was safe. But she got curious and followed. She saw what happened, only thinking it best to leave when the young man appeared.'

Quinn remembered with a pang of guilt Elyan's protectiveness of his sister during that first encounter.

'It's the description of the figure I wanted to relay with Ryia here, Quinn. It was a *Conductor*.'

Quinn's mouth dropped open. 'That's not possible...' he breathed, the pit of his stomach filled with icy dread. He knew he'd rubbed several people up the wrong way over the years, and he wasn't so blind that he didn't see that some felt him guilty of murder on the day of his banishment...But surely none felt strongly enough to try to *kill* him?

'Please, Quinn, let me explain.'

He nodded for her to continue, feeling queasy.

'Ryia says the man was tall, like you, but much older, around sixty or so years. He had a beard that was turning white, and white eyebrows that almost met. His pupils were very much like your silver one, only gradually Ryia saw a change in them, a deeper light. She apologises for not being able to determine the colour for you more accurately. She heard him reciting something, she said. But it was the amulet he was wearing that made her so sure that he was a Conductor, Quinn.'

Still he could not speak, a chill running through his veins as he fought to take her words in.

'It was exactly the same as the one your friend wears.'

Finally, Quinn found his voice and looked directly at the wolf. 'Could you see a ring? On his left hand…the stone shaped like the tip of a sword blade..?'

Alara looked at Ryia, who lowered her head in assent.

'Oh, *God*…'

CHAPTER 74. A STORM OF THOUGHTS

'I just can't take it in,' said Erelas, his pale face looking even paler by the sunlight glinting off the snow. 'It's not *possible*, is it?'

'That's what *I* told her.' Quinn was frantically whittling a stick with a knife as Cara dozed, one hoof raised.

'God – I've got a *hell* of a headache. I could have done without this.' Erelas rubbed his temples as he leaned his elbows on his knees. They were sitting on the rocks outside the cave entrance. It was early morning and he had slept the previous day and all of the night, but did not appear to have benefited from the rest. He still looked tired and drawn, but he'd brushed off everyone's concerns.

'It just doesn't make sense. He already had me banished, so there would be no *point* in killing me as punishment for killing Renn's father.' Quinn rose and began to pace in front of Erelas, stick discarded, knife gripped tightly in his whitening fingers. 'Besides anything else, the Keeper *forbade* it!'

'Which infuriated the Archdeacon.'

'Enough to make him go directly against the Keeper? Did he believe he would get away with it, if I *had* died?'

Erelas sighed, his head throbbing and his

body feeling as if it were being stabbed by talons of ice. 'I don't know, Quinn. Maybe he would have. If you didn't know it was him, what could *you* have told the Keeper? Also, *they* never come here. Except to see you, apparently.' His smile died as quickly as it had been born. He shook his head as if to clear the jumble in his mind. 'Sorry, Quinn, I'm racing away with myself...But the attempt on your life makes sense in *one* respect...'

Quinn spun around to face him, trying to ignore the protest in his leg. 'What respect?' he said his voice harsh.

'These visions. Just for the sake of argument, let's work on the assumption that they are the real reason he got you out of Delmoril...and let's assume Ryia is right.'

'I'm not following...'

'What if they *do* contain something that reveals another side to him? What if they offer evidence that he is the one the Keeper spoke of – the one he wants you to hunt down? This destroyer of souls...'

'The visions are of the man who took my mind hostage, killing people. I have not seen anything whatsoever to do with the Archdeacon in them—'

'Yet.'

Quinn shook his head. Clarity slipped away and he could not accept that it was even possible. 'No, Erelas. This is all wrong – *she* is wrong!' He gestured towards the cave, although the wolf was long gone and Alara was out gathering plants with Samien.

Erelas stood up, frustrated with Quinn. 'What are you *afraid* of?'

'What?'

'What is it you are afraid of happening? Is it accepting the truth, or are you afraid to bring the Keeper this news, any news, because once you do, you know you will have to *face* the Archdeacon – or whoever else it might be – and stop him…destroy him? Spell it out to me, Quinn, because while you spin yourself into a web, I can't help you to think straight!' Erelas sat down again, suddenly too tired to do or say anything else.

Quinn stared at his normally mild-mannered friend in silence for a few moments. Erelas reminded him of Galen, and how Galen admonished him repeatedly for not focusing on the real issues. He swallowed hard and sat down next to Erelas, who was shivering again.

'I'm sorry,' Quinn said, his voice calmer. 'You're right, I'm not thinking straight. I need to focus on what we do now…'

Erelas shook his head and bent forwards, interlocking his fingers behind his head and resting his elbows on his legs again.

'Are you alright? Erelas, you've not been yourself since you woke up…'

'It's just this headache. I'm not used to them. I don't think Kilora agrees me very much.'

'Maybe Alara can give you something for it

when she returns.'

'Are you going to answer the question?'

Quinn sighed heavily and began to prise the dirt from under his fingernails with the point of the knife. 'What am I afraid of? Well, yes, I suppose I *am* afraid of being forced to go against the Archdeacon, if Ryia is right. Wouldn't *you* be? Me, against the most powerful man in the whole of Delmoril!' Quinn gave a humourless laugh. 'I'm only alive *now* thanks to his badly timed shot and Aliena's care. If I have to confront him – I don't see that ending well. But it's not just that. What else is hidden in those memories? What if you're right and it is the Archdeacon Rook was working for? What if the Archdeacon isn't doing…whatever he's doing…alone? And I don't mean people like Rook, although even he must have *something* supernatural about him to have been able to do what he did to me. I mean other Conductors—'

'Alright! Stop, I get it!'

Quinn frowned at Erelas. 'What's the matter with you? *You* asked!'

Erelas stood up and turned to go back into the cave. 'I'm sorry,' he said, not looking back. 'I think I need to lie down until this headache goes.' He walked a few steps away and then stopped. 'We will sort this out, Quinn. We just need to talk to the Keeper again. Until we can reach him, try to rest, relax, talk to Cara, *anything*. Winding yourself into a frenzy won't help.' He turned and disappeared into the cave without waiting for an answer. When he reached the makeshift bed, he collapsed on to it, shivering wildly, with the sound of his own blood thundering in his ears. He barely had strength to pull the blankets over himself. Closing his eyes, he wished that all this trouble would go away and they could be back in Delmoril, by the waterfall, at peace again.

Outside, Quinn looked over at Cara, who was still dozing, and decided to leave her be. Sighing, he locked his hands together and pressed his thumbs to his forehead. If he was distressing Erelas so much, he really did need to pull himself together.

CHAPTER 75. MORBUS

Quinn stayed out of the way, wanting to be alone with his thoughts once Alara and Samien returned, with bundles of leaves and winter flowers in two shallow reed baskets. While they busied themselves sorting them out for drying, he tended to Cara, making sure she was clean and comfortable and talking to her for a while. He felt bad that Erelas had lost his horse so soon, but he still had hope that she would be found alive. She may have been young and new to the task, but Conductor's horses were smart and generally able to look after themselves. The wolves would not harm her – Alara had got that from Amis himself.

The snow began to fall again, so he led her to the back of the cave, past Erelas, who was restless but still barely visible under the blankets. Quinn felt sorry that their conversation had ended up being so fraught, but Erelas had been exhausted and they had both been confused by everything they had learned. Maybe Erelas was right; maybe it *did* make sense that the Archdeacon had a desire to see Quinn dead. And maybe it had something to do with him needing to hide his crimes. All Quinn knew was that they couldn't figure this one out on their own – they needed the Keeper.

Cara lay down in the soft dust of the cave

floor. Quinn sat against her shoulder and rested his head against her warm neck. He knew they all needed rest. Nothing could be done that day, so there was no use making everyone's nerves jangle by going over it all a hundred times. He would wait until they were in a better state to be able to sit and think logically and pool their information.

He was woken from his dozing by Cara snorting. His eyes snapped open and, as he sat up straight, he saw Erelas staggering to his feet from the low bed. He tripped over the blanket he had let fall and landed heavily on the floor with a grunt of pain.

Samien had been right by the bed and instantly bent down to help Erelas. Quinn felt something flash through him – he could not have named the feeling, even long afterwards, but he scrambled to his feet and rushed over to them. '*Get away from him!*' he shouted. He shoved Samien roughly away, so hard that he had to twist and fall onto his back, rather than put the stump of his arm out to catch himself. He lay still, eyes wide, clearly too frightened to move, while Quinn knelt at Erelas' side. Alara stood up from her place by the fire and walked over warily, unsure of what had happened.

'Erelas!' Quinn said as gently as his panic would allow.

Erelas looked even paler than before. He shook violently, and his silver-grey eyes were wide with fear. He was gazing at some random point in the distance, unfocused and unresponsive to Quinn's voice. A small trickle of blood seeped from his nose and his breathing was ragged and shallow. One fist kept clenching and releasing over and over, while the other hand lay limp on the floor.

Quinn felt his forehead and frowned with worry as he felt how hot his skin was. 'Erelas...look at me...'

Erelas seemed to hear him that time and blinked hard, his eyes watering. 'She hates me,' he said breathlessly.

'What?' Quinn said. 'Who does?'

'Anwenn,' Erelas said, louder this time, trying to look towards Alara. He tried to lift his hand to gesture towards her, but did not have the strength to do so and quickly gave up trying. He looked back up at Quinn and said: 'She sent the raven.' Then he shouted: '*No* – she wouldn't *do* that!'

'Erelas,' Quinn said, his voice shaky. 'You're not making any sense. You're sick...you need to get back onto the bed.'

'*Morbus*...'

'Yes, you have a sickness...'

'*Corvus*...'

'A raven? Erelas, what does—'

Erelas shook his head and suddenly coughed. '*Misericordia!*' he gasped. He coughed again, and Quinn could see blood in his mouth.

Alara bent cautiously down at their side, exchanging worried glances with Quinn.

'I didn't know,' Erelas whispered, his eyes starting to close.

'Know what?' Quinn placed a cool palm on his cheek. 'Erelas, what do you mean? Didn't know what?'

'The raven was sick...'

Alara took Erelas' motionless hand and leaned over him so he could see her. 'Where did it scratch you, Erelas? When?'

Erelas stopped clenching his fist and opened out his fingers. Across the centre of his palm were three deep scratches, red and angry against the paleness of his clammy skin. '*Cruciatus*,' he said weakly.

'What did he say?' Alara asked Quinn.

'He said it is agony...' Quinn could tell by her expression that she knew what was wrong with Erelas and that it was not good news.

Alara turned back to Erelas and stroked his left temple with her fingers. 'When was this?'

Erelas coughed again and seemed to fade a little, but then fought back and looked directly at her. 'Two nights.'

'Two nights,' repeated Quinn. 'That was when he met with this Salorean, wasn't it?' he said quickly, a flash of anger crossing his face. 'If this was *his* doing...'

Erelas grabbed Quinn's sleeve and pulled him closer, his eyes wide again. He shook his head as steadily as he could and tried to swallow again. With his consciousness failing, he barely managed to breathe the words: 'No! Maynard wasn't there...' Sudden pain seemed to strike him and he arched his back and squeezed his eyes shut. With a strangled yell he clawed at Quinn's arm, but despite Quinn and Alara trying to encourage him to hold on, he passed out. A dark trickle of blood escaped from his mouth and slowly made its way down his jaw.

'What did he say? I couldn't hear him,' Alara asked.

'He said Maynard wasn't there. This wasn't him.'

'That is just as well,' Alara said, looking fearfully into Quinn's eyes. 'Because we are going to *need* him.'

CHAPTER 76. AN UNORTHODOX INTRODUCTION

Quinn stood and watched helplessly as Alara fought to keep Erelas calm in between short periods of unconsciousness. He had been stripped down to his undergarments, but still he was soaked in sweat and shivering violently. He was greatly agitated; often he would speak to people who were not there, or start yelling in Latin. More than once Quinn heard him mention the Archdeacon, but he could not make any sense of what Erelas was saying about him.

'How much longer?' he asked Alara, even though he knew she did not know the answer. 'And how do we know he will even come?'

'He will be as quick as he can, Quinn. Amis will guide him along the swiftest path. I told him to tell Maynard that it is *me* who is sick...' She wiped blood away from under Erelas' nose and washed the cloth in cool water. 'He's going to have to go into the pit if this fever does not ease soon. It can be used to cool as well as to warm the body.'

'He *can't*,' Quinn said. 'We'd never keep him calm in there. He would only hurt himself more.'

'He is boiling. He will *die* if we cannot stop the fever rising further.' Quinn looked at the pit. It was a deep hollow, carved out and polished smooth by the Kilorans who had once lived in this cave, but abandoned it for reasons Alara did not know. The Saloreans allowed her to live in it and even got the pit working for her again. It was fed by a spring that ran through the floor of the cave and two openings in the side of the pit let water in or out, and could be closed by perfectly fitting rocks being slotted into them. The water was heated by a fire that was lit under one end of the pit, the smoke being channelled up through a shaft in the rock and out into the open. Quinn had never seen anything like it before – in Delmoril they kept clean using the waterfalls, and in Rivallen the people bathed in the rivers and lakes, if at all. He had never bathed in warm water before and the luxury of it amazed him as much as the fact that it had saved his life.

He knew Alara was right: she *could* control the temperature of the water in the pit to make it work in reverse by feeding cold water gradually into water that was at the body's temperature. It would be an effective, yet safe way to bring down Erelas' fever, but he was just too volatile now. He would likely panic and thrash about and Quinn could not bear to risk him smashing his head against the side of the pit in an attempt to escape the horrors flooding his tortured mind. All he could do was pray Samien returned quickly – and that Maynard had agreed to come with him.

'We can take him outside.' Quinn suggested. 'Use the snow...'

Alara shook her head. 'It would be too sudden. The shock would stop his heart.'

'*For the love of God...*' Quinn breathed, closing his eyes and crouching down at the side of the bed. He held out his hand and Alara passed him the cloth. Wetting it further in the bowl of cool water, Quinn dabbed Erelas' face, his own a mask of fear.

Alara stood up, placed a hand on Quinn's shoulder for a moment and then walked to the cave entrance to keep a look out for Samien. Cara, who had been eating outside, wandered over and nudged her and Alara whispered to her.

Quinn hoped she was praying, too.

Erelas suddenly gasped and as Quinn leaned in closer, grabbed the front of his shirt with his good hand. Quinn was surprised at his strength, for he could not break his hold. He froze as he saw turquoise sparks dancing in Erelas' eyes. At that moment, he had no idea what his friend was going to do to him...

Erelas looked straight into Quinn's eyes as blood began to flow freely from his nose. '*Get away from me, Devil!*' he shouted. Quinn heard Cara voice her alarm outside. He looked at Erelas, frightened of him, though it was a fear he could not explain. Erelas yelled again, shaking Quinn by his collar: '*Christ help me!*' His scratched hand was thrown up and reached for Quinn's throat. He tried to pull back, but Erelas' grip was too strong and all he succeeded in doing was lifting him from the bed.

Just as he was about to close his hand

around Quinn's throat, a hand was clamped onto Erelas' forehead and he was forced back down. The combined effort of that and Quinn's own struggle made Erelas lose his grip and Quinn leaned over him, pinning his wrists down at his sides. As soon as he knew he had control, he looked up.

The man he saw bending over the bed was huge. He was cloaked and much of his face was hidden, but his eyes were glowing slightly with purple sparks. Quinn could see finely-crafted, strong armour through the opening of the cloak, along with an enormous sword hanging from a leather belt around his waist. Erelas had described him in detail, but Quinn had to admit he was impressed by the man in the flesh. Maynard did not meet his gaze, but continued to keep his focus on Erelas.

Quinn looked back at Erelas. Maynard's hand still held him down and he was still fighting and cursing and pleading, but he was under control and losing his strength rapidly.

'*Miserère nobis*!' he gasped, his whole body going rigid.

The glow in Maynard's eyes intensified, the deep purple casting flickers of light on Erelas' deathly-pale skin as he leaned closer. 'Peace, now...' the Salorean said in a deep, but gentle voice. '*Rest*. It will all be over soon...'

Quinn looked past the man and saw Alara and Samien standing close to the cave entrance. Samien looked scared and out of breath. Alara shook her head slightly at Quinn and he understood that she did not want him to interrupt. Maynard was not going to harm Erelas.

He looked back and saw Erelas was beginning to relax his body a little, but blood was still flowing back into his throat and he struggled to breathe. It took all of Quinn's willpower not to interfere, and he was relieved when Erelas managed to cough, then swallow and clear his airway a little. As he gulped air down, he seemed to lose his tension and his wide eyes slowly closed. In just a few more moments he was completely calm, and Quinn was able to let go of his wrists and straighten himself up. Maynard stayed where he was. The purple sparks danced between his eyes and Erelas' face, some of them entering his nose and mouth as he drifted into darkness and peace.

Eventually, Maynard took his hand away and straightened up, his eyes returning to their normal silver-grey. Quinn stood up to face him. They eyed each other suspiciously and with caution, while Alara and Samien remained motionless.

Finally, Maynard pulled back the hood from his head and spoke. 'Well...' he said. 'It's not every day I get to meet a living legend.'

CHAPTER 77. HOSTILITIES

'So – you have the Devil in you?' Maynard asked mildly, as he looked Quinn straight in his good eye.

Quinn frowned as he looked at the larger man, taking him in properly now he was standing upright. He was not afraid of Maynard, but he considered how a Kiloran must feel when confronted with such a solid threat of a man. Sheer size aside, the unequal division of his rugged face by a vivid red scar made him even more intimidating and Quinn couldn't imagine the man ever smiling. He had the look of a nomad, but where Conductors from Delmoril would return home to fresh clothes and bathing in its waterfalls, Maynard looked as if he hadn't seen clean water for days. There was also a faint smell of damp about him, rather than the usual smell of horses, as was a trademark of the Delmoril Conductors. Quinn briefly wondered if he had an equine companion at all.

'I heard what Erelas said as I came in,' Maynard explained when Quinn made no answer.

'You didn't think I ended up a killer by *choice*, did you?' Quinn snapped. 'Unlike Saloreans.'

Maynard took a step towards him so that he was forced to look up to meet his glare. '*Go home*, Quinn,' he said, his voice taking on a sinister calmness. 'Take Erelas, forget his missing horse and go home. There is nothing but trouble here for you. I'm sure there's a limit to how many times even *you* can be raised from the dead.'

'Just what *is* it you and your kind are hiding, to hate outsiders so much that you'll murder them?'

'Stop it, *both* of you,' Alara said, stepping between them. 'Quinn, I understand you are still upset about what Ryia told you, but Maynard has helped Erelas and you should be grateful for that, if nothing else. And, Maynard, you should have more empathy for what he has gone through over the last few months. Leave each other alone, if you cannot get along.'

'I *am* grateful,' snapped Quinn. 'More than *he* will ever appreciate. And, as it happens, I'd like nothing more than for him to leave us alone.'

The two men glared at one another for several long moments, before Maynard pushed past them and strode out of the cave. He paused at the entrance and turned back to Alara. 'You lied to me. No more favours, Alara. You knew the rules and you broke them. You're on your own.'

Alara looked at the floor, not daring to argue with the big Salorean. She didn't look up until his footsteps receded.

Quinn sighed heavily and sat down on Erelas' bed. Taking his hand, he turned the palm uppermost and gave a slight nod of satisfaction when he saw that the scratches had vanished. He also checked his forehead and was relieved to find the fever had passed. Erelas would most likely sleep for the rest of the day now and wake up back to his old self. It was hard to believe that he'd been so close to death just a short while ago. The Saloreans had very strong healing abilities, it seemed.

He looked up and saw that Alara was crying and being comforted by Samien, his one good arm wrapped around her shoulders as she leaned into his broad chest.

Still, Quinn did not like the ex-guard. He felt guilt over his part in the man's circumstances, and he did not like anyone to be afraid of him, but something about him was distasteful to Quinn. He considered Samien a coward in general, and cowardice was something he had always despised.

He decided that if Alara wouldn't – or couldn't, after Maynard's threat – help him, the sooner they could return to Rivallen, the better.

He stood up and left Erelas to rest, deciding to sit away from all the misery he seemed to have brought down on them all.

CHAPTER 78. A COMPANION RETURNS

Quinn rushed out into the glare of the sunlight reflecting off the snow, still pulling one of his boots on. He squinted and cursed as he almost slipped, but then stood straight and found what he was looking for. '*Erelas*!'

Erelas looked up and smiled. 'Look who's back!'

Quinn's mind did not register what Erelas was doing until that moment. He held Einna, who was stood quietly, enjoying his attention, wearing her saddle and bridle and carrying all the things Erelas had left behind when he had raced off on Cara to find Quinn.

Quinn's jaw dropped. He looked completely confused and Erelas laughed.

'I'm sure she's pleased to see you, too,' he said.

'But how...no – never mind that. Are you alright? You *scared* me. I woke up and you'd gone!'

'Now who's fussing?' Erelas grinned. 'I feel fine. A little bit fuzzy and tired, like I've spent all night in a tavern on too much good wine, but without the headache. Look – Cara's followed you out.'

Quinn looked around to see his mare standing at the entrance to the cave, tossing her head up and down in approval at Einna's return. 'You should be resting,' he said to Erelas.

'Well, I was. But I heard Einna arrive.'

'How did she get here? With all her gear, too?'

'Maynard.'

'What?'

'There's a note...' Erelas held out a scrap of parchment.

Quinn took the note and read it. He raised an eyebrow and looked at Erelas, who was back to making a fuss of his mare. 'Charming man. How did he find her *and* all her stuff, I wonder?'

Erelas looked at Quinn, surprised. 'God – you're so cynical, Quinn. Maybe she was waiting by her stuff. She's a smart horse, she might have gone back to wait for us to find her.'

'If she was so smart she wouldn't have run off in the first place.'

'Be nice! She can understand you, you know.'

Quinn walked over and patted the chestnut mare's glistening coat. 'I am sorry, Einna. I'm grumpy this morning.'

Einna nudged Quinn gently and then snorted softly, turning her head back to her master.

'She looks well,' Erelas said.

'Better than you. Go back inside and rest. I'll take her gear off and she can rest inside with Cara.'

'Are we going to do what the note says?'

Quinn looked at the note again. '"Give heed to my warning and go home." That would depend.'

'On what?'

'Alara. He was very angry with her. I don't want to leave her if she is in danger of retribution.'

'She has Samien.' Quinn burst out laughing, making Einna jerk back.

'What's so funny?' Erelas asked.

'He's terrified of *me*, let alone Maynard.'

'I meant to *plead her case*, Quinn. Not everyone fights with swords. Besides anything else, what are you going to do to protect her – stay here and wait for the Saloreans to force us out, or worse? We're defenceless out here, our abilities don't work, remember?'

'Actually, they do.'

'Since when?'

'The night you arrived, when you were asleep. I was thinking about the Archdeacon. I got myself wound up into a bit of a state and went outside to cool off. I was squeezing a small rock in my hand and before I knew what I was doing, I did the exploding stone thing that used to make the scholars so mad...'

It was Erelas' turn to laugh. 'Well it did used to send every horse within earshot running for cover. Used to take them hours to round them back up again. You never did get bored with doing that.'

Quinn smiled. 'Well it didn't exactly go the same way that night; far less power than normal. Which is just as well, really, or I'd have blown my fingers off. But it did shatter into half a dozen pieces. So my power *is* weakened here, but it works. I've been testing it out of sight of the others. Small stuff...however, my sword isn't taking any power from me at all.' Quinn moved to Einna's side and undid her girth straps. 'Anyway, you do have a point about Alara. And I don't think she wants to help me, not deep down – and I don't blame her. So I guess we might as well leave at first light tomorrow. You need one more day's rest. And yes, I *am* fussing. It's time I repaid *that* particular favour.'

***

Erelas was delighted to be able to use the pit that afternoon; he still felt quite chilled and complained that he smelled worse than Einna. While he bathed, Alara took Quinn to sit by the fire with her and Samien.

'I want to offer you what help I can with your visions,' she announced.

Surprised, Quinn looked from her to Samien, who instantly looked at the floor. It irritated Quinn, but he said nothing.

'You came all this way and you have both been through hell. I don't want it to all have been for nothing. It wouldn't cost me anything to try to help you.'

Quinn still did not speak. This was what he had come to Kilora for, knowing it was a risky journey. He had now discovered the Archdeacon had tried to kill him, and that was proving hard enough to come to terms with. The thought that he might actually discover the reason behind it all – what it was in his head the Archdeacon wanted kept secret – suddenly gave him a feeling of dread that wrenched his stomach towards the ground. Once he had that knowledge, he would have to act on it and there would be no going back. And, the more he considered it, the more Erelas' theory made sense. If the Archdeacon was indeed the 'destroyer of souls', then he had no idea how he could defeat him – it was too much for him. The Keepers had chosen the wrong man...

'Are you alright?' Alara asked.

Quinn inhaled, deeply and slowly, looking into her green eyes. 'I don't know if I can do this...'

'I saw you last night, Quinn. You had the visions again, didn't you? I watched you go outside. I saw what they do to you.' Alara moved closer to him and took his hand. 'You don't deserve to have to live like this. Whatever may come of what you discover, you have a right to understand what it is you are forced to see. Maybe then we can find some way to rid you of them...'

'There *is* no way,' Quinn said quietly. 'Even the Keeper couldn't do anything for me. I will carry these visions for the rest of my life.'

Alara felt fresh compassion for him, and squeezed his hand. 'Then all that is left is for you to get justice.' Quinn said nothing, unable to help feeling a sudden sense of being trapped.

'Let's do this, Quinn. Don't walk away and miss the chance to get some sense out of your suffering. You don't want to have to make this trip all over again when it becomes too much to carry one day in the future. *Do it now*. Get it over with.'

Quinn knew she was right. He sighed, trying to suppress the sense of fear he felt, as if he were wading into cold, deep water and it was beginning to crush his chest. 'How do we do it?'

'That's the nasty part.' She squeezed his hand again. 'I am sorry. There is no easy way to do it. You must be asleep, and I must *force* you into that sleep. Your own subconscious must not be allowed to interrupt the flow of the memory. Which means you will not be able to wake yourself from it. You will be trapped in the visions until *I* wake you.'

Quinn swallowed. 'For how long?' His voice shook a little and he glanced at Samien, who was staring steadily at him. Quinn wondered what he was thinking...

Alara shook her head. 'I do not know. I will have to judge when you have seen enough. I will see what you are seeing, although I will remain awake—'

'Is there no way to unlock them without you seeing them?'

'No.'

'But...'

'Do not worry about me, Quinn. I will be alright.'

'But they make me sick...'

'That is because you do more than just see them, Quinn. You feel them. You experience them as if they are *your* memories, but you still keep your conscience, your sense of right and wrong. I will just be an observer. My telepathy is not the kind that feels empathically what the other person is feeling. I will be quite safe, I promise.'

CHAPTER 79. THE MEMORY MADE WHOLE

Quinn saw himself leave the tavern and go out into the street. It was dark and chilly and there were few people about at this hour, but voices could be heard from an alley not far away, just like before. The body he was trapped in turned towards the sound and Quinn saw the man and the woman again. He had tried to stifle the leering grunt that escaped his lips and replace it with a warning shout, but it didn't work.

The woman's dress was still pulled up and the man still stood between her legs. He was still supporting the woman's weight as he slammed into her and Quinn could hear him panting against her throat as he drew nearer to the couple. She groaned with him as he increased the speed and power of his thrusts further still. The man almost reached his climax and Quinn knew that those exhilarating moments would be his last.

Quinn found himself saying desperate prayers in his mind once again, for something to happen that would break their spell and let them know they were in mortal danger. But it was too late – too late by months, maybe even longer. Their lives had been stolen long ago, and even God could not change the past.

He felt his hand gripping the handle of the dagger as he approached the couple without a sound. Again, he stood directly behind the man and their loud passion hid his presence from them. Quinn watched helplessly as his left hand gripped the man's shoulder, while his right hand dealt the fatal blow. The hot blood sprayed over the woman's bare skin as his body stiffened, caught between ecstasy and pain, pleasure and terror. The woman cried out, then screamed as realisation hit her. Quinn's mind flinched, the noise assaulting his sanity, but there was nothing he could do. He knew from months of bitter experience that he could never win these battles and that this rogue memory had a vice-like grip on his consciousness until someone was able to rescue him by waking him up. Only this time, he had to stay with it right until the very end, until Alara judged that he had seen all he needed to see. He briefly wondered if she could read his thoughts about the trust he had placed in her, before the vision before him forced him into new territory...

The man's body slumped, lifeless, to the ground, as he – Rook – smashed his fist into the woman's face to bring an abrupt end to her screaming. Dazed, she stared wild-eyed and petrified at him, as he grabbed the front of her dress and began to haul her back towards the tavern. He said nothing, but Quinn felt the twisted smile of self-satisfaction crossing the alien face he was merged with. The woman whimpered as she stumbled along, trying to keep pace with him. Blood drooled from her split lips and min-

gled with that of her dead lover. As they reached the tavern, he shoved her through the door and locked it behind them, as she tried to comprehend the scene of carnage in front of her. She was not given much time to take it in, however, as she was pulled by her wild, dark hair towards the stairs, and half-dragged up to the room where the youth lay dead. The smell of vomit and urine hit the back of Quinn's throat and made him feel sick. The woman, too, gagged, and tried to dig her heels into the floor to prevent being shoved closer to the evil she didn't want to face. But, just as Quinn had to, face it she did. She was thrown to the floor, landing hard on her knees, where she gasped for air in between sobs of fright. The door was closed and he felt his face distort into the now-familiar grimace of sick pleasure the rogue derived from his task.

'Hush now,' he heard the parasitic voice say. 'I'm not going to hurt you. We wait here for a while, then I pass you over to someone else and I get paid. You never see me *again. How's that sound, eh?'*

The woman said nothing, but looked up at him, the plea in her tear-laden eyes plain to see.

Quinn tried to calm his thoughts as the body he was in stood by the door, listening. He was forced to keep looking at the distraught woman and the dead body on the floor mere inches from her. The trickle of vomit which had escaped the youth's gag had run down his face, mingling with the blood the injury from the floorboards had inflicted upon his skull. The urine had mostly been held in the fabric of his cheap clothes, but some had seeped into the wood, and it smelled as if the contents of his bowels had begun to leak from his corpse, too. Rook sniffed, coughed and turned away. Quinn thought the gesture one of mild annoyance rather than disgust at the results of his actions. He could not begin to fathom the workings of this man's polluted soul; how he could live with himself and the things he had done, what drove him to commit such acts of depravity. It was incomprehensible to Quinn. His inability to understand made him fear for his sanity afresh – he felt as if it was balanced on a brittle twig, and that twig was liable to snap at any moment...

Footsteps brought his thoughts back to the vision; someone was approaching up the staircase. Rook stood up straight and waited. A knock, then two more, then a pause, then two further taps. A signal. He opened the door, and at that moment Quinn's worst suspicions and Erelas' theory were both realised. There, in hooded black robes, looking more filled with fury than Quinn had ever known, stood the Archdeacon.

'Master...' he heard himself say, the smirk gone from his face, the tension in his body suddenly holding him rigid. 'I...'

'You what, you stunted monster!' bellowed the Archdeacon, inches from his face as he pushed his way into the room. 'What the hell have you done? What is that mess down in the tavern?'

Quinn looked at the floor, something akin to shame flooding through this borrowed body. 'It all got out of hand. I couldn't stop myself. I saved one for you, but I killed him by mistake, so I went and got her.' He pointed to the woman, who still quietly sobbed with her hands in her lap, staring like a hunted deer at the men in the room. *'I had to hit her to shut her up, but she's good. She's just been showing how healthy she is up the alley with her lover.'* He added this last bit of information with a chuckle which made Quinn's mind want to scream out...

'You disgust me, Rook. One task, that's all I give you, just one, and you end up turning the place into a butcher's shop!'

'I'm sorry, Master. It gets in the blood. Surely you understand. You can't resist what you feel when I give you what you need. I'm no different!'

Quinn's mind reeled along with Rook's body, as the Archdeacon backhanded him across the face. He stumbled as the woman shrieked, but stayed on his feet and looked defiantly at the Archdeacon. 'I want payment. I did what you asked. What I did before *I got her is no business of yours!'*

The Archdeacon took a step towards Rook, but he held his ground, licking blood from his lips.

'We're done,' spat the Archdeacon. *'After this night, we're done. I will find someone else. Wait for me outside, I will pay you when I am through here.* Get out!'

Rook stepped past the Archdeacon, stole a last glance at the terrified woman and left the room, pulling the door closed behind him. As Quinn tried to make sense of the events, Rook took him along the small corridor and into the adjoining room, careful not to make a sound. In the empty darkness, he crept to the wall between this room and the room the Archdeacon was in and slid his face along the boards until his eye found the crack that allowed him a view of the Archdeacon and his victim.

Unable to comprehend what the Archdeacon might possibly be about to do to the woman, Quinn could only clutch at the thought of his trust in Alara – that she would pull him out before he lost what was left of his tortured mind...

The Archdeacon approached the woman slowly but purposefully, lowering his hood and levelling his piercing silver-eyed gaze on her without sympathy for her fright. 'Stand up,' he barked suddenly, even causing Rook to flinch. The woman stayed where she was, visibly shaking, blinking hard, tears and mucus from her nostrils mingling on her top lip as she held back her sobs.

The Archdeacon reached down and hauled her to her feet by her upper arms, the pressure causing her to emit a squeak of pain. Once up, he grabbed the sides of her head, taking fistfuls of her curls to keep her from escaping his grip. Her mouth opened and closed like a fish drowning in air, but no sound came out. The Archdeacon's eyes began to change colour, deepening to a thick indigo, purple sparks dancing in front of them as her watery eyes widened still further. He inhaled deeply, his body seeming to shudder, as in an instant her eyelids began to droop as if she was falling into a faint. Her legs started to buckle, but still he held fast, the sparks drawing some kind of misty substance from her eyes into his own. He groaned and shuddered, almost as if he was in sexual ecstasy. His mouth dropped open to draw in extra oxygen as the mist increased. The woman's body weakened further, until he was holding her up entirely by himself, and still the mist flowed from her eyes. He cried out as if in a final peak of pleasure and then he let go of her. She crumpled into a heap beside the soiled corpse of the youth. The Archdeacon slowly sank to his knees, breathing hard, hands trembling. His face was a mask of serene satisfaction, with a hint of some intense energy flowing through his body.

Rook kept watching and Quinn fought to understand. The Archdeacon was killing people, drawing their energy out of them, feeding on their very souls...because it gave him a rush of pleasure? *It was just too abhorrent to contemplate, but he had now seen it for himself, through the memory of the man who supplied his victims. There was no backing away from the truth. The Archdeacon was responsible for all the souls that had gone missing. He had fed upon them, as if their soul energy was some kind of potion, something he was addicted to, craved, enjoyed. And he'd had this wicked man, whose memories were now trapped inside of Quinn, to bring him what he needed, time and time again. He couldn't help but wonder who was supplying the victims now Rook was serving his sentence in Hell...*

He was brought back to the vision sharply when the Archdeacon suddenly looked up, towards the crack in the boards. Rook pulled away, but it was too late – the Archdeacon had seen him and realised Rook had spied on his deeds…

In a heartbeat Rook was running, out of the door, crashing along the corridor and half-stumbling down the rickety wooden stairs, before slipping on a pool of congealing blood on the tavern floor. Righting himself, he glanced up the stairs and saw the Archdeacon pursuing him, steadier, more slowly, but without a shred of panic in his carriage. He knew he would catch Rook, no matter what the man did. Still Rook ran, sliding across to the main door and unlocking it. Throwing it open, he desperately searched for somewhere to hide, but he knew the truth – there was nowhere to hide from the Archdeacon. In a bid to do anything but stand still and wait to be caught, he began to run, his fists clenching as he heard the Archdeacon closing behind him.

Quinn panicked – this was where Rook died. This was the alleyway he had been called to that fateful night. He remembered the crooked houses, the stench, the wounds, the blood… Now he was going to feel Rook's death himself, every lingering, agonising second of it. Alara had to rescue him; she wouldn't let him endure that, surely? There was no need for him to see, let alone feel Rook's end…

He prayed and tried to transmit a plea for help to Alara, as he felt the strong grip of the Archdeacon's hand slam down onto his shoulder. His breath caught in his throat as his eyes confirmed what his own memory had brought to mind. The Archdeacon was holding a sword – Rook's own sword – ready to thrust into

his borrowed flesh.
    God help me*! his mind screamed.*

CHAPTER 80. CLASH OF THE BROTHERHOOD

Quinn snapped upright on the low bed, knocking Alara backwards to land heavily on the damp floor. As he jumped to his feet, rather unsteadily, the sweat pouring down his face and his eyes blazing with red sparks, she reached out in an effort to calm his obvious fury.

'*Don't touch him*!' yelled Erelas, snatching her arm back. 'He'll *kill* you – and he won't know he's doing it!' He pulled her up and ushered her behind him, glancing at Samien to make sure he, too, heeded the warning.

Quinn was almost catatonic. He took rasping breaths of freezing air as his legs battled to hold him up. The sparks danced; the turquoise of his functioning eye was barely visible through the red display of rage.

'What do we do?' asked Alara in a trembling voice.

'Nothing. There is nothing we can do. Except keep away from him and wait.'

'For how long?'

'I don't *know*, for the love of God!'

Alara fell silent, tears pricking her eyes. She felt a mixture of fear and guilt – she knew she should have pulled Quinn out of the memory sooner, but something had pushed against her efforts, and whatever it was had been strong. It had taken all her skill and determination to win the battle, but by then it had been too late. Quinn had witnessed the death of the rogue, from the rogue's point of view. Not just witnessed, but felt the pain, the fear, the disbelief. She could not imagine the trauma he was experiencing right now and she was not surprised by his violent reaction.

'I'm sorry,' Erelas said, placing a hand on her arm without taking his eyes off Quinn. 'I didn't mean to snap.'

'It's alright,' Alara said, looking at the concern in his face. She understood his fear. She knew he was wondering if Quinn had escaped with any shred of himself left at all...

Quinn sank slowly to his knees, dropping his gaze from some distant point to the floor underneath him, the sweat trickling down his nose and dripping into the dirt. His fists clenching over and over, he pushed against his knees with his wrists, fighting against complete collapse. 'I'll kill him,' he whispered, barely loud enough for his companions to hear. He looked up and there was a collective sense of relief among them as they saw the red sparks were thinning out and the turquoise light shone clearly from the iris of one eye – the other eye still black and sightless. As he searched for familiarity in the cave, Erelas slowly stepped forwards, indicating with an open hand that the others were to remain where they stood.

'Who, Quinn?' he said gently. Then he suddenly halted his progress as a fresh flare of red lit up Quinn's eyes.

Quinn's fearsome glare scanned the cave, turning to a look of confusion when he was unable to find his target. '*The Archdeacon*,' he hissed, digging his fingernails into his palms so deeply they drew blood.

'Alara, Samien,' Erelas said in a low voice, without looking round. 'Get out.'

'But...' the former guard began, his voice weak.

'There's no *time*!' Erelas shouted. 'Get *out* – and stay away until I come and find you!'

Quinn made a move to scramble from his knees to his feet as Samien rushed from the cave, followed by a more hesitant Alara.

'No, Quinn! Wait...*please*...he's not *here*!'

Quinn looked at his friend, his eyes unchanging, but, for now, he remained where he was.

'Tell me what you saw,' Erelas continued, taking another cautious step forwards. Racing through his mind was the fear that Quinn's abilities were recovered far beyond the destruction of small pebbles as the anger was directed back towards him.

'You let him go...' His voice was unnervingly steady and Erelas stopped again, now just inches from Quinn's reach.

'Listen to me,' he said. 'The Archdeacon was never here – we're in *Kilora*, remember? With Alara and Samien – and the Quinn I *know* you still are does not want to kill anyone, least of all innocent people. Let them go until you are yourself again. Tell me what is going on, tell me what the Archdeacon has done! We'll find another way to –'

'To what?' snapped Quinn, making Erelas flinch. 'Get *justice*?'

Erelas steeled his jaw before he replied. 'Yes. Isn't that what you've spent your whole life fighting for?'

Quinn glared viciously at him, but still made no move.

Erelas inched forwards and crouched down in front of Quinn, his gaze never wavering. He had to hope his friend was not lost and he was determined to help, however nervous he might feel. 'Tell me – what *happened*? What did you see?'

But Quinn stood up and Erelas mirrored the action, blocking Quinn's path as he saw his eyes flick towards the cave entrance. He could hear a man's voice, rising, panicked but also angry...

'That's Samien, Quinn. It's *not* the Archdeacon. *Don't...*' Erelas pleaded.

'Get out of my way, Erelas.'

'No! You don't want to do this. Fight the rage, Quinn. I know you can. I *swear* to you, that is not the Archdeacon!'

Quinn stepped towards him, his face barely able to adequately express his feelings. 'You don't know *anything*!' he hissed.

Erelas did nothing but stare in disbelief as

Quinn slowly turned and retrieved his sword from beside the bed.

The sharp scrape of the blade being pulled from the scabbard rang ominously in Erelas' ears. His long-time friend advanced on him, bringing the weapon up until the blade was pointing directly at his chest. 'What are you *doing*?' he asked, his voice loaded with confusion and more than a little hurt.

'Making sure this ends here.' Quinn's tone was flat, almost as if the words came automatically and with no forethought. 'Get out of my way, Erelas, or I will kill you,' he said, as he tossed the scabbard aside.

Erelas slowly drew his own sword, while still believing Quinn was bluffing and would never use a weapon on him. 'This is *madness*, Quinn! You're not thinking straight…The dream…'

'The dream made things clearer than ever!'

The point of Quinn's blade was now less than a foot away from Erelas and he was forced to bring his own weapon up to block it and adopt a defensive stance. It was a single-handed weapon, a beautifully crafted broadsword, but Erelas found himself brandishing it with both hands, unable to keep it steady enough with just one. The prospect of being forced to fight someone he considered his brother was turning his limbs to water. Even though he knew Quinn could not use the sword's power against him, a fellow Conductor, he knew the end result of the clash could nevertheless be disastrous.

He was, however, glad he had opted for the more secure grip, when Quinn suddenly flicked his blade up and across, clashing with Erelas' sword and scraping along the sharp edge with a metallic hiss. Erelas flinched, but did not lose his hold on the sword. Tightening his hands around the corded leather grip still further, he stared at Quinn, willing him to snap out of the delusion he was under. Words were pointless now.

But, far from coming to his senses, Quinn began to *mock* Erelas with his blade, perhaps recalling his superior skills over those of his friend when it came to combat. He flexed his wrist, left, then right, each time knocking Erelas' sword to the side, then waiting for it to be moved back into its precarious defensive position in the centre. Then he swung it in an arc, bringing it down towards Erelas' legs at an alarming speed. Erelas only just managed to block the move and jump back a step. His eyes flicked down to Quinn's blade momentarily, his shock evident as once again Quinn began to play games with him – a feint here, a jab there. All the while his vicious expression probed Erelas' face for clues to his next move…

Erelas began to get angry. He may not have been able to match Quinn's natural flare for the blade, but neither was he a novice – he had never beaten Quinn in training, but he had beaten plenty of other Conductors with his speed and lightness of foot. On Quinn's next move, another sweeping arc, this time towards his head, Erelas ducked, spun round and with a shout of defiance brought his blade around one-handed, with an audible rush of air, towards Quinn's body.

Quinn blocked, the clash of metal uncomfortable in the confines of the cave. But Erelas didn't miss the flicker of surprise in his eyes. However, that move came at a price when, faster than Erelas could dodge it, Quinn brought his still-booted foot up and caught him in the ribs. Snapped double, he lost his balance and fell to the floor, his hands jarred by the impact. Severely winded, he had to ignore the burning pain and scrabble to his feet before Quinn took advantage and cut him in half. He only just made it.

Again Quinn attacked and again Erelas blocked. Then Erelas retaliated and Quinn was forced into a defensive move. All the while, Erelas' hurt and frustration bubbled up and burst forth, channelling down his sword arm as he tried desperately to claw back some ground. And all the while, Quinn was tiring. Erelas didn't miss the slight unbalancing that occurred when his friend leaned too much on his back foot, the knee still not strong enough for rapid, harsh movements and the shifting of his weight. Erelas began to push forwards to take advantage of this weakness, at the same time drawing Quinn into a series of energetic swipes at his body and head in an effort to increase his fatigue.

At any other time, Quinn would have

worked out exactly what was happening and would have foiled the plan with a series of attacks designed to reverse the trend on to his opponent. But right now, sore, with limited vision, in a slight fog from the enforced sleep and lacking any true understanding of what was going on, he soon began to falter under Erelas' increasing aggression. Further and further back he was pushed with each strike, until finally, the heel of his right foot was forced into contact with the edge of the straw-stuffed mat he'd been sleeping on and his struggling concentration was at last broken. A glimmer of confusion crossed his face, and his body let him down with the smallest break in its tension. Erelas seized his chance and with a roar of fury, grabbed his sword with both hands and put his full weight against the edge of Quinn's weapon, which had been held vertically in between guards. Quinn's centre of gravity shifted disastrously and he fell backwards, out from under Erelas' sword and onto the low, straw bed. He broke his fall with his sword arm, twisting his wrist awkwardly as he landed. His looked at Erelas in shock, fearful that a finishing strike would come before he could react – and found the point of his friend's sword a mere finger's length from his throat.

He froze, while Erelas stood over him, breathing heavily, his eyes burning with resentment and outrage.

'Don't *ever* draw your blade against me again,' Erelas said, his voice low, but trembling

with his emotion.
    Quinn, exhausted and fully accepting his defeat, let his sword fall to the ground.

CHAPTER 81. SOLACE FOR ERELAS

'Is it done?' Erelas asked, looking up at Alara but not relinquishing the comforting hold he had on the hilt of his sword.

Alara nodded. 'He will sleep until sunrise, at least. But not,' she added quickly, 'like before...this is a near-natural sleep. If he dreams, he will wake up himself, or he can easily be woken by us.'

Erelas nodded his understanding, the tension in his shoulders visibly dissipating. He placed the sword against the wall beside the gently flickering candles she had placed there, not rising from the rock-seat he'd been sitting on since stumbling back into the cave; he had needed to rush out into the icy air to vomit, the cramped muscles in his assaulted abdomen finally releasing once the immediate danger of further attack from Quinn had passed. Turning back towards the fire in the centre of the cave, he watched Alara approach him, a small drinking vessel in her hand.

'For you,' she said, crouching beside him. 'For the pain.'

'I'm alright...'

'Drink it.'

Her steady gaze met his and he eventually complied with a wry smile. 'Thank you.'

'You should sleep, too. You're still recovering from the sickness the raven gave you. Even with Maynard's help, you must still be exhausted, *especially* after...'

'After the world stopped making *any* sense at all?' Erelas looked between his knees at his boots, cupping the warm draught in his hands.

Alara placed a hand on his arm. '*Drink* it.'

He complied, the bitter liquid going down in one mouthful, with a flinch at the taste. Before he could resume the soothing grip on the cup, she took it from him with her free hand. Placing it on the ground behind her, she kept her eyes on his, studying him with concern etched into her features. Suddenly her hand came up to his cheek and rested against it, her warm palm transmitting more emotion than her face ever could. He found himself leaning his cheek against it and closing his eyes, acutely aware of how badly in need of solace and reassurance he was at that point. All the trials of the past few months were catching up with him, and the day's events with Quinn had brought him to the very edge of the abyss.

He felt her move, but she did not take her hand from his face, and he did not feel ready to open his eyes. He still had them closed when, as soft as the snowflakes beginning to fall outside, her lips brushed his. His mental turmoil was too great for any surprise to register in his mind or his body, and when he did not pull back from her kiss, she increased the pressure gradually, until he responded by parting his own lips and allowing her in. He took his arm from under her other hand and placed it around her waist, pulling her gently to him as he leaned back on the rock. Soon she was sitting astride his legs, arms around his neck, both of them beginning to breathe heavily as the sensations of each other's touch overwhelmed them.

Nowhere in his thoughts was there any room for Anwenn. He was broken, used up, ready to turn into a worthless shell of a man – Alara was there, comforting, loving, making sure he did not pitch forwards into the black pit of despair.

CHAPTER 82. SAMIEN BRINGS TROUBLE

'I have never been so angry with anyone in my life. You're the *last* person I expected to feel that way towards!' Erelas moved away from the cave and stood in front of Quinn. 'But you left me no choice...'

Quinn shifted his position on the rock and hid his face in his hands for a moment. 'I know,' he said quietly, looking at Erelas with clear remorse. 'I have no excuses, Erelas. I've *never* felt like that before. Even when I – with Renn's father...'

'It wasn't you—'

'That's just it, Erelas. It *was* me. It's what I am now, it's part of me. No wonder the Keeper wants to use me to stop the Archdeacon.'

'When are you going to tell the Keeper what you found out?' Erelas decided it was futile to argue against Quinn's claim. He was not even sure he could.

'We leave today. I'll tell him the second we cross the border since we haven't been able to summon him here.' As Erelas' mouth opened to object, he held up his hand. 'There's no sense in trying to go back into the memories again, to see if there's anything else we need to know. It's too dangerous – for everyone.' He sighed, tired. 'We'll just have to get back to Rivallen as fast as possible.'

'Erelas...'

Both men looked up at the sound of Alara's voice. She was walking towards them from the direction of the river, her hands clasped tightly together.

'What is it?' Erelas asked, as Quinn looked searchingly at her.

'Samien has gone.'

'Gone? Gone where?'

'And why do you look so frightened?' Quinn asked, going to meet her.

'He's gone to ask....to get Maynard. I *tried* to stop him, but he's convinced you're both mad and that you're going to kill us in our sleep...I'm sorry.' She bit her lip and looked at the floor as Quinn reached her.

'Shit...' Erelas breathed, joining them.

'Don't worry, either of you,' Quinn said. 'We do not intend to be around by the time Maynard gets anywhere near us.'

'You're leaving?' Alara's face betrayed her pain at his words, a look matched by Erelas. He knew the predicament they were in, but wasn't ready to leave Alara just yet. 'But – do you not need my help anymore?' she asked, trying to sound neutral.

Quinn scoffed and shook his head. 'I've seen enough,' he said bitterly. Then, seeing her face, he took her hands and spoke more softly. 'I am very grateful for what you have done for me, Alara.

Without you I would not have the answers I have with which to go forwards. I am in your debt.' As she looked down shyly, he kissed her forehead. 'Thank you,' he whispered, and moved away to see to Cara, allowing Erelas to say his own farewell…

CHAPTER 83. MAYNARD'S MOTIVE

'Just shut up and let me *think*, for the love of Christ!'

Erelas glared, breathing down his rising anger. But Quinn wasn't even looking at him anymore and instead was focused on Cara's bridle, his tension apparent as he roughly cleaned the day's dirt from the leather. Erelas considered continuing his plea, but Quinn was in no mood to listen, so he turned and strode away, deciding space might be the better option.

He had tried to persuade Quinn that Maynard could be reasoned with, that no matter what Samien said in his agitated state, the Salorean was an intelligent man and would hear their side of the story before running anyone through with his longsword. But all Quinn wanted to do was race back to Rivallen where Maynard – and any other Saloreans – couldn't touch them. The only thing that mattered was getting to where they could summon the Keeper, get some guidance on their next move and get this whole crisis over with. When Quinn had rather unkindly suggested Erelas only wanted to delay because of Alara, the conversation had become strained.

Quinn hadn't meant to snap at his friend,

but he was frustrated with Erelas dragging his heels. Just days before he had been asked what he was afraid of, and now Erelas was the one who was clearly dreading what awaited them on the other side of the border.

He threw the bridle down onto the snowy ground with a heavy sigh. He knew he had been spiteful and should apologise. It wasn't Erelas who had been singled out by the Keeper for this task, yet he had refused to stay behind in the relative safety of Rivallen while Quinn went through with it all alone. Nobody had forced Erelas to go looking for him when he had been banished, or made him stand by Quinn's side as they took on the Sheriff – and it was Erelas' courage in summoning the Keeper that saved Quinn's life at the castle. Quinn owed him understanding and support, not snide remarks about his personal feelings and snap judgements about his motives. He didn't *deserve* Erelas...

A twig snapped behind where he was sitting, making him freeze and hold his breath. Erelas had walked off in the other direction...

'*Easy*, Quinn. Don't do anything stupid, now.'

Maynard.

Quinn slowly turned his head until he could see the huge shape of the Salorean moving steadily into view. He was relieved to see there was no weapon in his hand, but was not ready to entirely trust the calmness of his voice just yet.

'Where is Erelas?' Maynard asked, looking around as he drew alongside Quinn.

Quinn considered lunging for his sword as Maynard's attention was drawn away, but Erelas' arguments flashed into his mind and he stayed where he was.

'Cooling off. We had a disagreement. About *you*,' he added accusingly.

'Really?' Maynard said, with more than a little mockery in his tone. 'Who was on my side, I wonder?'

'Are you here to kill me quickly, or are you planning on irritating me to death?'

'*Kill* you? On the word of *Samien*?' Maynard laughed, a deep, almost booming sound that came from the face Quinn had never believed could look happy. 'Samien is nothing but a simpering coward. I'm sure you gathered that for yourself after a few days around him. It's not just the fact you cut off his arm. He'd love me to kill you for that alone. But your friend is also a threat – to his cosy existence with Alara. He lacks the balls to defend his territory, so he comes whining to me.'

'*His* territory?'

'It's actually my territory – my *people's*. But that is not the issue. I didn't come here to kill anyone. I made it clear to Erelas on the night I met him that I have no quarrel with you. Providing,' he added quickly, 'you leave, which you are doing. I came to escort you to the border.'

'Why? Why would you do that for us?'

'It isn't for you. As I explained to Erelas, I've no wish for more violence in this damned country. I'd rather my efforts to save his life didn't end up ultimately wasted. I was on my way to make you leave when Samien found me.'

Quinn had no time to respond to Maynard's assumption that they could be *made* to leave. Erelas appeared, stopped dead in his tracks and dropped the firewood he had absent-mindedly collected on his walk. Wincing as some struck his foot, he dared not take his eyes off the Salorean.

'Peace, Erelas,' Maynard said, raising a hand.

Erelas glanced at Quinn, who merely nodded and leaned back against the tree, fatigued already by this dance Maynard insisted they keep having.

'Maynard.' Erelas inclined his head in a belated greeting and walked forwards, the wood forgotten. 'I thought for a minute you'd come to chop off our heads.'

'I could have done that long before now, Erelas. I'm only here to make sure you get to the border safely.'

Erelas raised an eyebrow. Maynard suddenly seemed to lose patience with the suspicion that surrounded him and Erelas bit his lip as he saw the Salorean's expression darken.

'Why can't you just accept things as they are?' Maynard snapped. 'I have no damned hidden desires to harm you or your people! If you *must* know things that are none of your business, the family I spoke of is in *Rivallen*. I have a wife and daughter there.'

Quinn sat upright at this revelation, exchanging glances with Erelas.

'Trouble between our lands puts *them* in danger,' Maynard continued. 'If you leave and never come back, my people will not seek to deter others from coming here by leading raids into Rivallen.'

Erelas scoffed before he could stop himself. 'Why on earth would they raid Rivallen for that?'

Maynard glared viciously at Erelas and Quinn stood up, ready to defend his friend against the rising temper of the huge Conductor.

'It's happened before.' Maynard replied.

'What?' Quinn said.

'Your Archdeacon – the riot many years ago? That *bastard* killed many of my people. The peace has been kept by a mutual agreement to stay out of each other's territories, so if you *were* discovered here...Saloreans would love any excuse to have another go at revenge. That is why I have been so insistent on your leaving. Right from the moment I found Erelas that night.'

Erelas took a second to absorb this news and then blew through his cheeks. 'So it is true? Saloreans...' he said quietly. 'He beat God only knows how many Saloreans *on his own*?' He looked at Quinn, knowing exactly what he was thinking.

'Seventeen, to be exact. Fourteen dead. Three survived. I was one of those three.'

'My God.' Quinn stepped back until he bumped against the tree behind him and slid down, slumping on the damp floor, staring into the distance. Erelas stood, open-mouthed, waiting for Maynard to continue his tale.

'I was hurt, the other two were not and made it back to Kilora. I was taken in by the woman who would later become my wife. She cared for me, made me well again – my abilities were damaged for a long time, much like yours have been, Quinn.'

When Quinn said nothing – listening, but stunned by confirmation of the legend he'd refused to believe – Maynard went on.

'When I recovered, I wanted to stay with her, but I found out the Archdeacon was hunting for the survivors and I knew I was putting Loran in danger. We married in secret, but shortly afterwards I returned to Kilora. I wasn't trusted for a long time, due to my months of absence, and so I dared not tell my people about Loran. I visited in secret when I could, and then our daughter was born. I longed to stay, to leave Kilora behind for good, but they meant too much to me for me to endanger their lives like that – if not from the Archdeacon, then from my own people. I knew they would come looking for me and view me as a traitor if they found my wife and daughter. So I am stuck here, sneaking over the border when I can. If hostilities are raised further and my people decide to start attacking Rivallen again, they will be in grave peril.'

Maynard paused, as if telling his story had exhausted him. 'I'm sorry I did not clarify my reasons for making sure you were not discovered here, but I do not know you. Even now, I cannot be certain that you will not return to Rivallen and hunt my family down. But I know you and the Archdeacon are now enemies, Quinn, so I am putting faith in the possibility that because the Archdeacon hates *me*, you will take pity on my family. I don't expect friendship, only compassion for innocent lives. I know you both possess that.'

There was a long silence, with Erelas and Maynard studying each other, and then Quinn.

Finally, Erelas frowned and looked back at Maynard. 'What of your own Archdeacon? *Your* Keepers? What role do they play in all of this? Surely the Keepers don't sit back and allow all this to continue?'

'We have no Archdeacon. He was killed by yours when he tried to obtain retribution for the loss of the fourteen Conductors. They never replaced him. The Keepers never come here and I do not know why.'

Quinn folded his arms across his knees and sank his head onto them. 'Holy God,' they heard him mutter.

Erelas shook his head. 'No wonder your lands are in such a violent mess. No Archdeacon, no Keepers to guide or rebuke. And the Kilorans behaving just as badly. It's madness unleashed upon madness!'

'I saw a better life when I was stranded in Rivallen. I lack the power to change things here, but that does not mean I want to be an active part of it. I keep to myself, conducting on the fringes of society, rarely going near my own kind. I think losing Salorea to the floods was the worst thing that ever happened to this place. Now we have let ourselves loose to wreak havoc on all of Kilora – and who can blame its people for fighting back?'

'One man can change things. Look at Quinn.'

'*No!*' Quinn snapped, getting to his feet as fast as his stiff knee would allow. '*Don't* look at me, don't use *me* as an example of some righteous hero who saved the day from evil. I'm not that man and I never will be! The Keepers – and you – are putting their faith in the *wrong damned person*!'

'Quinn—' began Erelas, shocked at the outburst.

'I can't *do* it, Erelas, can't you *see* that? Have you listened to anything Maynard said?' Quinn waved his arm violently towards the Salorean, who was standing still but ready to react if he needed to. 'Fourteen dead, three injured. *Seventeen* Conductors *and* an Archdeacon, all destroyed by one person…the one person the Keeper will expect me to be able to destroy all by myself! I can't walk without a limp, I have only one working eye, my abilities are messed up and let's not forget you getting the point of your sword to my throat yesterday! I beat Garin through luck more than skill or strength and only then after he had brought me to the point where I had nothing else to lose. I was killed by *my own* power, Erelas, what the hell do you think the Archdeacon's power will do to me?'

Usually ready with words of encouragement, Erelas was dismayed to find he had none.

CHAPTER 84. REASSURANCE FOR QUINN

'I still don't understand why you, the Keepers, can't just deal with him with your *own* powers. Surely there's ample opportunity for you to strike at him when he's in your realm?'

The Keeper sighed. 'It's not that simple, Quinn.' He paced in front of the fire, the dancing shadows on his face made him look somewhat alarming. 'You know I cannot remain here long and it would take too long to explain. But just as God himself will not interfere in the free will of man, we also cannot act *directly* against the Archdeacon, or any other being, Conductor or human, who acts with evil in this world. You know as well as I do that punishment awaits in the afterlife – but while man is living in *this* world, he must remain able to choose his own path. But that will not protect him from *you*. You can destroy him dependent on what path you choose, as you are part of the same world. The only way to defeat him is to make *him* become the victim.'

Quinn looked down at his feet, not wanting the Keeper to see his anger. 'So I'm on my own. You need me to do this for you, alone, knowing the Archdeacon is far stronger than me – yet you possess powers far beyond mine.'

'You will have our support, Quinn. Trust in yourself – you will find a way. You are not alone…' The Keeper looked at the sleeping forms of Erelas and Maynard. 'Your friends will aid you in any way they can.' He crouched in front of Quinn and lifted his face until their eyes locked. 'Do not despair, Quinn. I have faith in you, as do they. Find where the Archdeacon is killing these people and *stop* him. He must be using somewhere like the tavern, and he must have another like Rook working for him to gather his victims. Once you discover where, you should be able to devise a plan of attack. We will be waiting for your arrival in our realm, with his severed soul. Once there, we, with the Guardians ready, will take over. You have nothing to fear from them.'

Quinn kept the Keeper's gaze. 'I don't fear them. I fear *him*.'

'You're forgetting that the Archdeacon is much older now, Quinn. And those Conductors were not like you. They were not as strong, they didn't possess the abilities you now possess. The Archdeacon who died was old and weakened by a life of violence in Kilora.' He took Quinn's face in his cold hands and looked earnestly into his mismatched eyes. 'You *must* swallow your fears, Quinn – or they will endanger everyone involved in this. You can defeat him. You have to believe that!'

Deciding not to reply to the Keeper's affirmations, Quinn asked: 'Why was the Archdeacon in

Kilora never replaced?'

'There was no-one worthy.' The Keeper released him and stood up. 'The situation remains that way to this day. Maybe the future will be different.'

Quinn had no reply, not wanting to voice his cynicism. He simply nodded his understanding and looked back at the ground between his feet.

'God *is* with you, Quinn. Or you would not be here today. Remember that.'

Quinn looked up, the anger gone from his face, in its place a kind of anxious weariness that softened his features in the flicker of the fire. 'Will you pray with me, my lord?'

The Keeper held out his hands and Quinn stood, taking them in his own. 'Of course,' the Keeper said, and closed his eyes.

***

The small ball of blue flame soared through the air, narrowly missing overhanging branches of oak, before plummeting to the ground and landing with a vicious hiss. A thick sphere of purple-grey smoke grew from the point of impact, growing at an alarming speed until several square metres of ground were enveloped in it, preventing Quinn, Erelas and Maynard from being able to see what had been there mere seconds before.

Erelas settled the skittish mares as Quinn stared, wide-eyed, at the results of Maynard's demonstration. A grain of hope settled in the pit of his stomach and dared to grow, slowly, almost faltering, but it steadied again when he looked at the triumphant half-smile on Maynard's face.

'It will work,' Maynard said, as if reading Quinn's thoughts. 'All we need is to get you in close quarters with the Archdeacon. You will know it's coming, *he* will not...that will give you precious seconds with which to gain an advantage.'

'And it's harmless?' asked Erelas, coming to Quinn's side as the horses resumed their grazing.

'Totally. It will make you cough and your eyes will water, but the effects are short-lived. Hold your breath for as long as you can and you will have ample time to overpower the Archdeacon.'

'Forgive me, Maynard,' said Quinn, looking earnestly at the Salorean. 'I still have a little trouble understanding why you are helping us, but I am grateful. Without this device, I see no way to any chance of victory.'

'I understand your trepidation, Quinn. But, as I've said, I am not like other Saloreans, and certainly not like Kilorans. I have tasted life away from both peoples, tasted contentment and happiness in Rivallen with my wife and child. The thought of that coming to an end tells me I *must* help you. And over the last few days, as it happens, I've come to respect you both.'

Quinn raised an eyebrow at Maynard's sudden openness. 'Well, I wouldn't say you're the most likeable person I've ever encountered, but you're not *all* bad,' he said, a wry smile escaping his lips as Erelas thumped him on the arm.

Maynard gave a brief snort. 'Funny – that's what Loran said when I met her.'

CHAPTER 85. ANWENN

It was three weeks since they had left Alara's home. The longer they travelled, and the more distance they put between themselves and the mountains, the milder the weather became. They moved on to the steady accompaniment of dripping water as the snows melted and slowly revealed the green carpet beneath their feet. They were even able to remove their cloaks for some of the daytime, when the weak sun would struggle through the clouds.

For three weeks Erelas had brooded. In the first week, he would spy one of the wolves among the trees, or on the brow of a hill. Following. Watching. He knew Alara had sent them to keep an eye on their progress, to reassure herself that they were safe. That he was safe. Then they had stopped following, and he felt even more desolate.

He had been surprised at the extent to which he missed her. Their brief stay in the cave had opened him up to the possibility of affection – if not love – after Anwenn. In his heart, he knew it was over between himself and Anwenn now. Too much had happened. He could not go back and undo his encounter with Alara – and nor did he wish to. But it left him now, miles away from Alara and with no hope of any real relationship with her, feeling somewhat empty inside. He knew that he would not seek out Alara again. He needed to adjust to life alone for a while, but his current emotions were alien to him. They were feelings he was unfamiliar with, which gnawed at him night and day, no matter how much he tried to focus on the troubles that lay ahead of them.

'Erelas?'

He looked round to see Quinn staring at him, frowning with concern.

'You haven't heard a word I've said, have you?'

'I'm sorry. I was miles away.'

'I bet I can guess where,' Quinn said, not unkindly. 'Do you know what you will do when you get back to Delmoril?'

'I'm not going back to Delmoril.'

'Ever?' Quinn was unconvinced by Erelas' faintly sharp tone.

Erelas shook his head, unable to hide the sadness in his face. 'There's nothing there for me now.'

'I'm sorry, Erelas,' Maynard said, walking alongside Einna, one hand resting on the hilt of his enormous sword. 'You will have to go there at least one more time.'

The dread in Erelas' face was plain for his companions to see, and Quinn especially felt bad for his friend. He knew how much the last meeting with Anwenn had upset him. Maynard knew nothing about Anwenn at all and Erelas preferred it to stay that way, so he looked away quickly.

'I don't know how else we can begin to track the Archdeacon's movements,' Maynard continued. 'I know Quinn remembers where the tavern was, but there is no guarantee the Archdeacon is still using it. We also don't know who – if anyone – is helping him. You have to go back to Delmoril and trail him with an orb. You're the only one of us who can get in...'

Erelas closed his eyes and sighed. 'Then I'm doing it at night,' he said.

***

Erelas left Einna tethered outside the settlement in Delmoril and walked silently towards the building which contained the Archdeacon's quarters. He wrapped his cloak tightly around him, hood up, in the hope that anyone who was up and about at this late hour would not realise who he was: the friend of the disgraced Conductor, who had abandoned his bride-to-be in order to assist that exiled friend on some mystery mission. Although none of them blamed Quinn for the death of the King, they all knew he was responsible for the death of Garin, something which confirmed in the minds of some that he was truly no good, that he had turned and was beyond redemption. Erelas didn't care for their opinions one way or another. He just didn't want to be seen creeping around the Archdeacon's quarters, considering what they planned to do to him. He was not good at looking innocent...

As he passed the chapel he considered going in to seek God's forgiveness for what they were about to do, but, fearing the presence of one of the priests or scholars, decided against it and offered up a brief prayer instead, mist escaping from his lips as he whispered into the chilly air. Spring had not yet reached Delmoril, but under his cloak he was sweating...

No light escaped the small window of the Archdeacon's room. But a faint shuffling noise made him stop in his tracks and look frantically around, holding his breath. After what seemed like an age, a Conductor appeared from the building behind the Archdeacon's, moving slowly away, towards the chapel. She had her hood up and did not look in Erelas' direction, so once she reached a safe distance, he breathed again, but his heart hammered against his ribs.

The Archdeacon's window was open slightly – a small measure towards preventing the room becoming completely fogged up with incense and smoke from the herbs he spent a lot of the day burning. Right now, Erelas could see that all that burned was a handful of embers in the dying fire and he had a clear view of the rest of the room by its dim orange glow. The Archdeacon was there, his thin, bony form on the bed facing away from the window, covered by a heavy wine-coloured bedspread.

Erelas' heart thumped ever harder as he looked at the sleeping form of the man responsible for the deaths of innocent people and had tried to kill the man he considered his brother. For a second, he wondered if it would not just be easier to sneak into the room and stab the Archdeacon in the heart, his hand even reaching out for the door handle. But he knew – from his and Quinn's pranks in the past – that the Archdeacon guarded his quarters at night with castings that would alert him to Erelas' presence before he got near him...and this time the old man would kill him.

Instead, he stuck to the plan and made a casting of his own. With words whispered in the weak moonlight, an orb flickered into life in his palm, this one no bigger than a ladybird. It started its existence a beautiful turquoise-blue, but soon became completely transparent. Erelas had to look very closely to make sure it was still there, looking for the rippling distortions in the background, before he gave it the instructions it needed. He had to leave to trust that it had gone through the window and attached itself to the Archdeacon's energy. It would later communicate with another orb and allow Quinn to track his enemy wherever he went in Rivallen. The hope was that he would lead them to his killing ground, where they would lay a trap which would enable Quinn to bring about his destruction.

Hope. It was all down to that little, simple word. Erelas felt sick as he slowly backed away from the window and offered another prayer for the orb to remain undiscovered for as long as they needed it to work. He longed for this to be over and for them to be able to put their lives back together in whatever way possible. And just as the thought of repairing his friendship with Anwenn was added to that hope for the future, he backed straight into her.

'*Erelas*!' she whispered, aware of where they were standing. 'What are you doing here?'

Erelas swallowed and tried to read her face in the gloom – was she angry, suspicious, pleased to see him or just plain surprised? 'I...I came back for some potions. I've used all mine.'

'Well, you have been gone for a long time,' she said, her voice betraying some disapproval. 'Nobody knew if you were ever coming back. I got sick of being asked.'

Erelas felt a stab of hurt at her tone. 'I am sorry. I thought it best I stay away for a while. For both of us,' he added quickly. 'Can we move away from here? I don't want to wake the Archdeacon...'

'Then how were you going to get the potions?' she asked, as they walked slowly away from the building.

'I thought he might still be up. I was just going to rest in the chapel until morning when you came along.'

Anwenn looked at him for a long time, her bright eyes reading him, making him more uncomfortable by the second. 'How is Quinn? I haven't heard anything about him since…since you left. Has he recovered from what happened in the King's tower?'

'Yes, he has. For the most part. His knee will never fully heal, but he manages.'

'Delmoril didn't stop talking about it for a long time.'

Erelas raised an eyebrow. 'And is Delmoril's general opinion of him good or bad?'

Anwenn frowned, stopping outside the chapel. 'Is that directed at me? Look, Erelas, I'm sure you think I was unfair – but I was *hurt* by your decision.'

She softened her expression and took his hands in hers. 'I didn't know what else to do but give you a choice between him and us. But now…'

Erelas pulled his hands away sharply, surprising both Anwenn and himself. 'There is no 'us' anymore, Anwenn. I'm sorry. I realised when… while I was away that we are no good together. I know you, and probably all of Delmoril, think I pay too much attention to Quinn and not enough to my own life. But, believe it or not, I have learned a lot about myself these past few months and I am not *just* Quinn's shadow, or whatever it is the rest of you think. There is more to life outside Delmoril and I'm discovering it with Quinn – because I won't abandon him the way his parents did and the way you seem to wish I would.'

Anwenn looked as if she couldn't speak at all for a few moments and stared at him, as if she were wondering if this was the real Erelas. 'But I thought that – I was *angry*! I thought once you had helped Quinn recover you would be back! You're a Conductor, you *belong* here!' Her voice was rising and Erelas took her arm and steered her further away from the Archdeacon's quarters, relieved that she didn't resist. 'Erelas – your life is here! Why are you following him into exile? You can't—'

'*Anwenn*!' Erelas hissed, cutting her off. 'Please, keep your voice down. I'm still a Conductor and always will be, the same as Quinn is still a Conductor, although he cannot do his duty any longer. *I* can. And I will. I don't need to live in Delmoril to do that.'

She looked close to tears now, and Erelas faltered, his resolve slipping.

But then her eyes hardened. 'Maybe the others are right,' she said, venom in her trembling voice. 'Maybe Quinn *has* brought you down to his level. You're ruining your life, Erelas,' she added, trying to restore some calm in herself. 'We could still be together, have a future together, like we always planned! You could still visit Quinn—'

'*No*!' Now it was Erelas' turn to raise the volume of his voice. Glancing around to make sure they were still unseen, he squared his shoulders and sighed. 'It's too late, Anwenn.'

'Why..?'

'I...' He ran his hand across his jaw as his stomach lurched. 'I met someone. A woman.'

'What? Another Conductor? Where? Who

is she?'

'Not a Conductor. A woman from Rivallen.'

Anwenn gasped and backed away. 'You mean you have abandoned me and taken up with someone who isn't even a *Conductor*?'

'You think that makes her any less *desirable* than you?' Erelas snapped, repulsed by her prejudice.

Anwenn gaped. 'You've...oh, dear *God*.' She turned away, her hands over her mouth and nose.

Erelas gritted his teeth. 'If you must know, it is unlikely I will see her again. But the fact remains I know now that we – me and you – will not work. I am sorry to leave you with such a low opinion of me, but I have made my choice, just as *you* asked me to.'

Anwenn swung back around and the look in her eyes almost made him step back, but he held his ground.

'You disgust me!' she spat, then pushed past him, striding back the way she had come.

Erelas sighed, trying to calm his galloping heart.

CHAPTER 86. MARKING THE PREY

'It is done.' Erelas swung his right leg forwards over Einna's withers and jumped down from the saddle. Taking her reins, he scratched her chin gently and gave a faint smile.

'What took you so long?' asked Quinn, getting up stiffly from beside the fire, where he'd stayed all night, waiting. 'Was there trouble?' he said, walking slowly over to his friend.

Erelas glanced around. 'Not for you – or us,' he said, unable to hide the discomfort he felt as Maynard strolled within earshot.

'Anwenn?'

'I don't want to talk about it, Quinn.' His tone was weary rather than sharp. 'It's done. And so is my task. Let's just forget about everything else and focus on that.'

'As you wish,' Quinn said, giving him an understanding smile and placing a hand on his shoulder. 'Good work. And thank you – I know it wasn't easy for you to go there.'

Erelas nodded and looked back at his horse, focusing on taking off her bridle so that he could not see whether Maynard was staring at him. As much as he was beginning to warm to the Salorean Conductor, he wasn't about to start revealing his private affairs to him.

'So...' Quinn said, turning to Maynard. 'You're still happy with this plan?'

Maynard shrugged. 'It won't be difficult.'

'But he might recognise you...from the...' Quinn wasn't sure what to call the battle Maynard had been in all those years ago.

'He'd have to *see* me first.'

'I wish I shared your confidence...'

'It'll work. Focus on yourself. You need to rest, pray and meditate. We could be setting our trap as early as two nights hence and you need to be ready.'

'You assume there *is* such a thing as me being ready...'

***

Maynard crept around the back of the building, a frown creasing his rugged features further. He was confused and he didn't like to be confused. He stood up straight and sighed with exasperation as the little blue orb changed direction again, floating back towards him.

'For the love of *God*, make up your *mind*,' he whispered into the chilly night air, not sure whether he was talking to the orb, or its intended target – the Archdeacon.

He'd been following it since dusk, over an hour ago. He'd been led in a circle and then on a zigzag path through the narrow streets of Ripley, a small town far north of Castle Rivallen. He was getting tired of ducking into low doorways and behind carts, trying not to look suspicious to the few residents who were out and about, ever conscious of the increasing chances that he might be seen by his quarry. All he could think was that the Archdeacon must be using the amulet to move from place to place, causing the orb to have to restart its trail – and that in itself might present problems; Maynard didn't know if he could determine that the Archdeacon was using a particular building for his grim indulgences if he was not in the building *long* enough for Maynard to spy on him…

Finally, as the moon reached an early apex in the night sky, the orb stopped outside a house which looked as if it was a hundred years old and built in a hurry. From the light of the lamps in the street he could see that the timbers were gnarled and crooked, its porch leaning at an alarming angle. The thatch was rotting and there were gaps where the door hung askew. Two tiny windows on the ground floor seemed to blink like the orange eyes of a cat as candles flickered from within.

Maynard waited, not trusting that the orb would remain long enough for this to be the right place to stalk the Archdeacon. After a few minutes, he gave it the benefit of the doubt and moved in closer from his vantage point on the other side of the empty street. He flicked the hood of his dark robes up and pulled them tight around him, concealing the magnificent sword at his hip. Reaching the corner of the house, he stood and listened for a good few minutes, until he heard sounds of someone moving about inside. He heard muffled voices coming from within, too, and then the steady tread and creak of someone climbing the stairs to the darkened upper rooms.

Peering around the corner as far as he dared, he craned his neck to see the flicker of light appear in the far upstairs window. It was almost immediately obscured by a shabby curtain, but he'd seen all he needed to see. With a few whispered words, he dismissed the orb and made his move.

He made his way cautiously to the back of the house, pleased to find an equally rickety door in the middle of it. Rats scattered, squealing, as his massive boots disturbed their foraging in the piles of refuse strewn about the yard. He ignored them and stood at the back door, senses sharpened. When he was satisfied the risk was not too great, he gripped the door handle, muttered some words under his breath and turned it.

The door opened silently and he slipped into the dark passageway, his eyes quickly adjusting to the difference in visibility. There were no objects for him to bump into, no steps to trick him and give away his presence. Inching forwards, he found an open doorway on his left and crept through, hardly daring to breathe. This was the room that had been closest to him as he lurked at the front corner of the house – the candle was still lit in the back corner of the room, but there was nobody there.

With his heart finally beginning to register his apprehension, he pushed on. He carefully negotiated the basic items of furniture in the room, conscious that any noise would travel well in this crooked old house. He neared the front of the house and, on his right, saw another open doorway, the door hanging precariously on one rusty hinge. Peering around it briefly, he discovered he had found the way to the staircase. Now was the time for extra help with his stealth.

He made his casting, the words hardly a whisper. His eyes flashed indigo for a moment, then returned to their usual silver. A transparent shield enveloped his bulky frame, as he offered a prayer for God to be on his side for the next few minutes.

A single, brief scream shattered the eerie quiet of the house, making Maynard jump violently. His right hand shot to the hilt of his sword instinctively, but he recovered quickly enough to not draw it. The shield protected against being seen, not heard. He did not want to risk the blade bumping against the timber walls of the staircase as he ascended. His heart was beating fiercely now, his instinct for survival screaming at him that he should not be here. This was an *Archdeacon*, after all. But he forced it down and began to climb, prepared for any further noise from above.

He heard a groan as he neared the top

step, one that was half pain, half pleasure. Then, a chuckle, a sinister kind of noise that raised the hairs on the back of his neck and made him grip the handle of his sword ever tighter. He knew that noise had not come from the same person who had groaned. And certainly not from the person who had screamed. Three people. One of them the Archdeacon. He would have to be incredibly careful...

CHAPTER 87. THE PERILS OF WINE

In the end, they decided that delaying the trap they were to set the Archdeacon a little beyond the two nights was a good idea. The plan they had constructed was one which depended on absolute plausibility, and Quinn had a lot of preparations to make – preparations he would never have thought up on his own. Erelas' idea was an unusual one, to say the least, but when Maynard had relayed to them the type of neighbourhood the Archdeacon was using, even Quinn had to admit to the ingenuity of it.

He stopped washing. He also stopped trimming his short beard. He went out in the rain, rode Cara at a gallop along muddy tracks to get his clothes splattered with the filth, then left them that way. He struggled with not washing his hands, particularly before eating, but his companions emphasised that he had to look the part in *every* detail. Clean fingernails simply would not do.

Then, most bizarrely of all – for him, for any Conductor – he got drunk.

Conductors were used to ale. Most water was not fit to drink, and if they found themselves too far from a safe source, they had to make do with ale. But as they could be called to a dying person at any moment, they never took more than was necessary to ward off a thirst. They certainly never drank enough to impair their functions to the extent a significant number of Rivallen's residents did on a daily basis. Especially residents of Ripley.

But now, Quinn had to look as bad as they did. He had to smell as bad as they did. He had to appear downtrodden, in despair, desperate, poor and alone – and ultimately vulnerable. And he had to practice.

So they gave him wine.

The first night, he drank quietly, not exhibiting any of the behaviour that he'd witnessed over the years – he wasn't chatty, or wistful, or provocative. He just sat by the fire in their makeshift camp in the woods on the outskirts of Ripley, and was his usual, thoughtful self. Then he was violently sick. He woke the next morning with a headache almost as bad as the one he'd experienced after falling off his horse many years previously. To his dismay as soon as he tried to get up, he began vomiting again. Maynard and Erelas refused to help him and he was in no condition to help himself.

'This is taking it too far,' he groaned, as he lay back down and pulled his filthy cloak over his head to block out the light. Sitting next to the camp fire, Maynard and Erelas tried not to smile.

'If we take away the effects,' Erelas explained, 'you won't look as rough as you need to before we set the trap. The Archdeacon isn't going to be fooled by *one-off* drunkenness, not from you. He needs to believe you have lost hope, and lost all regard for yourself – and if you look drunk from just that one night, he won't risk doing anything to you.'

After a long pause, Quinn finally said: 'Fine. Just leave me alone. And don't cook any food where I can smell it. Or you'll be *wearing* it, not eating it.'

Maynard snorted and Erelas couldn't help laughing.

Later that day, as soon as he was beginning to feel better, Maynard passed him another wine skin. Quinn's tired eyes made a plea that carried with it more than a little dismay, but Maynard simply cocked an eyebrow and went back to building up the newly lit fire.

'Drink up!' Erelas said cheerily, as he settled down with a skin filled with water from the nearby stream. 'I'm sure it won't be as bad as last night...'

'I hate you,' Quinn muttered, but did as he was told.

This time, his body was less traumatised by the onslaught of alcohol and he found he did not feel as burdened by the wine as he had been the night before. He could talk more, and before long he was talking more than he had for a very long time. Bemused, Erelas and Maynard joined in as he began to tell stories of the strange people he had encountered in Rivallen since the end of his training. The chat remained light-hearted, even if he didn't actually end up laughing his way through any of the funnier tales – but after a few hours he suddenly became subdued again. He shook his head firmly when Erelas tried to get him to drink even more.

He stood up from the fire and swayed. Trying to breathe the nausea away, he blinked hard as his companions and his surroundings seemed to pitch alarmingly as if they were all at sea in a storm. He staggered away to the privacy of the trees and threw up again. On his way back, his legs went from under him and Maynard had to help him to his sleeping place. Erelas hoped Quinn hadn't spotted him giggling behind his hands.

The next morning, they had a task ahead of them as Quinn swore he was never drinking again, to hell with their plans. Gentle coaxing, coercion and outright threats of having the stuff poured down his throat by Maynard all failed to convince him, until at last, in late afternoon, he was persuaded to eat something. Once he had food inside him, he recovered enough to agree to one last night of drunkenness – they had to carry out the next phase of their plan the following evening.

CHAPTER 88. MAKING AN IMPRESSION

Every night, since the first discovery of the Archdeacon's den of murder, Maynard had made brief journeys back into the heart of Ripley and made sure that it was being used each night – they did not want to put Quinn through any more than was absolutely necessary to secure the trap. Every night the orb had led him to the same house, at the same time. Now that he knew the Archdeacon had been there before, Maynard was able to secrete himself somewhere to watch him arrive and depart, sparing him the need to trespass and risk discovery and recognition.

He had not been disappointed. From his information, Quinn was able to prepare himself in ample time and get to the location at just the right moment.

That moment had arrived.

He felt terrible. His stomach was churning, his already impaired vision was blurry and he was desperate for a drink of cool, fresh water. He couldn't walk without bumping into things – people, horses, carts, buildings, fences – twice he ended up painfully on his knees in the dirt of the streets he was wandering around in. To any of the people he bumped into, his wandering was aimless, just the uncertain path of yet another drunk. The most that happened was that he learned a new term of abuse. But the plan had been checked and rechecked and drummed into him until even his horribly inebriated self couldn't fail to execute it. He knew exactly where he needed to be and when. Now, he was at his final destination.

Leaning for support against the crooked, wooden wall of the building, he sucked in air as that now-familiar feeling washed over him. Holding the nearly empty wine skin in his left hand, he gripped the door handle with his right, bending over and resting his weight against it. It didn't give way.

Good, he thought through the fog of alcohol. *Any minute now.*

Closing his eyes against the next wave of nausea, he tried to straighten up, but this one was too strong. His eyes snapped open again as he leaned further over and vomited on the doorstep, almost choking as the foul-tasting wine stung his throat.

He hadn't noticed the pair of boots peeking out from long, velvet robes appearing at his side.

'Well, I must say I'm surprised it took you this long to sink into the gutter where you belong. *Move*, you're in my way.'

Quinn's senses sharpened immediately, but he took care to maintain the image of complete helplessness. He straightened slowly, wiping his mouth with his filthy sleeve, and saw the Archdeacon's hateful glare fixed on him.

He was breathing heavily and having trouble making his one good eye focus on a single spot for more than half a second, but his legs were tensed into holding him up, and his knuckles remained closed around the handle of the door.

'Really?' he slurred. 'You claimed I was *more* than jus' a Conductor. Didn' I earn the right to cling on to hope a li'l longer?'

The Archdeacon looked him up and down in unconcealed disgust. 'You earned no rights at all,' he spat. 'Go *home*, Quinn, if you have one – which, judging by your appearance, I doubt very much. If you don't, just go away. Anywhere away from me. The sight of you makes me sick.'

'Oh, God...' muttered Quinn. Before the Archdeacon had time to react, Quinn threw up on his boots.

The Archdeacon's eyes flashed indigo for just a moment, but Quinn saw it and worried he had gone too far – he doubted the Archdeacon would believe that it was purely accidental. Then he seemed to gather himself and, drawing himself up to his full height, breathed in through his nose while glaring viciously at Quinn.

'With any luck, the other vermin of these streets will remove you – *permanently*,' he barked. 'I'd disappear, if I were you.' Then he simply turned and walked away. He had evidently changed his mind about visiting the house while Quinn was there. But that was fine with Quinn. The bait had been laid. All he had to do now was hope that the next night, the Archdeacon would grab it.

CHAPTER 89. THE PAWN

When the pain eased enough for Quinn to open his eyes, he found himself lying in a smoky, dimly-lit room with damp floorboards, seemingly devoid of furniture. As he slowly lifted his head for a better view, he felt the drying blood on his temple and a fresh trickle, as the shift in angle brought its route away from his hair and down his cheek. He pushed himself into a sitting position, willing his thoughts to clear, along with his already restricted vision – thanking God he had not needed to get drunk again that evening.

Someone was in the room with him. The trap had worked.

The man was sitting on a low stool, playing with a hunting knife without fear of, or even interest in his prisoner. He did not look up as Quinn got unsteadily to his feet, pressing the heel of his hand to the painful gash on his head.

'Any moment now,' the man said, still not looking up. 'No sense in trying to kill me, you're going to die anyway, when the Master gets here.'

Quinn was sickened by the hint of obsequiousness in the man's tone. '*Master*? Have you no dignity?'

Finally looking up, the man's eyes narrowed as he gauged Quinn's return to strength. 'Dignity is worthless. I get *rewards*.'

'You're just a pawn,' Quinn spat. 'You do know he will kill you when you have served your purpose? Or when you displease him? Like he did with his last pawn. I saw it happen. He was gutted in the street like a pig with his own sword. You have *that* reward to look forward to – how does it feel?'

In an instant the man sprang at Quinn and back-handed him. Still dizzy, the blow forced him to spin around and fall to his knees, blood streaming from his mouth and nose. He winced as a fistful of his hair was grabbed and his head wrenched back until he was looking up into the snarling face of the man. The knife was at his throat, the jagged, filthy blade pressed just hard enough to make him freeze, barely daring to breathe.

'We *all* have to die sometime,' the man hissed, spit escaping his cracked lips onto his greying stubble. 'Until then, until that empty black void, I get rewards.'

Quinn was considering debating the accuracy of the man's view of the destiny that awaited him, but was prevented from doing so by the door crashing open and the Archdeacon striding in. He grabbed the suddenly frightened-looking man and threw him backwards, away from Quinn. The movement resulted in the knife drawing blood, causing Quinn to gasp, but he relaxed again when, on touching the cut with his fingers, he realised the wound was just superficial.

'I told you not to *damage* him!' shouted the Archdeacon.

The man cowered, gradually shuffling back into the corner. He crouched low, hands raised in appeasement, yet gripped his knife tighter still. 'He put up too much of a fight, Master! You said he'd be blind drunk and easy to grab but he's *not*...I couldn't take him *without* damaging him!'

The Archdeacon lowered his voice and took a menacing step towards him. 'I wonder what I pay you for, at times...'

'Master, I—'

'*Be quiet*!' The man flinched and did as he was told, as the Archdeacon turned to Quinn. 'I *warned* you, didn't I?' he growled.

Quinn didn't answer the question. Instead, so low that it took too long for the Archdeacon to realise what he was doing, he uttered just a few words, and quickly breathed into his cupped palms. In a bright flash, an orb appeared and before the Archdeacon could react, it darted away, smashed through the tiny window and out into the night. The signal had been given.

CHAPTER 90. A CATA-STROPHIC ERROR

Puzzled, Quinn's captors stared at the broken window, wondering what the purpose of the orb had been. They soon had their answer. In through the gap in the filthy glass flew a small spherical object. It clattered to the floor, and for a second all three men looked at it. Then Quinn shielded his eyes. Before the man or the Archdeacon could gather their wits enough to do the same, there was a blinding flash and a boom like a strike of lightning. Thick white smoke quickly filled the room. Quinn held his breath and as he heard the two men begin to choke, he made his move.

Launching himself towards the Archdeacon's position, he barrelled into him, instantly regretting the amount of force he put into the move as his head began to swim. They crashed to the floor, the Archdeacon betraying his surprise with a shout. Quinn's eyes were stinging and he would not be able to fight the need for air much longer – he had to move fast. His hands found the Archdeacon's head and he clasped his fingers against his skull, forcing it down against the floor with a satisfying thump. He had to increase the pressure and lean all his weight against the heels of his hands to maintain his grip, as the Archdeacon began to struggle with all his strength. In a growing sense of panic, Quinn almost shouted the words he needed to complete his task, fighting across the urge to cough and the waves of nausea that swept over him.

But the expected response to his words did not happen. The rush as he ripped the Archdeacon's soul from his body didn't arrive. They remained in the choking atmosphere of the room, the man still coughing, strangled sobs escaping from his lips as he fought to get precious air into his burning lungs. Quinn and the Archdeacon remained in their battle of brute force, the Archdeacon beginning to gather himself as Quinn began to tire.

Quinn said the words again, forcing them out between the spasms his throat was going through as he fought to take in air, but keep the thick smoke out. He was not supposed to still be *here*, he was meant to be in the Plane of Shadows with the severed soul of the Archdeacon...

Still nothing happened and when the Archdeacon began to summon enough strength to almost make Quinn lose his grip with one of his hands, he knew he was out of time. In desperation and in fear of his life, he uttered the words he knew were his last hope.

In a sudden rush of air that almost froze all three men where they were, the smoke cleared. There, dark robes settling around him, stood the

Keeper. Quinn prayed that together they might defeat the Archdeacon and get him out of this plane to his eternal punishment, the pawn along with him.

But something in the Keeper's expression sliced through Quinn's hopes like a blade of ice. Fear. It was *fear*.

The shock of that look was enough to make Quinn lose his concentration and the Archdeacon seized his chance. All Quinn saw was a suggestion of shadow crossing his restricted field of vision, before the Archdeacon's forehead made savage contact with his right cheekbone. Quinn immediately lost his hold on the Archdeacon and could do nothing in his daze as he was roughly shoved aside, hitting the wall with his shoulder as he fell to the floor. His head throbbed as he fought to locate the Archdeacon with his clouded sight. A rustle of robes, a grunt of effort and a cry of surprise were all the clues he had to go on before he saw, for just a sliver of time, the Archdeacon and the Keeper locked in a deadly battle of strength – a battle that, to Quinn's horror, the Keeper appeared to be losing...

And then they vanished.

Quinn wasted no more than a second on his shock and disbelief before scrambling to his feet on trembling legs and lurching towards the man who was slumped in the corner, still gasping for air, his knife forgotten on the floor. He grabbed the weapon, seized the man's hair and with a vicious twist, forced his whole body around to expose his throat. With a roar of rage and frustration, he dragged the blade across the man's taut flesh, the jagged edge tearing through skin and sinew, ripping a great gash that brought forth a river of blood. With a shocked gurgle, the man's eyes widened, until they could widen no further. He looked up at Quinn, as if he were wondering why...then, as his brain was deprived of blood and oxygen, his eyes quickly closed and he became a dead weight under Quinn's grip.

He dropped the body and grabbed the amulet from under his blood-soaked shirt. As he opened his mouth to pray that it would work, it lit up and softly thrummed in his palm. Letting it fall back against his chest, he leaned over the man and placed his fingers at the sides of his head, ignoring the sticky, viscous mess covering them both as the body slowly drained itself.

Focusing all his thoughts on the immediate task, he recited the words he needed to follow the Archdeacon and the Keeper, trying to smother all thoughts of why things had not gone how he had expected them to...now was what mattered. Now and whatever happened next.

CHAPTER 91. THE FINAL STRUGGLE

The first thing to reach Quinn's senses in the Plane of Shadows was the man's high-pitched wailing. It pierced his already painful head, and in disgust and fury he pushed the man away from him, leaving him to crumple in the red dust to await the attention of a Keeper or a Guardian, he didn't care which.

He looked around, eyes frantically searching for the Archdeacon and his Keeper. He soon found them, locked together – the Archdeacon looked murderous and the Keeper still looked afraid.

Afraid.

Again, Quinn tried to make sense of it in the brief time he had before his own fear took over and forced him to move. He had to help the Keeper somehow – but *how*? He had summoned the Keeper because he hadn't felt able to defeat the Archdeacon alone. If the *Keeper* was helpless in the face of the Archdeacon's strength, what could *he* do about it?

As he raced towards them, his eyes stinging and his lungs still craving clear air, he found a wisp of hope in the arrival of two Guardians. Their dark, leathery bodies grew in his field of vision as they approached the scene of the battle before him, parting to come in from opposite directions. If anything could stop the Archdeacon, it was them.

But as he got closer, he was horrified to see the Guardians slow their descent, until they remained in the air several feet away from the Keeper and the Archdeacon.

'*What are you doing? Save the Keeper!*' he screamed at them, his voice raspy, a cough following close behind. But they took no notice, and suddenly he had reached the fight. He had no time left to think or worry.

He barged straight into the middle of them, knocking the Keeper flat on his back, forcing the Archdeacon to stumble sideways and unbalancing himself. As Quinn straightened and wheeled round, his eyes blazing red and his hands poised to strike, the Archdeacon recovered himself and with a roar of rage lunged at him. The old man's movements were slow, clumsy – Quinn felt a spark of confidence return as he easily dodged the attack. Positioning his feet firmly, and bracing himself for the next attempt, he saw the Archdeacon's eyes were as red as he knew his own to be. A sick feeling washed over him – he did not want to resemble this evil in any shape or form, he only wanted to destroy it. The thought of being anything like this man, the cause of all his heartbreak, drove him further into his rage and when the Archdeacon came at him again, he was ready with a surge of adrenaline that overrode the Archdeacon's superior, but weakening strength. His hands shot past the old man's forearms and locked onto his head, his elbows thrust outwards to prevent any chance of his own skull falling into the same kind of grip. He squeezed with all his might, his mind focusing on the Archdeacon, his eyes looking deep into those of his nemesis, probing, searching, invading...

At first he felt a sensation not unlike the one he experienced when killing Renn's father...a mildly pleasant influx of energy that filled his veins and created a gentle warmth. The sensation swelled within as each second passed and he drove his strength into the destruction of the Archdeacon's soul, until he felt he couldn't possibly take any more. He could almost have smiled in that moment.

But then the pain started – pain he had not felt with Renn's father. Pain that felt more and more like his horrific experience at the beginning of all this tragedy and strife. Pain he felt from Rook.

He swallowed hard, trying to ignore the gritty dust that scratched his throat and made it spasm in protest. Calling on God to aid him in his battle against this evil, he threw everything he had left at the Archdeacon, whose arms were now thrashing wildly at Quinn's in an attempt to dislodge himself from the trap he was in. Quinn closed his eyes, pressing the lids together as hard as he could, willing his power to hold on, to keep going, bolstering his faith that God would triumph over evil.

But the pain was becoming too much. As it coursed through every fibre of his being, it wrenched a cry from him and he almost lost his grip on the Archdeacon's skull. He tried to embrace his anger, gathering up every injustice that had been done in the name of this vile old man, every innocent life lost, every soul destroyed, every family member trapped in an endless search for loved ones who would never return to them. As he opened his eyes again and locked his piercing gaze onto the Archdeacon, he pushed every thought of justice and vengeance towards him, using the strength of his conviction to add to his power. The red sparks danced and darted and twisted every which way, before shooting into the glowing, red eyes of his enemy.

The Archdeacon screamed, almost drowning out the sound of the Guardians. But Quinn had heard them shriek, and for a moment he was distracted again, unable to fathom why they would not come for the man who was endangering one of their masters...why they would not do what they were *created* to do...

His grip weakened again and the Archdeacon pushed back at him once more, finding reserves of strength Quinn would never have believed possible. His own anguished voice returned as he felt as if every nerve in his body would snap. Suddenly he could no longer push forwards, but could only feel panic rising as his own energy was pushed back towards him. Fear, fatigue and a crisis of confidence were all the Archdeacon had been waiting for, it seemed. Quinn's grip began to diminish and he felt sheer terror as the Archdeacon's bony fingers grasped his forearms his nails dug into the flesh through the fabric of his tunic sleeve, the material squelching with his own blood and that of the nameless pawn.

He had no time to think of a way out, as something large and solid impacted with his legs, just above the knees. It hit his right leg first, and pain lanced through the site of his old injury. He fell to the ground heavily, winded, his vision blurring once again. Then something grabbed his left arm and it felt like a hundred needles were breaking through the skin, forcing another yell of pain from him. He was dragged through the dust, unable to see what had hold of him, before being lifted clear off the ground and violently thrown into a large boulder. His back, shoulder, and the back of his head slammed into the rock. Down came merciful darkness to take away his agony.

CHAPTER 92. FURY IN GRIEF

He woke up deaf, nauseous, coughing dust and feeling fresh agony at every spasm his muscles were going through. With his eyes watering and his limbs feeling like jelly, he slowly pushed himself up onto his hands and knees and forced himself to look around. He could feel a trickle of blood making its way down his spine and his arm was losing a steady stream of it; his sleeve was ripped and he could see dozens of teeth marks oozing at an alarming rate, running in rivulets along his skin. As sound came back to him like the headlong rush of river water over jagged rocks, he turned his head towards the Guardians, who were crying – no, *wailing* – not far from him.

Sitting up, he covered his ears with bloodied hands and tried to see what was happening. The Guardians were walking around on the ground – fretfully pacing a few metres this way, a few metres that way, raising their heads on curved necks and screaming at the magenta sky. The noise was more than mournful this time. It was grief-stricken.

Eyes stinging, Quinn scanned the ground and it wasn't long before he found what he had been dreading to see. The helpless, prone shape of a figure in dark robes, his face somewhat obscured by the distance and the dust, but unmistakably identifiable.

The Keeper.

'No...' Quinn breathed, scrambling to his feet, swaying a little as he moved forwards a few steps.

One of the Guardians swung its scaly neck around and screeched at him, sending him stumbling backwards again. Unable to keep his knee from giving way, he sat down heavily, fresh pain lancing through every inch of his body, knocking the air from his lungs.

'Be still, Quinn. Or they will knock you down again. Wait.' The voice came from behind the rock and Quinn was thrown into new confusion as he tried to look for its owner.

Another Keeper moved around the rock and drew alongside Quinn, pausing to look down at him before striding towards the Guardians. Muttering something Quinn could not understand, he seemed to bring the creatures under control in seconds and they lowered their heads and backed away from the body on the ground. Bending over the figure, he moved the hood of the robe away, and for the first time Quinn clearly saw the face of the man who had saved his life. His pale skin seemed even more starkly contrasted against the black cloth, and his gentle eyes were closed. A little blood had seeped from his nose and run down to his mouth, but, unlike Quinn, he had no heartbeat to force more of it from his body. Quinn felt sick as sorrow gripped his core. He wished he could have done for the Keeper what the Keeper had done for him, for it was obvious – he was dead.

As a veil of tears descended over Quinn's eyes, the new Keeper walked back towards him and uttered the words he had no need to say. 'I am sorry,' he added.

Quinn struggled to speak through the spasms of grief that gripped his lungs. '*God…*' was all he managed, then his head dropped, the tears hitting the dust between his knees.

When he was finally able to compose himself enough to stand up, Quinn looked at the new arrival. He was very much like the Keeper he had come to love and respect, but slightly taller, a little darker, with an intensity in his eyes that lacked any of the kindness Quinn had been privileged to know.

He felt his anger spark as he held that cold glare. 'Why are you doing nothing?' he asked, then coughed.

'Meaning?' the Keeper replied calmly.

'Bring him back!'

'I cannot.'

'Cannot? That's *ridiculous* – you're a Keeper, aren't you?' Quinn's voice became stronger and louder as he limped towards this new being, suddenly feeling as if he did not know their race at all, despite the dealings with 'his' Keeper. 'He brought me back, why can't you bring him back?'

'He was killed by the Archdeacon. There is

nothing *left* for me to bring back...'

The words slammed into Quinn as hard as if one of the Guardians had flown straight at him. He felt dizzy, empty, guilty, heartbroken – all at once. He could not move, but stood there, dripping blood into the red sand, his gaze locked with the Keeper's cold, silver eyes. He was willing him to un-say what he had just said, praying for it to be untrue, aching to see the events reversed and no body on the ground in front of him. But it didn't happen. His Keeper was gone, lost forever, his soul destroyed. He would never receive his reward for his kindness and purity of heart. And it was his fault.

'I am sorry. Truly, I am, Quinn. Things were never meant to end up this way. The Archdeacon was never meant to reach this plane alive –'

'It's my fault. I knew I couldn't do this. But you *used* me!' Quinn suddenly shouted, looking from the body to the Keeper and back again. As he stared at the corpse, he felt rage burning inside him, rising up and threatening to choke him. 'He knew – you *all* knew! You knew that none of you could defeat him and you needed me to do it for you! I was led to believe I was never alone in this fight, because you never *told* me that Keepers could not fight him! You knew all along that if the Archdeacon got his hands on any of you then it would mean death for you instead of him. *You used me!*'

'Quinn...'

'*That's* why the Keeper looked so terrified

when I summoned him – I was never *supposed* to summon him! I was supposed to kill the Archdeacon, and then bring his soul to you…that way you would have stayed safe.' Quinn began pacing, ignoring the pain in his knee. 'But, because none of you saw fit to tell me you were powerless against him, I summoned *him*,' he pointed, 'and I got him killed! You all got him killed!' Quinn strode up to the Keeper and grabbed him by the front of his robes. Pushing him backwards, towards the corpse, his eyes blazing red and his throat burning with rage-fuelled bile. He leaned his face in close and looked into the startled man's eyes. '*Where* is the Archdeacon?' he hissed.

'He is *dead*, Quinn! The Guardians –' he tried to prise Quinn's bloodied, sticky fingers from his clothes, but made no progress and quickly dropped his hands in submission. 'The Guardians have destroyed him. They knocked you out of the way in order to do so without destroying *you*, too. But they were not quick enough to save the Keeper. I don't know why they hesitated. *Please*,' he added, glancing nervously sideways. 'Let go of me before they see what is happening. You do not want to be hurt again…'

'I want *proof*.'

'There is no way to *give* you proof, Quinn. You know the Guardians leave nothing! Please-…you must trust me –'

Quinn let go of the Keeper's robes and stepped back, suddenly weary. He looked deep into the Keeper's troubled eyes and let his anger fall away from him. There was nothing else to be done.

'I'll never trust any of you again,' he said quietly.

Clutching the amulet tightly, he took one last look at the dead Keeper's tragic form, as he uttered the words that would take him home.

CHAPTER 93. A PROMISE KEPT

Aliena lifted the pail of fresh milk and patted the cow's rump with thanks. The brown calf still slept, half-hidden in the golden straw at his mother's feet, untroubled by sharing his evening meal with Aliena.

As she moved towards the barn door, Aliena thought she would have to tie it shut tonight. The storm which had blown up suddenly looked as if it was going to get wilder, and she didn't want the animals frightened by it. The door was already knocking gently, punctuating the creaks of the old building's roof.

Closing it behind her, she carried the pail to the cottage, trying to remember where she'd left the strongest twine – and then she stopped in her tracks. The cottage door was wide open, the light from her candles and the fire in the hearth shining out onto the path. She knew she had closed the door properly and that the wind wasn't yet strong enough to have blown it open.

Side-stepping a few paces, she approached the cottage away from the path so she could not be seen by anyone who might be inside. Placing the pail quietly on the ground by the wall, she listened intently for sounds of an intruder – and when they came, she was so surprised she couldn't stop herself from crying out. It was the sound of large objects colliding with some force...as if something had fallen to the floor and taken other objects with it, the largest of which was, by her guess, her table. One item smashed, another rolled noisily and the light dimmed as a candle was blown out by the force of movement it had been subjected to.

Then, silence returned.

Aliena waited. She was alone and unarmed, and although peace had been restored since the death of Sheriff Garin, thugs, drunks and thieves still roamed at night, looking for easy targets. As her eyes came to rest on the axe she'd been using that morning, stood up against the wall by the door, she decided she would not be an easy target. She grabbed it firmly in her hands and stepped into the light of the doorway.

The kitchen table, heavy as it was, had tipped over, depositing its varied load on the floor. There, lying stricken and bleeding next to the mess – wet, filthy and only wearing hose, his riding boots and a thin linen tunic – was Quinn.

'Oh, dear *God*,' she breathed, letting the axe fall. She ran to him, dropping to her knees and quickly assessing his condition, trying to suppress the overwhelming joy she felt that he had returned to her. He was lying on his left side, his left arm stretched out in front of him, bleeding badly from what looked like dozens of holes in the skin. He had a gash on the back of his head, the blood running down and staining his collar. There were other cuts and bruises about his face and neck. He was covered in mud and dust and had obviously not taken care of himself for days.

'*Quinn!*' she said, gently lifting his face towards her. His skin was warm, almost feverish, yet his right hand, when she took it, was ice-cold. He was breathing rapidly, but not weakly, still managing to squeeze her hand. 'Oh, what have they *done* to you?' she whispered, looking closer at his mauled arm and wondering who 'they' were...

His eyes fought their way open and he looked at her, clearly having some difficulty focusing, but determined to stay awake. 'It's over,' he said, his voice calm but weary.

'Where is Erelas?' Aliena asked, fear gripping her insides.

'Safe. With Maynard. He will find me...'

'Who is Maynard?'

'A friend.' He squeezed her hand again. 'Please, can you help me up? I'm so cold.'

'I'm sorry,' she said. 'Of course – let's get you onto the bed...I need to stop your arm from bleeding.'

With Aliena's help he was able to get to his feet, resting almost all his weight on his good leg and half limp, half hop to the bed that had been his since that first day they met. He winced as he lay back and shivered violently as she helped him out of the ruined tunic. She closed the cottage door and went in search of more blankets.

The glimmer in her eyes had not gone unnoticed and Quinn's heart seemed to leap as he realised how much he had missed her, how much he had buried his feelings for her. Now he knew that life was for living – and he was going to live it. Not for the Archdeacon, not for the Keepers, but for himself and for those he loved most. It would begin right here, right now, with Aliena.

She returned with the blankets and arranged them over him so that he would become warm and comfortable. She was about to go for clean water and linen strips to wash and bind his injured arm, when he caught her by the hand and pulled her towards him. Almost unbalanced, she sat on the side of the bed and leaned in close, expecting him to say something to her. Instead, he reached up to her face with his good hand and guided her closer, until finally, to her surprise, their lips met. He kissed her, and the kiss was loaded with a thousand things he had never said, a thousand wishes he was too scared to lend his voice to, and a thousand thanks for the woman he hadn't deserved to find. He did not rush, but made sure she felt the love and tenderness that went with it. When he finally let her pull away a little, he kept his palm gently against her cheek and looked into her eyes.

'What are you doing?' Aliena whispered through her smile.

'Keeping my promise,' said Quinn, finally smiling at her. Already he could feel his heart mending.

He was home.

CHAPTER 94. SAFE

Erelas leapt from Einna's back before she had even come to a halt, causing Maynard to raise an eyebrow at his agility. While he grabbed the mare's reins and kept her close to Cara – who had consented to being ridden by the huge Salorean without a fuss – Erelas sprinted to the open door of the little cottage and skidded to a breathless halt. Rapidly surveying the disorder within, his eyes came to rest on Aliena, who had stood in alarm at the noise of his entrance, away from the low bed. As soon as she recognised him, she put a finger to her lips. Looking from her to the bed, he understood – Quinn was fast asleep. Battered and bruised, but asleep and, judging by Aliena's lack of panic, safe.

'*Thank God!*' he said quietly, striding over to the bed. He took Aliena's hands in his and kissed her on the cheek. 'I guessed the orb was bringing us here, but dreaded to think what state he would be in. We expected him to return to the house he left us from...'

'Erelas – slow down. We? And what house? What *happened*?'

'Sorry,' he said, forcing himself to settle his nerves. 'It's a long story, and one I only know half of right now. Did he say anything to you about what happened?'

Aliena shook her head. 'Only that you were safe and that "it" was over...' She sat back down on the bed and lifted his left arm from the covers, which she had bandaged as best she could. 'He needs healing, Erelas. The bleeding won't stop. It looks as if something has bitten him badly...'

Erelas shivered as he realised that the only creatures that could have inflicted wounds like that on him were Guardians. 'I'll take care of it.'

'The horses are secure.' Maynard spoke from the doorway and Aliena and Erelas both turned to look at him. Aliena tried to hide her surprise at the size of the stranger, but Maynard had spotted it and bowed his head politely. 'I didn't mean to startle you.'

She rose from the bed again and walked over to him. Holding out her hand, she smiled and said, 'You are welcome here. I am Aliena – I guess you are Maynard? Quinn mentioned your name...'

'I am,' he said, taking her small hand in his and squeezing it gently. 'Erelas has told me much about you on the journey here. When he was not imagining all kinds of horrors that might have befallen Quinn...'

Erelas caught Maynard's sideways glance and pulled a face. 'You exaggerate,' he said, then sat on the bed, setting to work on uncovering Quinn's wounded arm. 'Have you given him anything to make him sleep?' he asked Aliena.

Returning to the bedside, she shook her

head. 'No. He didn't need anything. He is exhausted.' Her expression became one of concern again as she crouched down and gently stroked a stray bit of hair from Quinn's eyebrow.

'Good – unfortunately, I need to wake him as soon as I've dealt with this arm. We need to know the whole story...'

CHAPTER 95. HOME

'Are you sure you were *deliberately* misled?'

'No, not completely sure, and I'm not certain I ever will be. But this new Keeper didn't deny it, since he doesn't know exactly what the other Keeper told me. And, of course, the other Keeper is dead, so can't try to convince me otherwise.'

Quinn sighed, absently rubbing the arm that, until Erelas had worked on it, had been badly damaged. Now, just a week later, it was healed, leaving only faint scars that Erelas could not remove – scars that along with the ones on his ribcage, forehead and back, told a harrowing story that stretched back only half a year.

'It doesn't matter,' he went on. 'There's enough suspicion to prevent me from trusting them again. I won't be going back to their realm anyway – I'm no longer a Conductor in *practical* terms. And I certainly won't be summoning one of the Keepers.'

'*I* still have to deal with them...' mused Erelas.

Quinn looked at his friend and realised how his tale must have made him feel very uncomfortable about the future – he was still a Conductor, and now he and all the other Conductors would have to function without an Archdeacon, and with no way of knowing what the consequences of Quinn's actions might be in the Plane of Shadows. Keepers weren't immortal, by any means, but deaths among them were so rare...

'I am sorry, Erelas. I wish it had not turned out the way it had. I'm sure the new Keeper will not hold any grudge against *you*. He didn't even appear angry with me. Just *scared* of me. But he doesn't have to worry about seeing *me* again. It will all work out. I'm sure he will replace the Archdeacon in due course—'

'It's not your fault, Quinn.' Erelas stood up from the warm grass and began to pace in front of him. 'None of it is. Go right back to Rook...*nothing* you have done since then can be held against you, and if anyone in Delmoril says otherwise...'

'You're going back?'

'Well...no. At least, not unless I have to. For supplies and such.'

'You're sure you want to stay here?'

'The young king has offered me a home at Castle Rivallen. Renn told him I was seeking somewhere to live.'

'Very nice.' Quinn smiled as Erelas caught his eye. 'You'll get fat, though. Poor Einna...'

'Shut up!' Erelas laughed.

'Let's get back,' Quinn said, getting slowly to his feet, his knee still aching in the cool of the early spring morning. 'Maynard is leaving soon and Aliena will start fretting.'

'She suits you.'

Quinn smiled again. 'I learned a harsh lesson when it came to Aliena,' he said, the smile fading. 'If she hadn't the patience, or had not been as loving as she is, I could easily have lost her. I don't deserve her.'

'Ahh, of course you do. You *absolutely* deserve someone who can keep you in line.'

Quinn laughed – a carefree laugh that signalled he was ready to leave the past behind him – as they mounted their horses and raced each other down the hill, to the farm that was now his home.

For reasons Quinn did not care to find out, Rook's memories never returned. In their place, he began to make dreams of his own...

***

ABOUT THE AUTHOR

C. S. Evans

Born and bred in Somerset, C. S. Evans is a mother of 3 wonderful sons. She spent almost 20 years in Gloucestershire, but is now back in her home town of Wellington.

In former lives she has been a groom and a Special Constable. She is now owned by 3 cats, and collects swords and cookery books. She loves reading, cooking, history and watching cricket.